Ashley Cameron
POPPY
My little Wife
crime novel

2

Ashley Cameron

POPPY

crime novel

Impressum

Bibliographic information of the German National Library:
The German National Library lists this publication in the German National Bibliography; detailed bibliographic data are available on the Website http://dnb.dnb.de
©2021 Ashley Cameron
Editor: Uwe Raum-Deinzer
Translator: Carly S. Martin
Production and publishing: BoD – Books on Demand, Norderstedt
Cover ©ZERO Werbeagentur München, Germany
Image: © Alexandra Bochkareva / Trevillion Image
ISBN: 9783753491011
Publisher: BOD – Books on Demand

For Poppy

The girl from the village who everyone thought was weird.
You can be proud of yourself and have my utmost respect.

About The Book

"This is our new home," says Mommy.

"Poppy, you know you never have to hide from me, right?" *he* says.

"He's got a face like a bowling ball," says Grandma.

"Express yourselves clearly, class; just say exactly what you mean," says the teacher.

Help me, thinks Poppy.

Poppy is a six-year-old girl who lives with her mother in a run-down suburban neighborhood. One day, they move into a luxurious mansion with her mother's new partner. Poppy's mother is happy. She can finally buy anything she wants.

This new 'Daddy' or "Mr. Rich", as the young girl calls him, makes Poppy's every wish come true. He showers her with gifts, washes her hair three times a week and takes her on long journeys in his big car, just the two of them. He calls her his little wife.

In fact, everything would be just great, if it wasn't for one thing …

1976

Not all daddies let their kids sit in the front seat.
He says I'm lucky.
I turn to look at his big old head.
I think, *Mommy and I are really lucky. We're as lucky as can be.*
(Poppy, six years old)

The Black Car

The lights are on over at Mrs. Martin's. Her curtains twitch. She's already peeked out three times to see if we're still there. And yes, we're still here. I waved to her and yelled that it's my birthday today, but Mommy said, "Shut up, Poppy. You'll wake up the whole street shouting like that!"

We're standing with our bags on the steps in front of the apartment building. White snowflakes are floating down and landing on our shoes. I try to catch them with my tongue. Mrs. Martin thinks I'm sticking my tongue out at her and disappears back behind her curtains.

I don't know what time it is, but I think it must be very early in the morning because it's pretty dark. Everyone on our street is still fast asleep – everyone but Mrs. Martin and us. She's very rich. On the inside, her house is all white with lots of gold and pink. I was allowed to go in once when Mommy went to clean it. Well, she didn't really clean it at all. We watched TV the whole time. I drank some Coke and Mommy smoked a cigarette. At the end, she did a bit of dusting and let me keep watching TV.

Mommy doesn't like cleaning. She says it's not what she was born to do. But she saw a coat that looks like it's made of silver and she wants it. And Mrs. Martin would pay her twenty dollars.

At the end of the day, Mrs. Martin came back to her white house and said, "Well, you certainly won't be doing that again!"

"Fine by me," Mommy answered. "It's not my idea of fun anyway. I'm a hairdresser, I'll have you know!"

Today is my sixth birthday. I haven't gotten any presents yet but I'm sure I'll get some later. Mommy didn't even have time to sing *Happy*

Birthday to me this morning. She said she had to pack our bags *and* put on a really pretty outfit *and* shave every single hair on her legs *and* style her hair perfectly. I've already asked her twice what we do today, but all she did was put her finger to her lips and said "Shh" like it's a big secret.

So we wait. And wait. I look at our bags. Maybe we're going on vacation, but vacations cost money and we don't have any. I suddenly think about my Daddy.

Hooray, we're waiting for Daddy!

He's coming to pick us up because it's my birthday today. Ever since he started living with that other lady, Mommy keeps saying that he's a horrible bastard and that I'm not allowed to talk about him. So, I don't. But Mommy never said I'm not allowed to *think* about him. I don't really know what Daddy looks like anymore. A long time ago, when I was still five, I saw a picture of him at my grandma's house. I wanted to look at a big book and when I grabbed it off the shelf, the picture fell out and floated down to the floor.

"He's spread his wings and flew off for good, sweetheart. He's not coming back," said Nanna. She's got a very scratchy voice. Mommy says it's because she smokes so much.

Nanna picked up the picture of Daddy and looked at it. He was crouching in front of a radiator. He looked young and handsome in the picture, and it didn't look like he was growing any wings. He was smiling too, so I smiled back at him and asked Nanna if she knows where Daddy was now.

"I told you, he's gone for good. He's in the city. He decided to run off and join the circus," she said, throwing the lovely picture in the trash.

Just as I want to ask Mommy if we should go back inside, a black car turns into our road. It's big and shiny. Mommy suddenly stands up on her tiptoes and starts waving excitedly. The car drives towards us and stops like Cinderella's carriage. A man gets out. Who could it be?

It can't be Daddy. This man is really old. He's wearing a gray suit and he has giant ears, a graybeard, a huge nose and huge glasses. He looks like he's important.

"Wow, *Pick-up*, you're here," says Mommy.

"Like I promised," says the man calmly.

Three words. The less said the better; that's what Nanna always says.

"This is my Poppy," says Mommy, pointing to me.

"She's adorable," says the man in the same calm voice and after a pause, "Hello Poppy."

Four words.

Then everything happens too quickly. First, they put the bags in the trunk and once Mommy is sitting in the front and smiling, the old man with the gray beard picks me up and puts me in the back seat. Everything inside is made of leather and wood.

"Mommy...?" She doesn't hear me.

Just before we drive off, I see Mrs. Martin open her curtains again. Her eyes shine like a cat's in the dark because she can see the big black car and she always wants to know what Mommy and I are doing. I bet she's really wondering now.

Mr. Martin is now also standing at the window, in his dark-blue pajamas. I shout, "See you soon!" even though I don't want to see them again at all. They can't hear me anyway because it's so windy outside.

Mrs. Martin says something to Mr. Martin.

Mr. Martin just shrugs.

The Dark Brown Castle

Mommy shakes me awake. "We're here, Poppy!"

"Where?" I'm still tired.

"The place where we're going to stay forever." She points out the window. Through it I can see a house as big as a castle.

The old man is carrying our bags to the front door.

"This is where we live now," she says, getting out of the black car. She comes to my door and swings it wide open. "Come on!"

I almost start to cry because I'm a little scared, but she can't tell because she's already running up to the house. I quickly get out of the car, run up to her and grab her skirt.

She turns around and asks in an annoyed voice, "What's wrong, Poppy?"

"Mommy..."

"What are you crying about now? Let go of my skirt!"

"But everything's still at home," I say.

The man has already gone into the house. Mommy tries to get away, but I hold on tightly to her skirt.

"Are you crazy," she asks angrily. "There's nothing left in that shitty apartment. Everything is here. Now, let go of my skirt!"

I do what she says, and Mommy walks up to the front door. In front of the house is a big garden with short grass and tall trees. A cop is standing on the other side of the road. He's smoking a cigarette and waves at me. I wave back and quickly catch up with Mommy. I don't want her to close the door and leave me standing outside all by myself.

"This is our residence now, Poppy," explains Mommy. She doesn't sound normal. All posh and weird.

"What does residence mean, Mommy?"

She rolls her eyes and sighs. "It's our new home," she answers.

The entryway is tall and wide. There's a light with sparkling jewels and silver icicles hanging from the ceiling. I try to count them. When I get to seven, I suddenly realize that the old man is standing next to me.

"A little birdie told me it's your birthday today," he says.

I look at Mommy, who is standing by the coat rack and nodding her head really hard.

Yes, it's my birthday today and I nearly forgot all about it.

"Come with me," he says.

Four short words.

We follow him into another room. It's three times as big as the entryway. Everything is made of leather and wood, just like in the car. There's a big brown leather sofa and two dark brown leather armchairs. I look at the walls full of dark brown cabinets. One of them contains very thick books, which are made of leather too. I guess dark brown is his favorite color. In the middle of the room, I suddenly see a red bicycle with a silver bow.

I don't know what to say, but Mommy does.

"Oh Pick-up," she squeals, "that's crazy! Oh Poppy, look behind you, there's even more stuff on the table!"

I turn around and see a huge dark brown table with a big pile of gifts, more than I can count. Mommy counts them, all ten of them, and gives the man a kiss on the cheek and a pat on the bottom. The old man makes a face and takes a step away from her.

"And you know what's really funny, Poppy?" she says, pointing at him. "It's Pick-up's birthday today too!"

He doesn't look like it's his birthday at all. He's not smiling or wearing a party hat.

"How old are you now?" he asks me.

"Six."

"I am two times six," he says.

Five words. I bet he wants a present too.

Mommy blinks like she can't believe what she's hearing. "Two times six? Why two times six? You're not twelve, are you?"

"We don't have a present for him," I whisper in Mommy's ear.

"That's okay," says the man, who heard me even though I was being very quiet.

"Pick-up? I'm your present, aren't I?" she says with a funny laugh. "But don't unwrap me just yet."

The man ignores her and lifts me onto my new bike.

"What do you say, Poppy?" asks Mommy.

"Thank you, Mr. Pick-up."

"Mr. Pick-up? For goodness' sake, Poppy, are you stupid or what? That's my nickname for him. Think up your own."

I look at the man and say, "Thank you, Mr. Rich."

Mommy laughs so hard that she nearly falls over. "Mr. Rich?" she yells. "Mr. Rich! Oh Pick-up, do you know what that means? I think Poppy likes you. She's nearly as much of a jokester as me, isn't she?"

The man doesn't laugh, but instead opens the doors to the garden, puts his hand on my back and wheels me outside on my new bike. Once I'm in the garden, he gives me a push to start me rolling. "Cycle around for a bit and take a look at the garden."

Me and my bike fall over right away.

"She doesn't even know how to ride a bike, Pick-up!" shouts Mommy.

I get back up and laugh so that she knows I'm not hurt.

"Why don't you just go for a walk around the garden for now, Poppy?" says Mommy. "*Mr. Rich* will teach you how to ride your bike later."

I walk around the garden in circles, making them bigger and bigger and getting faster and faster as I run through the short grass, spreading my arms out wide like the wings of a plane. I make airplane noises too – I can't help it; I'm just so happy. Mommy laughs and claps her hands. I'm running so fast and shouting so loud that I suddenly have to cough.

"It's too cold out there; she'll freeze to death. Let's get her back indoors," says Mr. Rich to Mommy.

I go into the living room, but I can't stop coughing. Mommy hits me on the back to make it stop, but it really hurts.

"Go and get Poppy a glass of lemonade, Patricia," he says.

Mommy looks around. "Where do you keep it?"

"In the kitchen."

She walks out of the living room.

Mr. Rich comes closer to me. "You're all sweaty," he says in a worried voice, lifting my T-shirt and placing his hand on my bare back. He slides his fingers up and down my spine. "You're completely soaked, you poor thing."

I nod and make myself cough a bit more.

"You can have a lovely warm bath this evening, Poppy."

I think it's nice that he's so worried about me. Then we hear Mommy shouting. "Pick-up, I can't find the kitchen anymore!" The man leaves the room. When they come back with my drink, Mr. Rich says that he still has a lot to do.

Mommy looks at the table full of presents. "As do we," she says.

The moment Mr. Rich leaves the room, Mommy starts to unwrap everything quickly. I watch her -— it's so exciting! My presents are a baby doll with her own baby bath, a doctor's playset with a nurse's uniform, a tea set, markers in all colors of the rainbow, and a big bag full of marbles.

"Well, well," says Mommy. "If that's what he's buying us already, I can't wait to see what he'll get me for my birthday."

Because this was our first night in the brown castle, we got to have Chinese takeout. Me and Mr. Rich went to pick up the food in his big black car. Mommy stayed at home and set the table. In the car, I was even allowed to sit on his lap and hold the steering wheel. When we got back, I ate all the yummy food until I was stuffed full, just like Mommy.

She's now lying on the sofa and watching TV, and Mr. Rich is kneeling on the mat in the bathroom and taking off my T-shirt, pants and panties. The bath is nearly full.

Once I'm naked, I have to wait a bit while he checks that the water isn't too hot.

"Now," he says. "In you go." He grabs me under my arms and lifts me up over the edge of the bath. When I'm almost in the water, he pulls me back up again.

"Hmm," he says. "I think we can find a better way to do that, don't you?"

He keeps lifting me up to find out the best way to put me in the bath. He says "oops" and "oopsy-daisy" every time it goes wrong.

Hmm is a very short word, just like oops.

It's so funny. Every time he says "oopsy-daisy", I laugh louder and louder. When he finally finds the right way – with his hand under my butt like a pillow – he swings me over the edge of the bath and into the water, where the ducks and boats are floating. All the toys are new and they're all for me. I'm not allowed to play with them for too long though. Mr. Rich says I need to be washed too.

It takes him a long time to wash me and when we're done, the water is starting to get cold. When I'm finally allowed to get out, I shiver because there are no towels.

He tells me I can leave out the *Mr.* and just call him *Richie*. He says that would be a much nicer name.

I nod. Richie is good too. He really is nice.

Richie uses his hands to dry me off. He makes sure he doesn't miss a spot.

Far away, I can hear a funny song playing: *"This old man, he played one; he played knick-knack on my thumb."*

Apple Juice

"When Grandpa dies, we'll get all his money," says Annabella.

"Oh." I look at her with my eyes wide.

"Tough luck for you," she continues. "You won't get a penny. He's *my* Mommy's Daddy."

She points to her Mommy, who's called Phyllis and is drinking coffee with my Mommy, sitting in what looks like a pool of pillows in the middle of their living room. They also have a bar with tall stools and a white rug.

"Well isn't this fancy?" said Mommy when we walked in. She did a funny little sniff too, like there was a bad smell in the room.

I'm sitting on the floor in the corner with Annabella. They gave us some cookies and apple juice.

Mommy and I have been living in the big brown castle for ages now, and tomorrow is my first day of school here. Annabella is in my class too. She's always asking me questions and all at the same time.

"Is your Daddy dead?"

"No," I answer. "He's a plumber."

"But he's dead, right?"

"No, he's not."

"So, what's your Mommy doing with my Grandpa?"

"She lives with him."

"I bet it's because he's so rich," says Annabella.

I don't want to talk to Annabella anymore, but Mommy is still sitting in the pillows with Aunt Phyllis. We wouldn't have to talk if we had something to play with. "Why don't we go and play in your room?" I ask.

"We can't, my Daddy's upstairs."

"Oh."

"He's sleeping. He's very tired because he worked all day."

"Oh," I repeat because I don't know what else to say.

"He works for Grandpa. My Daddy is the best salesman in the whole showroom, and it's really big." She dips her cookie in her apple juice, and a piece falls off into the glass.

Annabella is the only person I'm allowed to play with. She's my new friend now, says Mr. Rich, because she's harmless. You see, when you're as rich as he is, you have to be careful. Anything could be stolen, even me. In fact, ever since we started living in the dark brown castle, I'm not even allowed to go outside on my own.

"Where did your Mommy get all those weird clothes from?" asks Annabella.

"She bought them." I don't know what she means; Mommy's clothes aren't *that* weird.

"Why are her eyelids so blue?"

"She likes them like that."

"Well, I don't."

I don't believe a word she says. Mommy is the most beautiful lady I know. She looks like Barbie. In fact, if I lined up all my Barbies – I have fourteen of them, all presents from Richie - and Mommy was the same size, she would fit in with them perfectly. She has exactly the same blonde hair and blue eyes. That's why she's my *Barbie Mom*. She also likes to wear soft sweaters that have glitter or shiny stars on the front or back – they're so pretty. She's always dancing around in them singing "Dancing queen, young and sweet, only seventeen!". I'm not sure why, but I always laugh along with her anyway. She really is young and sweet, just like my Barbies - all fourteen of them.

Annabella's mom is skinny. She's dressed in all denim and has a huge mop of ginger curls on her head, like it's on fire. A carrot top, as Nanna would say.

Me and Annabella watch our moms drink coffee without saying a word.

"Do you want to come and play at my house too?" I ask her. "We can play with my Barbies."

"No, my Mommy says I'm not allowed to."

"You're not allowed to play with Barbies?"

"I'm not allowed to come to your house. You can visit me but not the other way around."

"Why?"

Annabella doesn't answer and stares at her slippers with an angry face. Mommy finally gets up and climbs out of the pool of pillows. She has to pull her new skirt up really high to get out. I can even see her panties. Auntie Phyllis and Annabella can see them too.

"Ewww!" says Annabella, screwing up her nose.

Mommy pulls her skirt back down. "Come on, Poppy, let's go. Say goodbye to Aunt Phyllis."

I get up and walk over to my new aunt to shake her hand, just like Richie taught me.

"Goodbye, Aunt Phyllis!"

"Goodbye, Poppy." She doesn't smile; she just looks at me. She's got eyes like a dead fish.

When we're eating dinner in the evening, Richie wants to know what I think of Annabella.

"She's nice," I say. "Really nice."

Richie likes talking to me more than to Mommy. When she says something, he hardly listens. Actually, he doesn't even look at her. But when I speak, he listens carefully to every word. He often puts his hand on my head. Or on my leg, like now. He squeezes it and winks at me. I can't wink, so I just smile back. And then I smile at Mommy too, but she doesn't see it.

"Do you know what, Pick-up?" says Mommy. "Your Phyllis doesn't exactly have much to say, does she? Talking to her is like pulling teeth."

"I think Aunt Phyllis has pretty hair," I say, trying to make up for what Mommy said. "And they have a lovely house, right Mommy?"

"If you like that kind of thing. One thing's for sure: all that stuff certainly wasn't cheap. I wonder how they can aff…"

"Phyllis doesn't have any expenses," says Richie, interrupting her.

"What do you mean, no expenses? You're not telling me they live there *for free*?"

"Yes, *for free*, just like you live here."

"You mean you pay for *all* of it?" Mommy's voice is getting louder and louder.

Richie suddenly starts angrily mashing his potatoes with his fork. That means he wants Mommy to shut up. Mommy looks surprised and stares at his lump of mashed-up potato for a while. She laughs loudly and says, "Well, Pick-up, if you want to give *me* a pit full of pillows too, you can forget about it! I don't need one. They're too much hard work. You have to clamber around for half an hour just to get back out! And I bet that bar wasn't cheap either. But who wants to live like they're in a bar anyway?"

Mommy leans over and pinches Richie's cheek. I know that he can't stand it when she does that, but she just won't stop. "It's crazy, isn't it? That Phyllis has everything she could ever want, but it still feels like she's jealous of me. She kept giving me this weird look. Oh well, I guess that skinny bitch would give anything to have a sexy figure like mine."

Richie destroys his pile of mashed potatoes and finishes his plate.

Mommy's almost finished too.

I haven't even eaten half of my meal.

"And Annabella was such a show-off too, wasn't she Poppy?"

"She had yummy apple juice," I say.

"Annabella was bragging that her father runs the whole company all on his own."

Richie gives Mommy an annoyed look.

"Oh yes," laughs Mommy. "And you're always saying what a useless bum he is in the tent factory."

She's right. Richie's always saying that Aunt Phyllis's husband is as dumb as a doorknob and wouldn't be able to tie his own shoes without his help.

"What exactly do you mean when you say tent factory, Patricia?"

Mommy's cheeks suddenly go all red. "Oh, you know what I mean. What's it called again?"

"Do you know what it's called?" he asks me.

"It's a place where camper tents are made," I say. "For vacations."

"Exactly. And what are the tents called?"

"Liberty. That's another word for freedom."

"Excellent, Poppy." He strokes my hair.

"That's right, gang up on me again. You're as thick as thieves, you two!" says Mommy.

"We need to wash your hair again today, Poppy, don't we?" says Richie.

It's Sunday today. We wash my hair every Sunday, Wednesday, and Friday. I like it better when Mommy does it. But after dinner, Mommy always loads the dishwasher and afterwards lies down on the sofa with her magazines.

"Poppy's barely touched her food," she says. "That's because she ate too many cookies at Annabella's house."

I actually only had one, but Mommy doesn't know that.

"Just five more bites and you're done," says Richie.

They both give me a stern look: Richie because he thinks it's important for me to eat and Mommy because she thinks it's important for me to listen to Richie – he's the boss after all.

I feel like I have a frog in my throat, and I can barely swallow. But I'm too scared to say that I'm not hungry. I drink a sip of water after every bite to help it go down. The moment my plate is empty, Richie gets up.

"Come with me," he says.

Mommy looks at Richie. Maybe she doesn't think my hair needs to be washed again today. It's still clean from last time. But all Mommy says is, "Well, I'll tell you one thing: if I was as skinny as Phyllis, I wouldn't wear such ridiculous outfits."

She gets up and starts to clear the table.
Richie takes my hand and leads me to the bathroom.

Everything Is Perfect

His name is actually Eugene, but Mommy still calls him Pick-up because he *picked* us *up* in his big black car. That's what 'Daddy' told me when I asked him about his nickname, anyway. He wants me to call him Daddy, but I keep forgetting. I just think Richie suits him better.

We had a *real* conversation in the car this morning. That's what he called it: a real, serious conversation. I felt really grown-up. After all, being able to have a good chat with somebody is something special. And he said that he can have good chats with me. And that I'm very clever.

He was sitting behind the wheel of the black car and smoking a cigar. I was allowed to sit next to him where Mommy usually sits. I could hardly breathe, not just because of the smoke but also because he was being so nice to me. "You're a special child, Poppy," he said, putting on my seatbelt. "Very good and very clever."

He couldn't fasten the seatbelt properly, so we sat really close for a while as he continued trying. While I was waiting, I played with the electric button on the window.

He told me, "You're not allowed to touch the buttons. And if you see a cop, you have to duck."

"Okay." It sounded like a fun game.

There's a police station close to our house, but I hardly ever see anyone there. Richie says that the station is almost always empty. Our neighborhood is so lovely and peaceful because there are no black people there - that's what he told me.

When the seatbelt finally clicked shut, I felt Richie's warm breath on the back of my neck. "I don't think many daddies would let their child sit in the front, do you?

"No."

"You're a lucky girl."

I turned to look at his big old head. I thought, *Yes, Mommy and I are really lucky. We're as lucky as can be.* We started out living in a tiny place, where Mommy cut people's hair all day long. She didn't have any money to buy sparkly clothes or blue eye make-up. And I didn't have a Daddy or a bike. Now we live in a brown castle with shiny floors, white rugs, and vases from China. I'm not allowed to climb on anything, but I can be loud – if Richie isn't taking a nap, that is. We have loads of flowery plates and cups with gold around the edges and every week, Mommy buys new bowls and plates to match. Mommy now even has a fur coat and a cleaning lady and three pairs of diamond earrings. I have my own bedroom with a secret closet. And a bed with a pink blanket and posters of ponies on the wall.

"Do you know where we're going?" Richie asked.

"To the toy store?"

He nodded.

"And why are we going to the toy store?"

"Because of the Playmobil knights."

"Exactly," he said. "You need them."

I wasn't sure that was true, but I did really want the knights.

Is wanting something and needing something the same thing? I already had the American Indians, so I didn't need any more of them.

"Yes," I said. "I need the knights."

We drove down the road. "We need to go to a different store," explained Richie. "Playmobil isn't available in every shop in Long Island yet."

I nodded.

And then Richie spoke for a long time and said lots and lots of things, which he normally never does. That's why it was a real conversation, I think.

"Listen carefully, Poppy. I really like the fact that you and your mother moved into my house. It's truly wonderful. I'm not all on my own anymore. You like that too, right?"

I nodded again.

"I really like having you around. Your mother and I are quite different. But you and I, we're similar in a way. Of course, we are! We have the same birthday, after all. That's something special, don't you think?"

"Yes, I think so too." And because I noticed that he said the word *like* a lot, I decided to say it too, just to be sure, "I like not living in the apartment anymore too."

"I can understand that," he said. "And I would imagine that you never want to go back there. Because you lived in a ghetto."

I didn't know what a ghetto was, but I said yes.

"You didn't have much of anything there, did you?"

"No."

"No money, no pretty dresses, you never went on vacation and you never got any presents…"

"Nothing," I said.

"That must have been horrible."

"Yes, it was horrible."

"But now you have everything."

"Yes," I said. "Everything is perfect."

We drove past the fields full of cows. The sky was gray and gloomy. Nanna would call it, "The ideal weather for a funeral."

"And shall I tell you something else? You need to look at me to hear it, though."

I looked at him.

"Being friends with you, Poppy, is the most important thing for me. We make a good team. And that's why you and your Mommy are allowed to stay with me. Because we have such a great time together. After all, if you weren't such a good girl, I would have sent you back to your apartment on day one. Will you remember that?"

I nodded again.

"Do you think you can always be a good girl, Poppy?"

All this nodding is making my head hurt.

"Do you understand what I'm saying?"

"Yes, Richie," I said.

"You really don't have to call me that anymore," he sighed. "Why don't you just call me Daddy? You know I'd like that better."

I didn't know whether I should tell him the truth. He's simply not a daddy. He's a man. A rich old man. He's the boss, sitting there in his gray suit with an old man's head, glasses and huge ears.

"The thing is, I already have a Daddy," I told him.

Richie gave me a surprised look. Maybe he didn't know that, I think. Maybe Mommy forgot to tell him. I didn't want to make him sad, but I thought he needed to know.

"That's why I can't call you Daddy," I explained. "Because when my real Daddy comes back, I'll suddenly have two and things might get weird."

Richie smoked his cigar and shook his head. "You don't have a father anymore."

"Yes, I do," I said. "In the city."

"Pardon?"

"He's run off to the city to join the circus. That's what Nanna said."

We stopped for a while at a red traffic light, sitting in the black car and not saying a word. Richie carried on smoking, but he looked angry. He doesn't like my grandma at all. He's never even met her, and he says he doesn't want to. He doesn't want to meet Auntie Barbara or Uncle Carl either. Auntie Barbara is Mommy's sister. She lives with Uncle Carl and their three children in New Jersey.

And that's the best place for them, says Richie. I don't believe that because they never have any money and they live in the woods. It sounds scary. I bet they live in dark woods where children disappear and are eaten by witches with evil eyes.

Nanna has already called us seventeen times to ask when she can finally come and see our new house, but Mommy always says she's too busy at the moment. Much too busy...

As soon as she puts the phone down, she always says, "Too busy shopping, Poppy!" and laughs really loud, sounding anything but ladylike.

When the traffic light changed to green, Richie asked, "Do you know what *run off to join the circus* really means?"

I close my eyes and picture my young, handsome Daddy. He's standing in front of a huge striped circus tent, surrounded by clowns and elephants and acrobats. He's wearing a colorful costume and laughing happily as he juggles three burning torches, throwing them high into the air and catching them before they fall. The city is so far away, and everyone loves to run off there to join the circus.

"It means that nobody can find him," says Richie.

He realized that I still didn't really know what he meant. "Running off to join the circus means that he's left and never *wants* to be found again. Your father didn't want to be your Daddy anymore."

"Why not?"

"Because he didn't like you enough."

Mommy never told me that.

"The chances that you will ever see your father again are zero – it's not going to happen."

I played around with the zip of my coat and he kept on talking, on and on.

"It's a fact – do you know what a fact is, Poppy? It's something that is true, like the fact that your father doesn't love you and doesn't care about what happens to you. So, you're better off just forgetting all about him. Look at me, Poppy, damnit. I'm talking to you."

I looked at him.

"This whole time I've been trying to explain to you that you're a really good girl," he said. "That's why I want to be your father. I can look after you."

He put out his cigar, stroked my head and carried on driving with just *one* hand on the wheel. I felt safe with his big hand resting on my hair.

"Will you marry my Mommy?" I asked.

I know that Mommy really wants him to. She keeps tearing pictures of wedding dresses out of magazines and putting them on the brown table next to his plate at breakfast. He never looks at them.

"Will you always be a good girl?" he asks.

"Yes," I say.

"Yes what?"

"Yes, of course."

"No, Poppy. Not 'yes, of course'. Who am I?"

I wasn't sure what to say.

"Who am I?" he asked again.

And now I realized what he was talking about.

"Yes... Daddy."

He nodded at me and said, "Well, we just had a real adult conversation, Poppy. We understand each other."

He parked the car and turned off the engine and leaned over to undo my seatbelt. Unstrapping me seemed to be just as hard as strapping me in. He grabbed the seatbelt with one hand and slid his other hand down into my pants.

A lady with a dog was walking by our car. She smiled at me and I smiled back.

"There's a lady with a dog," I said.

He pulled his hand back out and was able to undo my seatbelt straight away.

When we got out of the car a bit later, he put his arm around me. We went to the toy store and he bought every single one of the knight figures on the shelf. He paid with lots of cash that he pulled out of the bag hanging from his wrist.

The man behind the counter smiled at me. "You're a lucky girl to have such a nice grandpa."

"I'm her father," said Richie.

"Oh, I'm so sorry!" The man's face had turned as red as a tomato, just like Mommy's did when Richie yells at her. Richie winked at me. I nodded back because I still can't wink but I wanted to show him that we make a good team.

Yes, I thought, I really am a lucky girl. If this is my Daddy, we're safe and people will like us *and* I will keep getting new Playmobil for the rest of my life. He looks after us. That's what Mommy wants and that's what she needs. And that's why she's as lucky as can be too.

A Well-off Dreamboat

"Money is no object whatsoever," sang Mommy as we entered Maria's Bridal Paradise. We'd driven all the way to Manhattan just to visit this huge shop. And because money was no object, we were served by Maria herself. My new Daddy is a *well-off* man. That's what it said in the advert: *"Well-off man looking for a home help".* Mommy cut it out of the newspaper and has kept it in her purse the whole time because she thinks it's such a good story. The tale of the lady who became more than just a home help, she calls it. Things turned out differently because Daddy fell head-over-heels in love with her the moment he first saw her. Mommy tells Maria the whole story and I listen carefully.

"It's like it was yesterday," says Mommy. "I can still see myself standing there with the advert in my hand. I ring the doorbell of this massive mansion and a gorgeous young man opens the door. I say, 'Hello, I'm Patricia from New Brunswick. I'm a single mom and I'm here to apply for the job as your home help.' He didn't say anything at first, but then he stuttered, 'Hello, I'm Eugene and I've never seen such a beautiful woman before in my life. Even though I'm extremely rich for a man in his thirties, I've never been as speechless as I am now. You're certainly far too stunning to vacuum my floors. Come in, come in!'"

Maria's mouth drops open.

"It's like a movie script, right?" asks Mommy with a big smile on her face.

Me and Maria both look surprised.

Shocked like a clumsy electrician, as Nanna would say. Maria looks like she doesn't think it would make a good movie at all, and I'm shocked because this is the first time I've ever heard this story. I have no idea who this young, attractive man Mommy's talking about really is. After all, Daddy has hair growing out of his ears.

"Oh yes, sometimes love just comes so naturally," says Mommy, still chattering away. "It doesn't always have to be hard work. You turn up ready to clean the floors, and a year later you're being whisked off on your honeymoon."

Maria says that it's a fantastic story and nearly enough to make her cry. She looks at me. "And how old are you?" she asks. "Five?"

"Nearly seven," replies Mommy. "She doesn't eat enough; that's why she's so skinny. He loves her like she's his own daughter. Isn't that just wonderful?"

When Mommy tries on the dresses, I'm allowed in the changing room with her to help with the zips. We spend hours in there, and Mommy tries on what feels like a million different dresses. At some point, my tummy starts to rumble, but Mommy can't stop trying on different white dresses and I understand why: they look so pretty on her. Maria must think so too, because every time Mommy comes out of the changing room, she says, "Oh my God! Your lucky *dreamboat* will absolutely adore this one."

She calls Daddy a *dreamboat*, but he doesn't look like a boat and I don't think she'd want to dream about him either. But Maria has never seen him, so she can't know that. Oh well.

"Be it a *dreamboat* or a *canoe*, they all sink the same way," is what Nanna always says.

When showing us some of the dresses, Maria tells us that they have a real certificate of authenticity, which sounds important. At some point, she says both things together: "This gorgeous dress has a genuine certificate of authenticity and your lucky *dreamboat* is sure to love it."

"I think they all cover up too much cleavage," says Mommy, pointing at her boobies.

"That's the latest trend," says Maria.

Mommy pulls the dress right up until you can see her panties and says, "And they're all too long as well. I've got lovely legs, right Maria?"

"Of course, there's no denying that."

"Therefore, it would surely be an absolute scandal not to show them off?"

Maria thinks that it would be a scandal too and takes us to the one corner of the shop that we haven't yet explored. She points to a big white wardrobe.

"This is where we keep our most modern designer dresses, Miss Brown. For customers with exquisite taste."

Mommy's eyes light up like a torch as Maria opens the doors. The dresses all leap out at the same time, like a big white fabric cloud full of lace and glitter and beads.

"And has your lucky *dreamboat* chosen his outfit for the big day too?"

"Who?"

"Your future husband; what's he'll be wearing?"

"Oh, him. He makes everything look good; sometimes it's enough to make me jealous," says Mommy. "In fact, with a body as young and firm as his, he could even get married in jeans."

Jeans? Daddy?

"But money is never an issue with him, so I'm sure he'll wear something very special.

"You certainly hit the jackpot when you found such a wonderful future hubby. I don't suppose he has a brother, does he?"

Maria and Mommy laugh. She gives Mommy a dress that isn't anything like any of the other dresses that she's tried on so far. It's as white as snow and sparkles everywhere you look. The top of the dress shows a lot of Mommy's boobies, and the bottom is really short in the front, but very long in the back. Maria says that this unbelievably stunning dress looks like it was made especially for Mommy and is sure to get lots of compliments. She says that on such a big day, the most important thing is to make sure it's unforgettable. Mommy thinks so too. Maria says that she can make a handkerchief for the groom's suit and a special dress for me from the same fabric as the dress. It will cost around $1500 and will take her three weeks to get everything made.

"What do you think, Poppy?" asks Mommy. "Shall we go for it? Do you want to be my flower girl?"

I nod. Maria asks if Mommy needs anything else.

"No, I think that's all for now, thanks."

"Do you already have something blue?"

"Blue? Why?"

"For luck, of course," answers Maria. "You always have to have something old, something new, something borrowed and something blue; that's what they all say."

"What a load of crap! I don't like old or second-hand clothes. And I don't need to borrow anything. The dress is brand new, surely that's enough?"

Nanna says that sometimes you need to make your own luck.

Mommy winks at the shop lady and says, "Do you know what, Maria? When the big day comes around, I'll just slip on my sexy blue lace thong. I'm sure that will bring me all the luck I need, if you know what I mean!"

Nanna also says that there's no such thing as luck and that Mommy wasn't lucky at all with my handsome young Daddy because he left her. I bet Mommy didn't wear blue panties when she married him. That's why Daddy ran off to join the circus. Not because he doesn't love me anymore.

Plan B

"Holy cow!" says Nanna when she's finally allowed to come and see our new house. Nanna is short, fat and always angry. Mommy says her waist is wider than her hips and Nanna calls it her spare tire, which is weird because she doesn't even have a car. Aunt Barbara and Uncle Carl didn't come, and that's a good thing. On the phone, Aunt Barbara told Mommy that she should stop acting like she's suddenly become the Queen.

"Oh of course, you're right," answered Mommy. "I only live in a mansion in Long Island with my millionaire while you're still stuck in your tiny shoebox in Jersey with your dream man Carl, his fake leg *and* his chronic bladder infection."

Aunt Barbara then said something weird: you can paint a turd gold, but it's still a turd. But why would anyone want to do that? Before I got the chance to ask Mommy, she'd already slammed down the phone. Later, we listened to the whole conversation again with Daddy on his new recording thingy. He keeps it in his office under a see-through plastic dome. Daddy says it starts recording the moment someone picks up the telephone.

Mommy didn't know that everything was being recorded, but when Daddy played us back her conversation with Aunt Barbara, she found it so funny that she asked him to rewind it three times.

"Damn, Patricia, it's certainly fancy here, isn't it? You even live near the park."

Mommy is so proud. She shows Nanna everything: the rooms, the plates, the vases and a photo of my new Daddy so that Nanna knows what he looks like, because he's at work today.

She holds the photo up really close to her eyes. "He's not exactly a looker, is he?" she said. "He looks like a bowling ball. What was his name again?"

"Eugene"

"Well, talk about a name that screams filthy rich!"

Nanna has a booming voice and isn't known for being polite. Pawpaw is the same. I don't like him, but I hardly ever see him because he's a drinker, and when you drink, you don't go out that much. Nanna tells us that he broke his nose in a fight at the bar yesterday.

"And guess who turned up at my place last week?" asks Nanna.

"Who?"

"Joshua."

"Joshua?" Mommy's forehead goes all weird and wrinkly. "What did he want?"

"To play ping pong with me, what do you think? He wanted to know where you live now, of course. He wants to see Poppy."

Mommy's face turns white.

"And what did you say to him?"

"I told him to fuck off."

"And then?"

"That was it."

"Are you talking about my real Daddy?" I ask excitedly.

Mommy and Nanna keep on talking as if I'm not there.

"Oh my God! Oh. My. God!"

I think Mommy is a bit shocked.

"He can't do anything. What do you think he's going to do?" asks Nanna.

"He might kidnap Poppy and demand a ransom," cries Mommy, pointing at me.

Nanna starts shouting too. "What are you getting all worked up about? He gets money every month already, doesn't he?"

"Who gets money?"

"Joshua, of course!"

"From whom?" Mommy is really panicking now.

"From Santa Claus, who do you think?"

"Santa Claus?"

"From the bowling ball, for goodness' sake!"

Because Mommy is breathing faster and faster and still doesn't know what Nanna is talking about – nor do I, by the way – Nanna points at the photo of my new Daddy.

"As long as Joshua stays away from you, he doesn't have to pay any child support. And he gets paid a fair amount every month too."

Mommy suddenly goes all quiet.

"Hello, anyone there?" asks Nanna.

"How do you know that?" asks Mommy.

"Joshua told me himself, when he was standing on my doorstep." Nanna speaks loudly and clearly, as if she's talking to a child.

Mommy is still as quiet as a mouse. After a while, she smiles at me. "Did you hear that, Poppy? Daddy's sorted everything out for us again."

"How come you don't know anything about it?" Nanna's eyes go all small like she's looking directly into the sun. "It's your money too, right? After all, you'll soon be married to the bowling ball."

"It's none of my business."

"Well, if I were you, I'd make sure that everything is down on paper in black and white," says Nanna.

Nanna explores the entire house, leaving nothing untouched. She starts off in the kitchen, where she opens all the drawers. She moves on to Mommy and Daddy's bedroom, where she even gets down on the floor to look under the bed. In the living room, she takes all the leather-bound books off the shelf to see if there's anything hidden behind them. But there's nothing there. Nanna sounds out of breath as she continues looking. Lastly, she wants to look in Daddy's office.

Mommy and I don't think that's a good idea. After all, Daddy might come home from work early. But Nanna doesn't listen to us and waddles into the room. She says she has the right to know if there are any skeletons in his closet. That's weird because she's already looked in his closet and found nothing but suits.

After looking at the recording thingy, Nanna finds something even more interesting: the safe. It's in the wall, covered by a painting of a big brown horse, but Nanna notices right away that the picture is only there to hide something else. She keeps turning the big knob full of different numbers on the front of the safe, but of course, nothing happens because she doesn't know the code. Mommy and I have no idea what's in the safe either.

"I bet that's where he keeps his millions," says Nanna. She's standing in the middle of Daddy's office with her hands on her hips, or at least on her spare tire. "You'll have to find out the code. It can be your backdoor. After all, you always need a Plan B."

"If I want to get out, I'll go through the front door, thank you very much!" says Mommy proudly.

"Are you really that stupid or are you just messing with me?" snaps Nanna.

I can tell that Mommy doesn't want to talk about it anymore because she sighs loudly and asks, "Would you like another cup of coffee before you finally leave?"

"You know where you can shove your coffee," growls Nanna, before angrily putting the painting back on the wall and taking a step back, right into Daddy's desk. "Shit!" she grunts.

An hour later, Nanna leaves the house with two shopping bags full of stuff. She's taken rice, pasta, chips and Crisco from the pantry, two bottles of schnapps from the bar, and cheese, Coke and butter from the fridge. Upstairs, three pairs of dark brown socks and two light blue shirts are now missing from Daddy's drawers.

"Did your grandma steal a lot?" He's flapping the photo around in the air. The paper is still completely black, but the picture will soon start to appear. It's like a magic trick.

"Not too much," I answer.

"Did she look in the closets?"

"A little."

"You don't have to lie to me. I always know more than you think. Don't you ever forget that."

Daddy has his own special tricks. He showed them to me, holding his finger up to his lips, and said "Shh!". He always lays out invisible thread or tape so that he can see whether anyone has come into his office and broken them.

"Come and look," he said. "I'm making you magically appear on this photo."

I'm standing in the living room. I'm naked and covered in goosebumps. Daddy flaps the photo a bit more to make all the colors come out.

"We do this every Sunday morning from now on. We need to see exactly how you've grown."

He puts me on the sofa and takes two more photos. In the first one, I have to keep my legs closed and in the second one I have to spread them wide. Next, he tells me I can stand up and he crouches down and takes photos of me from below. I have to stand very still. I stare at a spot on the carpet and close one eye and then the other so that it looks like the spot is jumping from left to right and back again. It's funny. After doing it a few times, I realize that I can make things move – almost like magic. Maybe even myself.

"What are you doing, Poppy?"

"Nothing."

He takes off his pajamas.

I look at the door.

"Mommy's allowed to sleep in on Sundays, she deserves a rest," he says. "And you and I need the time to get to know each other even better."

He turns around and folds up his pajamas neatly.

I wink at myself in the glass door leading out to the garden. He can never find out that I can do it now.

Winking is my special thing. It's my magic trick.

Liberty De Luxe

"My Daddy's company is on the other side of Main Street." I'm standing in front of my class. This is my first presentation that I've been practicing at home with Daddy.

Every Wednesday, someone can talk about their dad's work. I wrote the word 'Liberty' on the board and am pointing at it. "That's his brand: Liberty. They make foldable trailer tents for vacations. My Daddy invented them."

"Her dad is my grandfather", Annabella exclaims, "she's talking about my Grandpa!"

"Nice, Annabella, we heard you. Just like we did before", Mr. Thomas says.

This is the third time that Annabella has interrupted me. The teacher nods at me. "Go on, Poppy, don't let it bother you. You're doing a great job."

"The Libertys are produced in Mexico and when they're finished, they are brought on a train to New York."

"My father keeps that place running", Annabella interrupts. "Nothing would work without him!"

"Annabella!" Mr. Thomas's voice has a threatening tone to it.

"Yes, what?" The way she says it sounds a bit harsh.

"Poppy pretends to be something special because my grandfather gives her ten Barbies every week, but my father is the best salesperson in the entire company."

"Go take a timeout now, Annabella, and wait outside for a couple of minutes." Mr. Thomas has never sent anyone outside before. First Annabella blushes. Next, she opens her mouth wide and screams:

"Why do I have to go outside? That's not fair! It's about *my* grandfather! I know a lot more about him than she does!"

"Annabella, that's enough!" Mr. Thomas gets up from his chair.

"She gets everything she wants from him! She has the entire Indian village from Playmobil, she gets to wear new dresses every day, and she constantly goes on trips to the beach and when she turns seven, she will get her own horse! I only got a stupid hopper ballfor my birthday!"

"Annabella, damn it. I just told you that's enough." Mr. Thomas takes Annabella by the arm.

"Ouch!"

"No ouch. Be quiet. Go outside!"

But Annabella isn't having any of it. She points at me. "I know exactly why it's like that. You think nobody knows, don't you? But I know."

I'm getting goosebumps and am starting to sweat. That's not possible. She can't know. Nobody can. I watch Mr. Thomas struggle to get Annabella out of the classroom. He has to hold her with two hands and push the door open with his foot. Annabella keeps squirming and wriggling and is getting louder and louder: "I know exactly why it's like that! Why you're always getting everything from my Grandpa. My Mommy told me!"

I want the school to collapse and lava to come down from the ceiling. I want the floor to open up and swallow us all whole. For a fighter jet to fly through the room and burst everyone's eardrums. Then we'll either all be deaf or dead, and Annabella couldn't say what she wants to say. But nothing happens and everyone can hear her when she screams: "Poppy's mom is a whore!"

I don't know what a whore is, but I guess it's something bad because the entire class is staring at me in shock. I have never seen the teacher this angry.

I sit down and burp in relief.

Mr. Thomas thinks that I did quite well given the situation. And if Annabella hadn't been so stubborn, I would have been able to answer the questions from the class. Therefore, he puts a clown sticker on my forehead.

I am happy but also disappointed. I think Mr. Thomas can tell, because after the bell rings at 3:00pm, he asks me if I want to stay a bit longer to *really* finish my presentation. He asks a lot of questions about Liberty and I know the answers to all of them, and afterwards we eat an orange.

I smile at him. He smiles back at me. When Mr. Thomas smiles, his eyes smile too.

"Mr. Thomas?"

"Yes, Poppy?

"What is a whore?"

He needs to think about it. It takes almost a minute. Then he says: "It's an insult, a bad word. And it was very ugly of Annabella to say that about your mother."

"But what does it mean?"

"Something ugly."

"Oh!"

"And it's definitely not true."

"Okay."

He opens his mouth and closes it again. "Well", he finally says and looks at his watch.

"Yes", I say.

"Your mother has probably been waiting outside for a while."

"Yes", I say again.

"You must be hungry."

"I'm alright."

"Well, I could use some food right about now."

Mr. Thomas walks towards the door. I follow him slowly.

"Poppy?"

"Yes?"

"Do you want to tell me anything?"

I don't know the answer to that.

"What is going on in your head?", he asks.

"Nothing."

"I don't believe you", he says and puts his thumb on the sticker on my forehead. I close my head and gently lean against his thumb. I could stand there like this for the rest of my life.

But Mr. Thomas looks at his watch again and says that we really need to leave now, otherwise my mom will probably call the police.

Something In The Way He Moves

In the weeks leading up to the wedding, Mommy is happier than I've ever seen her before. She sings love songs and puts on self-tanning lotion every morning. She wants to talk about the big day all the time, especially with Daddy. But he doesn't answer. Mommy doesn't mind, she just keeps babbling. About her dress. About the cake. About the music. There won't be any guests, just me. Mommy didn't like that at first, but when Daddy told her she could choose between doing the wedding his way or not having a wedding at all, she chose to do the wedding Daddy's way.

"You know what your problem is?", she says to him from time to time. "Really, you're just incredibly jealous because you want to have me all to yourself. Because when you see me in that lovely white dress, you're going to freak out completely. It's insane! And I know that you don't want other guys to dance with your sexy bride."

When Mommy says things like that, her eyes sparkle, but Daddy just keeps looking at his newspaper or his food.

It's finally the big day. Early in the morning, Mommy and I sit at her dressing table to get ready. We've already put on our dresses and shoes. I have warm curlers in my hair. They're very close to my scalp and I can feel the heat on my skin. Mommy's using her finger to paint her eyelids with blue eyeshadow. Afterwards, she tousles her hair to make it as tall as a mountain and sprays hairspray everywhere. Even directly into my face.

Mommy put on a bit too much of the brown cream. Now her whole body is orange. "Look, Poppy, I look like an orange", she says. "Lucky that I'm beautiful either way."

Daddy's new suit is laid out on the bed. You can barely see it because it's as white as the sheets. Daddy doesn't want to wear anything special, he wants to wear his business suit, which is dark brown like everything else in this castle. Mommy knows that. She doesn't like it at all and yesterday she suddenly exclaimed: "Over my dead body will he get married in these rags." We quickly went shopping and found this white suit in a special menswear store. It's from Italy. Mary's handkerchief is already in the breast pocket, and Daddy will also be wearing some white patent shoes. Mommy hopes that the suit isn't too tight because Daddy hasn't tried it on yet. He went to work this morning and will pick us up at half past ten.

Mommy is becoming more and more restless. She puts both of her hands into a bowl filled with clip-on earrings. For herself, she chooses ones with shiny stones and pearls and for me, a pair with only pearls. They're heavy. I can feel my heartbeat in my earlobes.

We take the curlers out and when I look into the mirror, I'm startled by my curly hair, but Mommy says "Perfect", and ties my hair up with a white ribbon. I close my eyes just at the right time, as she grabs the hairspray can again. She sprays my curls until they're hard as a rock.

She takes me through the whole plan again. "You will carry the basket with rose petals, Poppy."

"Yes."

"When will you throw the petals?"

"At the end."

"Why do you keep coughing like that?"

"Because of the hairspray."

"The tape recorder. Where is the tape recorder?"

"Here."

"Does it have the right tape?"

"Yes."

"Do you know when to press *play*?"

"Yes."

"And *stop*?"

"Yes."

"And the B-side is for the end, after we've been blessed."

"Then come the rose petals."

"You're a smart girl."

I hear Daddy's car in the driveway. Mommy checks her watch and tells me it's time. She picks up her bouquet and stands in the middle of the bedroom. *One* arm is wrapped in silk, the other arm is bare. She extends an orange leg. Just like a model.

When Daddy comes in, all he says is: "Are you ready?"

"Can't you tell?" Mommy sounds a bit angry.

But Daddy doesn't even notice, not even Mommy's pretty dress and the white suit that is waiting for him. Mommy points at it and asks him to put it on quickly.

"Nonsense." Daddy leaves the room.

"What are you doing, Pick-up?", Mommy calls after him.

"I'll be waiting in the car."

"Damn it", Mommy says.

I take the tape recorder and my basket with rose petals and follow Daddy. When I get to the car, he's sitting behind the steering wheel smoking, but when he sees me, he quickly gets out and opens the door for me.

"What the hell do you have with you?", he asks.

"Nothing special", I say because I know that Mommy wants it to be a surprise.

"Well, you look beautiful", he says. "Should we run away together?" He smirks.

I giggle – he likes that. Daddy goes back to smoking behind the steering wheel. A few minutes later, Mommy comes out in her high heels. She has a cigarette in one hand and her bouquet in the other. She has quite a hard time getting into the car, especially because her dress is so long in the back. It's always getting stuck in the door.

"Mary should have included a user's guide", she moans.

"Do I have to help you?", Daddy asks after a while.

Mommy is gasping for breath. "You don't *have* to help, but you sure as hell can."

Daddy is staring through the windshield.

Mommy gets in. "Well, the cat's in the bag. We can go."

Daddy is the first one to get out of the car when we arrive at the clerk's office. He opens the door for me while Mommy tries to get out of the car. When she's finally standing on the curb, she says she wants to take a moment. She waves at all the people passing by in their cars or on their bicycles.

I've never been to a wedding. The office smells like a cleaned potty and our steps echo. In the middle of the corridor, a woman with an apron and a mop shows us where to register. A lonely man with very little hair and broken glasses is sitting at the registration desk. He sends us in the other direction. After a while, we find a small room where the county clerk is waiting for us. There are two rows of chairs. Mommy sits me, along with my rose petals and my tape recorder on a chair in the first row.

Daddy is already speaking to the clerk. I look down at the tape recorder, trying to remember what exactly the difference is between the button with the square and the one with the triangle. When Mommy nods 'Yes', I push ... the triangle, yes, that's it. And when she shakes her head 'No', I push the square.

Yes is triangle, No is square, No is square, Yes is tri...

"What do we need witnesses for?", Mommy exclaims.

She looks at Daddy angrily. Daddy looks at the clerk who says that it's not his fault, it's the law.

"Can't we do without?", Daddy asks.

"No", the clerk answers. "Two witnesses have to sign."

"Okay!", Mommy says and points at me: "What about her? Can't she sign?"

"The witnesses have to be of legal age. She's a child."

Daddy looks at his watch. Mommy's eyes look like those of a doll, that's how wide they are. She hurries out of the room. "Wait here!", she calls over her shoulder. "I'll be back in a minute!"

Daddy sits down next to me with his head in his hands. The clerk stays standing at the front of the room. We can hear Mommy running through the halls in her high heels, screaming nonsense things. All gets quiet. The clerk starts to whistle quietly, but he immediately stops when Daddy shoots him a look.

It takes a while for Mommy to come back. She brought the woman with the mop and the man from the registration desk with her.

"Well", Mommy says. "Here are your two witnesses. Thank you very much, please have a seat over there."

The cleaning lady and the man sit down next to me.

"Will this take long?", the cleaning lady asks. "I still have to mop the hallway."

"You'll be out of here in a few minutes", Mommy says. „Pick-up, give these people some money."

Daddy gives each of them fifty dollars. They look very satisfied.

The clerk clears his throat. "Can we finally get started?"

"Please", Daddy says.

"No", Mommy exclaims. "First, we have to walk in!"

"We are already inside, Patricia."

Mommy shakes her head and says that the wedding wouldn't get any seal of approval like this. Because she almost starts to cry, Daddy quickly says: "Okay, okay", and lets Mommy pull him outside into the hallway. They come back in, but this time, together. But Daddy is faster than Mommy, so she pulls him back by the arm. Passing by, she nods at me heavily. I nod back at her; it's going very well.

Then Mommy calls: "Triangle! Triangle!" I quickly push the triangle. Immediately, a woman sings beautifully: "Something in the way he moves." Mommy explained to me this morning that her name is Shirley Bassey and that she's already dead. Good that they thought to record her before she died.

Mommy looks lovingly at Daddy but glares at the cleaning lady because she's turning down the knob that controls the volume.

When Mommy and Daddy get to the clerk, they sit down with their backs turned to me. Mommy shakes her head and I understand what she means this time. Shirley Bassey isn't singing anymore. The clerk talks slowly and boringly and that's good, because it gives me time to turn the tape and rewind it.

It takes a while before the clerk finishes. Daddy has a long line of first names. When they're busy with the rings, Daddy calls me to the front. Mommy is getting a beautiful ring, full of shiny stones and I also get a ring with a pearl and a shiny stone.

"We are married now too, Poppy", Daddy whispers.

I don't know how to answer, so I say: "Okay", and sit back down.

After the cleaning lady and the man sign, Mommy nods her head again. I push the square on the tape recorder. Now we're listening to "Sugar Baby Love", and Mommy and Daddy leave the room together. I stay behind with the clerk, the cleaning lady and the man from the registration desk.

"Well", the cleaning lady says while also covering her ears, "I have never seen something so romantic. I almost cried."

"The dress was really expensive", I explain to her.

The clerk looks at me and points at the tape recorder and the rose petals. "You can turn the music off. And if you still want to throw those, now's the time."

The four of us leave the wedding room and step out into the parking lot, where Mommy and Daddy are waiting. I throw a few rose petals. Mommy quickly runs to the car to get the camera.

When she comes back, the cleaning lady takes pictures of Mommy and Daddy and as a thank you, Mommy throws her bouquet to the cleaning lady.

"Thanks! I've been married for twenty years, but you never know." She laughs and winks at me.

Daddy drops us off at home and immediately drives off to work.

"It was beautiful, really beautiful, Mommy", I say.

She doesn't say anything and takes me to the bedroom where she brushes out my curls. It hurts, I have tears in my eyes.

After I say "Ouch" one too many times, she takes a pair of scissors and cuts my hair without saying a word. She doesn't even tell me to sit still. She chops so wildly that I'm afraid she might cut off my ear. Looking at my hair all over the floor, she says defiantly: "The old fart is a lot older than what he told him."

I stay silent.

Mommy pulls out her cigarettes. The hand holding the lighter is trembling so much, she almost sets her dress on fire.

"Be careful, Mommy," I say.

"What?"

"The lighter, Mommy, be careful!"

Mommy smokes her cigarettes in seven drags. I count them. She takes ages stubbing it out and hisses: "He's the same age as your grandmother. Son of a bitch!"

Afterwards, she lies down on her bed. I don't know if I'm allowed to go, so I stay until she falls asleep. I don't dare pick up my hair. I look in the mirror and wonder if ugly short hair needs be washed as often as pretty long hair.

1977

I'd like to call Mr. Thomas.
But it's the middle of the night.
But if I did ...
... then I'd ask him if all of this really is normal.
If Mr. Thomas answers *Yes*, I'd say: *Thank you, Mr. Thomas, see you tomorrow!*
And if he answers *No*, I'd say: *Help*!
(Poppy, seven years)

Yellow Is A Color

It's Wednesday afternoon. I sit hiding and am as quiet as a mouse. We just ate some warm yucky food, which I threw back up into Barbie's carriage. I worry about the carriage, chunks everywhere, but maybe I can clean it in the sink without anyone noticing.

I hear him breathing. He's been standing there for a while. He calls my name softly, but I am not here.

My hideout is secret and deep. It lies hidden behind a narrow door in the wall and stretches far into the dark. The ceiling gets lower and lower because of the slanted roof. Every few feet there is a screen of boards and behind each screen I created a special room. There is a Barbie room (where I am now), a Monchhichi room, and a Playmobil room. The Barbie room is the best, because it is the farthest down and there is a castle where I can hide behind.

As soon as I hear someone coming up the steps, I creep behind the closet. If the door to my room is opened, I wait first to see who it is. If it's Mommy, I immediately jump out and shout "Peek-a-boo!" or "Haha, I got you!" If it's Daddy, I wait until he leaves. Sometimes that takes a while. He knows and doesn't know it. Maybe he senses that I am hiding, but he is not sure. He's never found me.

And when he asks, "Poppy, you know you never have to hide from me, right," I always tell him that I just don't hear him sometimes or that I was in the bathroom or outside. It is a game that we play. The only one that I always win.

I can sit still for hours, which he cannot do. I never get hungry, my legs never cramp or fall asleep, no matter if I am lying flat on my stomach under the bed, or hiding between the coats in the closet, or making myself small up in a tree outside in the yard.

He gives up. I hear him go down the stairs towards his office. I wait another minute, count to fifty-nine, and when I get to sixty, I crawl towards my Monchhichi dolls. Just as I am about to dress my Indian girl doll in the Monchhichi Rainbow Boy's blue overalls, I hear Mommy go down the stairs, the heels of her boots clicking on the marble. Quickly, I crawl back through the Playmobil room, out of my hiding spot. I open the door and run into the hall. Mommy is already downstairs putting on her new blue fur coat.

"Mommy!" I call from the top of the stairs.

She looks up.

"What are you doing?"

"Nothing."

"Where are you going?"

"To get cheese."

"Can I come?"

"Aren't you in the middle of a game?"

The door to Daddy's office opens. "Are you leaving?"

"I want to get us some cheese."

"I'm coming with you," I say and run quickly down the stairs to pull on my coat.

Daddy looks at me. "Were you upstairs?"

"Yes." I try to look at him like I always do.

"Why do you insist on going with your mom to buy cheese," he asks.

"Because... I want... I want to sing along to that song in the car!"

"What song?"

"About the yellow."

"Yellow? What yellow," Mom asks.

"Yellow is a color. Not a song," he says.

Now they are looking at me angrily. Daddy looks angry, because he understands, and Mommy because she doesn't.

My stomach hurts, but I manage to continue to smile at them, and sing "We're in the yellow."

It's quiet for a moment before Mommy laughs.

"She means the Beatles. I keep thinking, what does this child mean with yellow, but she means the Beatles. That's what you mean, right Poppy? They sing: *'We all live in a yellow submarine'*, not *'we're in the yellow'*."

"Yes," I say. "That's what I mean. We always listen to it in the car, don't we?"

Daddy goes back into his office, and Mommy helps me into my new white rabbit fur coat. It smells like a dead hamster (I used to have one), especially when it's raining, but I am so happy that she is taking me with her that I don't fidget. We have to go through Daddy's office to get to the garage where Mommy's blue sportscar is parked. He sits behind his desk and doesn't look up as we walk past him.

"Bye, Daddy, bye," I call. I hope he isn't upset with me. Or angry. *Is he angry?*

"See you later, Pick-up," Mommy says.

He doesn't look up and sorts through his papers. A few pages tumble to the floor. I bend down to pick them up. He also bends down.

As our heads move close together, he says: "Hypocrite."

It Comes From Within

"Can someone tell me what's happening in the Netherlands with the Malaysians?"

It's a warm afternoon in May, and Mr. Thomas is waving a newspaper around. He tries to cover a new current event every day.

"They hijacked a train," calls Sandra.

"And why did they hijack a train, Sandra?" asks Mr. Thomas.

"Because they're angry."

"You bet they're angry. But do you know why they are rebelling in this way?"

I raise my hand. Daddy talked about this at dinner last night, so I'm happy that I know a little about it.

"Enlighten us, Poppy."

"It's because they're black, Mr. Thomas."

"What exactly do you mean?"

"Black people are criminals and that's why they hijacked the train."

"Black people are what?"

"Criminals," I say.

Mr. Thomas wrinkles his forehead. I turn around and shoot a smile at Jeffrey, who is sitting behind me. Jeffrey is the only boy in school that has a brown father and a white mother. He is number three on my list of nice people (Mr. Thomas is in first place, followed by David, who has one green and one blue eye) so I don't want to offend him. Besides, he's not really black, but brown, like Daddy's armchair. But Jeffrey doesn't seem to be paying attention. He's been quietly singing *Yes Sir, I can Boogie* all morning.

"Jeffrey," I whisper because I want him to notice my smile.

"What?" Jeffrey asks.

"Are you laughing at Jeffrey, Poppy?" Mr. Thomas asks.

I turn around quickly. "No, no, of course not!"

Mr. Thomas has never looked at me this way before. It scares me. "The Malaysians came from Indonesia, Poppy. Jeffrey's father is from Aruba. So, Jeffrey has no connection to the train hijacking whatsoever. Where did you hear this nonsense?"

I hold my breath to keep myself from crying. The tears come anyway.

"Tsk," Annabella makes a sound.

"Be quiet, Annabella," the teacher says before looking at me

"My Daddy said that all blacks are criminals," I whisper.

"I'm sorry to say but your father is wrong."

"That's my Grandpa! Her father is *my* grandfather," Annabella yells. "Mommy says she has the face of a monkey."

Mr. Thomas ignores Annabella's words, as if he didn't hear her. "Poppy, will you please remember in the future that not all black people are criminals? That that's just nonsense?"

I nod quickly.

"What does it mean to be a criminal? Does anybody know?" he asks.

It's quiet. Jeffrey continues to hum the song quietly.

"My mother," David says suddenly.

"Pardon?" Mr. Thomas asks annoyed. "What about your mother?"

"My mother is a criminal," David brags. "You said so yourself."

"No, David, I said that your mom is creative. That's something completely different."

David's mom has a glass eye and bakes cupcakes for little children. For David she knits sweaters in all colors of the rainbow.

Mr. Thomas removes his glasses and rubs his eyes as if he is tired all of a sudden. "Okay, kids, we only have five minutes left until the bell. Should I put on the Flintstone's song?"

The whole class cheers. Mr. Thomas sticks one finger into his ear and one into the air.

"Under one condition. Remember this, whether it's today or sometime in the future, it doesn't matter if you're white like me, or brown like Jeffrey, or purple like Dino. – being good or evil has nothing to do with the color of your skin. That's something that comes from within. Do I make myself clear?"

Everyone nods.

Mr. Thomas looks at me. "Alright, Poppy?"

"Okay."

He winks at me.

I wink back.

Mr. Thomas is the only one that knows I can do that.

The Cold Shoulder

After the bell chimes, I run to my mom waiting outside of the school. She stands out even in a crowd of forty other mothers. It's not only because she is the only one waving and shouting my name, but also because she grew since this morning. It looks like she transformed her hair into a beehive on top of her head. Mommy also put on her new white boots that go over her knees and that have zippers and very high heels. She's wearing a short jean skirt with appliqués. It's November and cold, but her legs are bare, because Mommy doesn't like to cover them. She says that she would rather freeze to death than to wear one of those warm brown turtlenecks from Kohl's. In Long Island, everyone buys their clothes from Kohl's. Modern clothes at a discount for only five dollars!

I'm glad that Mommy doesn't wear turtlenecks, or else she would want to die. She always says, "I'd rather chew off my own foot!"

"Tsk, tsk, tsk," I hear left and right.

"Hi Mommy! Did you get new boots?"

"Yes, their nice, aren't they? I went shopping. In Manhattan! I got tired of the stores here in Long Island."

"I lost all of my marbles again."

"Crazy child."

"I'm allowed to play songs by *Blondie* during our Christmas party."

"That's nice."

"David plays the guitar and Jeffrey the keyboard."

"Jeffrey? His style fits better with *Boney M.*"

"And in two weeks on Monday, we're having picture day."

"Great! I will give you a fantastic make-over."

"But I don't want a beehive on my head."

"Are you deaf? You're not getting crazy beehive hair. You're getting a nice hairdo."

"But I don't have to sleep with the rollers in, right?"

"Yes. Without the rollers it'll be way too flat"

Mommy looks at the other mothers around us. "If everyone here would pay a little more attention to their looks, they wouldn't look like peasants in this god-forsaken place."

Three mothers overhear her and glare at us. But no one has ever spoken to her before.

"Do you still have to go shopping, Mommy?"

"Do you want to come along, or should I drop you off at the house?"

"I want to come with you!"

"You don't have to yell. I'm standing right here."

After we get done grocery shopping, we visit Mara, who has all kinds of household items and toys in her shop. Mara always listens with wide eyes to whatever Mommy has to say. Especially when she is talking about Saint-Tropez, then Mara is all ears, because Saint-Tropez is the most beautiful place she can imagine.

"Do you want a gingerbread cookie, Poppy?" asks Mara.

"Yes, please."

"You really raised her well," Mara says.

"Yeah, it's crazy, right? I don't have anything to do with that. Her father takes care of everything. He's really cultured and considers that important."

"Well, it is."

"She can even order drinks in French. Go ahead and show us, Poppy."

"Je voudrais un coca pour moi, s'il vous plaît," I say.

"What did she say," Mara asks.

"No idea," Mommy answers, "but it makes you feel like you're in Saint-Tropez."

Mommy eats the cookies, while Mara takes care of other customers.

"I wouldn't mind skipping this winter. Today's just another day with shitty weather," Mommy says after the other customer leaves.

"But Christmas is really pretty."

Mommy raises one of her eyebrows. She practices that in front of her mirror. "I always thought that Santa Claus was kind of a pervert, but I do love the Christmas season. It's such a wonderful time of the year: a big tree in the living room, decorated with large silver ornaments. Sitting together, relaxing with the whole family. Eating. Drinking. Long walks through the snow..."

Usually Mommy doesn't pose this much. It's always just the three of us. And Mommy never walks in the snow. She always says: "I'm a member of the *Why Walk When You Can Drive* club," whenever she starts the car.

"Now nice," Mara sighs.

"On Christmas day, Daddy always takes us to eat at a fancy restaurant, right Poppy?"

"Oui, to a five-star restaurant."

"And of course, we will be traveling to Saint-Tropez again this summer."

"I've never been outside of this city," Mara says with a sad tone in her voice.

"That's weird, I couldn't even imagine living like that," says Mommy. "Saint-Tropez is my home away from home."

Before we moved to Long Island, Mommy had never traveled. We were too poor living in that small apartment in New Brunswick , but she never mentions that. It's as if she is suddenly ashamed of the life we had before.

I pet Mara's dog that always sleeps underneath the counter. His name is Babu. Mommy thinks Babu is nothing but a dirty mutt because he is not a purebred and smells bad. I would love to have my own dog. A small white dog. Maybe when I turn eight, Daddy said. But that's still months away. Nowadays, Mommy talks about Daddy more often to other people. I don't like that. I'd much rather prefer her talking about long walks in the snow that she never takes, or other lies like that.

"Do you know what could be wrong? He barely ever touches me anymore, no matter what kind of sexy outfit I have on. But I'm left standing there, looking hot as hell, and think: This can't be normal."

Mara doesn't know either. I pet Babu a little harder. Mommy keeps talking and talking and gets louder and louder.

"When we first met, it only happened that one time. Didn't do a thing for me. Get in, get off, get out. But at least I knew I turned the old geezer on. But since then? He gives me the cold shoulder, no lie!"

"You don't think...," Mara whispers, "... no way."

"No way! That's what I'm saying. Do you think that's normal? Give me another cookie. Are these the ones out of the new *Food and Wine* magazine?"

"Well, yes" Mara says and smiles.

She is nice and honest.

"Babu's fur is so soft today," I call out from underneath the counter."

"Do you also want a cookie, Poppy?" Mara asks.

"No, thank you."

"I know a couple of guys who would love to have a shot at a tall glass of water like me," says Mommy. "I have options. Every day. Everywhere.

"Mommy," I say. "Are we ready to go?"

Mommy pretends like she can't hear me. "I still have a rocking body. Nothing's sagging, everything is tight and where it's supposed to be. So why does he act like he isn't attracted to me?"

"Well," Mara repeats.

I bite into my forearm.

"But I don't want to sound ungrateful," she continues. "As a single mom, you win the lottery if you find a man that takes you and your child. I would look pretty dumb if I left him. Then I will never have a nice roof over my head again like I do now."

"And then we would never travel to Virginia Beach again," I say and crawl out from under the counter. "On y va?"

"The next time you go on vacation, Poppy should spend some more time in the sun," Mommy laughs. "She's always been so pale. Even as a baby. Every time someone visited me in my maternity room, they would say how healthy the girl was. Although I only put on a little rouge and lipstick!"

Mara and Mommy laugh aloud, with wide eyes and hands covering their mouths. "Yes, I know, I'm one of those mothers," says Mommy. "But that doesn't bother us, does it, Poppy?"

"Are you a couch potato, Poppy?" Mara looks at me with twinkling eyes. "Exercise outside is good for you."

"Poppy can open the window and jump up and down on her bed," Mommy says, and they are laughing again. "Can you give us another bag of marbles, Mara? She always loses them."

Mara knows how to wink too!

In the car, I try to snuggle up as close to Mommy as I can. She pushes me away. "I can't steer like that, Poppy."

"I always want to be with you, Mommy."

"Well you are always with me, right?"

"Not always," I say. I give her a kiss.

"Stop that, you're not a baby anymore."

I stay quiet for a while. When we reach the intersection with the bicycle shop, she asks me if I want to hold my hands in front of her eyes.

"Why?"

"It's a game."

"I don't know that one."

"Silly girl. I just invented it," she says. "Now, do it."

"We'll crash."

Mommy laughs and says: "It can't get any worse than it already is. I'm so down."

I don't know what she means with down.

"Then I'll just do it myself, silly."

We drive onto the intersection and Mommy closes her eyes. Cars honk, two people fall off their bikes. Mommy squeals out of joy.

I squeal with her, but out of fear. She doesn't hear the difference.

Summertime

"Can't you sing a song for us, Poppy?" Mommy asks, her mouth full. She likes it when I perform for her like I'm in a band. But she's never asked me to do that in front of Daddy.

He looks up from his steak and says: "Please, can't you just act like a normal person for once?"

"What do you mean? Poppy is an excellent singer."

"We're enjoying a quiet meal."

Daddy often tells me that this is because my parents don't have anything in common. *"Your mother and I don't have anything to talk about. I can speak to you, though. You understand me because we are so alike. You're special to me, you know that, right?"*

Mommy rolls her eyes, "I'm not asking her to sing her ABCs, that's your job. I'm only asking her to sing us a little song."

"We're eating dinner right now, Patricia."

"Yes, and?"

"She needs to finish her plate first."

"The food is too hot. Once Poppy is done singing, she can still stuff her face."

Daddy sighs and looks at me helplessly. I smile and shrug my shoulders. He smiles back and makes an exhausted head gesture towards my Mommy, as if she was the child and Daddy and I the parents.

I don't mind singing for them. If I sing, then I don't need to eat. And what's even more important: If I sing, I don't have to talk about what I did this afternoon after swim practice. I'll tell them once we are done eating dinner. I don't think Mommy will be angry, but Daddy will probably explode.

"Fine," he says while looking at the clock.

We didn't expect that from him.

Mommy claps her hands. "Damn it, Pick-up, that's so nice of you. Sing that *Summertime* song by *Mungo Jerry!*" She looks at Daddy. "You're going to love this, I know it."

"I'm so excited," he says dryly.

I clear my throat and start to sing Mommy's favorite song.

"Chh chh-chh-chh, uh, chh chh-chh-chh, uh.

In the summertime...

Mommy hums along. Daddy looks serious and is sitting stiffly in his chair, but he drums his fingers on the table to the beat. I have never seen him so relaxed before.

Sing with us!

Yes, we are happy!

Dah dah-dah-dah

Dee-dah-do dee-dah-do-dah-do dah-do-dah-dah

Dah-do-dah-dah-dah-dah-dah-dah-dah."

I skip a few lines because Daddy is here, and he might get tired of listening, but Mommy likes it as much as ever and is bent over with laughter. Her face hangs over her plate and tears streak down her cheeks. Daddy sends her an irritated look, but she only laughs harder and elbows him in the arm.

"Fantastic," she says.

"Quiet now!" says Daddy.

I keep singing.

Chh chh-chh-chh, uh chh chh-chh-chh, uh.

Chh chh-chh-chh, uh chh chh-chh-chh, uh.

Sing with us!

We are so happy!

Dah dah-dah-dah

Dee-dah-do dee-dah-do-dah-do dah-do-dah-dah

Dah-do-dah-dah-dah-dah-dah-dah-dah."

I have to sing the last part really loud to be heard over Mommy's hysterical laughter.

Then she applauds.

"Very nice," my Daddy says. He says it harsh but also with a little surprise in his tone.

"Oh," Mommy sighs, "your voice is so nice, Poppy. I could absolutely melt."

"Yes," I say imitating Nanna's raspy voice. "It's like a gift from God."

"Now, finish your food, Poppy," Daddy tells me.

They're almost done with their plates. I dig a hole into the center of my mashed potatoes so that I can pour the gravy into it. Once the gravy is in, I demolish the potato volcano. Then I push the green beans around on my plate, from left to right and back again. I cut the steak into small pieces. I hide a few pieces underneath the destroyed potato volcano. In the meantime, I pretend to chew.

I'll tell them later. Maybe it's not so bad after all. Maybe he won't get angry. If I keep that in mind, it could be alright.

"This is really good," I say.

"You can't know that. Your mouth is empty," Mommy growls at me.

"I already had three bites."

"Don't lie to me, Poppy."

"Look, Mommy, my plate was so full and now it's almost empty."

"You will finish the whole plate," Daddy says without looking at me.

Everything goes quiet.

Silence. It's like I never even sung at all. I take another bite and try not to throw it back up.

"Eat up!" he yells.

I can only breath through my nose.

"Poppy, stop acting so childish," Mommy hisses.

But I am a child.

Something is wrong with my eyes. I see double. All four of them are staring at me.

"Take your plate and go into my office," Daddy orders.

The plate is so heavy and my knees so weak. I still manage to get up and go towards the door.

"And when you are done eating your dinner, call me. As a reward, I will wash your hair."

Now's the moment.

"Off you go," he says.

I turn around. He finished his plate and gives it to Mommy. She tries to stack the plates, the saucière (I'm not allowed to call it a sauce boat anymore), and the bowl with the remaining mashed potatoes.

I can't hold it in anymore: "You don't have to wash my hair today, Daddy. I can do it on my own. I've done it before." My voice is much louder than I intended.

"Damn it," Mommy curses as the bowl of potatoes crashes to the floor.

Daddy doesn't react to Mommy. He only stares at me. "What did you do?" His voice is like thunder.

"I washed my hair, Daddy. After swim practice."

Daddy sits there like a statue and turns white.

I feel snot coming out of my nose and traveling over my lips. I snort it back up into my nose.

"Is that it? Or do you want to tell me anything else, Poppy?" he asks.

"I'm almost ready to swim in the amateur class, Daddy," I answer. I keep calling him "Daddy" so that he won't get angrier.

But I think I'm crying.

Mommy is underneath the table and gathering up the spilled potatoes.

I pull my sleeve over my hand and wipe my eyes clean with it. "And Ashley Baker got an A for her science project, but I don't think she built that solar system on her own."

Daddy just keeps staring at me. I concentrate on the wall behind his head and sniff.

"You think you're so smart, don't you?"

My shoulders rise and fall.

"If you think you are grown-up enough to wash your own hair, then you are grown-up enough to finish your plate."

Just keep staring at the wall. It's almost over.

"Am I right?"

The plate shakes in my hands.

"Will you answer me today?"

I shrug my shoulders again.

"If you shrug your shoulders *one more time*, you're going to get a spanking. I'm not going to put up with that!"

I accidentally do it again and look at him in shock. He slowly shakes his head and holds up a finger in front of his white face. His mouth is slightly open, and his breathing is heavy.

He is very angry with me.

Mommy emerges from under the table.

"Understood!" she heaves. She gathered up all the mashed potatoes back into the bowl. They are covered in dust and hair.

I turn around and leave the room, with the plate.

Vivian

"Oh, you mongrel, aren't you a little stinker?" Mommy is talking to the dog in her arms. It is small and white and wagging with its short tail. When Daddy came in holding the dog, I thought it was for me. I immediately stretched my arms out for it, but Daddy walked right past me towards Mommy.

"Here," he said. "For you, Patricia."

Mommy clapped her hands and squealed how happy she was.

"Her name is Vivian, but I will call her Fifi for short. Got it?" she says.

"I will also call her Fifi," Daddy says.

"Why? You won't ever call her Fifi, that's my name for her."

I just hope Mommy won't toss Fifi into the trash when she's sleeping. That's what she did last year with my pet turtle because she thought it had died. Turns out, it was just hibernating.

We ride into Manhattan to buy stuff for Fifi. Mommy buys various leashes, outfits, and bows, and wants everything in all colors available. After all, Fifi's outfits will have to match all of Mommy's clothes. She also buys a pet carrier so that she can carry Fifi wherever she goes. Fifi gets tired quickly since she has such short legs. Daddy pays for everything, pulling out cash from his wrist bag.

The general rule is that I can get one gift for myself whenever we travel to Manhattan. Last time he bought two bottles of perfume: one for Mommy and one for me. Mine smells better, he told me when Mommy had her back turned to us. But today I won't get anything. It's been two weeks since I washed my hair myself, and I'm still being punished for that.

"Ok," says Mommy. "And now we need to buy a cake for Barbara and Carl, since they're coming tomorrow."

Daddy flinches. He must have forgotten. He mumbles: "Seriously? What time?" He is angry.

"Tomorrow around lunch time."

I haven't been able to think of anything else for days. Aunt Barbara and Uncle Carl are coming to visit us and are bringing their three children: Conny, Bobby, and Hannah. I'm afraid that they are going to want to play with my toys. Daddy doesn't like the idea of visitors either, but he must have given in when Mommy said: "You have the choice, Pick-up. Either we invite them to come here and get it behind us or they'll just show up one day on our front step and want to be let in. How I know Barbara, a herd of wild horses couldn't keep her away."

Daddy said that he can still decide who enters through his door.

"Maybe so," Mommy replied, "but when you're working in your tent factory and my only sister shows up at the door, I definitely won't just send her away!"

I watched as Daddy shook, but Mommy didn't see it. Then she said something that Daddy didn't see coming: "We'll just invite them. That way you can still be in *control*."

Mommy acts as if she knows exactly what she is doing, but she also keeps rambling at Daddy, like a parrot. Daddy uses that word a lot: *control*. Most of the time he doesn't even listen to a word that Mommy says, but today he did. He hates visitors and there's nothing he dislikes more than strangers sitting on the couch in his living room. And it's twice as bad when those people are Aunt Barbara and Uncle Carl. But he must have been thinking about keeping control.

"Fine. But only for an hour. After that they better be gone."

Instead of the expensive cake, Mommy buys cupcakes (you could just offer them some cookies, Daddy said) and gnashes her teeth. When Fifi decides to pee into her new pet carrier on the way back, she screams in anger: "Bad dog! Vi-vi-an!"

Sunday, Family Day

"Like trying to fit a square peg into a round hole," Aunt Barbara answers when Mommy asked her how things were going with Uncle Carl's work.

My uncle is standing in front of the glass cabinet with the forty-three crystal Swarovski figurines and is trying to open the door. When he realizes it's locked, he moves on to the *Precious Moments* collection that Mommy setup on the windowsill.

These little figurines are very cute and can be quite expensive. There are twenty-one that show small children in various poses: one is dressed like an angel, one is herding a sheep, while another is playing with a puppy.

Uncle Carl picks up one that shows a small child looking at a baby in a crib and asks Daddy: "And you paid for these?"

"Fifteen dollars and thirty-three cents," Mommy answers.

Daddy is keeping a watchful eye on Uncle Carl, who is wearing baggy, purple sweatpants and large snow-white tennis shoes. Aunt Barbara is wearing a matching outfit, but in pink instead of purple. An hour ago, when Mommy saw them standing on our doorstep, she asked if Aunt Barbara and Uncle Carl are going to a body building class together. Aunt Barbara didn't understand what Mommy meant and stared angrily at Mommy's finger. Mommy put on all of her rings and is constantly waving her hands around so that Aunt Barbara can clearly see the shiny jewelry.

Aunt Barbara doesn't laugh at any of Mommy's jokes. She doesn't laugh at all. I think that it's because she looks a lot like Nanna, but

Mommy says that the reason that Barbara doesn't laugh is because she doesn't want to show her teeth. Her dentures are too big.

"Oh yeah? Is that what you think? You have dentures too!" I heard Aunt Barbara scream at Mommy when I listened to a recording of one of their phone calls.

"Get a grip," Mommy answered. "You're just jealous because I still have all of my own teeth and never needed a root canal or braces." Silence followed; Aunt Barbara hung up.

Sometimes I'm not sure if Mommy lies or if she actually believes in what she is saying.

"Would you like some more lemonade," Mommy asks.

Conny, Bobby and Hannah, who are sitting beside each other on the couch, shake their heads. Conny is five, Bobby just turned eight, and Hannah is already nine years old. All three of them have curly, red hair. Bobby's front teeth are too large so that he is constantly drooling, and Hannah has such a pig-like noise, that it looks like someone is constantly pressing a finger against it. Conny, the youngest, eats boogers and always giggles at everything. Every now and then Bobby sinks his elbow into Hannah's side, which results in her quietly calling him a 'little shit.'

Mommy has Fifi on her lap and is petting her belly. They're both wearing blue sweaters. "Go show the other kids your room, Poppy," she tells me.

I shake my head, but Mommy doesn't see it. I look at Daddy frantically. Maybe he can ask them to leave, but he still has his eyes on Uncle Carl, who just found the drawer that contains the sterling silverware.

I stand up. Conny, Bobby and Hannah follow me silently. We haven't even made it to the door to my room, when they rush past me screaming and throw themselves onto my new toys: the Playmobil firetruck and caravan. Then Conny also discovers Skipper, Barbie's little sister. Daddy bought her for me this morning. He wasn't mad at me anymore, so everything went back to normal, like it always is on

Sunday morning: Daddy and me naked on the couch. He spent the entire morning telling me how to play with Skipper. "If you twist her arm like so, she gets boobs." Luckily, Conny hadn't figured that out yet; and I won't tell her about it either for sure.

Bobby and Hannah crawl into my secret hideout behind the closet and start messing everything up. I begin to sweat. I had taken care to build and organize everything the way I want it – every toy, every piece of clothing that I sorted, everything is being touched and thrown around the room. Conny is bending Skipper's legs the wrong way until one of them breaks off. Meanwhile, Hannah is tearing off the Monchhichi puppets' clothes. When Bobby wants to join her, she yells: "Get lost, you fucking turd. Asshole!"

Bobby crawls crying and wailing to the Playmobil room, where he collapses on top of my castle. I can hear several parts breaking. They scream and cuss and use words that I have never heard before, not even from Nanna.

"Go fuck yourself before I beat the hell out of you."

"Moron. Cock sucker."

"Shut your fucking mouth, you little shit."

"Fucking whore, you're nothing but a slut."

"Mother fucker."

At some point, I sit down on my bed and cover my ears with my hands, but it doesn't help. I can still hear them – as well as my father's footsteps. He's coming up the stairs, faster and louder than usual. I spring up, ready to go hide, but then I realize that he probably isn't coming because of me, so I sit back down. When he opens the door, his face is pale.

"What the hell is going on in here," he asks Conny.

She shows him Skipper and says: "I didn't do it. It was them. They did it." She nods towards the closet behind my bed where Bobby and Hannah are sitting still.

"Do you not have any decency?" My father keeps looking at Conny. His upper lip is sweaty.

"There," Conny says. "They're hiding behind there."

"Come out here now," Daddy yells into the closet.

Nothing happens.

"I'll count to three," he says. "One."

I would come out if I were them.

"Two."

Conny is keeping count with her fingers. Bobby and Hannah are still acting as if they weren't there.

"Two and a half," Daddy says and clenches his fists. His knuckles are white.

We hear noises. Bobby and Hannah crawl out of the hiding spot.

"I told you they were back there," Conny says.

"Shut your mouth, you ugly bitch," Bobby says.

Daddy's voice is shaking. "Go downstairs. Get out of my house. Out!"

Conny, Bobby and Hannah leave my room. My father follows them.

"Scum," I hear him say. And then again: "Nothing but scum."

"What a day," Daddy sighs.

"Yes," I agree.

"I'm glad they're gone. And you?"

"Yes, me too," I say.

I'm sitting in the bathtub and watch the two doors. One door leads to the hallway and the other one into my parent's bedroom. Both doors can be locked, but he never does it.

Mommy is lying on the couch in the living room. She also didn't enjoy the visit. Daddy gave her a bottle of wine and a couple of magazines. That always calms her down. We get our subscriptions every Thursday. After we are done, we donate them to the poor.

Whenever Mommy talks about the poor, she looks sad. (Because being poor sucks and makes you ugly, she said). That's why the magazines she reads only contains stories about rich people, with beautiful men and women. Sometimes they're sick or have heartache, but at least they are still rich and good looking.

Daddy lifts me out of the bathtub and dries me off with his hands. This way he can carefully examine my body. I hope that one day he won't have to do it anymore. But there is always something new to be found, he says. So, he keeps doing it, never growing bored. It's always the same for me. His hands rub over my skin. His finger enters between my legs. He closes his eyes and breathes funnily, as if he's been running all day. Just like when his new remote-controlled helicopter crashed into his own car. Daddy was standing a hundred feet away and started to panic. We've never seen anything like it before. "Look at that crybaby," Mommy called. "Can you believe it!"

When he removes his finger from me, he shows me his penis. He always says that I need to look at it closely, but I never notice anything new. Then I have to touch his penis and move it around, all the while moving my head from looking at one door to the other. Mommy is not allowed to come in. I always hope that she is reading something exciting. For example, she loves the actress, Joyce Delavigne, because she has beautiful hair and always wears the nicest designer clothes. Mommy likes to wear her hair like Joyce, but they don't sell the same clothes in Long Island. Mommy also likes to read about celebrities, James Bond, and about the royal family. And then she also has an affinity towards Monaco's Grace Kelly, because she is married to a rich prince, and her middle name is Patricia.

When Daddy pushes my head down, I can no longer turn it to look at the doors. He holds my head in both hands. I try to breathe through my nose so that I won't suffocate and think about trees. How can you tell what family a tree belongs to? That's a tough question, but I know a lot about it. For instance, you can tell what kind of tree it is by looking at its bark. If the bark is white and smooth, it probably is a birch. If the bark is whitish or gray, it is a poplar. If the bark looks like a soldier's pants, you can be sure that it is a plane tree. I climb up into a beautiful and thick plane tree, all the way up into the canopy. Nobody knows that I am sitting up there. Only Mr. Thomas is allowed to know. Because he loves trees as much as I do. Because he smiles with his eyes and sometimes his breath smells funny. That's a smell that calms me down, because it's not a bad smell, but something nice.

Daddy takes me into his bedroom and lies me down flat on the bed. Somewhere in my head is a place where everything is quiet. I can't find that place right now. I try to think about everything I know, I take a tour through my mind, and focus on small thoughts. It helps a little. If a tree has red leaves, it's probably a beech in Fall. Or a red maple. Our shampoo and body wash smell like fresh lime. The show with the talking dog is the funniest TV show that I know. Green beans, Playmobil, not all black people are criminals. Steaks. Barbie. Liberty – for a carefree vacation. And that my real dad's name is Joshua.

It's a quarter past three in the middle of the night, and I'm in Daddy's office. My head is full of curlers. Mommy put them in right before bedtime for Picture Day tomorrow.

She staggered a little and kept squinting. Her hands shook, causing half of the curlers to fall to the floor, but she didn't give up and said: "We'll make the most of it, Poppy."

"Okay," I said.

"Don't cry. You're a lady and ladies don't cry."

"Okay," I repeated. I wasn't crying because of the hot curlers in my hair, but because my butt was hurting. I tried to shift from one cheek to the other, so that the middle part could get some relief.

Mommy sighed. "Stop that. You need to stop crying and wiggling around."

Then everything was quiet for a while.

I turned around to try to look at her, but she turned my head to the side so that she could put in the last three curlers. When she was done, she pointed to my bed. "Early to bed, early to rise, makes a man healthy, wealthy and wise. Now, close your eyes and close your mouth." But that didn't help.

And now I'm here. It's dark and quiet. I know this room so well that I can move around easily, even when it's this dark. For example, I could find the telephone book with my eyes closed. But of course, I wouldn't be able to read it.

I make my way across the room with my hands held out in front of me, and within fifteen seconds I find it. I turn on the desk lamp to give me just enough light to read the pages.

There it is: *H. P. Thomas*. I know that his name is Hank Peter. He told me so. Park Avenue in North Hempstead. The phone number is 555-8493. Hank Peter Thomas. 555-8493. I won't be calling him, of course not, it's the middle of the night. But if I would call him, I would say: *Hello, Mr. Thomas! It's me, Poppy. How are you? Good? Did I wake you? Ok, good. Me? Yes, I'm doing good too. Mr. Thomas, I'm in my dad's office. I've been thinking and I have a question for you. It's about washing your hair. My dad does it for me. Three times per week: Wednesdays, Fridays, and Sundays. Yes, that's why it's always so nice and shiny. But I still hate it. Why don't I like it? Well, he always dries me off without a towel. He just uses his hands. No, really, he doesn't use a towel. And that's why I wanted to ask you – is that normal? So, what do you think? Is it normal?*

If Mr. Thomas says yes, then I would say: *Thank you, Mr. Thomas. See you tomorrow!*

And if he answers no, then I would say: *Help!*

I think it would be a good conversation, because it sounds like a simple chat. I start off explaining everything in a few words, just like Mr. Thomas likes when we write our essays, and then ask my question. I'm well prepared, because I have a response to each answer. But it is clear and direct, and Mr. Thomas likes it that way. "Speak clearly, children, and don't mumble. Just say exactly what you mean."

The only hard part about the conversation is that it would be recorded. It wouldn't be smart to break the recording device. Daddy and I had just made up.

I could just call to talk about something else and not mention the bathroom right away. Maybe talk about trees at first. Or even better, about squatters, blacks, and gays. Then Daddy would hear Mr. Thomas say that all people are the same, and he would understand. And then he would no longer think differently about black people or keep calling them niggers. Then Mr. Thomas would surely say that you shouldn't use that word, and Daddy would hear it and remember it in the future. If that works, then I can call him back and next time talk about the hair washing and bathing. Then Daddy would hear Mr. Thomas say that it would be better to use a towel. And then maybe Daddy would think: Yes, Mr. Thomas is pretty smart, he knows what he's talking about. I think he's right. How silly of me!

I take the phone to the recording device underneath the plastic dome. The cord is long enough. I pick up the receiver. The recording device clicks and starts to run. I dial the number, the phone rings. I see myself standing there with the receiver held in my hand.

"Elizabeth Thomas."

Oh, that's right. He's married. To Elizabeth. She sounds sleepy.

"Hello?" she says.

I cough and suddenly my mouth feels dry.

"Hello?" she says again.

"Good evening," I whisper politely. "Is Mr. Thomas available?"

"I'm sorry?"

"This is Jane Fonda," I reply.

Jane Fonda is often called Lady in the magazines. And Mommy called me that today too.

I hear Elizabeth mutter that Hank should come to the phone. Then there is a moment of silence.

"Hank Thomas speaking," the voice of Mr. Thomas says suddenly in my ear.

I flinch.

"Hello," I say quietly.

"Hello?"

I count to ten in my head. Then I say with a high-pitched voice: "Beans, beans the musical fruit: The more you eat, the more you toot!"

I hang up. The recording device stops.

Click!

A Terrible Tragedy

As I wake up the next morning to go brush my teeth in my bathroom, I hear Mommy crying. I run downstairs in my pajamas. At the breakfast table, Mommy is sitting with her head buried in a plate. Daddy is standing beside her with his hands in his pockets. He is bent forward slightly, as if he was comforting her. But as I get closer, I can see that he is actually trying to read the newspaper that is lying beside Mommy's head.

When he sees me, he says: "Good morning, Poppy!"

"Good morning!"

Together we look at Mommy, who continues to cry.

"What's wrong, Mommy?"

"Nothing," Daddy answers.

Mommy looks up and gives Daddy an angry look. Her eyes are red and swollen. She grabs the newspaper and holds it up, pointing at the front page. "You call this nothing!" she screams at Daddy.

On the front page is a picture of Joyce Delavigne with large letters saying: *THE BIRD OF PARADISE IS DEAD!*

"She's dead. Suicide, she shot herself. In the head. And you say it's nothing," Mommy says.

"I'll see you tonight," Daddy says and leaves.

"Go ahead! Leave me alone in my sorrow," Mommy calls after him. "Go to your tent factory! There everyone at least knows their worth."

I pour Mommy a cup of tea to help calm her nerves. I start taking the curlers out of my hair. Mommy looks up again and asks me what I am doing.

"I can brush it myself," I say. "That way you can take the time to grief."

If I brush my hair hard enough, maybe the curls will disappear on their own.

Mommy shakes her head and whispers: "The show must go on." She wipes away her tears with a tissue, gets hairspray and the hairdryer from the bathroom, and starts on my hair.

Monday morning, we always start the class off with a group discussion while sitting in a circle. Usually there's a fight about who gets to start, but today Mr. Thomas himself raises his hand.

"Me first, kids," he says while looking around the room, until we all sit quietly. "Ok, who called me last night?"

No one knows what he's talking about, except for me. I don't say anything and hope that my face isn't as red as it feels.

"I received a phone call last night from someone in this class, I am sure of it. I just don't know who it was."

Still no one answers.

"I won't be mad, I promise," Mr. Thomas says.

And because no one says anything, he continues: "If there is someone here that wants to talk to me about something, he or she can gladly do so after school. Again, I won't be mad. You can talk to me about anything. But to call me and then hang up, let's not do that again."

Then he looks at me and asks:" Ok, Miss Curls, how was your weekend?"

Everyone laughs. To divert the attention away from my hair, I say: "Joyce Delavigne is dead."

"Who?" Mr. Thomas seems confused.

"Joyce Delavigne," I answer. "It was in the papers."

"Joyce Delavigne..." Mr. Thomas thinks. "Joyce Delavigne... Isn't that the crazy French actress with the weird clothes and all that makeup?"

"Yes, that's her. She's dead."

The whole class is looking at me, but not because they think that I am a perfumed whore, or because of Mommy's high heels, or because I'm not allowed to play with anyone, or because I have a rabbit fur coat and get driven to school in a nice car, but because they want to hear what I have to say. Since I had to read the article to Mommy four times this morning, I know exactly what it said.

"Let's talk about something else, kids," Mr. Thomas says. But then everyone is screaming and yelling: "What? What happened? Who died?" Mr. Thomas lets me tell my story. "This is a serious topic and we need to be respectful. Okay, Poppy?"

I nod. "It was suicide."

"How horrible," says Mr. Thomas. "And it was in the papers?"

"Yes, she held a pistol in her right hand and shot herself through her left ear."

"Well, that's strange." The teacher pauses a moment to look around the room. "Does anyone know why it's strange?"

"Because it's pretty dumb, shooting yourself in the ear to kill yourself," says Ashley.

Ashley's father is a cop, so she would know a lot of about that.

"Well, of course you wouldn't normally do that," Mr. Thomas says, "but there is something even stranger about the whole thing. Do you guys know what I mean?"

Everyone shrugs their shoulders.

I raise my hand.

"Yes, Poppy?"

"It would be hard to shoot yourself in the left ear, using your right hand."

"Exactly," he says. "That's right." But then he shakes his head quickly. "Gee, kids, I think this is a dark topic for such a wonderful Monday morning."

"She died too young," I say quietly, "and she still had so many dreams."

"What did she dream about," Jeffrey asks.

"Her biggest dream was to be the first woman to go to Mars. In a space suite made from Chanel. That's a designer brand."

"Hm," says Mr. Thomas.

"But they only sell Chanel in Manhattan," I continue. "I think they're going to bury her in her favorite gold trimmed pants."

"Anyway," says Mr. Thomas.

"It's a terrible tragedy," I sigh just like Mommy did that morning.

"I'm sure it is," Mr. Thomas agrees. "But now it's Annabella's turn, or her arm may fall off. You can lower your hand now, Annabella. How was your weekend?"

"My mom and I baked."

"What did you bake?"

"Carrot cake."

"Oh, wonderful," says Mr. Thomas and he really means it.

Then Jane talks about her little brother's birthday party. They went to a petting zoo, where there was a giant pig, but then her brother fell off of the monkey bars. He broke his arm. Corinna stayed with her grandparents over the weekend and could stay up past ten o'clock. Nathan wasn't allowed to leave his room for most of Saturday, because he cut his father's Bugs Bunny tie in half. And David knitted a sweater all by himself without help from his mother. He's not wearing it today, because one sleeve is shorter than the other, but we're all going to be amazed tomorrow.

When it's finally time to take our class picture, there is a lot of chaos in the schoolyard, because everyone wants to stand beside Mr. Thomas. At some point he decides to lie down on the ground. He's lying on his side with an arm under his head. I kneel behind him, between David and Jeffrey, and try to hold my head in a way to hide my hair.

Dance With Me

Mommy has already finished a half a bottle of rose-colored champagne, and is winking at the singer, Barry Summer, who is singing on the stage. It's Christmas today and we drove to a dinner and a show at a casino hotel.

"Oh, Poppy," she whispers, "look at his smile. Good God, I'm totally crazy about this guy."

Barry Summer does have a nice smile, but he's not sending it Mommy's direction. He's smiling at his wife, whose name is Lala and is sitting at a table near the stage with their four children. Lala Summer has brown hair and a white dress, and Barry is in love with her.

"What is he doing with that cow? Do you know, Pick-up?" Mommy asks. "You have much better taste than him. Aren't I much prettier? Huh?"

Daddy doesn't answer. He's looking over the wine list and is stroking my leg with one hand. Daddy isn't in love with Mommy; he's in love with me.

Barry's and Lala's children are laughing at something their mother said. Lala has beautiful white teeth and she throws her head back a little when she laughs. Mommy does that too, but when she does it, she always looks around to convince herself that everyone is watching her laugh. Lala only has eyes for her children.

"I think she's wearing dentures. Poppy? Tell me: who do you think is prettier?"

"You."

"Well, I have to agree," says Mommy and blows a curled strand of hair out of her face. She purposefully styled it that way just for tonight.

After our appetizers – a disgusting shrimp cocktail for Mommy and Daddy, and a piece of watermelon for me – Mommy wants to dance.

"Don't let me stop you," says Daddy.

"I don't want to dance alone, Pick-up." Mommy nods in the direction of the dance floor, where more and more couples are gathering.

"I don't dance," Daddy says.

"Sure, we know that," she responds. "But I won't be sitting around like Piffy on a rock bun the whole night."

The waiter brings the pumpkin soup. He pours it from a silver pot into our bowls. When he leaves, Daddy repeats his words: "I don't dance."

"You never do anything that I like."

That's true. Daddy doesn't dance, he doesn't laugh, and hardly every speaks. He smokes and works. He gropes me or he lies on top of me to see how strong I've gotten.

Mommy looks around. Everywhere there are happy families sitting at the tables. The men are all younger than Daddy, and if they are the same age, they probably came along as the grandfathers. Mommy is now winking at all the men that she can see and laughs, but no one asks her to dance.

When our waiter returns to take the soup bowls, Mommy places her hand on his arm. "If you are interested in a round of Quickstep, you know where to find me."

The waiter looks at Daddy, but he's looking at the singer, Lemon, who joined Barry up on the stage. She has dark skin and is wearing a short, blue-metallic leather dress. Mommy would kill to own something like that.

Mommy's hand squeezes the waiter's upper arm and tells him how nice his muscles are. He would be able to easily carry her out to the dance floor. "See you soon? Then you can see how my skirt twirls in the air."

The waiter respectfully withdraws his arm, bows, and says that he is too busy. When he's gone, Daddy gets up.

"What are you doing now," Mommy asks.

"Bathroom," he says and disappears.

"Make sure not to fall in," Mommy mutters.

I laugh. Mommy laughs too – with her head thrown back. She looks around again.

So, there we sit, Mommy and me. She is wearing a red fluttery dress and her hair is styled. She has her diamond earrings in and all her rings on her fingers. I'm in a dark-blue silk dress with white stockings and black shoes. Mommy lights a cigarette and quietly hums to the music. I try to imagine how it would be if Daddy would never return from the bathroom. Would the money in Mommy's purse be enough to pay the bill? Would it be enough for us to go on alone? Probably not. But we could still find a job for me. Or we could find my real father and ask him if he wants us back. Or find a new father. He doesn't even have to be rich. Normal would be fine.

"Poppy? Poppy, look here!"

Mommy folded her napkin into the shape of a bra and is holding it up to her breasts.

"Do you want to play a game?" I ask.

Mommy closes her eyes for a moment. Then she tosses her napkin on the table. "I hope Pick-up gets lost on his way to the bathroom."

Before I can tell her no, she grabs my hand and pulls me onto the dance floor. When we get to the middle of the crowd, Mommy loudly says: "Ok Poppy, let's go, but just because you really want to." Then she begins to twirl her skirt around and snaps her fingers. Barry and Lemon sing *The Alternative Way*, and Mommy gets wilder and wilder, which makes the people around us step back, so Mommy has more room for her crazy dance moves. She jumps from left to right, then from front to back, and keeps yelling: "Yippee, here I am, Poppy!" It sounds happy and excited, but the further she jumps, the angrier she looks. She keeps running into the other dancing couples and stepping on other people's toes. When someone finally says something to her, she tells him: "Get over it, you wimp!"

"Shhh, Mommy," I say. "These people aren't doing anything wrong."

"I'm also a person. I have rights."

"Come on, Mommy, let's sit back down."

"I deserve the same amount of respect as others. Pick-up doesn't dance, but he's got a lot of money. He'll buy out this entire place, if necessary, including Lemon with her fat, black ass."

Thankfully, the stage is far away. I can't image that the singer would want to hear her say that.

Suddenly, Daddy is standing beside us. He grabs Mommy's arm.

"Oh, so you did come to kidnap me, after all," she giggles.

"We're going home."

"But I'm still hungry," she pouts.

"That's enough, Patricia, damnit. You're embarrassing yourself."

Daddy is the only one that can calm Mommy down. She never gets mad when he tells her to stop something. She only laughs and says: "Oops."

She knows it's better to do what Daddy says. He's the only one who never makes any mistakes. He knows how to eat properly with a fork and knife. That the silverware at a restaurant should be used moving from the outside in. That you are not supposed to show people that specific finger, or they'll chop off your entire hand.

Lemon finished all her songs and is done for the evening. "Thank you. Thank you very much," she says through the microphone. Everyone claps, while Daddy drags us to the coat check. Mommy turns around with a smile, as if the applause was for her. Then Daddy helps me into my coat. Mommy has to do it on her own. Just before Daddy can shove Mommy through the spinning doors, we can hear Lemon say that this was a night to remember and that she has never seen so many beautiful people together in one place.

Don't you think so, Barry?

Definitely, Lemon! But the most beautiful women is my wife, Lala.

Well, I would hope so, Barry.

Applause.

1980

Mommy can't make it on her own.
And I can't make it on my own with Mommy.
So I ran to a pay phone
and called Daddy... and Daddy came.
(Poppy – ten years old)

Hoping For Your Understanding

"Poppy!"

Mommy screams from the bottom of the stairs. I'm in my bed, hurting all over. My head, my legs, my arms. The flu. It's the second day.

Yesterday was a beautiful sunny day, so I woke up covered in sweat with a high fever. I didn't go to school because the first thing I did was throw up. Daddy didn't go to work either. He stayed home all day to keep an eye on me and so that Mommy could lay outside in the yard. She likes to tan until her body is golden-brown. As soon as the first rays of sun peek out, she grabs her white and gold bikini and lays in the yard, arms and legs stretched out wide. "Boys, I'm going to go soak up some sun!" she would always yell.

She did it yesterday too. Mommy soaks up the sun and I'm lying in my dark room with a fever. Daddy checks on me every thirty minutes to take my temperature. I can't stay here another day. I need to get away. To school.

What's today anyway? Wednesday. I have to make it. But when I try to stand up, a searing pain shoots through the middle of my head. There is pressure on the inside of my eyes and a loud ringing noise in my ear.

"Poppy!"

I want to let Mom know that I'll be down in a minute, but when I open my mouth, only hot air comes out.

"Poppy!"

Shut up, I want to yell back, *just shut your stupid mouth!* I take a deep break instead and call: "Coming!"

I throw on some clothes and head downstairs, where Mommy is already eating breakfast. One hand is pressing a chocolate-covered toast into her mouth, while the other hand is petting Fifi's stomach, who is sitting in her lap.

"Are you feeling any better?" she asks. Chocolate and breadcrumbs cover her lips

I nod.

"You're still looking rather pale."

I shrug my shoulders.

Mommy grabs another toast covered in chocolate and demolishes it in two bites. She's getting fat. Every time she buys something pretty, she has to get it a size bigger a few weeks later. I'm getting thinner. It's as if we're both growing in the wrong direction.

I sit down and place my head against the cool tabletop.

"You're not well yet," she says.

"It's Wednesday," I point out. "It's only for a few hours. I'll make it. Only P.E. will be hard, I think."

"I don't think it's a smart idea to bounce around like a monkey in a circus."

"Can you write me a note excusing me, Mommy?"

"Sure," she says. She gets up, leaves the kitchen, and returns with a pen and paper. I drink some tea. Then I take the pen and write:

Dear Mr. Thomas,

Since Poppy isn't yet feeling quite like herself, I believe it would be best that she not participate in P.E. today.

Hoping for your understanding.

Sincerely,

Patricia Grinberg-Brown (Poppy's mother)

"What does it say there," Mommy asks and points to the last sentence.

I read it aloud.

Mommy nods.

"Yes," she says, "hoping for your understanding. That sounds nice."

Mommy never cared that she could barely read or write. She doesn't have the patience to read a book, she likes pictures and photos, and likes to look at magazines. If something has to be read aloud and written down, either Dad or I will do it for her. When going grocery shopping, she draws little pictures of things she needs instead of making a list. It looks cuter too, she says. I could never go shopping using her drawings. She draws in a lot of detail and most things usually include some kind of smiley face or heart-shaped eyes. I can't tell her depiction of apples and bananas apart, and she uses the same picture of a chicken for both eggs and chicken breast. A smiling chicken means eggs; a crying chicken means chicken breast. If Mommy gets to buy a few things for herself, her shopping list ends in drawings of stars, hearts, flowers and fireworks.

Mommy copies my letter, sticking out her tongue in concentration. She writes slowly and draws a period after every word.

"You don't have to put a period after every word, Mommy," I tell her.

"Let me do it my way."

Mommy finishes the letter just as Daddy enters the kitchen. He's in his pajamas. He thinks that I'm staying home one more day.

"Why aren't you in bed," he asks.

"Because I'm feeling much better."

Mom hands me the note and I stick it into my school bag.

"What's that," he asks.

"An excuse note, so that she doesn't have to participate in P.E.," Mommy answers him.

He looks at me with his eyebrows raised high. "You're *not* thinking about going to school, are you?"

"Yes," I say, "I really am feeling much better."

He places a hand against my forehead. I shrink back a little.

"She's burning up with fever," he tells Mommy.

"I am not!"

"I think it's irresponsible to let her go."

I grab one of Mommy's toast and start chewing on it. "Look, I'm even hungry again."

"You're staying home!" Daddy says.

"I need to go to school," I reply, "we're practicing for the upcoming spelling bee."

"This is ridiculous, Patricia. Poppy is too sick."

"Listen," Mommy says, "if Poppy wants to go to school, I can't stop her." She sighs. She wants to go outside and tan in peace. Just like yesterday.

Dad and I look at each other. I count the seconds in my head. After five seconds, he looks away first. That's the first time I won. My legs are shaking out of fear and because of the fever. But there's something else, something new. *He* looked away first, not me. *He. Looked. Away. First.*

I push the plate away and get up. My father leaves the kitchen.

"Can we get going, Mommy?" It's way too early, but I don't want to see him again. Mommy finishes her forth piece of toast and then drives me to school. I'm probably the only ten-year-old in the world that gets dropped off and picked up from school every day (*but maybe there are others*).

I'm also the only ten-year-old that owns her own horse (*I'm fairly sure about that*). The only ten-year-old that isn't allowed to wash her own hair (*I'm sure because I've carefully asked others in my class before*). The only one with a surfboard (*I'm not so sure about that*). The only one with nightmares that are so bad that I sometimes lie awake all night long (*I'm sure, because they're always about my Dad and I can't imagine that other people would have dreams about their fathers like that*). The only one with a mother who can't even write her own name (*I didn't ask around about this one because I think it would embarrass Mom, but I can't imagine other mothers having that problem*). The only one that gets her picture taken every Sunday morning while naked (*I sense that this is true, but never asked anyone about it*). I also think that I am the only ten-year-old that knows what sex is (*but I don't dare ask the other kids if they know too, and if yes, who they learned it from*).

"Good morning, Poppy. Welcome back," Mr. Thomas is looking at me. He's alone in the classroom. I'm the first one here.

"Hello, Mr. Thomas."

I sit down at my desk and press a hand against my aching stomach. Because of the flu, but also because I know that I am the only ten-year-old like this. There are no other girls like me. I can tell by looking at them. They're different. I can read it in their eyes; they look happier. And dumber. Because they don't have to worry about a thing. I sometimes get the feeling that my head may want to explode from all the thoughts I have. And not just on Wednesdays, Fridays and Sundays. That could happen at any time. I don't drink anything before going to bed anymore, or he would hear me getting up to use the bathroom. Even at his age, his hearing is very good.

The last time I had to use the bathroom at night, he immediately came out of the bedroom to join me. He helped wipe and then said that it's not clean enough yet, so I had to take a bath in the middle of the night.

I'll never go downstairs again at night. If I really can't hold it anymore, I use the sink in my room. I even pooped into it once. It took forever to get rid of it, and the smell lingered for a couple of days. But that's not so bad. *Once* I went downstairs to Mommy because of a horrible nightmare. I dreamt that Mommy had died. She was gone and I would have to live the rest of my live alone with Daddy. I told him that I wanted to die too, but he said: "You don't want to die, you want to stay with me, and you know it. You're my little wife."

At Mommy's funeral, Nanna was cheering as if her life depended on it. When I asked her why she was so happy (*It's your daughter," I cried. "Don't you want her to live? That I have a mother? How can you be so happy?"*), Nanna answered that I was stupid; this was the moment to open the safe.

"Don't you understand, Poppy? This is *my* Plan B."

"You don't know the code," I reminded her.

"But of course, I know it," Nanna said. "The code is D-E-A-D."

Suddenly, Nanna was standing in Dad's office and she was opening the safe. At first, I didn't want to see what was in it, but then she started to cuss: "What the devil? That bastard! What am I supposed to do with this?" Now I wanted to look.

I approached the safe slowly. Nanna was still standing in front of it, so I poked her in the back. "Move over, Nanna."

She turns around. "Are you sure you want to see this, Poppy?"

"Is it really bad, Nanna?"

She didn't say anything and didn't move away. I started to panic. Mommy is dead, I thought, and there's something horrible in the safe.

"Why is all this happening, Nanna?"

"That's life, Poppy," she answered and finally stepped aside.

I shut my eyes tight for a second before opening them again.

It was me, as a baby, sleeping in the safe.

Nanna left the office cursing loudly.

"Shh!" I call. "Shh! The baby is sleeping!" At the time, I hadn't thought it was weird that I was the one in the safe. I covered the baby with a blanket and closed the safe carefully, so as not to wake myself up.

*

When I woke up, I was crying. I went to my parent's bedroom and threw my arms around my sleeping mother.

Daddy immediately sat up. "What's going on, Poppy?" he asked.

"Nothing." I was shaking Mommy hard. "Mom?" I whisper in her ear. "I had a nightmare."

Mommy doesn't wake up. She just mumbled something and then lifted the covers so that I can crawl in beside her in the large bed. But Daddy grabs me right away and lifts me over Mommy so that I was lying in the middle between them, just a little further down. Mommy kept snoring, and Dad took my hand and placed it on his penis. I withdrew my hand carefully and pressed my body as close to Mommy as I could, but he yanked me back towards him and put my hand back.

I tried withdrawing my hand a few more times, but somehow it turned into a game, that Daddy enjoyed more and more, and then I thought, it would be better just to get it over with as quickly as possible. So, I didn't try anything else to stop him, but I also didn't willingly participate. He covered my hand with his own and started stroking his penis. I was afraid that Mommy would wake up, but at the same time, I wanted her to wake up badly. I whimpered as quietly as I could. It seemed like it took forever for him to finish. Afterwards, he whispered: "You even moaned a little. You like this game, don't you? You invented it after all." His eyes were gleaming.

It wasn't the first time that he said something like that to me. He says things like that often. He's under the impression that I started the whole thing, right after we moved into his house. He tells me about it, that even on the first day I already grabbed his hand and pushed it into my pants, and that we both liked playing this game from then on. And he whispered that there was something special between us from the start.

Did I really do that? But why would I?
I can't remember.

Mr. Thomas is eyeing me suspiciously. "Everything ok with you, Poppy?" He tilts his head to the side.
"Yep."
"Are you sure?"
"Sure as can be."
"Okay."
In my head I scream: *Help me!*

Random Chances

Daddy is kneeling in front of me on the big bed, a tampon in his hand. I'm lying on the lounge chair, just like Mommy when she is outside tanning, but I'm not wearing a bikini. Dad asks if I understand what he is saying about blood and menstruations and tampons.

"But all this doesn't apply to me yet," I tell him. "I'm only ten years old."

"I didn't ask you how old you are, I asked if you understand," Daddy says.

"Yes!"

"Ok, then I will insert the tampon now. Then you will know what it feels like." He always says that. "Then you will know what it feels like." He says that all this will come in handy in the future when I'm married. Because I will know how to do everything. ("You will make your future husband very happy").

I don't ever want to get married. Especially because I *do* know what it feels like.

His insert the tampon with his fingers. It's deep. And it hurts. Daddy starts to breath heavily.

This morning, Mommy and I drove into the city, because Dad gave her some more money for shopping. We went to see Marie's at her Modern Paradise store, where Mommy has been a regular customer for years ("I've been spending a fortune in this store!") and they know exactly what Mom likes. They line up the newest collection of short, tight, and sparkly dresses. If Mommy notices a dress that she particularly likes, she yells: "Jesus, that has my name written all over it!" There's always coffee and champagne for Mommy. Lemonade for me and a bowl of water for Fifi, and after Mommy tries on all the dresses, she will have a boring conversation with the salesperson.

Today it was a little more interesting, though. They talked about a baby disappearing in Australia. The parents claimed that it was eaten by a Dingo, but the police believe that the mother killed her baby. I find it hard to believe that any mother could do that to her own child. Well, maybe except mine.

"Sometimes babies can make you angry, Poppy," she tells me. "Because they ruin your perfect figure. But still, it's total nonsense: Dingo's only eat fish and their wings are way too small to be able to lift a baby."

No one dared tell Mommy that a Dingo is not a penguin.

We left the store with three bags full of silk and polyester, and made our way to the children's boutique, where they just received a new collection.

"The early bird catches the worm, Poppy. It's best to be the first through the doors, or the nicest items will be gone." Mommy is absolutely sure about that.

"Oh, what a shame, we're too late," I teased her as we entered the store. "All the nice things are already gone." It was a joke. The whole store was full of cardigans, pullovers, and winter coats. But Mommy looked at me in shock and frowned: "Are you stupid? These are all the latest rave! You must be blind!"

She pushed me into a dressing room and proceeded to hand me all kinds of winter clothing to try on. It was extremely hot, and everything itched. Then Mommy suddenly had the idea to bring me very tight and very thick turtlenecks that I couldn't even put on without her help.

While I was trying to squeeze into a violet specimen with silver thread, Mom whirled on the sales lady, took a deep breath, and let lose: "By the way, you sold the same rose-colored dress that you sold to my Poppy, to my husband's granddaughter. You know, the one with the bow and the golden butterfly."

"I don't remember that..."

"Yes," she said. "You do remember. If you're going to sell something exclusively to me, then I should be able to expect that you're not going to sell the same thing to just anybody. Especially not to Phyllis and her spoiled brat, who doesn't do anything but try to imitate me because she doesn't have good taste herself."

"I'm sure that it was just a mistake. It… it won't happen again," the saleslady stammers.

"I would like to hope so. I mean, I laughed about it, but my husband was furious," Mommy lies. "What's your name?"

"Sylvia."

"Wonderful, a royal name. Good for you. That means that you aren't a complete moron, right? Just remember, Sylvia, that I spend a lot of money here, so I expect the appropriate level of service, or else I will take my money elsewhere!"

Sylvia's neck was turning red. Mine was too, but you couldn't see them because of the turtleneck, which was starting to choke me. The tight corduroys were also not comfortable, but the stupid sweater was really trying to do me in.

Sylvia must have noticed the sweat forming on my forehead. "I think you daughter isn't feeling too well, Mrs. Grinberg-Brown," she said.

"What? Why?" Mommy turns around and for one moment it seemed she had forgotten who I was. She looked at me in shock. It's the same look she has when Dad uses too many complex words in one sentence.

"Maybe she's a little hot in that sweater," the saleslady says.

"And you know that how?"

"Well," says Sylvia. "I just mean that she is such a nice and quiet little girl who never says a word, and it looks like she's struggling for breath."

"Are you trying to suggest that I don't know what's best for my own daughter," Mommy asks sharply.

"Mommy," I croak, interrupting her. "Can you please help me get this off?"

"Why?"

"I'm feeling dizzy."

She looked at the sweater. "Is it not comfortable? It fits you perfectly."

"No! It's way too tight! I can barely breath or lift my arms..." I answer. "Mom, please."

"This violet is such a distinctive color. Stop making a scene! The material is flexible, silly," she said. "Hm, why don't you put on this red coat over it, Poppy."

"Mommy..."

She grabbed me by the shoulders and shook me roughly. "You're going to put that coat on right now," she yelled in my face. "Don't argue!"

The saleslady lifted a hand as if she were about to help me, but in the end, she let it drop again. She even took a step back.

I forced myself into the red winter coat, and then I couldn't move anymore. It was as if I was one of those statues in the art museum that everyone gawked at.

"Now we're ready for winter. You'll be the prettiest girl in school, Poppy!" Mommy said and shot the sales-lady a triumphant look.

Sylvia only nodded.

"I can't go to school wearing this, Mommy," I said. "I won't be able to play. I can barely move."

"So?" Her face was red with anger. "You're not supposed to run around in this anyway. Just walk back and forth. That's what you do during recess, right? Walk around?"

"But Mom..."

"Are you trying to tell me I don't know what you do during recess?"

"No."

"So, what is it that you do?"

"Walk around."

"I knew it!" she exclaimed, looking around as if expecting applause.

The saleslady nodded again, but this time at me, as if to say: Best not to argue with her.

Mommy bit her thumb and then hit her knee with the same hand. "Can you believe this? You know what, we'll take it all. You only live once, right Poppy? But then I don't want to hear another word out of you, understand? Not all mothers would let their daughters dress so nicely, so don't expect too much more. Got it?"

"Yes," I said.

"Promise?"

"I promise."

We had almost made it to the car. Mommy was strutting ahead with all the shopping bags. I wasn't allowed to carry anything (except Fifi), since Mommy likes to walk around with shopping bags from different stores. She hopes that someone will take notice and say something like "Wow, you sure did go all out," because then she can answer with: "Well, if you don't buy the most expensive things, are you even living at all?"

If she had been carrying fewer shopping bags and would not have worn her leopard boots with five-inch heels, she probably wouldn't have tripped. But she was, and so she fell while crossing the street. She didn't get back up, but just laid there crying like a baby. I tried to pull her up, but she cussed before pushing me away, and then just cried louder.

I had never been this embarrassed before. I stayed close by for about five minutes. When I realized that she would not stand up and that a line of honking cars was piling up on both sides, I grabbed Fifi and crossed the street to stand with a hundred other people – to look at the sobbing woman lying in the middle of the street amid a pile of shopping bags.

A man standing beside me said: "Look at her and the state she is in. She must be drunk!"

I nodded. "Do you see that, Fifi? The lady over there is acting crazy. Thank God we don't know her."

A cop finally showed up and helped Mommy stand. It seemed to be working out well (maybe because the cop had a mustache and

Mommy loves those), but then she looked like she might collapse again, so the cop picked her up and carried her over to the sidewalk. Her legs were spread-eagle (she should have worn pants instead of a miniskirt!) and her head lolled around from side to side as if an ocean wave had washed her into his arms.

The cop deposited her on a bench off to the side. First she whispered helplessly: "Where am I? What happened? Everything is spinning." Then she suddenly remembered her shopping bags and yelled: "Poppy! Poppy! Come here, now! Where are my bags? Where are you? And where the hell are my bags!" She yelled at an elderly couple, who only gaped at her with open mouths: "Get lost, old timers!"

I gathered all the dropped bags from the street and gave them to her. The cop was saying: "You only fainted for a moment. Take a second to catch your breath. You must have collapsed from fatigue." (I thought that was a weird thing to say. Could he not see my Mom clearly?).

When Mommy noticed blood on her knee, she exclaimed that she needed medical attention and could no longer drive the car. "Couldn't you take us home in your cop car?"

The cop shook his head and pointed to his bicycle. "We don't have the personnel for a personal escort."

Mommy can't make it on her own. And I can't make it on my own with Mommy, so I ran to a pay phone and called Daddy... and Daddy came.

"What happened, Poppy?"

"I fell. Are you stupid? Can't you see that," Mommy yelled.

Daddy didn't say anything and took us home.

"Poppy, that's not a band aide," they said in chorus.

"I know, it's a roll of gauze." I was getting angry. They shouldn't laugh at me as if *I* was the crazy one, as if *I* was the one that all of New York was laughing at, as if *I* was the one too dumb to walk, as if *I* had bought a thousand dollars' worth of clothing that doesn't even fit me.

"That's not gauze either, you little angel."

"Then what is it, Mommy?"

Mommy and Daddy only laughed louder. It rang in my ears, and I hated them both so much in that moment that it scared me. In my mind, I could see both Mom and Dad lying in the middle of the road as a large truck came and ran over them, honking its horn. Forwards, and then backwards too. And then forwards again.

"What is it," I asked again.

"You'll figure it out, Poppy," Daddy said, while petting my head and winking at me.

Oh no, winking was supposed to be my thing!

And now I figured it out. Your life is nothing but a collection of random chances, Nanna Brown would say. Daddy explains it to me and sticks the not-gauze into me and then pulls it back out by the string, as if he was playing a game. Then he grabs a new one and gives it to me. It's my turn now. It's important that I know how to pull it out myself. He sniffs it with his large nose. He's gasping and grabs his penis.

After I pull the tampon out, he sticks his penis in my mouth.

Mommy is downstairs on the couch watching TV. She's eating a bowl of chocolates to help calm her nerves.

The Swimming Cap

This evening I am laying on the couch and Mommy is in the bathroom with Daddy. He is getting black hair.

During our Sunday morning breakfast, we waged a silent war because I did not come downstairs to have my pictures taken, I stayed in bed. When Daddy came upstairs to check on me, I hid in my secret closet. He called out quietly at first *(so as not to wake up Mommy)* and then he kept getting angrier and louder (because he can't stand it when I hide from him and don't answer his calls).

In the end, Mommy yelled from the bedroom: "Quiet, damn it!" and Daddy went back downstairs.

He kept giving me angry looks during breakfast. I was scared and kept my eyes trained on Mommy, who was gossiping about Aunt Barbara and Uncle Carl.

"She keeps calling, asking for money, but she can kiss my ass."

"Hm…," Daddy growled.

"And Barbara keeps talking and talking. She doesn't realize how much money her phone calls cost."

"Hm…"

"She says that they need a thousand dollars for the dentist, but her and Carl don't even have their own teeth anymore. Who do they take me for?"

I laughed. Daddy didn't like that. He was looking for something that would allow him to explode verbally. It ended up being the cheese. Cheese is one of the few things that I like to eat. I take the slices of cheese of my bread, but Daddy doesn't like when I do that. He also doesn't like when I loudly sip my tea. Or when I lick my knife clean. I know what would happen if I continue to do it: First, he would rap his knuckles against the table. Then I would look up and feign surprise: "Who is it?" And finally, he would hit me upside the head. Everything happens within a few seconds; it could have been a skit on TV. It doesn't hurt. I withdraw into my thoughts and hardly feel anything. Like I'm doing right now.

I picked a slice of cheese of my bread.

Daddy knocks on the table.

"Who is it?"

He hits me upside the head.

Nothing out of the ordinary so far. But Mommy stopped eating and was looking at him with furrowed brow.

"Is something wrong," Daddy asked.

"Yes," she said. "There is, but..." Mommy looked at me and back at Daddy.

"What is it," he asked her.

Mommy never talks back to Daddy, it would be a first.

Her forehead scrunched up even more. "You know what I think, Pick-up?"

"I don't have the slightest idea."

She started chewing on her thumb, like she always does when she's searching for the right words.

"What do you want to say, Mommy," I encourage her.

"I think, that with enough effort and support, we could make you look fifty again."

Silence. Daddy looked irritated.

"You think, Patricia," he asked with a hint of suspicion.

"Yes!" she answered as if the entire world suddenly made sense to her. "Yes! This whole week, I was thinking about nothing but how old you look, but now I know why: It's your hair color."

Daddy ran a hand through his hair.

"And it's not like you don't have enough hair left on your head. We could work with it. You just seem so old because your hair is such a washed-out gray color. Don't you think so, Poppy?"

102

I didn't know how to answer her.

"Poppy?"

"Hm?"

"Your dad has a full head of hair, so it's the color, right?"

I looked at Daddy. "What color do you want it to be?"

"Black, of course," Mommy says.

"Black?" Daddy seemed shocked.

"Black," she said again. "Black is refined and timeless."

"I don't know, Patricia…"

"Sure, Pick-up," she said. "Trust me. There are a few things that I am an expert in, and hair is one of them."

"Hm…"

"And certificates of authenticity," she said, "I know a lot about those as well."

Within a week, a pretty blue package from France was delivered via mail, containing a special hair dye. Daddy had already said at least twenty times that there was no way in hell that he would dye his hair, but when he saw the package, his resolve faltered. The man pictured on the package had beautiful black hair. He looked mysterious, kind of like Pierce Brosnan.

"All the good that could come from a pretty head of hair, huh Poppy," Mommy sighed.

Now they are both in the bathroom, and I am watching *Columbo* – I have it on mute, or they would hear it upstairs. Daddy specifically told me not to watch *Columbo*, because the show is about crimes, and those can be contagious. But I like Columbo. He punishes fathers that hurt their children. But it also shows heartbreak, robberies, sex, and sadness. He always finds a way to get the bad guy in the end.

When I hear them coming down the stairs, I turn the TV off.

"What were you watching," Daddy asks.

He's wearing a purple swimming cap on his head and his t-shirt is stained with black spots. His eyes are also different. I can see a hint of fear in them. He's bent over, as if the swimming cap weighs a ton.

"What were you watching," he repeats himself.

"Nothing," I answer. "Is your hair black yet?"

"It has to sit for twenty minutes," Mommy says and turns the TV back on. She sits down next to me on the couch and watches the screen, where Columbo is talking to his friends.

"Were you secretly watching this," she asks me.

"Yes, but I didn't know what kind of show it was, Mommy."

Daddy is just standing there, not saying a word. So, we watch the end of Columbo. All good. Mommy and I are sitting together on the couch, and Daddy is standing beside us. The alarm on Daddy's watch chimes and they go to wash out the dye.

They ask me to come help hold the showerhead over his head. He kneels in front of the bathtub and Mommy bends over him to wash his hair. The water running into the tub is black as night. When Mommy is finished, Daddy is allowed to stand up and look into the mirror. He looks like a clown. A very scary clown with an ugly black wig on his ugly old head. Daddy looks just as horrified as me.

But Mommy says: "If I didn't know any better, I would say you look like you're fifty-three, Pick-up."

My father keeps looking into the mirror and runs a hand over the remaining black spots on his forehead. "How long will it be like this?" he asks.

"It's permanent color," Mommy says. "It'll probably last a few months."

"Awesome," I giggle.

Daddy stares at me. His shoulders are sagging. Black spots on his forehead.

The swimming cap was removed but his head still seemed to sag underneath its weight.

"Awesome," I say again.

1983

I am not just *one*. There are *two* of me.
The Poppy that no one can see
And the Poppy that everyone knows.
The inner Poppy is getting stronger.
But the outside Poppy can't keep up with the lies anymore.
(Poppy – thirteen years old)

Maya Horn Disease

I faint a lot. Mom thinks I have the same disease as Maya Horn, because she was also very skinny and fainted a lot. Maya died six months ago. Dad finally sent us to the doctor. Nanna is with us. She has insomnia. When she heard that we were going to go see a doctor, she immediately joined us so that Mom can pay for her medications.

It's four o'clock in the afternoon, so Mom had already had a few glasses of wine. As Dr. Bowman – his glasses on top of his head – peeked around the corner into the waiting room, he frowned and wrinkled his forehead. "Ok, so the whole family, huh? Whose first?"

"We're here because of Poppy," Mom says. "But since we came all this way, you might as well take a look at Grandma Brown too." Mom points to Nanna beside her.

Dr. Bowman looks at Nanna.

She raises her finger. "That's me, Brown, always at the ready."

The consultation room only has two chairs.

"No problem," Mom says. "I'll stand. I still have strong, young legs."

But Dr. Bowman notices Mom swaying a little, so he goes and gets an additional chair. Then he sits down behind is desk and appraises me. "Well, Poppy, it's been a while since we last seen you here."

"Yes, Dr. Bowman."

"How are you feeling?"

"Good."

"We think that she has the Maya Horn disease," Mom says.

The doctor raises an eyebrow. "What kind of disease?"

"She's not eating," Mom explains.

"We were starving during the war," Nanna says. "But let's start with me. My bus leaves in twenty minutes."

Dr. Bowman eyes Mom, who found a stray piece of thread on her new yellow sweater. She pulls it loose and stares at it as if it were a worm. He looks at me. I smile and shrug my shoulders.

"Ok, Mrs. Brown, where's the fire?"

"Huh? Fire? There's no fire. I suffocate at least forty times every night. That bothers me!"

I like that Dr. Bowman immediately knows what's wrong with Grandma. She has sleep apnea. She stops breathing at night for a few seconds.

"You're a clever young man, I could tell that straight away," Nanna says. "But the question is, what can we do about it?"

"There are several options," the doctor explains. "You could start by going on a diet to shed some weight. It would be healthier either way if you..."

"If, if," Nanna interrupts. "Hindsight is 20:20. If I could go back to being twenty years old, I would be smarter."

Dr. Bowman clears his throat. "Do you smoke?"

"Hardly ever," Nanna croaks.

"Do you drink?"

"I don't go out getting hammered in a bar if that's what you mean. A shot of whiskey every now and then, right before dinner."

"I assume you sleep on your back?"

"Just like Dolly Parton."

"You could sow a tennis ball to your nightgown," he says. "In the back."

Nanna is silent for a moment and only stares at Dr. Bowman, her mouth hanging open. "Excuse me?"

"A tennis ball. Or maybe some bottle caps. To keep you from sleeping on your back."

"You're pulling my leg, aren't you?"

"I'm being serious," Dr. Bowman answers. "And sleep apnea is a serious condition. It's essential that you get a good night's rest, or it could start affecting your everyday life. It's not healthy. Furthermore, it can start affecting you mentally."

I think it's the last comment that really gets through to Nanna.

"Well then, can you get me a prescription for a tennis ball," she asks.

"You can buy one in any sports store, Mrs. Brown."

Grandma nudges Mom, who had almost fallen asleep in her chair. She reaches out a hand and Mom gives her ten dollars for the tennis ball and the bus ride home.

Nanna nods at the doctor. "I hope for your sake, young man, that you are not trying to make a fool out of me."

And then she is gone. She needs to hurry and catch her bus.

Dr. Bowman returns his attention to me. "As for you, Poppy, how are you sleeping?"

"Very well," I tell him.

Unless my father comes in and wakes me up. That happens almost every night now.

"How old are you?"

"Twelve," my mother answers.

"Thirteen," I correct her.

"Close enough," Mom mutters.

Dr. Bowman crosses his arms and leans forward. "Are you eating?"

"Yes."

I don't eat anything. I'm too tired to eat.

"But why are you so skinny?"

"Because... I don't like it very much."

"It? You mean eating?"

"Yes."

"But... but I am such a fantastic cook," Mom complains.

Mom is the worst cook in the western hemisphere, Dad told me once.

Dr. Bowman asks Mom if she would rather wait outside. She could get some coffee. Mom laughs and thinks that's a wonderful idea. She stands up and stumbles towards the door. For a moment, I'm worried that she will run into the wall, but then she is out of the room and closing the door behind her.

"How do you see yourself, Poppy," Dr. Bowman wants to know.

That's a weird question.

"Do you think you're skinny, fat or normal?"

"Skinny, I think."

Dad also thinks I'm too skinny. But still pretty. Should I tell Dr. Bowman about that? Mom's not here right now.

"Do you eat breakfast every day?"

"Yes."

I get up at six in the morning. I go down to the kitchen where I toss a few crumbs and pieces of bread onto a plate and put some butter on my knife. When my parents come in, it looks like I've already eaten.

"Lunch?"

"Yes."

I make my own sandwiches for school.

"Have you ever thrown up your lunch?"

"No."

I toss it in the trash at school.

Dr. Bowman threads his fingers together and looks at me. I smile back at him.

He seems nice. Should I ask him if it's normal?

"When you look around the classroom, do you think that the other girls are thinner than you?"

"No," I tell him. "I think I'm the skinniest."

"Do you like that?"

"Not really."

But I'm glad that I don't have breasts yet. Dad would probably want to play with them all day.

"Do you like that you... Do you enjoy having control or power over something?"

"But I don't have power over anything."

The light-headedness doesn't bother me all that much. It's almost like I'm floating on air.

"And yet, it's up to you whether you eat or not."

I'm suddenly exhausted.

"I do eat."

"But not much. Not enough, Poppy."

I sigh. My eyes feel heavy and I can barely keep them open.

"Do you want to know what I think, Poppy?"

"Right now?" I'm trying to look at him.

"Poppy, why are you looking at me like that?"

Because I have to keep my eyes wide open or I'll go to sleep.

"I'm sorry!"

"I think, that you're about ready for some summer vacation. Am I right?"

"Yes," I answer.

"Are you guys going back to Myrtle Beach this year?"

I shrug my shoulders. "The usual."

"Do you go swimming? Read a book? What do you do there?"

"Mostly things with my dad."

"What kind of things do you and your dad do?"

"Things."

"Games?"

I shake my head.

"Something else, then? Something fun?"

"No."

"Nothing fun? Ok then." He takes off his glasses and cleans them with his sleeve. I guess there is a stain on the lens that he can't get out. "It just won't go away," he mumbles to himself.

Behind Dr. Bowman there are two posters that depict the human anatomy. The left one shows a naked man and the right one, a naked woman. The doctor holds his glasses against the light. The stain is gone.

"Look," he says and puts his glasses back on. "I know exactly what you're going to be doing this summer, Poppy."

I stare at him.

"Get some rest, don't think about school, eat and enjoy your vacation. What do you think about that?"

"That sounds wonderful," I say.

"Tell your dad I said 'hi'. We will be taking our trailer and the Liberty tent for camping in the mountains this year. To Colorado."

"I'll let him know."

"And after you get back from vacation, I would like to see you again, Poppy. With a little tan and a little more meat on your bones."

"Okay," I say. I stand up and shake his hand, like Dad taught me to do.

Mom is snoring in the waiting room, her legs spread as wide as her miniskirt allowed. I go to the receptionist and get a follow-up appointment set for after summer break.

Not Just One

"Can you feel how much you've grown, Poppy?"

I'm lying on my stomach, counting to a hundred in French in my head. Dad and I are in our shiny camper, and Mom is stretched out on a floatie in the campsite pool. He wants to do it every day when we're on vacation. Every morning, as soon as Mom leaves (she always heads out early so she can get the best spot by the pool), Dad closes in the door to the camper.

"Can you feel it, how much you've grown?" he asks again.

"I hope we get a lot of wind today," I say.

"I'm sure. This is nice, right?" He's gasping. "It's great."

"I want to go surfing."

"Your back is getting a nice tan."

"When are we going to the beach?"

"We'll see. We're not done yet."

I suddenly hear a noise outside

"I think someone's coming," I tell him.

He doesn't hear me because he's groaning and gasping too loud. Then I hear my mother's voice.

"Pick-up? There's this black guy by the pool that is selling fantastic sunglasses out of a box. I need some cash."

Dad and I look at each other. He smiles a little as if to say: "Isn't she something?", and winks at me. I blink with both eyes. He still doesn't know that I've learned to wink.

"Hey, Pick-up, open up!" Mom calls. "I need some cash."

"Go on ahead, Patricia, I'll be down to the pool in a few minutes."

"But he'll be gone by then," she mutters.

Dad shakes his head. "Your mother, Poppy. She really is a weird one!"

I am not just *one*. There are *two* of me. The inside Poppy that no one can see, and the outside Poppy that everyone knows. It's always been like that, as far as I can remember, but here lately, the two Poppys don't get along anymore. I want to hurt myself every time I force myself to tell him: "Yes, I also like this. Yes, I understand that you would rather be married to me than to my mother. Yes, what we have is nice and something special."

The inside Poppy wants to break out, while the outside Poppy wants to get in. The inner Poppy is getting stronger, while the outside Poppy can't keep up with the lies anymore. She won't last much longer. Then the other Poppy will win, and she isn't going to be very nice.

It's hot in the room. On the other side of the door, in the trailer tent, I can hear Mom opening a bottle of wine. She pours herself a glass and mutters to herself. Dad is smoking a cigarette while sitting on the edge of the cot. He does that often *afterwards*. But it's not over yet.

I stare at his hands. Mom will go back down to the pool again soon and return later. I'm dizzy, my mouth feels dry, and there is a large fly sitting on Dad's head.

Where does Mom think I am right now?

At home I'm not allowed to leave the house without supervision, so why would I be allowed to roam around the campsite all by myself?

"When is she going to leave us alone," Dad whispers. My heart is racing. Then I call out: "Mom!"

Dad's cigarette flies to the grown. Mom doesn't answer. Dad is looking at me, shocked and angry all at once.

I hold my breath.

He picks up his cigarette and takes a long drag. Then he coughs a few times. A dry cough, and he's trying to keep it in, but he can't ignore the scratching in his throat. He starts a coughing fit and points to his back.

I pretend like I don't understand him.

Mom still hasn't said anything.

Then I hear her flip-flops. She's leaving.

When Dad's fit stops, he hits me upside the head. "No surfing today!"

Loud screaming wakes me up at night. It's mostly Mom's voice that I can hear, high and shrill. I can't understand a word she's saying. She had two bottles of wine for dinner. Now she's throwing things across the camper and is crying. She starts to scream and is sobbing even louder, but finally it starts to fade. She must have gone outside.

Dad comes to my cot. "Go after her or she's going to wake up the entire camping site." He goes back to bed.

I follow the sounds. A couple of people are already awake and aren't too happy about the commotion. "Je m'excuse, je m'excuse," I say and run towards the pool. I can see my mom's nightgown fluttering in the wind between the oleander bushes.

Mom is lying in the kiddie pool. Her flat hands are clapping on the water, like an overgrown, angry baby.

"Mom," I say. "Come on, let's get you out of there."

"I'm getting everything wet, but I don't care."

"You're being ridiculous. Come on out!"

"My life is hell."

"Your life is not so bad."

"Are you crazy? You have no idea!" She keeps splashing around and yells: "No idea!" My pajamas are getting wet.

"Please stop, Mommy," I beg her. "Please."

"You have no idea what I'm going through!" She's sobbing loudly. "He's nice to you."

I swallow my bile. "Come on. You might catch a cold."

"You don't understand how it is," she sobs.

"How what is, Mommy?" I want to go back to bed, I'm tired and cold. "What's so bad about your life?" I yell at her.

She stares at me in alarm. She's no longer crying but is still shaking a little. I don't buy her act. She always just puts on a show. She's only a mother on the outside; inside, there is nothing. Absolutely nothing.

"What were you guys fighting about," I want to know.

She wipes her nose with a hand.

"Mom?"

She crawls out of the kiddie pool with some effort, and approaches me, dripping wet. An old wet ghost with curlers in her hair. Some of her locks have come loose.

As she tries to get around me, I block her path. "I called for you today, Mommy. Did you hear me?"

"You don't know how it is."

"Did you hear me?"

"One day," she says, "I'm going to cut my own wrist. Because he..." She points towards our shiny trailer. "... because he broke me!"

She slowly shuffles away. Her nightgown is soaking wet. You can see the large, white underwear hanging off her sagging ass.

Columbo Did It

Dad and I are standing in front of the check-out counter of our favorite Chinese restaurant, waiting for our food. I'm nibbling on a fortune cookie, while Dad watches TV. The restaurant owner is a *Columbo* fan and records every episode so that his customers can watch them while they're waiting on their to-go orders.

Dad says what he always says when watching the show: "I think Columbo did it. That man keeps asking questions to throw people of his scent."

When my father said that the first time, Mom and I had to laugh out loud. But Dad meant what he said and continues to think that he is the only one that figured out Columbo's game.

Aunt Phyllis and Annabella enter the Chinese restaurant unexpectedly. Dad's forehead wrinkles. He's not in the mood to talk to Aunt Phyllis. She got divorced last summer and blames Dad that Annabella's father now lives in South Africa. Annabella didn't go with him, unfortunately. But I don't understand what Dad had to do with the divorce.

Aunt Phyllis looks thinner and weaker than ever before. She walks past us without saying a word. She retrieves a menu from the bar. Annabella says "Hello!" and reaches into the bowl in front of me to get a fortune cookie. Dad looks at Annabella disapprovingly for a second, before asking her how she's doing.

"You're taking home economics classes now?"

Annabella nods. "And I joined a ballet studio and the track and field team."

"Aha," says Dad.

"I can jump over hurtles this high, Grandpa. These cookies smell like fish sticks. Yummy."

"Can you Mom afford all this," Dad wants to know.

"Wott?" Cookie crumbles fall from Annabella's mouth.

"Wott? Don't speak with your mouth full," Dad says irritated.

"Wott?" Annabella says again.

"He wants to know if your Mom can afford to pay for the dance classes," I explain.

Annabella's brows furrow and she looks at her mother, who has her back turned to us as she orders two portions of Lo Mein.

"Mom?" she calls. "Can you afford to pay for my dance classes?"

Aunt Phyllis turns around. "Leave the child alone, Father!" She spits out the last word.

"If you need more money, Phyllis, all you have to do is ask!"

"I'm getting by just fine without you," Aunt Phyllis says.

"You're not getting by at all. You don't have a husband and your child has no brain."

"And you say that about your own granddaughter. You should be ashamed of yourself."

Annabella laughs and says that she doesn't need a brain. She's going to grow up to be a supermodel. She tries to stick a piece of fortune cookie up her nose because it smells so good.

"Annabella looks a lot like you," Dad tells Aunt Phyllis.

She gives him a hateful look. "Oh yeah? And what about *her*?" She points at me. "Does she look like *you*?"

"*She* at least has a brain," Dad says and places his hand on the back of my neck.

"She has a brain," Aunt Phyllis repeats quietly. She shakes her head and makes a weird snorting noise. There are suddenly tears in her eyes. She grabs Annabella's arm and drags her outside. She left without her two portions of Lo Mein.

Dad just shrugs his shoulders and goes to the bathroom.

I run outside. It's already dark. Aunt Phyllis and Annabella hadn't made it far, mainly because Annabella was trying to walk backwards.

She's bumping into parked cars and benches. My aunt tries to make her stop, but Annabella screams and kicks at her.

"Aunt Phyllis, wait," I call. "Please wait!"

She waits. Not because she wants to, but because she can't keep going with Annabella acting the way that she is. I stand in front of my aunt, out of breath, and say: "My mom's not doing well."

"That doesn't surprise me. I could have told her that this was going to happen." Aunt Phyllis's eyes are dry, but her voice sounds tight. She looks up, shakes her head, as if she has to convince herself that the sky is still there. "Tsk!"

I search for the right words. I don't think they've been invented yet.

The wind blows through my aunt's flame-colored locks. I'm getting goosebumps; my jacket is still in the restaurant. Aunt Phyllis is still not saying anything and keeps slowly shaking her head.

"I don't know what to do anymore," I say quietly.

Aunt Phyllis perks up. "Oh!" And again: "Oh!" Then: "In my opinion, *you* know exactly what you're doing. You're going to be a great actress when you grow up."

"Why does Poppy get to be an actress?" Annabella is done walking backwards.

"Because she's already great at acting," Aunt Phyllis explains. "Poppy has played a part her entire life, isn't that right, Poppy? Aren't you tired of always pretending that everything is alright? Or does it come natural to you now? At some point in time, it's like second nature, right?"

I don't know what to say to that.

Aunt Phyllis looks at something behind me.

I turn around.

My father is standing on the sidewalk. He's not doing anything, just standing there watching us.

Maybe Not Today

Ashley Baker is smoking a cigarette behind the bleachers at school. David and I are watching her. Ashley is holding the cigarette as if it were a joint and called us homos because we did not want to join her.

"You whore," David mutters.

"You got to grow a pair and smoke some," says Ashley. "Or you'll end up at the bottom of the social ladder. Fifth grade is no joke. You gotta be cool."

This morning, a group of fourth graders pushed David into a trash can. His eyes are still red from crying.

The first few weeks in fifth grade are the worst, Ashley tells us while taking another drag. Then things get a little better. Ashley has a seventeen-year-old sister, so she should know what she's talking about. Plus, she's got a wild card. Her father is a cop, so she earns a lot of respect for that. Sometimes I see him enter the police station near our house and wave to him.

Ashley visited him there once. She rang our doorbell, but I'm not allowed to answer. Ever since then, Ashley thinks I'm weird. She never rang the doorbell again. She also doesn't wave back when I'm at the window; instead, she shoots me the bird.

David and I don't have a respected father like Ashley to help our social standings. David is seen as a wimp, with his sandals and oatmeal cookies. I don't fare much better. My body is like a twig (according to David), my clothes are too expensive, and every day my mother drives me to school in her sportscar, yelling: "Oh, Poppy, he's cute. Is that your biology teacher? If he ever wants to study my human anatomy,

I'd gladly let him. I would even let him take a peek through one of those zoom devices." She means a microscope.

The bell rings. Ashley takes one more puff and throws her cigarette on the ground, before disappearing into the gym.

"Back to the shitshow," says David. He stomps his feet a few times and swings his backpack onto his shoulders. "Are you coming over later?"

David's mother tutors me in math every Thursday after school. "Not this time. I'm visiting Mr. Thomas this afternoon and see the baby."

"Cool."

I don't think David heard me. He doesn't think babies are cool at all. He takes a deep breath before bending down and assuming a start position, like the kids in track and field do before the race.

Suddenly, David says "Bang," and sprints towards the school.

This afternoon, Mom is driving me to Mr. Thomas's house. Dad thinks she's coming with me, but Mom decided to go shopping instead. She does the same thing while I'm getting tutored. She drops me off and gets her hair done, or sometimes she goes downtown.

I brought a present, but I don't know what it is. Mom bought it since I don't get an allowance. If I want something, I have to ask Dad and he'll buy it for me. As payment, I have to ride in the car with him for a few hours. He only steers with one hand. His left hand.

"I think it's very nice of you to come by, Poppy," says Mr. Thomas when he opens the door. He smiles widely. His hair is a mess and he looks pale, but his eyes are shining as if today was his birthday. I smile back and extend my hand. He grasps it with both of his and looks me up and down. "Come," he says. "Come in, please!"

There are garlands hung throughout the living room. It smells like cake and coffee. Elizabeth Thomas is sitting on the couch with the baby. Elizabeth is blonde and a bit round, with freckles around her nose. She also looks tired, but just as happy as Mr. Thomas. The baby is bundled in a blanket against her breast.

"Hello, Poppy!" she says. "I've heard so much about you. It's so nice to finally meet you. Julia just woke up."

"You can take off your coat, Poppy," Mr. Thomas offers. "I'll go into the kitchen and get us some cookies and lemonade."

"You can come closer and take a look," Elizabeth says.

She pushes the blanket back a little so I can see Baby Julia's head. I can see black hair, red cheeks, a pink finger... I hold my breath.

"Cute, isn't she?" Elizabeth whispers.

I don't think I've ever seen anything so beautiful in my life.

"I still can barely believe it," she says. "This is my baby. So small." She gives Julia a soft kiss on her forehead. And another one. "You want to feel how soft she is?"

I reach out a finger and touch one cheek, holding my breath again.

Mr. Thomas comes back with cookies and lemonade. We sit down next to Elizabeth on the couch, Mr. Thomas on one side and me on the other. We talk about my new school and about babies. And about Mr. Thomas and Elizabeth not getting a lot of sleep at night. Mr. Thomas also wants to know if I'm eating enough. To make him happy, I eat an entire cookie. I hand Elizabeth the present because she wants to open it herself. I get to hold the baby in the meantime.

Elizabeth says that she's never seen such a funny-looking pink badminton birdie with so much glitter, but that Julia would surely play with it in a few years. Very carefully, I smell the baby and place a kiss on Julia's head.

Mr. Thomas asks how my parents are doing.

"Good," I say. "They're doing good."

"That's great. I'm happy to hear it."

"Me too."

We fall into a comfortable silence.

"Yes," I say.

"I only ask because sometimes I got the feeling like you were having a hard time. At home, I mean."

I look at him and try my best to look surprised.

"I always hoped that you would come confide in me if there was something that you wanted to talk about."

I feign even more surprise. I'm very good at that: drop the corner of your mouth, raise your eyebrows, lift your shoulders.

"Hank," says Elizabeth.

"Yes?"

"Maybe not today."

Mr. Thomas is quiet. It makes me start to cry.

Elizabeth quickly takes the baby from me.

"Oh, Poppy, what's going on," Mr. Thomas asks. He sounds worried.

"It's nothing," I tell him. "I just have something in my eye."

Elizabeth watches Mr. Thomas. "I told you that today wasn't a good time to bring it up."

"I understand," I say. It sounds much ruder than I intended. I get up, shake their hands quickly, and announce a little too loudly that I need to go because I still have homework to do for tomorrow. Mr. Thomas follows me into the hall and helps me back into my coat. He even helps me with the zipper and buttons. I stand there like a little child, my arms hanging uselessly by my side.

He watches me when he finishes and nods. I try to smile at him, but he's not looking at me anymore. He keeps nodding. Very seriously he says: "Okay." And again: "Okay."

"Bye, Mr. Thomas!"

"Maybe we should... I think, we should... wait a second," he says. "I need to think." He runs a hand through his hair and glances at the ceiling.

I can hear Julia start to cry in the living room.

"Go and check on your baby," I tell him. "And thank you for the cookie."

I assume he's watching me through the window, so I skip happily until I'm out of sight. Around the corner, I sit down on the sidewalk and wait for Mom.

Maybe not today. Not a good time...

I bite down on my finger until I can taste blood.

During dinner, Dad wants to know how my visit with the Thomas family went.

"Such a darling baby," Mom answers. "I can't say it enough. His name is Taylor."

"Taylor?" Dad's eyebrows shoot up. "Isn't that a girl's name?"

I don't say anything. It would only complicate things more if I try to correct her. I push my plate to the side. I no longer have to sit in Dad's office until I finish my plate. I won that battle.

"It's a very sweet baby," Mom continues. "Everything that you would expect. And what a set of lungs! I think he must be teething already."

"The baby was just born two weeks ago," Dad says.

"Yes," Mom responds. "And it's really cute."

Dad looks at me. I shrug my shoulders.

"I am so happy that Poppy doesn't wear diapers anymore," Mom says.

"Poppy's already in middle-school, Patricia."

"Like I don't know that!"

"Well," Dad says. "Poppy is going to clear the table today. You're late."

"For what," asks Mom.

"Your art class."

"Oops, is it Thursday again already? Damn it, I need to get ready," Mom says and stands up. She's taking night classes at the local community college: art and cooking. Technically, Dad enrolled her. He says it's never too late to keep developing yourself. That's four evenings in a week that I am now alone at home with Dad. We still wash my hair three times a week. That's exactly seven days per week.

Seven... Dad's lucky number!

1984

I'm going to tell Mr. Thomas everything.
And this time, I won't cry.
(Poppy – fourteen years old)

Mr. Thomas

"I would like to become anorexic too. Is there a pill for that?" Mom wants to know. "Then maybe I'll be able to fit back into my old yoga pants."

My eyes are closed. Everything feels heavy. My right leg is stiff and hard.

"That's not funny, Mrs. Grinberg-Brown. This is a serious situation." An unknown female voice.

"I'm only joking," Mom responds quickly.

"Besides, we don't know if that is the cause of all this," the woman says. Probably a doctor.

I fainted at school again. The last thing I remember is falling towards the gym's green floorboards.

"Why does she have that thing in her nose?"

"Your daughter is receiving special nutrients. She is extremely malnourished. Did my colleague not mention that?"

"I didn't know that she wasn't eating."

"What happened?" My Dad enters the room.

"Pick-up, I was so surprised. I'm still shaken by all this. Poppy fainted during gym and was out cold for ten minutes. She also broke her shin. She is very malnourished. You can see her bones... did you know that?"

"Poppy? Poppy? Can you hear me?" He sounds concerned.

"Are you the father," the doctor asks.

"My daughter should be transferred to a private room," Dad mumbles.

"Do you have insurance?"

"I'll buy out this whole hospital, if need be."

"You don't have to do that. You just need to pay for a room."

"So, she can be transferred?"

"Let me see if we have a private room available."

"Please do that right away!"

The doctor is silent for a moment. "As you wish."

They wait until the doctor has left the room. I can hear Mom say loudly into my ear: "Honey? It's Mommy. Everything's will be ok. Your Daddy is here. You're going to get a private room. Even if it costs him an arm and a leg. You're worth it. Can you hear me, silly?"

*

"Poppy? Can you open your eyes?" It's the unknown female's voice.

I wait a moment, but I'm sure that my parents have left.

"Poppy?"

I open *one* eye. She has her blonde hair tied up in a ponytail and is wearing glasses.

"There you are," she says. "My name is Dr. Thaler. Sandra Thaler."

"Hello," I say meekly.

"Can you open the other eye as well?"

Well, ok.

"What pretty blue eyes you have! It's a shame to keep them closed."

I like her.

"And a pretty smile to boot. That's the first time I get to see that too."

I am indeed alone in the room. To my right, there's a door that leads to a hallway, and to my left are two chairs. The doctor is sitting in one of them. Behind her is a window that looks over a parking lot, covered slightly by yellow curtains.

"How are you feeling?"

"Good."

"As well as can be, probably?"

"Yes, given the circumstances."

She takes hold of my wrist and looks at her watch. "Are you not in the mood to talk to your parents right now?"

"I was sleeping."

"It's great that you can sleep with all this noise and excitement around you."

"When are you removing the tube from my nose?"

"Is it uncomfortable?"

"It's ok. That's a lot of plaster around my leg."

"You broke your shin bone."

"Yes, I heard."

"Ha." Her laugh is pleasant. "I knew you were awake the whole time."

"Will it be ok?"

"Sure. But the most important thing is to get you eating again."

I nod.

"I'm being serious, Poppy."

I nod again.

"If you don't start eating properly, you're going to die."

"Really?"

"Really."

"I didn't know that."

"I would take better care of myself, if I were you." Dr. Thaler strokes a finger down my cheek. "It's a lot to take in, isn't it?" she says.

I nod and cry. I can't hold it back anymore and once it starts, I can't stop it. I hear myself make weird sounds, sounds that I've never made before: like a small child that is too tired to cry, but does it anyway because it relieves some stress. It's quiet, it sights heavily, it gasps for breath. My sorrow floods over me like a wave, but I don't drown; I float above it, because the nice doctor is sitting beside me, holding my hand.

*

"Look, Poppy, flowers. Your classmates brought them by." Mom and Dad enter my room with a large bouquet. There's a small card with a bear on it. He has an icepack on his head, a thermometer in his mouth, and above him it reads: GET WELL SOON!

Mom places the flowers on the table beside my bed. My father's shirt is soaking wet and he keeps blinking his eyes.

"They can go ahead and get a bed for your father as well. He's completely out of it, worrying to death," Mom says. "I keep telling him that everything's going to be ok. The doctor agrees with me. Right, Pick-up? She says that Poppy will be back to normal soon. She just needs to relax a little and eat right."

"Can you get a vase, please?" Dad asks.

Mom had already sat down. "I'll ask the nurse when she comes in."

"No, go ahead and do it now. They're already wilting."

Mom gets up with a sigh and leaves the room.

Dad shuts the door behind her. "Did you sleep well?"

My first night away from home. I was alone. It was wonderful. Now it's over. And the door is closed.

"I missed you so much," he says. His left eye is twitching.

Mom please come back. Hurry, Mommy!

"Did you miss me too?"

He sits down beside my bed and pushes his hand beneath my blanket. He pulls down my panties a bit and inserts his finger between my legs. I want to press them together, but the cast on my leg doesn't allow it.

"I missed you so much," he says again.

Mom enters the room again.

He keeps his hand still and leaves it under the blanket. From where Mom is standing, she can only see his left hand, laying on top of the blanket. His nails are dirty. The chair beside my father is empty. She should come and sit down. But she doesn't; she remains standing.

"They're cutting the stems a little first," she says.

"Great," my father says and pushes his finger deeper inside me. I make a squeaking noise.

"What's wrong," Mom asks me.

I don't say anything. Neither does Dad.

"Is your leg hurting?"

Silence.

"Well, this really sucks," she sighs.

"Mommy, won't you come sit with me?"

She's still standing in the doorway. Mom and Dad glance at each other... then Mom looks away.

"I need a cigarette," she says.

"Come sit with me, Mommy. Please!" I'm begging her.

"I'm not allowed to smoke here, silly."

"You can smoke later when you leave. You can smoke as much as you want to, but please just come here..." I try to catch her eyes. She's digging in her purse without looking up.

"Go ahead, Patricia," Dad says. "We shouldn't stress her out. I'll be right behind you."

He moves his finger in and out, as if he wants to prove his power over me.

I bite down on my tongue. I taste blood.

"Mommy, please, come here!"

"What?"

"Go ahead," my Dad says again.

"Mommy!"

"Poppy, everything will be ok, that's what the doctor said. Stop overreacting! I'm going to take a smoke break, Poppy. But we'll see each other tomorrow, ok?"

She leaves the room. She closes the door.

*

"I can't help you if you won't say anything."

I'll never talk again. I won't eat either. There's a bowl of yogurt and a banana on the table beside me. The psychiatrist told me: "That looks good! Don't you want to try it?" I just shook my head. His name is Dr. Kroger. He has red hair, pointy ears, and is always squinting at me. As if he can't open them all the way.

"Let's just start from the top, Poppy."

I've been in the hospital for five days. In the beginning, Dr. Thaler and her blonde ponytail would visit me every day to see how I was doing, but when they noticed that I had stopped talking, she stopped coming. Yesterday, Dr. Kroger came instead.

"You know what? You can just nod. Or shake your head like you just did. Yes or no. Do you want to try that?"

He thinks he's so smart.

"Do you want to try that, Poppy? Yes or no. Just nod or shake your head."

I'm frozen, not moving at all anymore. Not even my eyes.

Dr. Kroger writes down something on his notepad.

I can read it upside down. *Apathetic.*

Good. That sounds about right.

Dr. Thaler came and saw me again yesterday. The day before that, Nanna Brown visited me. And the day before that it was David with his mother. No one stays long because I don't say anything and don't look at them. Mom and Dad come every day and stay for about thirty minutes. Twenty-five of those minutes, Mom is outside smoking.

Dad sits by my bed and touches me. Sometimes he runs his tongue over my mouth, even though my lips are pressed tightly together. Sometimes he opens his fly so that he can guide my hand to his penis.

I am apathetic, so I don't do anything.
*

"When can we take her home?" My father hasn't shaved in a while. And he stinks.

"You need to discuss that with the doctor," the nurse tells him, while changing my IV. His name is Mike and he's from Africa. Dad has yet to even look at him. Black people are all criminals, even if they work in a hospital.

I can tell that Dad is slowly falling apart. He keeps driving here from work, and back again. I don't talk, and the cast on my leg hinders him. He's stressed because the doctors keep coming and going without knocking. He doesn't dare do anything more than move his fingers underneath the blanket.

The day after tomorrow, he must go to a factory in Poland for five days. When he tells me, he sounds like we will never see each other again. I stare past him. For a moment, it seems as if he's crying.

"Do you at least have some kind of idea?"

"Poppy needs to be able to eat on her own," Mike explains.

"Are you practicing with her?"

"Daily."

"What is she eating?"

"Mainly liquids and soft foods, like yogurt."

"Please get me a bowl of yogurt," my father says. "I'll do it myself."

For fifteen minutes, Dad tries to get me to eat the yogurt. My lips stay pressed together.

Mike watches us to make sure that Dad doesn't get angry or mad. But Dad just keeps pressing the spoon harder against my mouth. When my face is covered with yogurt, Mike says that we should try again tomorrow.

8:10 AM

"Can I have a clock in my room?"

I finally spoke again, but I am only allowed things once I eat my vanilla pudding. This was Dr. Kroger's idea. He thought it over and decided that I needed a firmer hand. It's for the best, he said.

"As long as I'm not eating, no one is allowed to visit me," I ask.

He shakes his head. "No."

"Not even my parents?"

"I'm sorry, Poppy, but that's the way it's going to have to be."

"Okay," I say.

Dr. Kroger places the yellow bowl filled with pudding on the tray and heads for the door. A cherry is in the middle of the pudding. It's cute, like Baby Julia.

"I think it's fantastic that you're speaking again, Poppy, just so you know," he says. "But we still have a long way to go."

"I hope not," I say.

I look at the clock on the wall across from my bed. It's a large round clock, white with black numbers and red hands.

I want to know how late it is.

10:57 AM

Dr. Kroger enters the room and beams. "Poppy, your parents are here."

We both glance at the pudding bowl sitting untouched beside my bed. The cherry is still sitting in the middle.

"Oh well," I say.

Dr. Kroger narrows his eyes at me. "You didn't even eat a spoonful?"

I shake my head.

"You know the consequences?"

I nod.

"Your father is leaving for a few days, Poppy. If you want to say hello…"

"…I have to eat my pudding."

"Exactly."

"I'm not hungry."

Dr. Kroger is silent for a moment before he says: "Alright. If that's how you want to play the game, then I'm sorry."

He disappears through the door.

I can hear my father raise his voice in the hallway. I'm able to pick up a few words: "…absurd! … I will decide… my own daughter."

"Responsibility… consequences… behavior pattern…"

"A disgrace… police… mind your own business."

Dr. Kroger wins. My parents leave.

2:41 PM

"Someone wants to say hi to you, Poppy. It's your former teacher from elementary school." Dr. Thaler pokes her head into my room.

"Mr. Thomas?"

That's not possible.

"You know Dr. Kroger's new rules: eat and you can have visitors."

"Is it Mr. Thomas?"

"Yes, that's his name."

I place my hand on my chest. My heart is beating so fast and hard, that it scares me.

Dr. Thaler inclines her head. "Everything ok, Poppy?"

"Yes."

"Is he a nice man?"

"Very nice."

Mr. Thomas suddenly appears beside Dr. Thaler.

"Oops, you scared me," she says dryly.

"My apologies," Mr. Thomas says and looks at me. His eyebrows furrow. "Hey, toothpick!"

"Hello, Mr. Thomas," I say.

"May I come in?"

"It's not allowed," I tell him.

"Says who?"

"Dr. Kroger, the smarty pants."

"Why?"

"Because I'm not eating."

"Are you being punished for something?"

"I think so."

Mr. Thomas turns to Dr. Thaler, who is still standing beside him by the door. "Are you Dr. Kroger?" he asks.

Dr. Thaler turns red. It looks good on her.

"No," she says. "My name is Thaler."

"Is Dr. Kroger nearby?"

Dr. Thaler looks at her watch.

"He's on break right now," she says. "It's almost visiting hours."

"Aha. And?" Mr. Thomas asks.

"Very well, you may go in."

2:56 PM

Mr. Thomas is sitting beside my bed. We're silent. Every now and then our eyes meet and we nod at each other.

3:00 PM

Neither one of us wants to go first. The silence continues.

3:02 PM
Mr. Thomas sighed heavily a couple of times. Sometimes it looks like he's about to nod off. He takes my hand, lets it go again.

3:06 PM
"You disappoint me."

Mr. Thomas and I look up.

Dr. Kroger is standing in the door. He really does look disappointed. "I said no visitors unless you eat, Poppy. That was the deal."

"It's not like we're talking," I say.

"That's not the point." Dr. Kroger rests his hands on his hips. "I have to ask you to leave immediately."

"Just one moment," Mr. Thomas says.

"No! Sorry, but you're going to have to go."

Mr. Thomas stares at the vanilla pudding and then at me. "What do you think, Poppy?" he asks.

I take the bowl and scoop the pudding into my mouth. I keep eating. While I swallow, I stare pointedly at Dr. Kroger. His eyes are wide.

I eat another spoonful of pudding. Then another. And another. After six spoonful's, the bowl is empty. I give the cherry to Mr. Thomas.

"Would you look at that," Dr. Kroger says amazed.

"Out!" I tell him.

Mr. Thomas turns towards Dr. Kroger. "We would like to have some privacy."

3:12 PM
I'm going to tell Mr. Thomas everything and this time, I will not cry.

3:28 PM
I told Mr. Thomas everything. I did not cry.

Masterplan

Dr. Thaler and Dr. Kroger are in my room listening to Mr. Thomas.

Sandra Thaler keeps running her hand over her mouth; Dr. Kroger is flipping through his notebook as if it contained more information on me.

Their lips are moving, they take turns talking but I can't hear what they're saying. They take turns staring at my direction. No sound reaches my ear, it even stopped ringing. I can't hear a thing.

*

"Are you awake, Poppy?"

A cold finger on my cheek. Dr. Thaler... *Sandra*. My room is dark.

"Would you like something to drink?"

Sandra helps me sit up and hands me a glass of sweet tea.

"Mr. Thomas went home after you fell asleep," she tells me.

I nod.

"We talked about it and we think it's best if he speaks with your mother first."

"Oh!"

"Does that surprise you?"

"A little."

"He volunteered. And Dr. Kroger and I agree that it's for the best. Mr. Thomas has known your mother for a while after all."

I don't know what is for the best. Does such a thing even still exist?

But Dr. Thaler says: "You did good, Poppy."

I don't think I'll ever be able to look Mr. Thomas in the eye again.

"You did great," she says again. "That took a lot of courage, Poppy."

And soon, everyone will know. The entire city will know; my school will know.

"Do you think you can sleep?"

And Mom.

"Or do you want a sleeping pill?"

"Yes."

"Everything's going to be alright, Poppy. We're just taking this one step at a time."

*

I'm dreaming.

Mom is sitting beside my bed. I tell her everything. When I'm done telling my story, she says: "I've known all along, silly." She winks at me.

"Does Dad know that you can wink?

"He knows everything."

"I can do it too," I whisper.

"Really?"

"Yeah, look."

"That's not winking, Poppy."

"Yes, it is."

"If that's winking, then I'm wearing dentures."

"But Mom, you are wearing dentures!"

She hits me upside the head.

I wake up. My pillow is wet. My face is too.

The room is pitch dark, but my door is open. The figure of my father appears in the doorway, blocking out the light shining in from the hall. He's wearing a raincoat and is carrying a suitcase.

I scream.

*

Everyone is being very nice to me today. The nurse that helps me wash, the woman that brings me breakfast, Mike, who's been making me walk up and down the hall (this morning my cast was changed to allow more movement, and I'm getting used to the crutches). They are all friendly and concerned.

Dr. Thaler tells me she spoke to Mr. Thomas. He's talking to my mother at eleven today. My father won't be there at that time; they made sure of it.

"And then?" I ask.

"Then we will see."

"Step by step?"

"Yes, step by step," Sandra says.

*

"I'm completed flabbergasted. I can't believe it!"

Mom is standing in the doorway. She's not wearing any makeup and her ponytail has come loose, making stray hair fall into her face. She is dabbing her eyes with a crumbled tissue with one hand. With the other, she's holding onto Nanna.

Dr. Thaler and Dr. Kroger are standing behind them.

"I've been crying the whole time, Poppy. If only I had known! But I didn't know anything was wrong," Mom says.

"You couldn't have known," Nanna says. "Who can imagine something like that? He always seemed like such a respectable person."

Mom lets out a loud wail and rushes into my room. She throws herself on top of me. Nanna turns to Dr. Thaler. "It's like in World War II. With the Jews. No one knew what was going on. I didn't know either," she says. "And many people respected the Nazis."

*

I can go home tomorrow. We will have three more days before Dad comes back from Poland. Enough time for us to pack up our stuff and to look for a better future. We also need to file a report against Dad. It's a lot to do, but Sandra Thaler wrote everything down for us. Police, support resources, social services. Sandra and Dr. Kroger also give us their private phone numbers.

Take it step by step. Everything will be alright.

When it's time to say goodbye, Mom gives me a seven second kiss. After the kiss, she stays crying on top of me for an entire minute.

"Come, Patricia. We have work to do. I have a master plan. Step 1: We go home. Step 2: We call Barbara and Carl."

I Am The Situation

"Who asked you to come here?" Nanna Brown asks the two men standing at the door. The door to the hall is open so I can hear the conversation from the living room.

"Carl called us," one of them answers.

"Why?" Nanna's voice doesn't sound friendly.

"Because we have experience with certain types of situations."

"What kind of situation are we talking about here?"

"You don't want to know, Mrs. Brown."

"Do you think I was born yesterday? Do you want me to close the door on you?"

It's quiet for a moment.

"Well?" Nanna asks dryly. "What kind of situations?"

"Situations in which you have to take the law into your own hands."

"Would you look at that! I guess we can have a real conversation after all."

Ten seconds later, she enters the living room, followed by the two men: George and John, friends of Uncle Carl. One of them has a tear drop tattooed on the side of his face. The other is carrying a six pack of beer.

"Sit down at the table," Nanna says and goes to get my Mom out of bed.

They stay silent.

"Hello," I finally say. "I'm Poppy."

"George," says the man with the tattoo.

"John," says the man with the beer.

No one says anything else after that.

*

I feel weak and unsteady. I'm nauseous. This morning, a taxi picked me up from the hospital because Mom overslept, and Nanna doesn't have a driver's license.

It feels weird being at home without my father. I know he's in Poland. Still, it feels like he could walk through the doors at any moment.

I try to concentrate on the positive: I'm no longer alone. I can share my secret with my family, with Aunt Barbara and Uncle Carl. And it seems I can also talk to George and John.

The doorbell rings a second time.

Nanna runs down the hall.

"Patricia," she yells. "If you don't get out of bed this instance, I will drag you out myself."

A minute later, Nanna enters the living room followed by Aunt Barbara and Uncle Carl. Uncle Carl claps George and John on the back and then points at Nanna. They laugh. John doesn't have a lot of teeth. Mom enters the room – in her bathrobe. She didn't tie it properly; you can see her nightgown which doesn't leave much to the imagination. She has mascara marks underneath her eyes and her mouth is hanging open.

Aunt Barbara shoots her an angry look. "What have you been smoking?"

"I guess everyone is here." Nanna gasps for breath. She looks tired. The tennis ball therapy doesn't seem to be working.

"Is it too late for coffee," Aunt Barbara asks.

"Damn it!" Nanna stomps out to the kitchen.

"Where is he?" Uncle Carl glares at Mom.

"Who?" Mom is clinging to the back of the chair for support.

"My father is in Poland," I answer and try to help Mom sit down.

"Let go, I can do it myself!" Her voice is pitchy and childish.

Uncle Carl looks at my father's recliner for a second before dropping into it. Aunt Barbara watches my Mom struggle into the chair and sits down beside me. "Stop making a scene, Patricia."

140

"You're just jealous. Always have been."

"Yeah, yeah," Aunt Barbara says. "Have you even looked into a mirror today?"

"People! Calm down, all is good," Uncle Carl interrupts.

"Nothing is good," Mom says. "Everything is not good."

"That's not what I meant. I'm not stupid." Uncle Carl lights a cigarette. "I still don't know why you wanted me to come here. I couldn't understand a word you said on the phone. But one thing is certain: when a woman calls me crying her eyes out, my alarm bells go off. That's how it is. My fifth sense. I have eyes in the back of my head, is what I always say." He taps his fingers against the back of his head.

"That's right," says Nanna. "He's always had this fifth sense."

"It's the sixths sense," my aunt corrects. "You already have five senses."

Uncle Carl looks angrily at his wife. "Shut your trap, I'm talking to you sister. Is this about the old scarecrow?"

"Who?" Mom looks at him, terrified.

"Who do you think? Uncle Fester."

Mom nods slowly. She keeps nodding. She's like a little child who just discovered that she has to use her feet in order to take a step.

Aunt Barbara's eyes are wide, and she lowers her chin. The look she is giving Mom is full of contempt. "She's lost her marbles, Carl!"

"Quiet now! Patricia... hello, anybody at home? What did that son of a bitch do?" Uncle Carl wants to know. "And stop bobbing your head like that."

Mom stares at him wide-eyed. "It's terrible," she whispers. "Terrible."

"Don't beat around the bush. What did *he* do, Patricia?"

"I can't talk about it." Mom drops her head onto the table and cries.

Aunt Barbara is watching me, but I don't say anything. Nanna returns with some coffee and cookies. George gets three bottles of beer and opens them with his teeth. He has more teeth than John, but I highly doubt that they are real.

Mom bangs her head on the table. She sobs loudly, groans, screams. Aunt Barbara looks at me again. Sweat runs down my back.

"Alright," Nanna begins. "I suppose it is best if I start this meeting. This is the situation."

"Should she really be here for this," Uncle Carl nods in my direction.

This family nods way too much.

"She is the situation," Nanna answers.

"Why is *she* the situation?" Aunt Barbara asks. "I thought the situation is the one screaming her head off and trying to break the coffee table with her face."

Nanna gives Mom a nudge. "Will you tell them, or should I? Patricia – stop it! Stop acting crazy and pull yourself together!"

My mom listens, but leaves her head laying on the table.

"Fine, I will tell them," Nanna decides.

Everyone is looking at Nanna, except my mom.

"What is it, Mom? Tell us what's going on!" My aunt is almost bursting with curiosity.

"The situation is as follows: Mr. Grinberg is a pedophile."

Finally, it's out in the open.

"I'm sorry, pedo-what?" Uncle Carl shakes his head as if he doesn't understand.

"A pedophile?" Aunt Barbara says, stunned. "A child molester?"

"What?" Uncle Carl asks.

"He sexually abused Poppy," Mom yells without lifting her head.

Nanna sighs. "And not just once, but consistently over the years. It shocked the hell out of me."

Everyone is quiet for a few seconds until Uncle Carl jumps up from the recliner and throws his bottle of beer against the wall. "I knew it! That dirty, greasy fagot! I've always had this feeling that there was something off about that guy, that fucking cocksucker!"

"He didn't suck any cocks, Carl," Nanna Brown whispers. "Just our Poppy."

Our Poppy. Nanna has never called me that before.

The glass shards from the beer bottle flew all the way to Mom's *Precious Moments* figurines on the windowsill. Uncle Carl's outburst is also the trigger for George and John, who throw their own beer bottles at a picture of my father standing on the cabinet, yelling "child molester" and "perverted asshole."

Aunt Barbara seems to be in shock. She lights two cigarettes with shaking hands. One for herself and one for Mom. Nanna says that this is a game we cannot afford to lose, so we need to use our brains.

"Yes, and? What's the plan?" Carl asks.

"Dr. Thaler jotted some important things down," I say and reach into my pocket to get the piece of paper with the numbers for social services and support resources. The note was still on the table in my hospital room when I left. Mom had forgotten to take it with her.

"Dr. Thaler doesn't live in reality," Nanna growls.

"But it says here what we need to do," I say. "Step by step."

"We don't live in Dr. Snuggles's world!"

Nanna rips the piece of paper from my hand and holds it in the air. "We have *this*," she says, "but we also have *this!*" She taps the side of her head. "Our smarts!"

"Let me see that," my uncle mutters.

Nanna gives Uncle Carl the note.

He reads through it. "I don't believe this. What are the cops going to do? We can take care of this ourselves!" He holds his lighter underneath the paper, setting the numbers on fire.

I'm having a hard time breathing. *We'll do it step by step*, Dr. Thaler told me. *Then everything will be alright.* Now I don't know what the next step is.

I need to pee. "Nanna, where are my crutches?" She doesn't answer. This morning she cleaned the entire house and took away my crutches, because she wanted everything to be nice and clean for Aunt Barbara and Uncle Carl. ("Crutches aren't nice to look at. I'll put them away.")

I get up and slowly limp towards the hall. I hold onto chairs and cabinets along the way. Half-way there, I stop, close my eyes and suck in a deep breath. I can hear Uncle Carl guarantee that he will make sure that my father will burn in hell for what he did.

"A bunch of crazy niggers need to fuck him in the ass until his hemorrhoids bleed," Nanna adds.

"I'm telling you, Grandma, those inmates in prison would take care of Mr. Pervert for us. Right, George?"

George nods and gets another beer. "Yeah, they're not too gentle with child molesters. I've seen it myself."

Nanna laughs. "I hope you got a piece of the action too. But you got to take it slow, make it last so they learn their lesson!"

Everyone laughs.

When I open my eyes, my mom has moved to stand close to George. "I should get a tear drop like that tattooed on my face. For Poppy. So that everyone knows that her pain is also my pain." She sobs again. "I will never get over this pain!"

She watches George open the bottle.

"I could never do that. I still have all my own teeth," Mom mumbles.

The phone rings. Everyone freezes. In the silence, the rings echo loudly. Once, then twice. Three times, I count.

"Well," Nanna says. "I guess that's *him*."

Four times.

"Where did you say that asshole is?" Aunt Barbara asks.

"Poland," I answer.

"Answer it already, Patricia!" Nanna says with an annoyed voice.

"What am I supposed to say?" Mom's voice has gone higher in pitch.

Five times.

"That everything is ok, of course! He can't have any idea what's going on here."

But what is going on here? I wish someone would explain it to me.

Six times.

Mom goes into my father's office. Five people trot after her. I limp after them, bringing up the rear.

Seven times.

Mom is standing beside the phone, her hands hang limp by her side. It rings an eighth time.

"To hell with it!" Nanna pushes Mom out of the way and picks up the phone. The tape recorder turns on. Carl, George and John stare with open mouths at the recording device underneath the plastic dome.

"Brown speaking," Nanna answers the phone.

"What are you doing in my office?" My father's voice can be heard on the recording device. He sounds furious.

"Answering the phone. A good morning to you too!"

"Where's Patricia?"

"She's sleeping. Stomach bug. She has a high fever."

"And how is Poppy?"

"Still in the hospital."

"I know that!"

"You don't have to yell!"

"I want to know how my daughter is doing."

"She's doing wonderful, for a girl that weighs eighty pounds soaking wet."

"Is she eating yet?"

"Like a horse."

"Stop joking around, damn it."

"I'm not joking. She's eating again."

"Really?"

"I have to go now. Your wife has got the runs and we're out of shit paper."

"The what?"

"Toilet paper!"

"Tell Poppy to call me. The number is on my desk."

"I'll let her know."

"Today please."

"I don't know when I'll be back to the hospital. I can't leave Patricia alone. When are you coming back?"

"The day after tomorrow."

"Take your time. Life is not a fairy tale."

She hangs up and looks at Uncle Carl, who is standing in front of the safe turning the knob. "You can mess with that thing until your gray in the beard," she says. "We need a locksmith or safe cracker."

I'm suddenly very hot.

"Goodness, Poppy," Aunt Barbara says.

I look at her.

"You peed in your pants."

To The Other Side...

The next morning, I go downstairs, and everyone is still here. Or here again. I don't know where they all slept. No one is talking to me, so I go into the kitchen to make myself a grilled cheese sandwich. I promised Dr. Thaler that I would eat right.

I can hear them screaming at each other in the living room. George and John leave the house with a lot of commotion. As I am putting my plate into the dishwasher, Nanna enters the room.

"Good morning, Nanna!"

"I've had better."

"What do we do now?" I ask her.

"Start packing your bags."

"So, we are leaving?"

"Did you want to stay here?"

"No, I just thought that..."

"Leave the thinking to me."

"But I don't know what the plan is."

"Pack up everything and disappear. That is the master plan."

I pack the most important items into four bags: Clothes, toothbrush, my piggy bank, Mom's jewelry, my schoolbooks. I try my best to decide what's important and what isn't. Our pillows and blankets I stuff into trash bags. I have no idea how we're going to get all this stuff out of the house.

When I'm finished, I hear a car pull up the driveway, and look out of my bedroom window. A battered moving van stops in front of our door. George and John get out. They're brought a jackhammer with them, and a new six pack of beer.

"Poppy!" Nanna calls. "Come here!"

They want me to cross the street and enter the police station in order to file a report. Uncle Carl tells me to waste as much time there as possible and says: "You need to keep them busy, Poppy. We can't clean out the house in five minutes."

So that is the master plan.

"What are you looking at?" Carl asks.

"I don't know if taking stuff from the house is the right thing to do, Uncle Carl."

"Let me worry about that, Poppy. You just concentrate on doing your part. You want justice, don't you? That's what we're doing."

I have my doubts.

"Don't start acting stupid now," he says. "You said 'A'. Now we're not just doing 'B' but are going to go through the entire alphabet."

I remember Dr. Thaler writing down that I should go ahead and file a report. *It's a step, so I need to do that.*

"Ready, set go!" Uncle Carl pushes me towards the front door.

"Dad's going to be furious if you take all his stuff."

Nanna joins us in the hallway. "Why is she still here?"

"She's leaving right now," my uncle answers.

"Shouldn't someone go with me?" I ask.

Nanna clears her throat. "Why, are you scared?"

"I'm a minor."

"That's a good think," she says. "That's exactly the point we're trying to make here. The younger, the better."

"How old are you?" Carl asks.

"Fourteen."

He thinks for a moment. "Tell them you're twelve."

"But this would be a lie."

"Don't worry your pretty little head about it. It'll shock the coppers even more and that'll keep them busy," Nanna says.

"We're on the side of the law, if you think about it," Carl explains.

"Right. We're only helping it along a bit." Nanna is giggling like Mom. She disappears into the kitchen.

"It doesn't really matter what you say," Carl says. "But feel free to use your imagination and embellish a little. Do you get what I'm saying?"

I wish he would stop talking.

He places his hand on my shoulder. "It needs to sound really bad. Don't forget to cry a lot. That pig will end up in the electric chair. Mark my words."

"New York doesn't have the death penalty anymore, Uncle Carl."

He shrugs his shoulders. "Oh well, I'll just have to think of something else!"

The hospital wasn't all that great, but at least I had people around me telling me that everything would be alright. Now, no one is saying that everything will be ok.

Outside, I hear Uncle Carl call my name. "Poppy?"

I turn around.

"Tell them he stuck his tiny dick into all your openings."

In the police station, two police officers are sitting at a desk. One of them is Ashley Baker's father.

"Hello, Poppy," he says. "I didn't expect to see you here."

"Yes."

"How's your leg doing?"

"I'm doing ok. This cast is a lot more flexible."

"How did that happen again?"

"I fell during P.E."

"Ah yes, Ashley told me about that."

"Yes."

He points to the fat cop sitting beside him. "And this handsome fellow here is Mr. Scott, Poppy."

"Hello, Mr. Scott!"

"Good morning, young lady!"

"What can we help you with, Poppy?" Ashley's father asks.

"I want to file a report."

"Oh, Poppy, really?" Ashley's father acts surprised, but winks at Mr. Scott. Mr. Scott elbows Ashley's father in the ribs, and he elbows him back. And then they do it again.

Why are they doing that?

Amid the horseplay, Ashley father's asks: "Did your bike get stolen or something?"

I shake my head.

"Did your dog run away?"

"No, Fifi is at home."

"You didn't steal candy from the store, did you Poppy?"

"No."

"Started a fire?"

"No."

They stopped elbowing each other.

Mr. Baker rubs his arm. "Well, what is it your reporting then, Poppy?"

"It's about abuse," I say. "Sexual abuse."

Mr. Baker and I are sitting in a small, warm room without windows. If the room had windows, maybe it wouldn't be so stuffy. And we could see Nanna Brown, Uncle Carl, George and John clear out the house down the street. They would be taking anything of value. I can see it clearly now: the Persian rugs, the silver utensils, the *Precious Moments* collection, the Chinese vases, the TV, the fax machine, my surfboard, the recording device. And if they can manage it, the safe too.

Mr. Baker clears his throat and places a piece of paper into the typewriter that is standing on the desk in front of him. He hasn't said anything in a while.

"How is Ashley doing?" I ask him.

"Very good, very good. She has a boyfriend."

"That's nice."

He glances at the door. There wasn't anyone else around to take down my report, except for Mr. Scott, but he had to go pee all of a sudden.

"So," he says. "Where were we?"

I don't answer.

I'm not going to help Mr. Baker. He's supposed to be the one helping me.

He laces his fingers behind his head. It's an uncomfortable position that only creates the illusion of being comfortable. Mr. Baker soon realizes this and puts his hands back on the table. "I'll tell Ashley you said hi."

I nod.

"When will you go back to school?"

I shrug my shoulders.

"Excuse me for a moment," he says and leaves the room.

In the last ten minutes, Ashley's father hadn't looked at me once.

A different cop is now sitting in Mr. Baker's chair. He's from the Special Victims Unit, he says. Captain Hart is older than Ashley's father. He has a round face with a large, white beard, just like Santa Claus.

"Alright," Captain Hart starts. "We'll talk through this together, Poppy. Is that ok?"

"Okay."

Captain Hart takes a sip of water and hammers away on the typewriter. He listens to me without looking up from his typing fingers.

"Poppy, this abuse that you mentioned, what did you mean by that? Can you give me some details in your own words?"

"Well, it happened. It happened often."

"What happened?"

"The abuse."

"Was it done to you?"

I nod.

"And who was it?"

"Hm?"

"Can you tell me who abused you?"

I stare at his beard.

"Poppy? Who sexually assaulted you?"

"My father," I mutter as quick and quiet as possible. Maybe he won't hear me, and we can just skip this question.

"Your father?"

He has good hearing.

My left eye twitches and itches. I rub at it. It doesn't help.

"Your father abused you. Did I hear you correctly?"

I blink a few times and close my left eye for fifteen seconds. When I open it again, the twitching stops.

"Do you know what sexual abuse is?"

I wonder how far along Uncle Carl is at the house. Maybe they already have everything they want. Then I can put an end to this quickly.

"Poppy?"

"Yes?"

"The reason I am asking is that this is a serious allegation. Do you understand?"

"I'm sorry."

"So, it's not true?"

"No."

"Really?"

"Well."

"Is it true?"

"Yes."

"And you are absolutely sure you understand what abuse is?"

"I think so."

"Tell me about it!"

I clear my throat.

"Poppy?"

"Yes."

"What is sexual abuse?"

"It's ok later."

"What?"

"It's ok later when you're married. But if you do it too early, it's abuse."

Captain Hart is silent for a moment. Then he asks: "Can you give me an example please?"

I shrug my shoulders.

"What exactly did your father do?"

"He was always groping me."

"With his hands?"

I nod, but he doesn't see it because he's still typing.

"I can't hear you. Yes or no?"

"Yes."

"More than once?"

I nod again.

"I can't hear you. Yes or no?"

"Yes."

"Were you wearing anything when he did that?"

"Hm?"

"Were you wearing any clothes when he was groping you."

"No."

"What?"

"Not really."

"You weren't wearing anything?"

"No."

"So, you were naked?"

It's hot and my mouth is parched.

"Were you naked?"

"Yes."

"And your father?"

"Him too."

"Him too what?"

"He was also naked."

"Always?"

"Most of the time."

"How often?"

"Very often."

"But not always?"

"Almost always."

"Where did he touch you?"

I think I'm running a fever. It's hot and I feel like I need to throw up.

"Where did he touch you?"

"Everywhere."

"What do you mean, everywhere?"

"Well, a little here, a little there."

Captain Hart keeps typing and typing.

"Did it... uhm..."

I try to imagine what it would be like for Mom and me to live in a different place. It doesn't work, I can't see anything. Not even a color, just gray fog.

Do I really want to live alone with Mom?

"Did your father ever... how do I say it?"

Mr. Thomas explained once that if you are in doubt, you should stay still. Because if you are still enough, you can hear your inner voice, which will let you know whether what you are doing is right or wrong. I close my eyes and wait.

"Do you know what sex is?"

I must not have an inner voice. I can't hear a thing.

"Poppy?"

"Hm?"

Captain Hart stops typing. He coughs and takes another sip of water. Then he rubs his nose and stares at the ceiling. "Sex is when... when the man takes his... well his... but I'm sure that didn't happen with you."

He stays quiet for a second.

"Where did the abuse happen?"

"At home."

Captain Hart mutters something. He types again. "Only at home?"

"No, together."

"What?"

"We were together."

"No, yes, I understand. But I was asking if it only happened when you were at home, or in other places too?"

"Sometimes in the car."

He types.

"In the shed."

And types.

"In the trailer with the Liberty.'

He looks up.

"That's a camper tent," I explain.

"I know what Liberty is," Captain Hart says.

"I'm sorry!"

"Is that it?" he asks.

"Once in the tree house."

"In the what?"

"The tree house. He built it with one of his business colleagues. He's very good at that."

Captain Hart types an awfully long sentence.

I wait for him to ask me the next question.

"When did the abuse start?"

"When we moved in."

"How old were you then?"

"Not very old."

"How old exactly?"

"Six."

He stops typing again and stares at me. "Six?"

Captain Hart's eyebrows always go up when he has his doubts.

"That seems a bit exaggerated. How do you remember it so exactly?"

"I turned six on the day it started. It was my birthday."

He shakes his head slightly.

"With a six-year-old child! That is..."

Now he looks like he is furious.

"I'm sorry!" I say again.

"How old are you now?"

"Twelve."

"Twelve?"

"No, I'm sorry, I'm a little confused. I'm fourteen."

I look him in the eyes.

Does he believe me?

The thoughts in my head go silent.

Later, I shake Captain Hart's hand and thank him for his help. There are black spots in my vision. In the lobby, I run into Ashley's father. He's standing at the coffee machine and is talking with Mr. Scott and another police office. When they see me approach, they stop talking.

"See you later, Mr. Baker. Have a good day!"

The black spots are getting bigger.

"Bye, Poppy," Ashley's father says. "Good luck with the move!"

I don't know what to say so I just keep staring at him.

"There's a moving van in front of your house." He points outside with his coffee cup.

"Yes," I say. "We're getting new furniture."

"Ah." Mr. Baker nods. "Wonderful."

I stagger out of the police station. It took me thirty steps to get to the station; it took me seventy-two steps to get back.

... And Back Again

The crystal chandelier lies in pieces in the entryway. There is no furniture left in the living room, and all the rugs are gone. Fifi is barking nonstop, her back is covered in red paint. It's the same color that I later find in the dining room: PEDO is written on the wall in large letters. Below that it says "HOMO" in quotation marks. My ears are ringing, and I've gotten so used to the pounding in my head that it takes me a while to notice another sound coming from Dad's office.

The jackhammer.

"That perverted freak!" Uncle Carl is trying to crack open the safe. There are enormous holes in the wall. You can see through some of them to the other side. George and John are standing nearby covered in sweat. Uncle Carl lowers the hammer when he sees me.

"Where's Mom?" I ask.

"She went to the bank with Grandma Brown," Carl rasps and throws himself back at the wall.

"And Aunt Barbara?"

"She's getting a welding torch." The veins on his forehead are popping out. Uncle Carl swings the jackhammer through the air and straightens his back: "Back to it!"

Large pieces of wall fall to the floor. Mortar flies through the room. But the safe is still locked securely into the wall.

"Fucking safe." John wrinkles his nose.

For a few seconds, nothing happens, but then the wall collapses with the safe.

"What's with all the noise?" Nanna enters the office followed by my mom. She has my pink gym bag slung over one of her shoulders, which is throwing off her equilibrium. She hangs on to my mom for support. "You idiot! The whole neighborhood can hear you!"

Nanna is angry.

"Don't get so worked up! There's plenty of construction done around here," Uncle Carl says.

Nanna notices the safe on the floor and smacks her forehead with her hand. "We should have called in the experts!"

"How much did they give you, Patricia?"

Mom is staring at the safe. George and John are staring at the pink gym back that Nanna is struggling to keep on her shoulder.

"Patricia!"

"What?"

"I'm asking how much is in that bag."

"Two hundred thousand," Mom answers.

"Two hundred? Dollars?"

"All in one hundred-dollar bills."

"And they just gave it to you? Just like that?" Carl can't hardly believe it.

"I've got the power," Mom says proudly.

Nanna rolls her eyes. "No, she just has the power of attorney."

"That's what I'm saying. I've got the power."

"How did it go at the police station, Poppy?" Nanna asks.

"Good," I tell her.

"Did you tell them the truth?"

I nod.

"Good girl. You can't hide it forever."

"Hide what forever, Nanna?"

"The truth, Poppy."

Nanna was right. No matter how hard you try to hide it, the truth will always come to light. No matter how thick the wall around the safe is, how complicated the code, in the end, nothing matters. The biggest secrets are the ones that want to be made known. Because they are lonely. And because they keep growing. The longer a secret is kept, the bigger and lonelier it gets.

When Aunt Barbara comes back around six with the welding torch, and the safe is conquered at last, they don't find any money or jewelry, but the truth. Painfully exposed. One hundred, two hundred, three hundred, four hundred times. At first, I wonder how many different girls there were. There are some that are very young, and some that are older, and some around my age. Yet, they all look alike. They're all pale and skinny, with blonde hair and blue eyes. Sometimes they're looking into the camera, but most of them are looking away. At the wall. At something behind the photographer. They're ashamed. I want to cover them up with my hands. But there are so many of them. I don't know where to start. I'm in a lot of them.

As soon as my mom realizes what kind of pictures these are, she grabs two handfuls and throws them across the room. The photos fly like confetti through the air. No one moves to pick them up. Everyone freezes. Only their eyes react to the impossible.

Mom sinks down crying among the pictures. She folds in on herself into a fetal position. She's fleeing into her own world, leaving me alone again.

Aunt Barbara is the first to speak. "I don't want to ruin your moment of misery, but what can I take home with me? An old rug or maybe a bundle of bills?"

Nanna answers that patience is a virtue and that she would make sure that the money from selling the house would be divided fairly."

"How," Uncle Carl asks. "It's his house, isn't it?"

"He's going to prison for sure! Think about it, Carl. This pervert will give us compensation for the damage he's done after we sue him."

"What about until then? What do I get until that happens?" Aunt Barbara is almost frantic.

Nanna reaches into the bag and hands Carl a bundle of cash. He counts it, I do too. It's at least a thousand dollars.

"I'll consider this a down payment, Grandma Brown," he says and gives a hundred dollars to George and John. "A down payment! Make sure you keep that in mind! And I suggest that I'm the one to take care of the bag."

"*You* have no right to suggest anything!"

"Carl's right. That's how we should do it," Aunt Barbara says. "If we leave the cash to you, Mom, you'll just spend it all gambling within a week."

Nanna almost chokes out of outrage. "And that's coming from my own daughter?" She stems her hands into her sides and spreads her legs wider to keep her balance. "Who came up with this master plan, huh," she asks angrily. "Who is the only one with a clear head in this family of imbeciles? Who kept the child fucker in Poland at bay? Huh?"

"But we did all the work," Aunt Barbara screams.

"And hired additional needed personnel." Uncle Carl points to George and John. "And we got the jackhammer and welding torch."

"They are just henchmen. The only ones who matter are those two!" Nanna points at me and Mom. "These two are the ones that suffered. Without them we wouldn't even be getting anything. My granddaughter paid the price."

"But she got through it and everything's behind her now," Barbara says. "The pig is going behind bars."

For the second time today, Nanna slaps her forehead with her hand and rolls her eyes. "My God, where did I go wrong with you? Even if that perverted asshole goes to prison, he still ruined Poppy's life. She'll be lucky if she turns out somewhat normal. And to do that, we need to invest in her future. I'll put my neck on the line for that!"

Aunt Barbara stares gaping at Grandma. "Well, we wouldn't want to risk your neck."

"Don't worry about it. I'm elastic," Nanna responds.

Mom suddenly stands up again. "Give it to me," she says and extends her hand towards the pink bag. "Give it to me now!"

"The money belongs to me!" Nanna looks at her with distrust and quickly adds: "I'll take care of it for Poppy."

"But I'm her mother!"

"Technically, yes," Nanna says.

"Not technically, literally!" Mom yells.

Nanna grudgingly hands Mom the bag.

"And now?" Carl looks around the room.

"Now we leave the crime scene!"

Uncle Carl and Aunt Barbara leave with the car that has the shiny camper hooked to it. Aunt Barbara is sitting in the front and is holding the box with the *Precious Moments* and Swarovski figurines on her lap. Mom didn't mind her taking those. ("I can just buy them again later"). The backseat of the Toyota is packed with silver utensils and crystal glasses. In a hurry, Aunt Barbara wrapped everything up in newspaper and magazine pages. If you had to hit the breaks unexpectedly, everything would fly through the windshield. But I keep quiet.

Nanna is riding in the moving van with George and John. She's sitting in Dad's recliner, between plastic bags filled with plates, surrounded by furniture, the books, the bikes, the TV, the couch, the Chinese Vases and several pieces of art.

I lug the suitcases and trash bags outside. Mom is sitting on the steps on top of the pink gym bag and is lighting a cigarette. Fifi is running around barking.

After I put the last trash bag into the sports car, I go inside one last time. In the office, I pick up all the pictures and put them into a plastic shopping bag from the toy store. Next I get a piece of paper and write the word *Sorry!* on it and place it on his desk. I take the bag filled with pictures with me and stuff it into the bottom of my backpack.

I'm actually not sorry at all. I don't feel anything. I'm not sorry for the chaos. I'm not sorry for the broken wall or the empty rooms. And if Dad has to go to prison, well, I'm not sorry about that either. Maybe that sounds harsh. But I am sorry that I am not sorry at all. It's as if I'm trying to explain to him that Hitler wasn't all that bad ("Of course that man was bad, Poppy. Right is right, bad is wrong. Are you trying to say that Hitler was good?") But Hitler wasn't good. Gays aren't sick. And the color of your skin doesn't make you a criminal. And Columbo was never the bad guy.

I force myself one last time up the stairs into my room. Standing in the doorway, I say aloud: "Ciao!" without knowing why or to whom I was saying it. I think about Mr. Thomas, who I will probably never see again.

I forget how to breathe suddenly. I hit my head against the wall a few times, until there are spots running across my vision. It helps a little. I limp back downstairs and lock the doors behind me. And because I don't know what to do with the keys, I throw them with all my might into the rhododendrons.

Our Last Chance

Mom is taking a shower for the first time since checked in to the hotel three nights ago. We're on the fourth floor. The room is large, but because we have so many bags, suitcases and trash bags, there's only room to sit on the bed or in the bathroom. We don't allow housekeeping to come in.

Mom mostly just slept the past three days. I bathe often. If I'm not in the bathtub, I'm watching TV. I watch the news because I want to know if we're wanted yet for theft, vandalism, or slander. So far, there hasn't been any news about us. Still, I have a bad feeling.

I know Dad is back from Poland by now. I don't know if he's been arrested yet. I begged Mom to call Grandma. We're in hiding, and she doesn't know where we are. So, if she hears news about my father, she would not be able to get in contact with us. Mom rejected the idea. "If we call your grandmother, she'll just take control again, Poppy," she said. "I like it much better like this. Everything is good now. Just the two of us without a chaperone."

Mom gets out of the shower and dries her hair. After she leaves the bathroom, she empties all the suitcases and trash bags in search of her white, leather miniskirt. It's in the last trash bag.

"I need to get out of here, Poppy," she says. "We're on our own now and can't afford to waste any time daydreaming. We need to learn to stand on our feet again." She combines the miniskirt with a red and white checkered blouse, and the knee-high white boots. "I wish I had a cowboy hat, then the outfit would be perfect." She presses her finger into the small box with the blue eyeshadow. When she's done, she calls: "I'm ready to rock this place!"

"Where are you going, Mom?"

"Downstairs to the hotel bar."

I count the money in the gym bag to pass the time. It really is almost two hundred thousand dollars. Minus the thousand dollars that Nanna gave to Uncle Carl. I wonder how long we can survive on this. It's an impossible math question, but it calms me somewhat. We will make it, Mom and me. It's our Plan B.

I put on my pajamas. They're way too small on me. My midriff is exposed, and the bottoms ride up high on my thighs. It's cold, so I cover myself up with some of Mom's clothes that are strewed across the bed.

I placed the plastic shopping bag from the toy store back into the gym bag and slung the bag across my shoulder. I turn off the lights and fall asleep immediately.

There's a man in our room. I can tell by the sound of the laughter that it's a man. Since I know there is no way that it's my dad (he hardly ever laughed), I'm not that worried. The man is bent over a figure on the floor. Mom must have tripped over the suitcases, but the man is not able to get her back up. They're both giggling while Fifi is barking hysterically, and Mom farts.

"Oopsie, I made a poopsie."

I turn the lights on. The man is wiping tears from his eyes. Mom gets up.

"Mom, is everything ok?"

"Poppy, this is Edward!" Mom giggles.

"Apologies, we didn't mean to wake you up," Edward says.

"No problem." I wave it off.

Edward is tall and thin. He's wearing gray pants and a white turtleneck. He's messing with the collar; he must be hot. "My goodness, your mother is hysterical," he says and laughs.

"What time is it," I ask.

"Edward and I had a couple of drinks together, Poppy."

"Oh. Just you two?"

"And Rudolph, the bartender with the huge butt. He didn't want either of us."

"No," says Edward. "I don't understand that at all. After all, we're both so good looking."

"Rudolph is gay," Mom snickers and disappears towards the minibar.

"Ah, that explains it. But why didn't he want me then?" Edward can't get a hold of himself and ends up sitting at the foot of the bed, petting Fifi.

"Your mother has a great sense of humor. That's rare," he says and looks around the room.

"Yes."

Edward takes everything in. The chaos of our hotel room, Fifi, Mom in her leather skirt, me in my too small pajamas, and the pink gym bag slung across my shoulders.

"I'm aware of your situation," he says.

I give him a suspicious look. *How much does he know?*

"I will help you two," Edward says. "I have the perfect place for you."

"That's very kind of you," I say.

"Edward is in real estate." Mom takes a small bottle of vodka from the minibar and hands it to the real estate agent. He unscrews the cap and downs the entire bottle in one swig. Then he gives Mom a kiss goodbye.

"We'll see each other tomorrow in my office. You still have my business card, Patricia?"

Mom reaches into the inside of her bra. "I've must have lost it. Oops!"

Edward gives her a new card. "You don't look like someone who often loses things," he says and leaves.

Edward has several houses in mind. We're riding in the car with him. Mom is in the front seat with Fifi on her lap, and points to all the houses she likes, whether they're for sale or not. I'm in the back and lean forward so I can hear what Edward is saying. Sometimes I have to give Mom a gentle shove and shush her because she keeps interrupting him. I want to understand what he's talking about. He mentions our budget: somewhere between seventy-five and one hundred thousand dollars. I told him the amount myself. With the rest of the money, we will be able to survive until I graduate, as long as we eat at McDonald's every night. Afterwards I can find a job and we can go from there.

Edward believes that we inherited the money. He's a lot more serious today. He doesn't talk about Mom's great sense of humor anymore but tells me I can be proud of her. "Not every woman has the courage to leave a domestic violence situation, Poppy. It must have been hard for your mother to have to endured so much physical abuse over the years. And you're just a child. You couldn't have helped her."

"Hm…"

"Not to mention the emotional damage. It's a miracle that she is still able to be so happy and optimistic. You should be proud of her."

"Humor is my secret weapon," Mom says. "Can we go back to the first house we looked at?"

Mom means the mansion in the suburbs. If we were to buy that house, all the money in the gym bag would be gone all at once, and we would even have to borrow some.

"We can't afford that house, Mom. What will we live from?"

"You need to believe in yourself more, Poppy. Confidence is my second secret weapon."

Edwards parks the car in front of a house on a busy street. We get out.

"This is the last place," he says and points to an apartment on the first floor.

Mom glowers at the 'For Sale' sign on the small balcony. "Let's keep going," she says. "I won't go back into an apartment!"

"At least take a look at it," I tell her.

"I can already tell that I'm not going to like it."

"Just come on, Mom!"

"You guys can go ahead. I'll wait outside." Mom lights a cigarette. Her eyes shift from left to right.

"Are doing ok?" Edward asks.

"I feel great," Mom says. "As long as I can stand here and smoke."

"Ok," I say. "Edward and I will go ahead and go inside. You can follow us when you're done smoking your cigarette."

"We'll see," Mom answers. "Or maybe I'll just disappear all of a sudden."

She takes the pink gym bag from the back seat and slings it over her shoulder. In the past few days, Mom entrusted the care of the bag to me. It bothers me that she now wants to hold on to it herself. Somehow it feels like the bag now contains something dangerous. A hand grenade or a venomous snake.

"Mom, please don't be ridiculous!"

She rolls her eyes dramatically. "Your mom is going to make a run for it, Poppy. Soon she'll be across the country."

"That's not funny, Mom."

"We can continue looking tomorrow," Edward says. He's also acting nervous. I don't think he knows what to think about my mother right now. The more time he spends with her, the more distant he seems. No matter what he says.

Mom wraps her arms around herself and starts rocking back and forth, her cigarette dangling from her lips.

Edward clears his throat. "It's just that this apartment will probably be off the market by the end of the day. There's already been eight offers, all of the buyers are excited. It really is a nice place. And very affordable."

Mom stopped listening. She's talking to herself. If I ask her again, she'll just start screaming or turn away. But if I leave her outside alone, she might actually run away before I get back outside. But we need a place to live. I need to go back to school. Our lives need get back to normal.

"Mom? I'll only take a quick look inside, ok? I'll be right back."

She shakes her head violently and closes her eyes, as if that would make the rest of the world disappear. Edward is watching me. I can see his uncertainty, his bewilderment.

"You know what, Mommy, I think you're right," I say happily. "But since we're already here, it would be rude to not at least take a peek inside. You can wait here; we'll be right back. Come, Edward, let's get this over with."

I go towards the apartment. It's working. Edward is following me. Before we enter, I turn around. She's still there crying.

Of course, she's still there. Where would she go?

The apartment has two bedrooms, a living room and a kitchen. It's not very big but at least it's clean. The walls are white. The windows have pink curtains and all the rooms, except for the bathroom and kitchen, have a brightly colored carpet, just like Mom likes it. I keep limping back into the living room, because it has three large windows that look out front, so that I can check to make sure that Mom is still there.

"What do you think," Edward asks me.

"I like it a lot," I say. "How much is it?"

"Fifty-seven thousand."

"That's a good price. We'll take it."

"I think that's a great choice. But don't you have to talk it over with your mother first?"

"She usually lets me decide these kinds of things. You know the horrible life she left behind her."

"Indeed."

"Do we pay now?"

"We'll take care of all that during the signing."

"Can we go there right away?

"We need to make an appointment first, Poppy."

"Tomorrow?"

"Let me see what I can do."

"We're in a hurry."

"Understood."

"No, I don't think you understand. We need to get this done *immediately*. We desperately need a home."

"What's going on with your mother, Poppy? Does she have some psychological problems? Is she on medication? She needs help."

"It looks worse than it is. She's just exhausted."

"Are you sure that's all it is? That she's ok?"

"Well, given the circumstances, of course it's hard for her, but we need a home so that she can stabilize. Everything around her needs to go back to some semblance of normal. This is, as you say, our last chance."

My high-pitched voice bothers me. It sounds like I'm about to have a panic attack. And I'm using the word "normal" too often. Nothing is normal anymore. "Do you understand, Edward?" I urge him. "I'm so glad she met you. A nice guy who's helping us find a home. You are our last chance."

Edward doesn't respond. I go to the window and look outside. Fifi is pooping. Mom is gone.

Edward and I stand in front of his car. I have the apartment's sales pamphlet in one hand and am holding Fifi with the other. Nothing more. We've already waited for five minutes.

"Maybe we should call the police," Edward says.

"No," I say quietly. "That's not necessary."

I don't want him to see that I'm about to cry. Because the whole plan will fall apart, and we'll never get a new home.

"But where did she go?

"Probably to my grandmother's," I say. "She lives a few roads down." I point into the distance.

"Are you sure," Edward asks.

"I know where my grandma lives."

"That's not what I meant."

"Listen," I say. "We'll take the apartment. No ifs, ands or buts. I like it and we can afford it. I'll call you later about the signing appointment. I have your number."

"I'm taking quite a risk on you."

"That's very nice of you, but you don't need to worry. You can count on me."

"If I don't hear anything from you by this afternoon, I will move on to other interested buyers. You understand that, don't you?"

I nod.

He glances at his watch. "I'll give you until 3:00pm."

"Pas de problème," I say. I wish that Edward would finally leave so that I can take a moment to sit down on the sidewalk, but he doesn't move. I shake his hand and limp away. Self-conscious, I turn around before turning the corner.

I have no idea where I am.

I drag myself breathing heavily through the streets. I keep asking people, but no one has seen my mother. In the last half hour, I took turns running (as much as my cast would allow) and walking. I've been carrying Fifi the entire time, hoping that the beast would have enough energy soon to do as I ask. I place the dog on the ground and give the only command I can think of: "Seek Mommy, Fifi. Go search!"

Fifi doesn't do anything but bark. "Seek!" I say again but she only goes to sniff at a dirty napkin that's laying on the sidewalk. Then she licks the hamburger bun beside it.

"Fifi! Seek!" I growl. I feel nauseous. I throw up out of despair and anger. Everything pours out of me, sour and cold. A few passersby stop. A woman with a child in a wheelchair yells: "Yuck!"

"What the hell are you looking at," I snap at her.

"It's a shame that kids these days start drinking so early," she says with disgust. "What would your mother say?"

"My mother is a dumb bitch," I respond.

"Someone should call the cops!"

I can't control myself anymore and cry. The woman shakes her head and keeps walking. I wipe at my mouth.

"Fifi, go find Mommy," I beg her.

Fifi turns around and runs away. I don't know if she's just running away because I scared her, or because she picked up Mom's scent. I trot after her, tears streaming down my cheeks. I keep running into people. My limp is getting worse. More and more people are in my way. I trip and almost fall. People avoid and stare at me, while I scream at them: "Watch where you're going!"

Standing in the middle of the crowd, breathing hard, I close my eyes and try to imagine where Mom would go with a bag full of money. I suddenly know where she is.

The boutique isn't far. I ask people for directions and since I'm no longer crying and screaming, they are much friendlier and helpful. Fifi disappeared and I couldn't find her. I'm now on a known street and go into the familiar shop. The people working there recognize me.

"Yes, Mrs. Grinberg-Brown was just here. She bought out half the store."

I keep going. Mom was also in the next shop. She must be nearby. I find her at the register of an expensive boutique store. She doesn't even act surprised to see me.

"Oh, Poppy," she says. "There you are. What happened to you? Your hair is a mess."

I hug her.

"Stop that," she says. "You're not a baby anymore."

"You're spending too much, Mom."

"Would you like to put some of this on layaway," the cashier asks, looking at the huge pile of clothes that she just rung up.

"What's new?" Mom asks me.

"Fifi is gone. I lost her."

"Oh, that's too bad... but whatever. We'll just buy another dog!" she says.

"I'm so happy I found you, Mommy."

"So, tell me: Do we have a new home?"

"Yes. If we act fast, it'll be ours. I think you'll really like it."

"Well," Mom says while she's stuffing change into the shopping bag, "I think this has been a successful day, all in all. Have a wonderful day everyone!"

The Whole City

When I used to imagine the future, I always saw myself in a nurse's uniform: one of the earlier ones, with a white apron over baby-blue scrubs, and a white nursing cap. I lived in a pretty Playmobil house with a garden. The grass was fresh and green with small blades that swayed in the morning breeze. There were rose bushes and orange-colored flowers. The yard was surrounded by a white picket fence; the paint was still wet, so a "fresh paint" sign hung from it. Two kids who looked like Peter and Bobby from the *Brady Bunch* were playing in the yard. They wore overalls with brown hiking boots and threw rocks into a rain barrel. A gray tabby cat slunk between the children's legs. I stood in the doorway of the pretty house in my chic nursing uniform. I laughed at the playing children Peter and Bobby (I think they were mine) and clapped my hands together in joy. "Children, children," I called. "Don't cause any trouble, you hear?"

"We're not doing anything," the kids laughed.

"Sure, you're not," I said. And I smiled and shook my head with the nursing cap, causing a bobby pin to come loose. I pushed the pin back in with practiced fingers. At this moment, a young man in a dark blue suit and shining hair would always come up to me. I was never able to make out his face, but he smelled good. He carried a small briefcase that he would take to work every day. At the end of the day, he would come home and work in the garden – his sleeves rolled up - under the setting sun. He never kissed me.

"You need to open your mouth," Tim Stone says. His tone is friendly but also a bit impatient. We're kissing in the park amongst the playing dogs. Or at least that's what we're trying to do. But I keep my lips pressed tightly together. I never know when the right time is to open them, and now it's too late. Again.

Tim looks at his watch. I'm in love. Or I think I am. I think about this boy at least five times a day after all. When I think about him, I start to dream. But ever since I realized that I'm in love, my father pops into my head more often. "Why are you acting like this? I did everything to properly prepare you," he says. That's the reason why I can't enjoy it.

Furthermore, I don't even know if Tim loves me back. Ella Dean, one of the many girls who have a crush on Tim, is much prettier than me. She's been after him for weeks. Tim says that she's been around the block. But then I feel like I've seen the whole city. Tim doesn't know that though. He thinks I've never been kissed before.

"I need to go to soccer practice," he says.

"I have a lot of things to do as well."

"I'll see you later. Bye!"

"Bye."

Tim is gone. I head home.

It's a little bit like my mother's lipstick, it smears across her lips. When we lived in Long Island, her lips were always perfect. Now she can't stay within the lines. Since we moved into our new place, she's unable to do anything right. She bought a fruit bowl, but it's filled with Skittles. Only the red, yellow and orange ones. She thinks that the other colors are boring. We have curtains, but no chairs or tables. We're sleeping on air mattresses and eat various items from McDonald's every night while sitting on a couch that I found on the streets. We have a TV, but the picture is staticky. Mom doesn't seem to mind.

Nanna just came in. Now that she knows where we live (at some point in time I called her, even though Mom didn't think it necessary), she comes by to see us once a week. She claims it's only for fun, but she is never fun. She also never helps. She's only here for the money. Mom always gives her two-hundred dollars. It's the same today.

"Thank you, my child!"

"Please be quiet," Mom says. She wants to watch TV.

"You're lucky that I had to live through a *war*," Nanna says.

"Why does that make me lucky?"

"Because it taught me to live cheap, Patricia. You're also lucky that I haven't told Barbara and Carl where you live yet."

"Don't move, Mom. Great! Just keep standing right there."

Now that Nanna is standing beside the TV, the picture cleared up. Maybe it's because of Nanna's new corset that contains iron wires. It's personalized to her measurements and she is proud of it. Recently, she also started wearing a silver wig. The color difference to her yellowish white hair is still noticeable though. Nanna claims that it's still her real hair. "My hair seems fuller because of my new corset. It makes me stand up straight like an exclamation mark. I feel like a new person."

"Yeah, yeah," Mom mutters.

"Any news out of Long Island, Nanna?" I ask her.

"No news is good news," she tells me. "The pedophile Nazi still has money to spare. I heard he spent half a day at the police station. He denied everything. I'm sure he's got the law on his payroll."

Even though I filed a report, nothing seems to be happening. As far as we know, Dad never told the police what happened to his house on the day that Mom and I left. The furniture and the money, he let it all go. Mom too. And even me.

"Which is why we won't pursue the process any further," Nanna exclaims. "After all, we got away scot free."

Caught

Mom is lying on the couch in her underwear, a cigarette dangling from her mouth, while flipping through a magazine. I doubt I can leave her alone today.

"Mom, please put on some clothes."

"Don't wanna."

"But you need to get dressed. It's not proper."

"You're one to talk."

"At least I'm wearing clothes, unlike you."

"You call what you're wearing *clothes*?"

"It's costume day at school. I told you about that."

"I thought you were joining the circus. You look like a clown."

I *am* a clown. I'm the female version of Bozo the clown. Complete with a red wig, red nose, blue jumper, white collar, and large clown shoes. I did my makeup myself.

"We're having a costume party, Mom," I say. "There is a contest too."

"Why don't you choose a funnier or crazier outfit? Everyone is going to look like that."

I like my costume. It fits me. I still haven't made a lot of friends. Maybe today will be the day – as Poppy the clown, who hides her pain beneath a funny mask. But the people that laugh at her will never know.

But when I talk through the doors at school, no one laughs.

The auditorium is dark and the music too loud. The boys have gel in their hair and are wearing sunglasses.

All the girls are dressed like Madonna: red lips, eyeliner, fishnet stockings, and leather skirts. They all stare at me. I want nothing more than to run back home, but that would be admitting defeat. One advantage my outfit has: it seems that no one recognizes me with all this makeup on. To keep it that way, I don't say anything. And when I do have to say something ("I would like a Coke please"), I imitate Bozo's voice, which I'm really good at.

For two and a half hours, I sit in a corner and watch the people on the dancefloor. I pretend to be enjoying myself. Suddenly, Tim appears beside me.

"Poppy? Is that you?"

"Wowie-kazowie," I imitate.

Tim laughs. I immediately feel a lot better.

"Nice voice impersonation."

"I've seen him live once," I say.

With Dad.

"You can talk normally. You've really seen Bozo live?"

"Yep, in Long Island," I say with my own voice.

Tim smiles again. I do too.

"So, you're from Long Island?"

I nod. We don't know that much about each other. That's because we usually spend our time together kissing. Oh well, if that's what you want to call it. Tonight, I'm going to make sure to open my mouth for him. I just know it.

"Did you live there with your mom?"

"Where?"

"In Long Island."

"Yes."

"And your father? Where did he live?"

"With us."

"Where is he now?"

"Still in Long Island."

"Are they divorced?"

"Yes."

Ella Dean dances towards us. She's wearing stilettos that make her legs look like they stretch on forever. She looks older, like she's eighteen. Ella pretends to twirl a lasso above her head and throws it at Tim. He jumps up as if the lasso caught him. She pulls on the imaginary rope. I glance at Tim. But he's looking at Ella. He's laughing, but not in the same way he does with me. In that moment, I can see the difference: he's laughing at me. He laughs with Ella. She keeps pulling on the rope and he stumbles towards her laughing until he's in her arms. She loosens the lasso, takes his hand and drags him towards the dancefloor.

Tim has to go, I get it. He can't help it.

He doesn't look back. I get that too.

I'm putting on my coat as soon as they make the announcement. In a few seconds, we will know who won the costume contest. Since I can already sense the storm clouds gathering above me, I hurry as fast as my clown shoes allow towards the exit.

But of course, I'm too slow. They catch me. Of course, I'm forced to go up on stage. Of course, everyone is laughing when I thank them with Bozo's voice. Of course, I receive thunderous applause.

I not only win first place for having the best outfit, I also get a prize for the most creative costume. Two plastic trophies with glitter and colorful stars that my mother would love. I thank the jury (the principle, the art director and the drama teacher) and wave happily at the audience. The entire auditorium is singing *"Everything is for Poppy."* Ella and Tim sing as well – as much as they can in between them swapping spit.

I raise my arms, one trophy in my left hand, the other in my right, and start directing my singing classmates.

Always

Every time someone rings the doorbell, I worry that it's Uncle Carl. He's been bugging Nanna for weeks, because he's convinced that she knows where we are. Even if she keeps denying it. Nanna is afraid of him. It used to not be like that, but ever since he got involved in "this situation," he turned into a ticking time bomb, says Grandma.

Uncle Carl wants money. Lots of money. He says that he has a claim to it. He did all the hard work after all. If Grandma is to be believed, she told him the last time she saw him, that money can't buy happiness and that true happiness can only be found from within. For that, my uncle gave Nanna a black eye, which has since turned yellow.

"I'm risking my life for you two, God damn it," she often tells us. She only dares to visit us on Sundays when the football games are on; only then can she be sure that Carl won't follow her. She never stays long.

As soon as Mom gives her money, she leaves. But she always comes back.

Sometimes

Sometimes, usually on Wednesday afternoons, I go to a pay phone and call into Long Island. The conversations never last long, and I'm always sad afterwards, but if I never hear Mr. Thomas's voice again, I would be even more miserable. Which is why I call him every now and then so that I can lie to him about how much I love my new school. That I have a lot of friends. That we found a wonderful home and that my mother is like new. She even has a job, I lie, working at a travel agency. And since she already won "Employee of the Month" twice in a row, we will be able to afford a trip to Las Vegas over Christmas.

I still feel terrible about everything that happened, I tell him, but we were assigned to a nice social worker who I can confide in.

Mr. Thomas is glad to hear that I'm doing well. Before he hangs up, he holds Julia up to the phone and I can hear the baby breathing.

Sometimes she says: "Bah!"

Often

When I'm at school, Mom often goes into the city. I don't know where she goes or who she's with. When I get home around four o'clock in the afternoon and she isn't there, I stand in front of the window and wait until I see her.

I can't eat or drink until she comes home. I don't even take off my coat. I only calm down when I see her come up the sidewalk. Since we moved to the suburbs, she no longer walks normal; instead, she dances, hops, and skips across the streets. I press my face against the cold window glass and watch the strange being that crosses the busy street. Mom only wears oversized, bell-shaped white coats these days. Thankfully, the coats make her standout since Mom likes to dance across the streets without looking. The sound of squealing tires is oddly calming for me, because it means that Mom is coming home.

"Yoo hoo, Poppy, I'm home!"

"I see that, Mommy."

She's dancing across the living room. Every time she hits a wall, she closes her eyes and rests her cheek against the wallpaper. She stays like that for a few seconds and looks around her with a shy smile and rolls her eyes. She keeps her cheek pressed against the wall and I think she's counting backwards in her head. Because, she suddenly yells: "Zero!", and jumps towards the other wall to start the whole process again.

"I'm jumping from tree to tree, Poppy."

From tree to tree in a house without plants.

"What do you want to eat, Mommy?" I ask her.

"I would prefer going out to a restaurant."

"That's too expensive."

"Have you looked in the bag, Poppy?"

"The bag will be empty one day, Mom."

"No way. It's going to last forever, Poppy."

"No!"

Mom looks sad.

"You need to stop buying all this stuff."

She looks even sadder.

"And you need to stop giving money away."

"To whom?"

"Everyone. The homeless, living statues, the mime. You've given them enough."

Mom always throws twenty dollars into the living statues' hats. She tries to break the mime's concentration by waving a hundred-dollar bill in front of his face. She pretends to be in a basketball game and throws one-dollar bills at the plastic cups of the homeless people.

"And maybe we need to explain to Nanna again that we need the money ourselves."

"What does Grandma have to do with anything?"

"You're still giving her money, Mom."

"No, yes, yes, I get it!"

"No, you don't get it, Mommy. Nanna gambles it away and Pawpaw only fills up on whiskey. Two hundred dollars per week is too much."

"Really?"

"Sometimes you give her three hundred. Or four hundred." I'm not sure so I'm just guessing at this point.

"Well damn it. That much? But think about Carl, Poppy!"

"If he finds out that Nanna's been getting money from us, she's done for. She would be stupid to rat us out."

"You think? And you really think the money in the bag is all gone?"

"No, not yet, but soon, if you keep doing what you're doing."

"Thank God! So, we still have plenty left, Poppy."

"But not for long, Mommy, and I can't get a job yet. I need to go to school."

"And after school?"
"After school I'll take care of you."
"Why?"
"Because I want to."
"You don't have to do that for me."
"Yes, I do."
She shrugs her shoulders and turns on the TV.

Keep Calm

The girls in my class are taking turns jumping off the diving board. Angelina can do a backflip into the water; Mia always jumps up and down a few times before she jumps; and Ella takes the opportunity to show off: she jumps high into the air before doing a perfect swan dive into the water, like a seagull on the hunt for prey.

I'm in the water guarding the floaties, which will come in handy later when the waves start. We're at the nearby indoor water park, where they just installed a new wave machine that they plan to turn on today for the first time. After that, there will be free hamburgers and French fries, and a reporter that will take pictures for the local newspaper.

In fifty-four minutes, Mom will be home alone for two hours. That's the limit; I can't leave her alone any longer in the afternoons.

Everyone is excited and nervous. The girls are wearing waterproof makeup and fluorescent bathing suits. The boys are skinny, pale, and hyperactive. I look more like a boy on the outside, but on the inside, I know that I'm different. After six and a half months at my new school, I still don't fit in. Not really. They like me, but also think I'm weird. That's what Mia told me in the locker rooms while we were changing into our bathing suits. I would have preferred my own changing room, but the other girls insisted on sharing a room.

"You're really nice, Poppy. Funny and all, but weird."

I smiled. "Why do you say that?"

"I don't know. You just are."

I smiled even more.

"And it's not only that you still look like a child because of your flat chest."

I shrugged my shoulders, turned away from her, and slipped into my bathing suit.

"Or do you think the twins will be growing sometime soon?"

"Well, not really, no," I said.

"Let me see."

"No." I shook my head. "If there is any change, I will let you know."

Everyone laughed at me. I'm nice, funny and weird.

A loud siren sounds. The lifeguard yells through his megaphone that today is a day to be remembered, and that he hopes that the students will enjoy the new wave pool experience. The wave machine is turned on. Angelina, Mia, and Ella swim towards me and hold onto my floaty. There isn't enough room for four people, so I only hold on with one hand. The waves start off slow, but then grow higher. The girls are squealing, the boys are hollering. Within a few minutes, the waves are so high that everyone is holding on tighter to the floaty. Angelina starts to cry, and Ella yells at anyone that comes near us that they should find their own floaty. The chlorine burns my eyes.

Tim floats past us, goes under, and comes back up coughing. I yank him towards the floaty.

"Damn," he gasps. "This is way too rough!"

The waves are now so high that they break over the edge of the pool and flood the locker rooms. Angelina isn't the only one crying. Panic breaks out. The lifeguards are fighting with each other and can't seem to get the waves under control. One of them retrieves the megaphone and orders everyone out of the pool.

"Keep calm," a lifeguard shouts. He keeps repeating the words until everyone is out of the water. The reporter from the newspaper is taking tons of photos.

In the end, no one drowned. Still, the headlines the next day read: *Students barely survive at indoor pool park.* Beneath is a picture of the dangerously tall waves. You can see the swimming pool filled with terrified teenagers, including Angelia, Ella, Mia, and myself in the middle, hanging onto our float.

I'm the only one in the picture that is smiling.

An Eye For An Eye

Uncle Carl followed me home from school. I noticed him standing off in the distance, but at first, I wasn't sure if it was really him. Then he was gone, and I didn't think anymore of it: *Oh well.* But I should have been more alert. Even Uncle Carl reads the newspaper and he must have recognized me and figured out which school I now attend.

Presently, he's standing on our doorstep, looking at the house and at the first story windows. He's rang the doorbell a hundred times already. I'm hiding behind the curtains and hope that he gives up before Mom comes home. But he doesn't. He smokes five cigarettes and is still there when my mom shows up around seven o'clock, trying to commit suicide again by walking across the street with her eyes closed and her arms stretched out wide.

My uncle tries to cut her off halfway across the street, but she screams and hits him in the face. He hits her back. Mom screams louder. Cars honk; a man gets out of his car. He tries to calm Uncle Carl and my mother down. Uncle Carl yells at him to fuck off. The man listens. My uncle grabs Mom by the hair and drags her to the sidewalk. He rings the doorbell again, holding on to my wailing mother. I don't have a choice but to open the door.

He lets her go when he enters our apartment. Mom keeps screaming as he searches through each room. I follow him.

"Uncle Carl, please leave. She'll only get more upset."

"Don't worry, Poppy, this won't take long."

He finds the pink gym bag underneath my bed. As he pulls it out, my mom throws herself on him and grabs onto his legs.

My uncle kicks her in the stomach to make her let go.

"Let go of me, you stupid whore! Let go!"

"Please, Uncle Carl, don't do that!"

"Tell her to let me go, Poppy."

"Mommy, let go of Uncle Carl," I beg her.

"I won't allow it," Mom hisses. "That belongs to me."

"Shut your mouth, you dumb bitch!" Uncle Carl kicks Mom in the head and I think I hear something crack. She lets go and crawls into a corner where she lies down crying and bleeding.

I think as long as she's still crying, it can't be that bad, right?

"An eye for an eye, Patricia!" Uncle Carl shouts at the crying pile hunched in the corner. "This is what happens when you betray your family!"

"We really need the money," I try to say as calmly as possible.

"You better keep your mouth shut too, you arrogant, little hussy. Without me you'd still be in Long Island spreading your legs."

"Uncle Carl, please..."

"Go fuck yourselves! You're dead to me, both of you! You had six months to handle this fucking situation with some respect. One phone call would have been enough," he snorts and leaves. I go to my mom and kneel beside her, holding up four fingers in front of her blood-covered face.

"How many fingers am I holding up," I ask.

"What am I? A monkey?"

"No," I say relieved.

I get up and go to the bathroom. I get the plastic bag with the pictures from behind the toilet. It contains a thousand dollars that I added, because you never know.

That's all we have now going forward.

188

Because You Never Know

One week before Christmas, the money is almost gone, the heat doesn't work, and Tim and Ella broke up. I don't care that their relationship is over; all I can think about is food. I even hid a few coins in each of my socks, because I am always hungry. You never know.

Nanna comes by once a week to drop off some leftovers. She is more dejected than usual and keeps saying that things would have turned out differently, if we would have just listened to her. When I ask her what we could have done differently or better, she never answers.

In the past couple of days, Mom only talks about snow and Santa Claus. She stole fifty-four Christmas ornaments from the store. They all fit underneath her bell-shaped coat.

"I need to go this way, Tim," I say. He's been following me around like a dog for a few weeks.

"Me too."

"No, you live in the other direction."

"I'll walk you home."

With each step the money slides further down my socks. I stumble. My head hurts.

"Are you feeling ok, Poppy?"

"No!" The coins slide down past my ankles to my feet.

"Can I do something to help?"

"Go and get me some French fries."

"Come with me."

"I'm tired. I'll wait here."

"Really?"

"Yes."

Tim runs to the next snack bar. As soon as he disappears around the corner, I run home. The coins press into the soles of my feet.

At first, I thought the hunger was causing me to hallucinate. But at the same time, I realized that what I was seeing, was maybe not all that crazy after all. Not any crazier than what I've witnessed from her in the last few years. It is, however, much more dangerous. If she continues, she'll set the entire apartment complex on fire. I can hear sirens in the distance. I hope they can get through, because the whole neighborhood has gathered. Cars are blocking the road, the drivers getting out so that they have a better view.

I'm waiting for the fire department to arrive. The police are already here, along with an ambulance. They burst into the apartment, which wasn't hard since the door was left open, and quickly overpower my mother, who was waving two burning candles through the air. The entire incident lasted no more than five minutes. Everyone out on the street had a front-row seat to the action, which they could easily see through our three large windows. It's a miracle that nothing caught on fire.

Mom is wrapped in a foil blanket. She must have been cold; either way, nobody wants to look at her aging naked body.

The burning candles are doused. Her limps keep twitching as if they want to continue the bizarre dance she was doing. She babbles something, her mouth is moving. She's missing all her teeth. *So, she was wearing dentures.* I knew it. Two cops pull her out of view. She looks like a crazy old lady.

I move forward strategically so that I can watch without being noticed, as they load her up into the ambulance. If she were to notice me, she would call out and therefore everyone would know that I belonged to her. They would place me into a foster home, and everything would have been in vain. Everything I've done and everything I didn't do.

The ambulance drives off with my mother. I walk twice around the block until I'm sure that everyone has left. I go inside and lock the door.

It's quiet. It's cold. It's dark. I'll stand in front of the window and wait, even though I know that Mom will probably not come back for a while. I stand there until I can't feel my legs anymore, and then I stand there a little longer. Until I sink to the floor and pass out from exhaustion.

Girls Need A Mother

Mia's father places a hand on my leg and brings his face close to mine. "You like it, don't you, Poppy?"

"Yes, of course," I answer.

Mia turned her head away a few minutes ago in disgust. But I'm starving, so I keep stuffing the gorgonzola pasta into my mouth, as if my life depended on it.

"Mmm, it's good, Mr. Roberts." I don't want to be rude.

Mia's father slams his fist on the table in triumph. "I knew it! There are still normal kids in this world!"

"Don't act like an idiot, Dad," Mia says. "It tastes disgusting. I'm going to throw up. Poppy is only eating this slop because she's trying to be nice."

"Oh my God!" Thomas Roberts pretends to be insulted and looks at me. "Is that true, Poppy? Is it that bad?"

I shake my head and repeat that it tastes good.

"You," he looks at his daughter. "You're a terrible human being. You have no manners and no taste."

"And you are a horrible cook," Mia counters and blows her father a kiss.

Mr. Roberts laughs out loud. While he's laughing, Mia laughs too. I should also start laughing, but I don't know how. And I don't dare to try. I still think it's a miracle that they asked me to come in. When I rang the doorbell, I knew it was dinner time but now that I'm actually sitting at the table, I'm scared that they'll kick me out soon.

When Mia and her father are done laughing, a moment of silence follows. They first glance at me and look at each other. I notice that they raise their eyebrows and their forehead wrinkle.

"Shouldn't you call home?" Mr. Roberts asks.

"No. My mom is gone for the night. She's a flight attendant."

"What does your father do?"

"He's an HVAC mechanic."

"Oh, wonderful. Your house must always be nice and warm."

"My parents are divorced, Mr. Roberts."

Mia clears the table. I get up to help her, but she says: "Don't worry about it," so I sit back down. Her father lights a cigarette.

"And you live with your mom, Poppy?"

"Yes."

"Very good," he says. "Girls need a mother. Only having a father would be hard on any girl."

"It wouldn't be so bad, Mr. Roberts."

"Yes, it would be." Mia grabs the cigarette from her father's fingers and runs away with it.

"If you value your life, Mia Roberts." He gets up, cussing.

Mia runs to the other side of the room and takes a long drag. She coughs like my Grandma. Her father goes towards her and Mia climbs on top of a stool, holding the cigarette in the air.

"Poppy," she calls. "Help me!"

I can't move. I want to but my legs aren't working. I watch Mia and her father. It's like I'm watching them through a glass wall, or like they're on TV. Mia squeals, laughs, cusses, smokes and skips across the room. Her father corners her and takes the cigarette from her mouth, twisting her arm playful against her back. Mia squeals again, maybe out of pain, but mostly because she's having fun. He releases her arm and kisses her cheek. She throws her arms around his neck and wraps her legs around his waist. She hangs on to him like a monkey.

I stand up and approach them. I ask Mia if I could borrow her English textbook. I don't know what I'm doing. They both look at me a little irritated.

Then Mia says: "I'll get it for you."

"I'm sorry, Poppy," Mia's father says. "Were we being too loud?"

"Not at all, Mr. Roberts."

Mia walks me out and mumbles: "See ya tomorrow!" She quickly slams the door shut.

Outside, tears start running down my cheek. The sky is crying too. I'm cold. I can't breathe.

Snow flurries around me.

The Proposal

After three weeks, Mom still has not returned. Christmas break is over, but I don't go back to school. I just lie in bed all day; not only to keep me warm, but also because I have nothing else to do. When it gets dark, I visit the nice houses in the neighborhood to ask for donations for the Salvation Army. No one asks why I'm not carrying a collection jar. I ring the doorbells during dinner time, so people always give me money to get rid of my quickly. I use the money to buy a hamburger. *Once* I tried calling Mr. Thomas in Long Island, but Elizabeth said that they were busy moving out of the state, so I didn't get to talk to him.

I eat in my bed. I fall asleep, I wake up. I don't think about what I will be doing next. I've done that my whole life and it wasn't useful in the end. If I count all the hours I spent worrying about the future, I probably wasted six years of my life thinking about what to do. And now I'm lying here. So no, I don't have a plan anymore. Sometimes I let myself think about Mom in the hospital. Is she thinking about me too? Does she miss me? I miss her very much. I miss everything that could have happened and maybe will still happen if Mom gets better one day. That she will listen when I tell her something. That we will laugh about Nanna's corset together. That I will introduce her to Tim, and she gives me the thumbs-up behind his back. That I will kiss my mother without her telling me I should stop because I'm not a baby anymore.

"Poppy!"

Nanna slaps my cheeks with her flat hand. Left, right, left, right, left, right. My face is burning in the places her hand touch. At the same time, I can feel the coolness of her wedding band.

"Poppy! Stop daydreaming already. Wake up!" Left, right. "Open your eyes!"

I'm sitting on a mattress in the corner of my room, my back against the wall. "Go away!" I keep my eyes shut.

"What are you doing?" she asks.

"Nothing. I'm sleeping."

"You smell like shit."

"They turned off the water, Nanna."

"Well, at least put on some deodorant."

"I don't have any."

"Then go to a pharmacy and spray yourself with one of the samples."

I open my eyes. Nanna gasps for breath.

"How did you get in here?"

"The door was open."

I jump up and run to the door.

"Calm down, Poppy."

"Damn it!" I stop.

"It's not like there is anything in here someone would want to steal," she says.

I cry.

She rests her hand on the spare tire around her waist. "Don't start that crap, Poppy. This is no time to have a breakdown."

"Ok, ok. I'm ok."

"From your lips to God's ears."

"I was only sleeping."

"You look like a zombie."

"Why are you here, Nanna?"

"I spoke to your mother."

"When?"

"This morning."

"This morning?" My heart skips a beat.

"Are you deaf?"

"And what did she say?"

"She's coming home."

I cry again.

"Don't start that again," she repeats herself.

"When is she coming?"

"Any moment now." Nanna looks at her watch. "She told me that someone would bring her by."

I run to the window and wipe the window with my sleeve, but it doesn't do much; the dirt is on the outside. I rest my forehead against the glass.

In the reflection, I can see Grandma try to sit down on the mattress. Her butt sways back and forth, but the mattress is too low for her.

Finally, she lets herself fall.

The man helping the woman out of the white van is wearing a nursing uniform. The woman seems smaller than I remember. The roots of her hair are gray. She's wearing brown pants, black sneakers, and a short, gray winter coat. Her movements are unsteady, and she keeps placing a finger against her mouth, as if she keeps forgetting what she wanted to say. The nurse retrieves a white plastic bag from the car and hands it to the woman. Finally, he looks up and notices me. He asks her something while pointing at the window. Her eyes follow his finger. I step back, but not far enough. The man shoots me a smile and waves. Mom and I don't do anything. We just stare at each other.

"She's here," I say without turning around.

Nanna coughs. "Well, let her come in with her lackey."

But the lackey stays outside. He waits until my mom enters the building before he gives me a thumbs up. I copy the gesture. He gets back into his car and drives off.

"Help me up, Poppy." Nanna reaches out her hands towards me.

As I'm pulling her to her feet, I can hear my mother enter the apartment. I take my time helping Nanna up. When she's standing upright, I still don't know what to do, so I straighten out the sheets on the mattress.

"There you are," I hear Grandma say.

"Yes." Mom's voice sounds tiny.

"Did you have a good time?"

"Yes."

"What did they give you?"

"Hm?"

"What did they give you?"

"Yes."

"No, not yes. What? Pills?"

"Pills, yes. Here." Mom lifts the plastic bag.

"And are you feeling better?"

"Yes."

Nanna looks at me. "Poppy, stop that nonsense and come say hello to your mother."

I turn around and approach them. Mom blinks and does something weird with her mouth. I think she's trying to smile, but I can't be sure.

"Hey Mommy!"

"Hi Poppy!"

She's gained weight. Her face is rounder; her eyes are no longer blue but gray.

"How are you, Mommy?"

"Yes. Yes. Good," she answers.

"Good," Nanna says. "Give each other a hug and then I want to see a couple of smooches."

I give Nanna a look.

"Go on," she growls. "You must have missed her."

I give Mom a kiss on the cheek. Her skin feels clammy and cold.

Mom is shaking. "Cold," she whispers and looks around.

"Yes, this isn't a luxury mansion with heated floorboards, Patricia. And since it will never be, I have a proposal to make to you two ladies.

The Italian sausage burns in my stomach. Mom takes the last bite out of a sandwich. Nanna is stabbing a pink-colored fork into the remaining pile of French fries. I'm drinking chocolate milk, Mom has lemonade, Nanna has beer.

Nanna just told us her plan. My mom and I sat in a booth at the local snack bar and listened to her. Mom held a strand of hair between her fingers the entire time and kept pulling on it.

"Do you have any questions?" Nanna wants to know.

Mom and I lock eyes, but no words come to mind. We both know what's going on: We didn't make it. We won't make it. Not together, not alone.

"Well, that settles it then," Nanna celebrates. "I'll set the plan in motion when I call Long Island later."

Mom looks up surprised. She lets the strand of hair fall onto the table.

Grandma stands up with some effort. "Personally, I don't see this as a defeat," she says. "It's important to note that sometimes you have to take a step back to move forward." She's glaring at the slot machine in the corner while she says this. Then she goes up to the counter and asks for the check. "Come on, we're leaving."

"I need to go pee first, Nanna," I say.

"Hurry up, child," she says.

I run to the restroom. It takes at least seven minutes for me to stop throwing up and choking.

Mom and I are laying shivering beside each other on the floor. The moon is almost full and is casting its light into the room. Mom is smoking a cigarette she got from the cook at the snack bar. There are smoke clouds also coming out of her mouth, but it's from the cold.

When she's done with the cigarette, Mom closes her eyes. Her breathing is slow. I try to match it.

"Poppy?"

I jump. I'm scared.

"Yes?" My voice is shaking.

Silence. For a moment I think she didn't say my name out loud, but that I must have imagined it in my head. But after a minute she says it again:

"Poppy?"

"I'm here," I say.

"Me too," she responds.

"I'm glad you're back."

"Yes," she sighs.

"How was it where you were?"

She doesn't answer and rolls over. I contemplate if I'm allowed to place my hand against her back. I don't know if we would enjoy that or think it strange.

"Poppy?" she whispers.

"Yes?"

"What do you want to be when you grow up?"

She's never asked me that before.

"Do you know what you want to do, Poppy?"

"Yes, I think so, Mommy."

"What is it?"

"I want to be a banker, Mommy."

"But they are so boring."

"Then I want to be the first banker that is not boring."

And I'll be rich.

"Yes."

"And I'll buy a house."

"Yes."

"And you can come visit me anytime you want to."

"Yes, that sounds nice," Mom says. After a moment, she adds: "We'll see."

We remain silent.

I'm happy that I didn't lay my hand against her back just now.

Him

He is thin and trembling.

"Parkinson's," Grandma Brown says before we walked into the restaurant. "Just like Arafat and the Pope."

He has a mobile phone with him, a leather briefcase, and a man with sunglasses, who introduces himself as his lawyer. The phone is tied to a black suitcase laying on top of the table in front of him. *He* isn't looking at anyone.

I thought I would be scared, but I'm not.

We order coffee and apple juice. And a glass of water for Mom so that she can take her medication. Grandma wants a beer.

He's forced to put the black suitcase with the phone on the floor to make room for all the drinks. He knocks my mom's glass over while doing so.

She giggles. "Oops! Look, a small lake!"

The waiter hurries over with a towel. While the table is being wiped down, *he* orders Mom another glass of water. She looks up at the waiter.

"We're keeping you on your toes, huh?" In the last two minutes, Mom has made more jokes than in the last two days. She even put makeup on this morning that Nanna bought her. We wait until the waiter leaves.

"Great," Nanna says after Mom took her pills. "Let's put the cards on the table."

He gets a piece of paper out of his leather briefcase and pushes it across the table. Nanna reads it and nods. "Yes, that's crystal clear," she says and passes the note to my mom. Mom furrows her brows and acts like she can read the lawyer's note. I try to read it too but I'm too far away.

Mom brings her face closer to the letters and starts sounding out each word. We wait.

"You don't have to understand it all," Nanna says after a while.

"Oh, ok." Mom seems relieved.

"I'll summarize it for you," Grandma says. "Poppy can't take back the report, you have to do that. Just sign here on the dotted line."

"And will that take care of all the finances," Mom asks hesitantly.

"It's all there, don't worry!" Nanna answers.

He grins. It's a short and angry grin. Mom, Nanna and I glance up.

"You have no idea," *he* says, looks at his lawyer, and says it again louder: "They have no idea."

The lawyer notices that we don't understand what *he* means. "What my client had to go through; I wouldn't wish that on my worst enemy."

"It wasn't easy on me either," my mom whispers.

The lawyer shakes his head and raises his right hand, as if he was waving my mother's comment away. "Were *you* in a prison cell? Were *you* interrogated for hours? Do *you* have a disease that only worsens under stress? Did *you* have a flawless image that was completely destroyed from one day to the next? Did *your* house get vandalized? Did *your* personal belongings get stolen? Did *your* trust in humanity get reduced to nothing?"

"I didn't know any of that," Mom says helplessly.

Nanna is shifting back and forth on her seat. I don't like the direction this conversation is going.

"Well, I spent a couple of days in isolation," Mom giggles. "Does that count?"

"Shut your mouth, Patricia!" *He*'s beside himself. "Please shut your mouth or I'll lose it."

Mom raises her hand and pretends to lock her lips with a key.

He looks at me. "And you? Do you have anything to say to me, Poppy?"

I don't have anything to say to him.

"I can't believe this! You almost ruined my life, Poppy! Do you realize that?"

Even the lawyer shakes his head in disappointment.

"Poppy is very sorry," Nanna says. "I already told you that. We're all very sorry; that's why we're here. And that's why we'll sign. Right, Patricia? You're going to drop the charges."

Mom chews on her thumb. "I would love to, but I don't have a pen." She snickers.

No one has a pen, not even the lawyer. *He* tells me to go to the bar and ask them for a pen. They go silent. I stand up and walk away. My mind is blank. I don't think they spoke a word to each other during the time I was away.

My mother signs her name on the dotted line with shaking hands. "There," she says, "looks good, right? Patricia Grinberg-Brown."

He reaches into this jacket pocket and produces a thick envelope that he shoves at my Grandma. She rips the envelope out of his hand and stuffs it into her purse.

He takes his briefcase and his mobile phone and gets up. The lawyer helps him into his coat. The waiter comes and asks if everything is alright. *He* nods in my Grandma's direction: "She's paying!"

"How kind," she says. "A gentleman until the end."

He shoots Nanna such a hateful look that it makes her narrow her eyes.

"Do you have everything you need, Poppy?" *he* asks me.

I don't answer.

We finally lock eyes. An invisible barrier forms around my soul. It's as if *he*'s trying to break through. As if *he*'s trying to touch me with his eyes. But *he* can't do it.

I break the connection and focus my eyes on Grandma.

She shrugs her shoulders.

Mom mumbles: "Thank you, Pick-up."

I still don't say anything.

He leaves with the lawyer.

At the door, *he* turns around one more time. "Poppy, can you come, please?"

I nod and go to him. I'm not afraid.

"I'm glad that you came back, Poppy," he says quietly.

I shrug my shoulders and go back to our table.

Nanna is paying the bill with a hundred-dollar bill from the envelope.

The Black Car

It's snowing, just like nine years ago. Thousands of snowflakes are falling from the sky.

We're standing on the sidewalk in front of our apartment. We didn't have anything to pack, so we don't have any bags. I'm only carrying the plastic bag with Mom's pills. I shredded the pictures, burnt them and scattered the ashes on the lawn.

Mom wanted to take the mattress with us. I tried to explain to her that it made no sense. "There's nothing here, Mommy. Everything is there, remember?"

"Oh, yeah," she said.

We're standing stiffly beside each other, our hands shoved deep into our pockets. Everything is white. Everything is still. Snow lands on my eyelashes.

"There was a garden," Mom says suddenly.

I nod.

"And a little dog too?"

I nod again.

She stares at the tips of her shoes for a while. They're covered in snow. She furrows her brows. Takes a deep breath. Looks at me. She knows that the snowflakes that were once pure and a pretty, virgin white, where now dark spots that twirled dangerously from heaven.

Just as Mom opens her mouth to say something, the shiny black car comes to a stop in front of us.

He gets out and walks towards me. "Hello Poppy." His eyes are undressing me.

My mom and I get in the car without saying a word.

1998

I sneak through the rooms of the empty mansion. The light is slowly fading outside. Like black tar, the shadows crawl over the fixtures inside while I go through the house and enter each room after another. Just like I did back then on the day after my birthday, when I was woken up too early. A feeling of numbness tightly surrounds me.

I cross the large hallway, through the kitchen and dining room, up towards the second story where my parent's bedroom is. No one is here.

When I was younger, I thought there had to be something important to make it worth getting up early in the morning. I got up for Mom, so that I could give her a good-morning kiss on her forehead; she always turned her head away. Maybe I shouldn't have put so much effort into taking care of my mother. At some point in time, I stopped believing that anything was worth it all.

I enter my old room and suddenly feel very young again – six, perhaps – and I'm hiding in my hidden Barbie room. Toys are strewn around the room, castle towers lie in ruins, and the eyes of the dolls are too large. The house is dark, the air in the room cools down, it's dusk. Eugene is home (I deleted Richie, Daddy and Father from my dictionary when it comes to him – and saying *he* gives it too much meaning); Mom is gone. I can hear his footsteps. He calls my name once, twice. I keep quiet. I hear a rustling and the echo of his footsteps. That's how it must have been. When I was six, I hid in the closet, I slept there and when I woke up – after one rare night where I was left alone – I was suddenly seven.

I sigh and leave the room, closing the doors of the past behind me.

Now I'm standing in front of the bathroom door. It's maybe four or five seconds until I push it open. The bathtub is empty. It seems abandoned. A forgotten shirt hangs over the back of the chair. Above it, on the white wall, is a large, black mold spot, that, according to Mom, is shaped in the form of Africa. ("The Negro-land, Poppy").

I open the door a little more. It swings back. I often wished to find Eugene there behind the door, hanging in the corner from a belt in his robe.

The earliest memory I have of my mother in this bathroom, is her cold hand on my butt. I was sick, had a high fever, and she gave me a suppository. ("A Poop-canon.") The first memory I have of Eugene was his "oops" and "oopsie-daisy," as he placed me in the bathtub at six years old.

With a pounding heart, I glance around the corner. There's nothing and everything there: the smell of death, of pain, of stolen innocence and other scents of the past – memories, that lie buried deep within me like wine bottles in a cellar.

My mother died six months ago; Eugene soon after. The old man had already signed over the house and inheritance to me while he was still living. His company, Liberty, will go to Annabella's father. However, I don't think he's interested in keeping the business – like I'm not interested in keeping the house.

The only people at Eugene's funeral were the pastor and me. The pastor, because it's his job, and me, because I wanted to see what freedom felt like. But I didn't feel anything.

I try to imagine now – just like I did back then - the worst thing I could find inside the mansion, so that the reality behind it won't be as shocking.

And that would be my mother: sitting crumbled on a chair in her bathrobe, empty pill bottles around her, empty wine bottles, and her head hanging between her legs, foam on her lips, blood running from her nose, and a fizzing effervescent tablet in her open mouth that her confused mind tried to swallow. That's how I found her.

And *him* a week later: in the bathtub (how else could it be?), with a thin sheet of blood floating on top of the water, like a spilled kettle of stale black tea. His sex like a deserted little island bobbing just above the water, brown and disgusting. Beside him on the edge of the tub, was the case with nail files, scissors, and razor blades. His forearm, all the way to his wrist, was cut open, the top of a pair of scissors stuck vertically in his artery.

In Eugene's case, I would have loved to have helped out. The last few years with him were hell. He never missed an opportunity to demonstrate his dominance and to put us down. Due to his Parkinson's disease, he was no longer able to abuse me; I wouldn't have allowed it anyway. I stayed in the mansion for my mother. He took care of her and I would not have been able to do it alone.

If I had killed him, *he* would have probably just stared at me and nodded (there was too much nodding going on this house). I imagined killing him many times, and he knew that. Maybe that's why *he* took his own life. He took an overdose of his Parkinson's medication and got into the bathtub.

"A suicide is not uncommon in such a case, Poppy," the doctor told me later. There was no evidence of foul play. No one had any doubts. Maybe Grandma Brown if she had still been alive. But she would have been wrong. The thought of murder is not a crime, the act of murder is. I didn't want to live with that type of guilt.

"Life's just a sum of circumstances, chances, , and cash," Nanna would always say. "If you don't get that, you're going to wind up sick or crazy."

My mother went crazy and I ended up sick. But life is not a sum even if you reduce yourself to zero.

I leave the bathroom and close another door to the past. Today I understand that the brain works similarly to the digestive system. It can process everything, except a few things. These weird traumas are often recalled during unexpected moments, sometimes brought about by specialized doctors who are actually looking for something else, maybe something that they're missing themselves: a piece of their childhood, a young love. Some things swirl around in our heads for years.

Someone calls my name downstairs. "Mrs. Grinberg?"

I go down the stairs. At the bottom, the real estate agent who I hired to help sell the house, beams at me. As does the young married couple beside him with their two small children, Tina and Casper.

"We made a decision, Mrs. Grinberg," the father says and grips his wife's hand. "We'll buy this beautiful house. It just needs some fresh paint."

His words are like a beam of happiness on a rainy day. This family will fill this house with new life. I could – depending on my mood and motivation, I'll either be silent or talkative – simply show this family through the rooms. But I already said goodbye and don't want to take a step back again, so I'd rather the agent take care of the tour. He listens to people who don't say anything.

The estate agent guesses my thoughts and claps his hands together. "Would you like to take a tour of the house?"

Four heads nod happily.

I shake each of their hands and say goodbye. Outside, I turn around one last time and ask myself how long it takes for memories to decompose. I took the first step. The doors to the past are closed, the holes filled in, the curtains shut.

I raise my gaze to the window of my old room. Tina and Casper are there, waving at me. I smile. Wink at the kids

Then I get in my car – and live.

Acknowledgement

Mommy can't make it on her own.
And I can't make it on my own with Mommy.
So I ran to a pay phone
and called Daddy... and Daddy came.
(Poppy – ten years old)

Child abuse is shocking and concerning. Writing about it is hard. Sexual abuse means that an adult or teenager uses their position of power, their physiological and psychological advantage, the trust and innocence of a child, in order to get their own sexual gratification.

Poppy told me her story when she was already an adult, and I knew that I would one day write about it.

We've known each other since we were kids. As a seven-year old, I often asked myself, why she was so weird, and why she wasn't allowed to play with me, and why I wasn't allowed into their house (the mansion). Now I know why.

Children can sense when something is wrong. I remember the strange feeling that I got when I wanted to pick her up for a playdate, and her stepfather told me that Poppy was too busy. She was standing at the first-story window, looking at me pleadingly. I will never forget that look.

The list of possible clues to sexual abuse is long and not specific, so that it is often difficult to read the signs correctly. However, in almost all cases involving children, there is a change in behavior. As there was with Poppy. She stayed quiet – out of shame and because her stepfather threatened to throw her and her mother out onto the streets. Poppy was his favorite, and he was her secret, a secret that grew too big at some point in time.

Poppy was always afraid that no one would believe her. That's why she never said anything. She kept retreating back into herself, reacting dismissively. Only at school was she the funny girl that I knew. School was a place of comfort for her.

Due to Poppy's mother cluelessness, she chose to ignore her daughter's behavioral changes and the typical signs of sexual abuse. She preferred to go shopping.

I had many conversations with Poppy and my intuition back then was right. Instinctively, I knew that there was something very wrong. I feel responsible because I never told my parents about it.

Poppy is now married and has four children. Her family doesn't know anything about what happened in her past. But Poppy did determine that after her death, her family will receive the manuscript of this book with her own comments included.

I want to thank Uwe Raum-Deinzer the final editing.

The book *POPPY* was also reviewed by my wonderful editor, Christine Hochberger, Buchreif. As always, thank you very much.

I also want to thank Carly Martin and Francie Schmidt.

And final, a special thank you to my friend Poppy (pseudonym), for her courage to tell me her story. You can be proud of yourself and you have my utmost respect. You will always have a place in my heart.

AUTHOR BIO:

ASHLEY CAMERON

Originally born in the Dutch city of Heerlen, the author now lives with her family in Essen, Germany. She studied Economics at Maastricht University and after graduating, founded a pharmaceutical company, which operated worldwide. Bestselling author Ashley Cameron specializes in suspense thrillers, psychological thrillers and thrillers. She also writes short stories and screenplays. Her thrillers have made the top ten bestseller lists in Germany. The scripts were awarded several times in Los Angeles and filmed.
Ashley Cameron is the pseudonym of bestselling author Astrid Korten.

KAPITEL 21

Ich spüre, wie die Röte in mein Gesicht steigt. Ein eisiger Schauer läuft mir über den Rücken, die Härchen auf meinen Armen stellen sich auf. Mein Herz rast.

„Mifepriston und Cumarin", fährt die Ärztin fort, „sind nicht in Apotheken erhältlich, sondern können nur von Arztpraxen oder Kliniken, die Schwangerschaftsabbrüche durchführen dürfen, bezogen werden."

Ich stehe auf, abrupt.

Dr. Olafsson zuckt zusammen. Sucht meinen Blick. Sie legt einen Arm auf die Lehne ihres Stuhls. Als müsste sie sich abstützen. „Das sollte nicht sein."

„Was sollte nicht sein?"

Sie ignoriert meine Frage. „Woher hatten Sie diese Substanzen, Frau Sandvik?"

„Ich weiß überhaupt nicht, wovon Sie da reden."

Die Ärztin sieht mich entsetzt an. „Dass sie einen wirklich netten Medikamentencocktail in ihrem Blut hatten? Wie konnten Sie nur so eine gefährliche Kombination einnehmen? Das kommt fast einem Selbstmordversuch gleich."

„Nein ... Nein! Ich wollte dieses Kind. Ich habe nichts dergleichen eingenommen", antworte ich mit zitternder Stimme.

„Wollen Sie damit sagen, dass es Ihnen ohne Ihr Wissen verabreicht wurde? Nach dem Gesetz wäre das ein Tötungsversuch. Ist Ihnen klar, dass – falls es sich wirklich so verhält – es jemand gar nicht gut mit Ihnen meint?"

„Aber ... das kann nicht sein. Nein, das kann nicht sein. Sie müssen sich irren. Das Labor hat Mist gebaut."

Mir wird übel.

„Mifepriston hebt die Wirkung des Gelbkörperhormons auf und verhindert die Weiterentwicklung der Schwangerschaft. Der Fruchtsack mit dem Embryo löst sich. Cumarin hingegen erhöht unter anderem das Risiko für Spontanaborte. Sie hatten eine sehr hohe Konzentration beider Substanzen im Blut und wurden mit einer massiven, lebensbedrohlichen Abbruchblutung eingeliefert."

Ich schüttle den Kopf. „Nein ..."

Dr. Olafsson seufzt. „Überlegen Sie bitte, wer Ihnen das angetan haben könnte. Gehen Sie unbedingt zur Polizei. Erstatten Sie Anzeige. Irgendjemand wollte dieses Baby nicht und hat es in Kauf genommen, Ihnen physischen Schaden zuzufügen. Das gefällt mir ganz und gar nicht. Es ist definitiv eine strafbare Handlung."

Ich will weg aus diesem Zimmer. Weg aus den Albträumen - an einen Ort der Zuflucht. An dem mich niemand sieht, an dem mich niemand findet. Ich bin total erschöpft und will das alles nicht hören.

Aber plötzlich begreife ich, dass Dr. Olafsson recht hat. Und wenn sie recht hat, dann ist der Gedanke, dass mich etwas bedroht, nicht nur Einbildung, sondern eine Tatsache.

Die Ärztin steht auf, kommt auf mich zu und legt den Arm um meine Schulter. „Und jetzt verordne ich Ihnen viel Bettruhe und frische Luft. Also ordentlich schlafen, aber außerdem gut lüften und am besten öfter mal rausgehen, Wir treffen uns nächste Woche wieder. Dann sehen wir weiter. Aber überlegen Sie sich das mit der Polizei."

Meine innere Panik schwappt fast über. Nur eine Person kommt hierfür infrage: Jonas.

Jonas und ich verlassen das Krankenhaus. Draußen schneit es wieder. Ich will nur noch nach Hause. In meinem Zimmer den Duft frischer Bettwäsche einatmen, ein wenig heile Welt schnuppern.

Ich warte vor dem Eingang und fühle mich schwach. Stehe unsicher auf meinen Beinen. Ich will nach Hause, ins Bett. Nachdenken.

Mom kommt heute Nachmittag zu mir. Annika ist in Madrid, sie hat Blumen geschickt. Auf der beiliegenden Karte stand nur: *Ich umarme dich. Alles wird gut.* Kein Wort über ein Baby, das nie mehr kommen wird. Diese geplatzte Frucht muss totgeschwiegen werden.

„Du wolltest das Baby behalten", fragt Jonas plötzlich. „Es ist doch so, oder? Und das völlig zu Recht, es war die richtige Entscheidung."

Ich sehe ihn überrascht an. „Du hast mir dieses Kind gegönnt", stelle ich erstaunt fest.

„Aber ja, natürlich." Er sucht nach Worten. „Du wärst gewiss eine wundervolle Mutter, Jonte. Weißt du, woran ich die ganze Zeit denken muss? Es ist immer noch möglich. Du könntest von einem Spender besamt werden. Das ist heute nichts Besonderes mehr. Viele Frauen machen das."

Hält er dich zum Narren? Zuerst verabreicht er dir diesen miesen Cocktail, und dann schleppt er dich zur Samenbank. Warum stellt er nicht gleich seinen eigenen Samen zur Verfügung, um dich zu trösten?

Ich ignoriere Back-Vocals hysterisches Gelächter. „Warum sollte ich mich künstlich befruchten lassen?"

„Aber, Jonte, du hast keinen Schwangerschaftsabbruch durchführen lassen. Ich finde das bemerkenswert. Dein Kinderwunsch ist also immer noch da."

„Ich weiß nicht ... Ich konnte wirklich erst nicht glauben, dass ich schwanger war, wollte nicht darüber nachdenken. Besonders nachdem du gesagt hast, dass ich in meinem eigenen Haus vergewaltigt worden sein könnte. Allein der Gedanke daran …"

„Ich hätte das nicht sagen sollen. Es tut mir leid."

„Nein, es war richtig. Du hast mir damit geholfen, mich ernst genommen. Mir klargemacht, dass da etwas außerhalb meiner Kontrolle passiert ist. Ich weiß immer noch nicht, wie ich damit umgehen soll. Ich wurde offenbar vergewaltigt, auch wenn ich mich nicht daran erinnere. Meine Seele ist verletzt worden, meine Privatsphäre auch, ich bin total verunsichert. Das wird mir alles zu viel. Und jetzt das mit dem Baby …"

Halt! Behalte es für dich. Denk erst mal in Ruhe darüber nach.

„Ich verstehe, dass du das alles hinter dir lassen möchtest. Das ist eine vernünftige Entscheidung. Solltest du dich für einen Samenspender entscheiden, dann helfe ich dir. Du kannst mich auch gern als Vater leasen." Er lacht. „Natürlich kostenlos."

„Und was hält Haakon von dieser Idee?"

„Es war Haakons Idee."

Er erwartet, dass ich etwas Nettes über Haakon sage, aber mir fällt nichts ein. Ich kann nur denken, dass etwas nicht stimmt.

„Du hast noch nicht über unsere Scheidung gesprochen." Ich höre das Zögern in meiner Stimme.

„Das ist doch auch gar nicht nötig, Jonte. Natürlich habe ich darüber nachgedacht. Aber Haakon findet es lächerlich zu heiraten. Er ist nicht eifersüchtig. und wir haben doch nach wie vor unsere gemeinsamen Projekte. Wir sind das Architektenpaar *JO*. Eine Scheidung könnte negative Auswirkungen auf unseren Ruf haben. Eine richtige Trennung ist später immer noch möglich, ich habe es damit nicht eilig. Und du sicher auch nicht."

Wir sind zu Hause. Ich bin zu Hause.

Ich nehme den Schlüsselbund aus meiner Jackentasche und öffne die Haustür. Im Wohnzimmer erwartet mich ein riesiger Blumenstrauß in einer viel zu kleinen Vase. Eine Karte liegt bei.

„Willkommen zu Hause, gute Erholung und herzliche Grüße", liest Jonas und lacht breit. „Wie aufmerksam von Haakon."

Dieser Heuchler hat deine Freundschaft nicht verdient. Beende deine Zuneigung! Mach endlich ernst! Meine innere Stimme ist schrill und laut. Mein Kopf dröhnt

Ich würde den pompösen Blumenstrauß am liebsten in den Mülleimer werfen. Er ist anmaßend und aufdringlich.

Wie kommt er überhaupt in dein Wohnzimmer, Jonte?

Jonas verabschiedet sich. Mit einem Küsschen auf die Wange.

Ich warte einige Minuten lang, dann wühlt sich leise ein Kichern durch meinen Körper, quillt auf meinen Rachen zu, lässt meine Kieferknochen mahlen, platzt aus mir raus … als erlösender Weinkrampf.

In meiner Brust schwappen schluchzende Schreie über.

KAPITEL 22

Das Gehirn funktioniert nicht viel anders als das Verdauungsorgan. Es verarbeitet bis auf ein paar Dinge fast alles, und Traumata werden meist in unerwarteten Momenten wieder hervorgeholt. Ich habe meine tief vergraben. Will auch nicht über all das nachdenken, was die Gynäkologin mir gesagt hat, denn ich gehe mittlerweile davon aus, dass hier eine Verwechslung vorliegen muss.

Die Stille, die ich in den vergangenen Tagen in meine Ohren habe fließen und in mein Hirn habe eindringen lassen, hat kapituliert, sie ist geschlagen worden, hat sich zurückgezogen. Und die Panik mitgenommen. Jetzt ist alles wieder gut. Ich atme.

Ich habe mit dem zweiten Entwurf für das Klosterhotel angefangen. Der Stift fliegt fast von selbst über das Zeichenbrett. Sobald sich meine Hände der Tafel nähern, entsteht aus zwei Klosterzellen ein behagliches Zimmer, ohne den Charakter der Zelle zu verändern. Der Raum geht in das Badezimmer über, getrennt durch halbe Milchglaswände. Ich brauche zehn Zeichenstifte, um mit dem Tempo meiner sprudelnden Ideen Schritt zu halten.

Obwohl ich erst seit drei Tagen an den Entwürfen arbeite, sind bereits dreißig unterschiedliche Zimmer entstanden. Wenn das so weitergeht, kann ich dem Orden die Entwürfe in sechs Wochen präsentieren.

Ich hatte nicht die Absicht, mich länger als ein paar Tage krankzumelden, wollte meine Arbeit im Kino wieder aufnehmen. Mich und meine Gedanken bewegen.

Mein Vorgesetzter und meine Kolleginnen im XD Cinema Norge waren sehr herzlich und mitfühlend. Einige erwähnten sogar, dass sie ebenfalls eine Fehlgeburt hatten, aber sie warnten mich davor, dass plötzlich ein intensives Trauma erwachen könnte.

Ich verdrängte ihre Worte, die nur die Angst schürten, und mit einem solchen Vorgefühl möchte ich nicht leben.

Ich stehe allein auf weiter Flur. Halte inne, bewege mich nicht, bin aber dennoch auf der Hut. Niemand ist da, niemand zu sehen, niemand zu hören. Niemand. Ich bin mit meiner Vergangenheit allein auf der Welt. Stehe allein auf dem Feld des Lebens. Verkatert, obwohl ich nichts getrunken habe. Erschöpft auf eine Weise, die schmerzt, aber zugleich voller Tatendrang.

Ich verdränge auch jeden Gedanken daran, wie es zu der Schwangerschaft kommen konnte. Es ist passiert, und es ist vorbei. Wie ein Albtraum, aus dem man erwacht. Ich will nichts mehr davon wissen. Die

Verdrängung funktioniert fantastisch, weil ich das Tempo bei meinen beiden Jobs stetig erhöhe. Mal tauche ich in die fiktive Welt des Kinos ein, mal in die bislang noch imaginäre Verwandlung der Klöster. In gewisser Weise macht mich das unerreichbar für alle Rufe aus der Vergangenheit.

Ich zeichne. Zahlreiche andere Kirchen und Klöster blitzen mir durch den Kopf, die ich in den Urlauben mit Jonas besichtigt habe. Rasch schiebe ich diese Gedanken weg, will nur für mein Projekt *Zwischen Himmel und Erde* Platz in mir lassen. Sobald es abgeschlossen ist, werde ich sofort mit dem nächsten beginnen. Die Aussicht darauf sorgt bereits für ein Gefühl der Aufregung. Aber auch des Zweifels, der immer irgendwo in meiner Nähe lauert.

Und er hat einen Namen: Back-Vocal.

Was spricht dagegen, den Weg fortzusetzen, den Jonas und du begonnen habt?, fragt er. *Wenn du ihm ein bisschen mehr entgegenkommst, gebt ihr weiterhin ein tolles Duo ab. Zier dich nicht immer so, Jonte. Ich habe deine Stimmungsschwankungen langsam satt. Das steht dir nicht mehr zu, du bist nicht mehr schwanger …*

Ich stelle mich dem Gedanken: Spricht etwas dagegen, dass wir weiterhin unter *JO* firmieren? Die Rollen sind gut verteilt. Ich entwerfe die Gebäude, und Jonas repräsentiert uns nach außen hin. Ich muss nicht im Rampenlicht stehen. Jonas erfüllt diese Aufgabe dagegen mit Begeisterung. Er genießt es, bekommt dabei immer mehr Selbstvertrauen, wird immer selbstbewusster.

Bist du sicher, dass diese Annahme stimmt? Back-Vocal hört sich zweifelnd an. *Oder hat ihm etwas ganz anderes den Rücken gestärkt?*

„Jonas ist aufgeblüht", murmle ich, „weil er sich endlich geoutet hat. Die Liebe zu Haakon hat ihn verändert. Sie hat ihn gestärkt."

Hast du es endlich geschnallt? Er wird nie zu dir zurückkehren, aber er braucht dich, um weiterhin zum Mythos JO zu gehören. Dadurch erhält er Aufmerksamkeit, Anerkennung und viel Geld. Und du verschaffst es ihm …

Meine innere Stimme hat recht. Ich möchte das Projekt *Zwischen Himmel und Erde* unter meinem Namen veröffentlichen. Unsere Ehe ist zu Ende. Das Paar ist Geschichte, warum das Duo aufrechterhalten? Wir sollten uns scheiden lassen und unser Geld und unseren Besitz aufteilen. Aber …

Zieh endlich den Schlussstrich, statt …

„Aber ich bin noch nicht so weit, Back-Vocal."

Das solltest du langsam werden.

„Sei still! Ich muss mich konzentrieren …"

Ich möchte mich in das Klosterprojekt vertiefen, möchte, dass meine ganze Welt nur noch aus einem Zeichenbrett im Format DIN A0 besteht. In meinem Kopf ist kein Platz für komplizierte Gedankengänge, ich brauche kein soziales Umfeld und ganz besonders keinen Ex-Mann, der mit einer schwulen dänischen Qualle liiert ist. Der große Unbekannte, der meiner Meinung nach ruhig anonym bleiben kann.

Eigentlich will ich keine Trennung bei dem Projekt, denn dann müsste ich Veränderungen akzeptieren und mich nach neuen Partnern umsehen. Andererseits hat der Gedanke an diesen allzeit souveränen Haakon mir vor Augen geführt, dass die Kluft zwischen uns zu groß ist.

Jonas hat mich kürzlich gebeten, ihn zum Notar zu begleiten, um das Testament seines Vaters anzuhören. Da wir noch verheiratet sind, sei es eine Angelegenheit zwischen ihm und mir.

Was hast du mit diesem Testament zu tun? Nichts! Er braucht wohl einen Begleitschutz …

„Ja, was habe ich noch damit zu tun? Aber es wäre eine gute Gelegenheit, das Thema Trennung anzusprechen", konstatiere ich, denn ich habe jetzt einen Entschluss gefasst.

Ich habe mich entschieden, allein weiterzumachen. Der Rest wird sich finden.

Niemand weiß, dass ich der kreative Kopf von *JO* bin und dass Jonas nur für das Marketing zuständig ist. Das soll auch so bleiben. Ich werde darüber schweigen.

Mit Schweigen kenne ich mich bestens aus.

Mein Bauch schmerzt immer noch. Mir wird übel. Schweißtropfen perlen auf meiner Stirn. Das Atmen fällt mir schwer, und mir ist klar, dass meine Sinne durch die Schmerzmittel im Blut beeinträchtigt sind. Ich nehme den Nudelauflauf aus dem Ofen und stelle ihn auf den Tisch.

Meine Mutter sitzt mir gegenüber und legt das Besteck beiseite. „Du bist so blass. Geht es dir wirklich gut?"

Ich ignoriere ihre Frage. „Das wird schon wieder", sage ich rasch und versuche, heiter zu klingen.

„Was wird schon wieder? Deine Schmerzen? Deine Verlustgefühle? Deine Trauer? Was ist nur los mit dir, Jonte? Was genau verspürst du im Moment? Mich beunruhigt deine Ruhe. Es ist, als würdest du einfach abtauchen. Ich bin deine Mutter, keine Fremde. Wenn du nicht mit mir darüber reden willst, dann sprich zumindest mit Annika. Sie fragt sich auch, warum du dich so abkapselst."

„Ich kann im Moment einfach nicht, Mom", versuche ich ihr zu erklären. „Ich bin irgendwie blockiert, als hätte mich jemand in mir selbst eingesperrt." Ich sehe sie mürrisch an und füge dann schnell hinzu: „Außerdem habe ich gar keine Zeit, weil ich an einem neuen Projekt arbeite."

„Tatsächlich? Nun, das ist doch gut. Arbeitet Jonas auch daran?"

„Was meinst du damit?"

„Du hast zwar noch nie erwähnt, dass Jonas auf diesem Feld besonders talentiert ist, aber ihr habt doch damals dieses erste gemeinsame Projekt auf die Beine gestellt und sogar eine Auszeichnung dafür erhalten. Du hast ja schon als Kind gerne Häuser gezeichnet. Weißt du noch, wie du immer wunderschöne Märchenschlösser für die Poesiealben deiner Freundinnen gemalt hast? Ich wusste immer, dass du großes Talent hast, aber Jonas … Der kann gut reden, das ist aber auch schon alles."

„Was willst du denn damit sagen?"

„Ich wiederhole gern meine Frage. Arbeitet Jonas auch an diesem neuen Konzept mit? Geht er dir dabei zur Hand? Du kannst einfach mit Ja oder Nein darauf antworten."

Ich schweige.

„Keine Antwort ist auch eine Antwort. Ich bin immer noch in der Lage, eins und eins zusammenzuzählen, Jonte."

Mir reicht es jetzt. Ich stehe auf und räume den Tisch ab. Dabei erkläre ich: „Als Nächstes werde ich mit Jonas über die Scheidung sprechen. Er hat es damit nicht eilig. Aber ich möchte alles regeln. Das Haus werde ich behalten und Jonas seinen Anteil auszahlen. Genügt das fürs Erste?"

„Und dein Projekt? Welcher Name wird auf der Tafel des Bauherrn stehen? *JO* oder *Dr. Jonte Sandvik*?"

„Bitte, Mom, lass mich jetzt in Ruhe."

Sie steht auf, nimmt meine Hand und drückt mir einen Kuss auf die Stirn. „Ich will dich nicht länger drängen, aber vergiss bitte nicht, dass ich immer da bin, wenn du mich brauchst, Jonte."

Die Nacht ist voller dunkler Träume. Selbst bei Schlaflosigkeit. Vor ein paar Monaten war meine Zukunft noch in ein schimmerndes Licht getaucht. Jetzt weiß ich nicht einmal, ob ich noch eine Zukunft habe. Ich hatte meine Traumata tief in mir vergraben. Doch sie bahnen sich jetzt wieder einen Weg an die Oberfläche. Die erste Hautschicht haben sie schon verbrannt. Sie bröckelt ab. Trocken und kalt.

Mein Kopf dröhnt. Ich halte mir die Ohren zu. Meine mühsamen Versuche, halbwegs klar zu denken, ertrinken in einer Welle aus Panik.

Ich spüre die Gefahr, die in mir heranwächst. Kann mein Atmen hören. Lausche nach innen. Ich muss durchhalten.

KAPITEL 23

Etwas Seltsames geht vor. Ich erkenne mich selbst nicht mehr. Die hingebungsvolle Jonte, die Streitgespräche nahezu gänzlich vermeidet, ist anscheinend nicht mehr vorhanden. Jene Jonte, die dem Mitgefühl die Vorherrschaft überlassen und sich lieber selbst ins Abseits gestellt hat, ist nicht mehr zu erreichen. Sie ist weg, einfach so. Eine neue Jonte lebt jetzt in meinem Haus, und ich mag sie. Sie ist streitlustig und wetzt die Messer. Kämpft wie eine Bärin und bittet zur Kasse.

In mir lodert ein glühendes, zorniges Feuer, das versucht, auszubrechen. Wenn ich mich auf diese Wut konzentriere, sehe ich ein ganzes Bataillon gleichförmiger schwuler Dänen in Flammen aufgehen. Und ich genieße es bei jedem Einzelnen.

Vielleicht sollte ich mich nicht zu sehr bei diesen Visionen verausgaben. Mein Vorrat an Energie ist in den letzten Wochen bedenklich geschrumpft. Ich schlafe am Abend völlig erschöpft ein. Mein nächtlicher Tiefschlaf ist traumlos. Träume wurzeln in der Realität, im Leben – dieser Tiefschlaf dagegen baut den Kontakt zum Tod auf.

Morgens hebe ich mich aus dem Bett. Mein Blick streift sofort das Zeichenbrett, dann gehe ich ins Bad und schaue aus dem Fenster. Dort ist das Weiß ohne Rot, und zwei Gedanken prallen in meinem Hirn aufeinander: *Ich muss die nächsten Entwürfe zeichnen* und *Ich will den Zorn gebären.*

Ich werde eines Tages wieder eine Kehrtwende machen und meine Wut zügeln, da bin ich mir sicher. Ich wäre vielleicht besser dran, wenn ich gleich wieder die alte Jonte werden würde, die jeder kennt. Jene Jonte, die mir so vertraut ist, die jeden Ärger meidet und sich stets fügt. Die immer hoch über den Wolken ihre Runden dreht. Aber nun platzt mir die Wut aus allen Nähten und hält mich in ihrem Würgegriff gefangen.

Jeden Tag ertappe ich mich dabei, dass ich dem Badezimmerspiegel immer die gleiche Frage stelle: *Ist das mein Gesicht, das mir da entgegenblickt?* Ein Feuer brennt hinter meinen Augen, ein hässliches Lächeln vibriert auf meinen Lippen. Die Wangen sind gerötet, die Schultern hochgezogen, die Hände ständig zu Fäusten geballt. Eine Fremde starrt mir hasserfüllt entgegen.

Ich wende mich ab. Begreife plötzlich, dass ich nie wieder die alte Jonte sein werde, jetzt, da ich ein mein eigenes Gedankenkind zur Welt bringe. Meine früheren Arbeiten konnte ich noch mit Jonas teilen, weil unsere Doppelexistenz eine Mission war, die ich erfüllen musste. Ich wollte unsere Beziehung aufrechterhalten, stärkte seinen Lebenssinn und steckte dabei meinen Kopf in den Sand. Vielleicht weil die Chemie zwischen uns nicht gestimmt hat und meine Vorstellung von Liebe immer eine andere war als seine. In Wahrheit bin ich gar nicht so überrascht, dass Jonas nicht heterosexuell ist. Ich spürte immer, dass ich nur sein Alibi war – ein Deckmantel, der sich freiwillig um ihn schmiegte.

Jahrelang hat unsere Ehe auf diese Weise funktioniert. Ich stand in einem Bild, das nicht stimmte. Die anderen bemerkten es nicht, sodass ich manchmal darüber fast lachen musste. Denn ich kam mir fehl am Platze vor. So wusste ich denn auch tief in meinem Unterbewusstsein, dass unser erstes gemeinsames Projekt im richtigen Moment kam, um die Illusion der Partnerschaft zu retten. Es hat uns tatsächlich einander nähergebracht, die Architektur war das Band, das uns enger zusammengeschweißt hat. Symbolisiert in dem magischen Zeichen *JO*. Ich fühlte mich darin geborgen. Doch jetzt ist alles zu einem erstickenden Gefühl geworden, das ich mit Gewalt abschütteln möchte. Ich will mich endlich von Jonas befreien, will die alleinige Anerkennung. Sie steht mir zu, denn ich allein bin der kreative Kopf von *JO*!

Ich möchte dieses Gefühl einer Vorspiegelung falscher Tatsachen loswerden, um mich zu befreien. Denn wenn ich eine neue Jonte bin, eliminiere ich mit der alten auch den Gedanken an einen Eindringling, der mich vergewaltigt und geschwängert hat, sowie den an einen Unbekannten, der mein Baby getötet und womöglich auch mir nach dem Leben getrachtet hat.

Und ich will nicht länger das Anhängsel eines Mannes sein oder mich hinter ihm verstecken. Auch ich möchte mich outen. Als die wahre Architektin der neuen Entwürfe. Die Anerkennung steht mir allein zu. Ich will den Erfolg nicht länger teilen.

Dies ist mein Baby. Ich habe es geschaffen, getragen, geboren. Jeder *soll* wissen, dass das hier mein Kind ist.

Jeder *muss* die Wahrheit erfahren.

KAPITEL 24

Schritte auf der Treppe. Jemand setzt seine Schritte, als würde er auf einem Schachbrett laufen, als fände er Halt auf Flächen ohne Boden. Es sind Schritte, die sich entfernen und mich lähmen. Ich liege regungslos in meinem Bett. Müsste aber die Schlafzimmertür abschließen. Jetzt! Schnell! Aber ich kann mich nicht bewegen.

Das Licht im Flur ist an, ich beobachte die im Lichtstrahl schwebenden Staubteilchen. Meine Gedanken ballen sich zu einem Wort zusammen: *Mörder.* Ich verstehe nicht, was hier passiert. Warum es *mir* passiert. Weshalb ich getötet werden soll. Wieder horche ich in die Stille. Nichts. Die Schritte sind verebbt.

Hey, du hast nur geträumt!

Es ist zehn vor drei. Der Vorhang bewegt sich mit dem eisigen Wind, der durch das offene Fenster strömt.

Hast du das Fenster vor dem Zubettgehen nicht geschlossen?

Ich krieche tiefer unter die Bettdecke. Da ... da sind sie wieder. Die Schritte gehen langsam die Treppe hinunter. Sekunden später fällt die Haustür leise ins Schloss.

Ich warte zehn Minuten, erst dann bringe ich den Mut auf, aufzustehen und unten nach dem Rechten zu sehen. Der Schlüssel der Haustür hängt am Schlüsselbrett neben der Garderobe, dort, wo ich ihn gestern Abend hingetan habe. Die Tür ist verriegelt, ebenso das Nachtschloss.

Ich habe mir die Schritte nur eingebildet, habe das alles bloß geträumt. Hat mir die Angst einen Streich gespielt? Ich glaubte, sie unter Kontrolle zu haben, aber ich habe mich wohl überschätzt. Bin ich am Durchdrehen? Über der Treppe nehme ich einen schwachen süßen Duft wahr. Er kommt mir bekannt vor.

Ich verspüre das dringende Bedürfnis nach einem Glas Wein, obwohl ich mich entschlossen habe, nur noch am Wochenende ein paar Gläser zu trinken. Die Alkoholabhängigkeit liegt immer auf der Lauer. Ich habe in letzter Zeit wieder zu oft ein Glas über den Durst getrunken. Das muss sich ändern.

Später – jetzt kannst du dir ruhig ein Glas Wein genehmigen auf diesen Schrecken!

Ich nehme die Weinflasche aus dem Kühlschrank, schenke mir ein Glas Rotwein ein und leere es in einem Zug. Schenke sofort nach. Nach dem dritten Glas merke ich, dass ich ruhiger werde. Ein weiterer Beweis, dass es gegen die Angst, die in mir schlummert, hilft.

Ich inspiziere das ganze Haus. Nirgendwo etwas Verdächtiges. Alles an seinem Platz. Der Geruch ist ebenfalls verschwunden.

Ich fürchte mich, obwohl ich mir die Schritte offenbar nur eingebildet habe. Ich gehe die Treppe hinauf. Meine Beine zittern, ich muss mich am Geländer festhalten. Zu viel ist passiert. Ich sollte das alles aufschreiben, um mich daran erinnern zu können. Alles genau beschreiben, sodass sich später in meinem Kopf ein exaktes Bild entwickeln kann.

Morgen werde ich Annika anrufen und sie bitten, ein paar Wochen bei mir einzuziehen. Ich werde ihr alles erzählen. Fast alles.

Ich wache mit starken Kopfschmerzen auf. Habe zu tief geschlafen. Jemand klingelt Sturm. Rasch werfe ich den Morgenmantel über, gehe die Treppe hinunter und öffne die Haustür. Jonas steht davor.

„Habe ich dich geweckt? Wir haben heute doch den Notartermin. Hast du das etwa vergessen?" Er mustert mich. „Du siehst nicht gut aus. Hast du die Nacht wieder mal mit einer Flasche Wein verbracht?"

Das hätte er besser nicht sagen sollen. Heute ist *mein persönlicher D-Day* – der Tag *meiner* Entscheidungen. Ich werde keine Sekunde länger warten.

Aber ein Gefühl der Ohnmacht lähmt mich.

Jonas klingt komisch, denke ich. Noch komischer als sonst. Nicht mehr warten. Kein Morgen … Kein Später …

Nach dem Notartermin gehen wir zu mir zurück. Jonas kommt kurz mit rein. Er ist gut gelaunt. Tore hat ihn nicht enterbt.

Der perfekte Zeitpunkt, um reinen Tisch zu machen.

„Ich werde die Scheidung beantragen", beginne ich schnell, „und als Architektin alleine weitermachen."

Er wird bleich. „Das kann nicht dein Ernst sein", stammelt er sichtlich schockiert. „Du kannst mich doch nicht einfach im Stich lassen."

Vielleicht liegt es an der Angst, die ich in der vergangenen Nacht durchgestanden habe, dass mich seine Worte jetzt nicht berühren. Meine kurze Schwäche war wohl nur dem Rotwein zuzuschreiben, der mir nicht bekommen ist. Ich weiß es nicht genau, und es ist mir auch egal. Denn jetzt spüre ich wieder die neue Jonte. Der Hass ist wieder da und die Wut und das Misstrauen. Und die Energie. Das Gefühl der Ohnmacht ist versiegt.

„Es ist mein voller Ernst", erkläre ich knallhart. „Es war von Anfang an eine falsche Entscheidung, das Architektenduo *JO* ins Leben zu rufen. Das weißt du genauso gut wie ich. Dieses Duo hat in Wahrheit nie existiert. Es gibt eine talentierte, kreative Jonte, die wunderbare Gebäude entwerfen kann, und einen eloquenten, blendenden Jonas, der sich als Marketingprofi erwiesen hat. Du bist der geborene Verkäufer, ich die Schöpferin. Das war kein Problem für mich, solange wir verheiratet waren. Aber jetzt leben wir getrennt, Jonas. Du hast dich für einen Mann entschieden. Das ist auch gut so, und ich wünsche euch beiden viel Glück. Aber lass mich jetzt auch mein eigenes Leben leben."

Er steht auf. „Du enttäuschst mich, Jonte. Das hätte ich nicht von dir gedacht. Aber wie du willst. Das musst du mit dir selbst ausmachen." Er geht wütend weg, dreht sich noch einmal um: „Wirst du auf der Hälfte meines Erbes bestehen?"

„Das liegt bei dir, Jonas. Wenn du auf deine Hälfte der Tantiemen verzichtest, kann ich deine Frage mit einem klaren Ja beantworten."

Ich halte seinem Blick stand. Sein Gesicht wirkt merkwürdig weich gezeichnet, als wäre es nachträglich bearbeitet worden. In seinem Blick liegt keine Spur mehr von der Sympathie, die mir in Erinnerung geblieben ist.

Er schlägt die Wohnzimmertür hinter sich zu und wenig später die Haustür.

Ich kann mich nicht auf meine Entwürfe konzentrieren und rufe Annika an. Sie reagiert überrascht.

„Wow! Kannst du Gedanken lesen? Ich habe gerade an dich gedacht."

„Könntest du für ein paar Wochen zu mir ziehen, Annika?"

„Was ist los? Geht es dir nicht gut?"

Annika erhält eine kurze Version der vergangenen Nacht. Sie schiebt es weder auf Einbildung noch auf meine alkoholisierte Verfassung, sondern schlägt besorgt vor, die Polizei einzuschalten.

„Da stimmt doch etwas ganz und gar nicht", sagt sie. „Wir müssen so schnell wie möglich mit einem Ermittler sprechen."

Annika ist überaus freundlich zu mir, und dennoch habe ich den Verdacht, dass sie meine wirre Geschichte insgeheim infrage stellt. Vermutlich glaubt sie, dass ich nach der Fehlgeburt verwirrt bin und Zuspruch brauche. Ich liebe sie dafür, dass sie mich dennoch ernst nimmt und alles unternimmt, um mir zu helfen .

„Nimm das nicht auf die leichte Schulter", beschwört sie mich. „Ich muss heute noch nach Paris und kann erst morgen zu dir kommen. Wenn du willst, können wir dann mit der Polizei reden. Aber versprich mir, dass du gleich deine Mutter anrufst und die kommende Nacht bei ihr verbringst."

Ich verspreche es.

Der Gedanke, ein paar Stunden nicht in diesem Haus sein zu müssen, gefällt mir plötzlich sehr gut.

Ich trete ins Freie, gehe mit meinem kleinen Koffer auf den Taxistand zu und denke dabei an das Baby, das aus unerklärlichen Gründen meinen Körper verlassen hat.

Ich glaubte, ich könnte dieses alte Leben abschütteln, aber nun frage ich mich schon wieder: Wer trachtet mir nach dem Leben, und warum?

Ich weiß, dass alles irgendwann angefangen hat, dass es begonnen hat … irgendwo in diesem Dunkel.

KAPITEL 25

„Bente hat eine Freundin in Drammen besucht, und ich habe sie spontan eingeladen." Meine Mutter zieht mich in ihre Arme und küsst mich stürmisch auf die Wangen. „Sie ist im Wohnzimmer und freut sich schon, dich wiederzusehen."

Ich frage mich, ob ich ebenfalls das Bedürfnis verspüre, sie wiederzusehen. Aber warum sollte ich mich von Jonas' Mutter fernhalten? Ihm bin ich sowieso keine Rechenschaft mehr schuldig. Nach der Scheidung werde ich den Kontakt mit meinem Ex-Mann auf das Notwendigste beschränken.

Bente winkt mich mit einer freundlichen Geste zu sich. Sie hat das Handy am Ohr und tuschelt verhalten. Ich lasse mich in den Sessel fallen.

„Hallo, Jonte!" Sie legt auf.

„Hey, Bente!"

Mom betritt den Raum. Mir fällt auf, wie vertraut die beiden miteinander umgehen, wie gute Freundinnen, die sich seit Jahren kennen.

„Du siehst blass und mitgenommen aus, mein Kind."

„Es war etwas viel in letzter Zeit, Mom." Ich versuche, dennoch unbeschwert zu klingen, denn von meinen Ängsten will ich ihr nichts erzählen.

Bente legt ihre Hand auf meinen Arm, sieht mich forschend an. „Es tut mir sehr leid, dass du das durchmachen musstest, Jonte."

Meine Mutter holt den Rotwein aus dem Schrank und schenkt uns ein. „Heute kannst du dich mal richtig entspannen", sagt sie und zwinkert mir zu. „Wir werden eine Pizza bestellen und uns betrinken. Auf einen schönen Abend!"

Den ersten Schluck Wein spüre ich überdeutlich: Feuchtwarm gleitet er meine Speiseröhre entlang, sinkt wie ein warmes, feuchtes Tuch in meinen Magen und belebt meine Sinne. Köstlich.

Bente sucht meinen Blick. „Ich freue mich ja so, dich wiederzusehen, Jonte. Auch weil ich dir gerne etwas erklären würde."

Ich antworte nicht. Es gab zu viele Erklärungen in letzter Zeit. Und meistens waren es Lügen.

Meine Mutter mischt sich nach einem genussvollen Schluck Wein ein. „Bente will sich gewiss nicht aufdrängen, aber du warst jahrelang mit ihrem Sohn verheiratet, der dir Ammenmärchen über seine Mutter erzählt hat. Da muss doch endlich mal die Wahrheit ausgesprochen werden."

Bente zögert. „Du hast auf der Trauerfeier angedeutet, dass du nicht verstehen kannst, wieso ich Jonas einfach so im Stich gelassen habe."

Ich blinzle. „Habe ich das gesagt? Ich erinnere mich nicht mehr."

„Ich bin damals nicht wirklich darauf eingegangen. Aber ich würde es dir wirklich gerne erklären." Bente nimmt einen kräftigen Schluck Wein. Ihrer Stimme hört man es kaum an, dass sie schon beim zweiten Glas ist. Ich bin demnach nicht die Einzige mit einem kleinen Alkoholproblem.

„Ich habe mein Kind nicht einfach so über Nacht verlassen. Dieser Prozess hat siebzehn Jahre gedauert. Siebzehn Jahre, in denen ich immer verzweifelter versucht habe, eine Beziehung zu Jonas aufzubauen. Bis zu seinem elften Lebensjahr funktionierte es sogar einigermaßen, wenn man mal davon absieht, dass Jonas auf seinen Vater fixiert war: Papa musste ihn füttern, wickeln, ins Bett bringen – Papa war der Star. Tore hat den Jungen schrecklich verwöhnt, er konnte ihm nichts abschlagen. Jonas war sein Heiligtum, und der Junge genoss das. *Vaterhunger*, nennen Experten dieses Phänomen. Anfangs dachte ich, es sei nur eine Phase, aber bald manipulierte Jonas seinen Vater, sodass Tore alle Regeln der Erziehung vergaß, um seinem Sohn zu gefallen. Es gab keine Abgrenzung mehr in ihrer Bindung."

„Der Altersunterschied zwischen dir und deinem Mann war aber auch sehr groß", fällt meine Mutter Bente ins Wort.

„Ja, sicher. Dreißig Jahre. Als junge Frau arbeitete ich als Arzthelferin. Es ist kaum zu glauben, aber der allererste Patient, dem ich in der Praxis begegnete, war Tore. Ich war noch sehr unsicher, aber er näherte sich mir überaus freundlich und behutsam. Ich war es nicht gewohnt, dass mir jemand Aufmerksamkeit schenkte. Ein Jahr später haben wir geheiratet. Da war ich bereits mit Jonas schwanger." Bente trinkt ihr Glas aus, und Mutter schenkt ganz mechanisch nach.

„Hast du ihn geliebt." Ich schäme mich sofort für meine indiskrete Frage, aber die Antwort ist mir sehr wichtig.

Bente schaut mich überrascht an. Ich sehe ein Glänzen in ihren Augen und die leicht verzögerte Synchronisation ihrer Bewegungen. Es gibt nicht den geringsten Zweifel. Der Alkohol zeigt erste Auswirkungen, aber ihre Stimme ist fest und klar.

„Zumindest dachte ich, es sei Liebe. Er war fürsorglich und verwöhnte mich. Ich war jung und hungerte nach Aufmerksamkeit. Das war mir damals sehr wichtig. Das hatte ich nie gekannt. Erst später habe ich begriffen, dass das, was ich für Liebe hielt, vor allem Dankbarkeit war und dass ich die Sehnsucht nach Liebe für welche hielt. Aber in den ersten Jahren meiner Ehe verdrängte ich solche Gedanken. Erst als Tores Verhalten immer mehr aus den Fugen geriet, ließ ich sie zu. Und da Jonas ..." Bente schluckt und zupft nervös an ihren Fingern.

Meine Mutter hat in der Zwischenzeit den Esstisch gedeckt und schenkt schon wieder nach. Ich frage mich, warum Bente uns ihre Geschichte in dieser Ausführlichkeit erzählt? Belastet es sie so sehr, oder steckt irgendeine Absicht dahinter?

„Jonas war in der Pubertät ein sehr schwieriges Kind. Wir haben sein loses Mundwerk und seine Stimmungsschwankungen so weit wie möglich ignoriert. Er war sehr leicht reizbar. Ich war der verbalen Gewalt, die aus Jonas geradezu herausexplodierte, nicht gewachsen. Er schrie, fluchte, beleidigte und machte mich dann für seine Wutausbrüche verantwortlich. Nannte mich eine dämliche Schlampe. Offenbar nahm er mir übel, dass ich eine Frau war. Ich war nie Teil dieser Männerwelt zwischen Tore und Jonas geworden." Bente stockt. „Jonas brachte der Weiblichkeit nur Verachtung entgegen. Alles, was bei ihm schieflief, führte er auf Mädchen oder Frauen zurück und ganz besonders auf seine Mutter, auf mich. Ich war eine empfindsame Frau, umso mehr laugten mich diese Kämpfe aus, marterten mich seine ständigen Vorwürfe und Schuldzuweisungen, bis ich im Alkohol Zuflucht suchte, um dieser unbarmherzigen Umgebung zu entfliehen. Denn Tore stellte sich nie hinter mich, sondern tat eher so, als würde ich Jonas provozieren. Er war schon lange nicht mehr zärtlich zu mir gewesen, aber Jonas' Verhalten mir gegenüber war noch schlimmer: Er ekelte sich vor dem Anblick meines Körpers. Und er beschimpfte mich immer wieder, bis ich mir wie das minderwertigste Geschöpf vorkam. Tore schloss sich in seinem Arbeitszimmer ein, wenn es zwischen Jonas und mir krachte. Er meinte, alles andere würde Jonas nur noch mehr aufregen." Bente sieht konzentriert ihre Hände an.

Ihre Worte drücken meine Brust wie eine Zange zusammen. Mir ist warm vom Alkohol. Auch ich nehme einen Schluck nach dem anderen, um mein Entsetzen zu überspielen. Wir haben auch beide angefangen zu schwitzen.

Bentes dunkelblaue Bluse ist leicht zerknittert und bis zu den Brustansätzen aufgeknöpft. Man kann die Form ihrer Brüste erkennen. Ich versuche, sie mit Jonas' Augen zu betrachten, und mit einem Mal verstehe ich. Erinnere mich. Nichts ist ausgelöscht, alles ist wieder da. Überdeutlich.

Ich sitze völlig erstarrt auf dem Stuhl, denke an das erste Mal, als ich unbekleidet unser Schlafzimmer betrat. „*Zieh dir etwas über, zeig dich nicht so*", fuhr Jonas mich an. „*Ich finde das vulgär. Du siehst aus wie meine Mutter, die lief auch ständig entblößt herum wie ein billiges Flittchen.*"

Meine Bluse klebt an mir, vor meinen Augen verschwimmt alles. Ich will, das Bente aufhört, über Tore und Jonas zu reden.

„Ich sprach sogar mit unserem Hausarzt. Er riet mir, Jonas' Verhalten nicht allzu ernst zu nehmen. Mit sechzehn werde dieses pubertäre Verhalten nachlassen. Also versuchte ich ihn zu ignorieren. Zuerst brachte das Jonas noch mehr in Rage, doch dann trat eine neue Phase ein. Ich wurde wie ein belangloses Möbelstück behandelt, das nur ab und zu in Gebrauch war. Aber man verschwendete nicht allzu viele Worte an mich. Jonas sprach kaum noch mit mir, ich war meist Luft für ihn, und Tore wurde ohnehin immer wortkarger. Seit er seinen Dienst beendet hatte, steckte er seinen Kopf am liebsten in irgendwelche Bücher. Er war mir keine Hilfe in diesem Kampf, und er wollte auch keine sein. Manchmal schickte Jonas mir Textnachrichten von einer Vulgarität, die man nicht mal seinem ärgsten Feind zumuten würde, und allmählich verspürte ich Angst. Denn was gibt es Entsetzlicheres, als dass einem das eigene Kind den Tod wünscht?"

„Meine Mutter ist gestorben", höre ich Jonas' Stimme, und plötzlich verstehe ich, dass dies vielleicht nie als Tatsache gedacht war, sondern seinen innersten Wunsch ausdrückte.

„Wie hast du das nur ausgehalten?", fragt Mom derweil.

„Irgendwann gar nicht mehr. Eines Tages habe ich begriffen, dass ich niemals Zugang zu diesem Kind finden würde, nicht zu Lebzeiten seines Vaters und vielleicht nie mehr. Ich sah nur einen Ausweg, wenn ich nicht zugrunde gehen wollte: Ich trennte mich ohne ein Wort von Tore und Jonas und entschied mich für mich." Bente sucht meinen Blick. „Ich habe Jonas nicht *einfach so* verlassen, Jonte, es ist mir sehr schwergefallen, aber ich wusste, wenn ich auch nur eine Sekunde länger bleibe, würde ich kaputtgehen. Ich bin buchstäblich bei Nacht und Nebel auf Nimmerwiedersehen verschwunden. Es hat Monate gedauert, bis ich wieder in den Spiegel blicken konnte, jahrelang fühlte ich mich innerlich zerrissen, Nacht für Nacht träumte ich von ihnen. Erst als ich meinen jetzigen Mann traf, kam ich allmählich zur Ruhe. Mit ihm konnte ich reden; er hat mir klargemacht, dass fortzugehen für mich die einzige Chance war, um zu überleben. Vielleicht wäre aus Jonas ein ganz anderer Mann geworden, hätte ich ihn mitgenommen. Aber ich bin davon überzeugt, er war schon zu alt, es war schon zu spät, und wir hätten uns nur beide ..." Sie bricht ab.

Stille.

„Warum bist du dann nach all der Zeit und vor dem Hintergrund dieser leidvollen Erfahrungen zur Einäscherung gekommen", frage ich verständnislos.

„Um mich endgültig von Tore zu verabschieden. Ich habe diesen Schlussstrich gebraucht." Bente wirkt seltsam schwermütig. Sie weint nicht. Und sie lacht nicht. Sie sitzt einfach nur regungslos da, bis sie leise hinzufügt: „Und weil ich mich davon überzeugen wollte, dass er wirklich tot ist."

Ich fange einen Blick meiner Mutter auf, den ich nicht deuten kann. „Ich habe immer gesagt, dass diese Geschichte zwei Seiten hat", sagt sie und entkorkt eine weitere Flasche Rotwein.

Ich rutsche auf dem Stuhl neben ihr hin und her, hinter meiner Stirn ist ein seltsames Summen. Wie das der Wespen über der toten Katze in

Malvis Garten. Urplötzlich kreisen mir Lügen und Wahrheiten wie Insekten durch den Kopf. Ich kann sie nicht unterscheiden.

Ich nehme einen weiteren Schluck Wein, doch es reicht nicht, um das heftige Klopfen meines Herzens zu beruhigen. Ich denke an meine eigene Wahrheit. Jeden Tag meines Lebens droht sie herauszukommen und das dunkle Geheimnis zu offenbaren, das ich all die Jahre gehütet habe – diese eine Sache, die ich nie jemandem erzählen darf. Niemals.

Letztendlich sind all deine Lügen ein hoffnungsloses Unterfangen, Jonte.

Bente stellt ihr Weinglas ab. Das Geräusch klingt hell und hoch.

Wie ein geflüsterter Schrei.

KAPITEL 26

Ich träume von hellgrünen Wiesen, von duftenden Wäldern, einem himmelblauen Raum und halte inne und – ist es wieder Sommer?

Ich öffne die Augen und starre aus dem Schlafzimmerfenster dem Winterweiß entgegen. Draußen ist es schon hell. Der Wecker zeigt die achte Stunde. Der Kopf brummt mir ein bisschen. Meine Mutter und Bente sind bereits aufgewacht. Ich höre sie unten kichern. Ich erinnere mich schwach, dass meine Mutter und Bente sich in der vergangenen Nacht noch angeregt unterhalten haben, mittlerweile auf Likör umgestiegen, aber über Tore und Jonas wurde nicht mehr gesprochen. Ich sah fern, Wortfetzen flogen an mir vorbei, ich gähnte ... Dann: Filmriss. Blackout.

Bente ist anders, als ich sie mir vorgestellt habe. Sympathischer, freundlicher, humorvoller. Sie kann über sich selbst lachen und ist weit entfernt von dem abscheulichen Monster, das Jonas so plastisch an die Wand gemalt hat. Dennoch misstraue ich ihr noch immer ein bisschen und möchte sie nicht zu nah an mich heranlassen.

„Jonte, bist du schon wach?", ruft Mom unten an der Treppe.

Ich springe aus dem Bett.

Aufstehen! Duschen! Ab in die Küche!, knurrt Back-Vocal. *Das Tribunal wartet unten auf dich. Erzähl ihm doch auch ein paar Geheimnisse. Man muss doch alle Seiten hören ...*

Der Duft von frischen Brötchen und Speck weht mir entgegen, als ich die Treppe hinuntergehe und in die Küche komme. „Guten Morgen, Ladys!"

„Ich habe ein englisches Frühstück zubereitet." Mom lächelt mich an. „Gut gegen den Kater. Guten Morgen, mein Schatz!"

Bente sieht ziemlich mitgenommen aus. „Es ist lange her, dass ich mir so richtig die Rinne verzinkt habe. Ich habe einen fürchterlichen Kater."

Ich nicke. „Likör und Wein ist eine teuflische Mischung, Bente. Ihr hättet nicht ganz so oft anstoßen sollen", erwidere ich und stürze mich sofort auf das Frühstück. „Hm, das schmeckt köstlich, Mom. Seit Jonas fort ist, habe ich mir kein anständiges Frühstück mehr gemacht."

Eine seltsame Stille fällt wie ein Vorhang über uns. Ich spüre ihre Blicke auf mir ruhen und zögere einen Moment, bevor ich den hauchzarten Speck probiere.

„Wo wohnt Jonas eigentlich jetzt", fragt Bente.

Ich zucke mit den Schultern.

„Möchtest du lieber nicht darüber reden, Jonte?"

„Er war in letzter Zeit nicht mehr er selbst", sagt Mom. „Die erste Auszeichnung, die die beiden erhalten haben, hat ihn verändert. Ich denke,
dass ihm der Erfolg zu Kopf gestiegen ist."

Bente nickt, sieht mich aber dabei an.

„Kennst du den Architekturband, den Jonte und Jonas anlässlich der
Auszeichnung veröffentlicht haben, Bente?", fragt Mom.

„Ja, natürlich habe ich ihn mir angesehen, er enthält sehr schöne Häuser.
Aber ..."

„Aber was ...?"

Worte schweben auf mich zu, die ich nicht hören will.

„Aber ich kann mir beim besten Willen nicht vorstellen, dass Jonas davon irgendetwas entworfen hat."

„Ich auch nicht", stimmt Mom zu.

Bentes Stimme nimmt einen weniger zögerlichen Ton an. „Nein, wirklich nicht, Jonte. Er hatte als Kind keine Fantasie, war technisch vollkommen unbegabt, konnte auch keine Zeichnung anfertigen. Er hat sich noch
nie für die Funktionalität und die Schönheit von Gebäuden interessiert.
Zumindest zu anderen war er immer freundlich und korrekt, ja höflich
und zuvorkommend, besaß aber keinen Funken Fantasie und war nicht
im Geringsten kreativ veranlagt."

„Du hast ihn seit Jahren nicht mehr gesehen oder mit ihm gesprochen,
Bente. Du hast ihn nur als Kind gekannt", verteidige ich ihn und füge an
meine Mutter gewandt hinzu: „Und dir gegenüber hat Jonas sich kaum
geöffnet, Mom, was weißt du denn schon über ihn?"

„Das mag ja alles stimmen", hält Mom dagegen. „Aber ich habe Jonas
jedenfalls nie am Zeichenbrett erlebt, du hingegen verbringst nach Feier-
abend jede Stunde davor, soweit ich das beurteilen kann. Das hast du
schon als Kind gemacht. Schule, Hausaufgaben, Zeichenbrett, schlafen."
Sie beugt sich ein bisschen vor und starrt mich herausfordernd an: „Sag
uns jetzt die Wahrheit, Jonte, du musst ihn nicht mehr beschützen. Ihr
werdet geschieden!"

Ich möchte etwas Unumstößliches erwidern, kann sie aber nur wütend
anfunkeln. „Du gehst zu weit, Mutter!"

„Dachte ich es mir doch", fühlt sie sich bestätigt.

„Möchtest du nicht lieber darüber reden?", mischt sich Bente ein.

„Nein! Ich möchte mich erst selbst um alles kümmern. Es ist ein sehr
heikles Thema."

„Macht mein Sohn dir etwa Schwierigkeiten?"

In mir brodelt es. Ich schließe die Augen, um mich zu fassen. „Ich sagte
doch, es ist ein sensibles Thema. Punkt. Fertig. Aus. Ich habe keinen Bock
mehr auf solche Gespräche!" Ich springe auf.

„Du musst ins Leben zurückkehren, wie ich damals auch", sagt Bente langsam, jedes Wort sorgfältig abwägend, jedem Buchstaben Gewicht verleihend, als wäre der Satz sonst substanzlos.

Plötzlich bemerke ich die Linien in Bentes Gesicht. Sie kommt mir jetzt viel älter vor. Die Stille erdrückt mich. Ich möchte sie aufbrechen und entschuldige mich für meinen Tonfall, während ich mich wieder setze.

Das Frühstück geht weiter, als wäre nichts geschehen.

Ich rede als Erste wieder. „Bist du noch berufstätig, Bente?" Eine unverfängliche Frage.

„An zwei Tagen in der Woche. Mein Boss will mich nicht verlieren, weil ich besonders viel Geduld mit den schwierigen Patienten habe." Sie lacht auf. „Aber es war genau diese Geduld, die meiner Ehe geschadet und mich für immer meinem Kind entfremdet hat."

„Meine Mutter und meine beste Freundin behaupten ebenfalls, dass ich zu viel hingenommen habe."

„Wir sind uns sehr ähnlich, Jonte." Bente lächelt. „Und jetzt bringe ich dich nach Hause."

KAPITEL 27

Ich bin in Gedanken, während Bente in die *Griffenfelds gate* einbiegt und einige Meter vor meinem Haus abrupt auf die Bremse tritt. „Was ist denn hier los? Schau mal, Jonte, da vorne ist anscheinend etwas passiert."

Streifenwagen blockieren die Straße. Hinter uns jault plötzlich eine Sirene auf. Bente fährt das Auto ein Stück zur Seite. Ein Krankenwagen rast vorbei, Türen schwingen auf.

Ich steige verdutzt aus. In der Menge lacht jemand über die Worte eines anderen, ein taubes Gebrüll liegt in der Luft, das von mir abprallt, plump zu Boden fällt, wie Müll liegen bleibt.

„Bente, das ist mein Haus, in das diese Leute hineingehen", flüstere ich. „Was zur Hölle geht hier vor?"

„Nichts Gutes, vermute ich. Ich komme mit dir." Sie nimmt meinen Arm. Ich lasse mich willenlos von ihr führen.

Back-Vocal kichert hinter meiner gefurchten Stirn: *Morgenstund hat Blut im Mund.*

Ich kann die Gegenwart von Unheil spüren und gehe wie in Zeitlupe auf das Haus zu. In der Menge entdecke ich meine Nachbarin. Malvi sieht mich und kommt weinend auf mich zugerannt.

„Da bist du ja endlich, Jonte. Wo warst du denn?" Ihre Tränen lassen mich fast straucheln. Mir wird schwindlig.

Ich umfasse ihre zarten Schultern. „Weißt du, was hier passiert ist, Malvi?"

„Nicht genau. Sie wollen mir keine Auskunft geben. Aber in deinem Haus soll eine tote Person liegen." Malvi fährt sich fahrig durchs Haar. „Ich bin zu alt für derartige Aufregungen. Erst diese tote Katze in meinem Garten und jetzt auch noch das hier." Malvi wirkt entnervt. „Wo warst du denn nur, Jonte?"

Ihr Blick ist voller Entsetzen, die Emotionen darin drohen mich zu überrennen. Ich bin wie in Taubheit gehüllt und kann meine Lippen kaum mehr bewegen. Bente lenkt mich in Richtung des Hauses. Die Haustür steht offen, ein Polizist kommt uns entgegen und hebt die Hand, als wollte er uns stoppen.

Ich finde meine Stimme wieder und erkläre leise: „Das hier ist mein Haus. Was ist hier los?"

„Wir wissen es noch nicht genau. Der Notarzt kümmert sich gerade um das Opfer. Es ist eine Frau in Ihrem Alter. Ihre Schwester möglicherweise? Sie sieht Ihnen nämlich ähnlich."

Annika? Ich versinke in Schwärze, und zittere vor Angst am ganzen Körper. Schweiß rinnt mir über die Stirn. „Ist … ist sie tot?"

111

Ich will die Antwort eigentlich gar nicht hören, möchte am liebsten die Zeit zurückdrehen: mein feindseliges Verhalten ablegen, das gemeinsame Frühstück nicht so in die Länge ziehen, mich früher von Jonas' Mutter heimfahren lassen, Bente zu einer Tasse Kaffee einladen ... vielleicht wären wir noch rechtzeitig gekommen. Annika kann unmöglich schon lange hier sein. Wenn es wirklich Annika ist ...

Einige Sekunden lang gelingt es mir, den Lärm um mich herum auszublenden, die Polizeifahrzeuge, den Krankenwagen, die Schaulustigen. Dann durchbricht die Stimme des Polizisten meine feige Flucht vor der Realität.

„Sie lebt noch", antwortet er. „Aber sie ist in einem sehr ernsten Zustand. Warten Sie bitte einen Moment, ich sehe drinnen mal nach."

Hinter mir höre ich schnelle Schritte näher kommen. Ich muss mich nicht umdrehen, um zu wissen, dass es meine Nachbarin ist.

Malvis Neugierde hat über ihre Tränen gesiegt. „Hast du etwas in Erfahrung bringen können, Jonte? Wo warst du überhaupt? Ich habe dich gar nicht wegfahren sehen."

„Ich habe bei meiner Mutter übernachtet, Malvi. Hab gestern ein Taxi genommen." Warum erkläre ich ihr das? Was geht sie das denn an?

Sie nickt und plappert dann drauflos: „Ich habe den Notruf verständigt, weil deine Haustür offen stand. Ich habe sofort erkannt, dass da etwas nicht stimmte. Du lässt sie niemals auf. Außerdem war da noch dieses fremde Auto – zwei Häuser weiter auf dem Parkplatz. Ich erkannte gleich, dass es deiner Freundin gehört. Du weißt schon, dieser mageren Stewardess." Sie zeigt auf einen weißen Toyota.

„Kennst du das Auto?", erkundigt sich Bente bei mir.

„Ja, es ist das von Annika."

„Hattest du denn eine Verabredung mit ihr?"

Ich schüttle den Kopf. „Annika ist noch in Paris. Sie kann es gar nicht sein. Das ist unmöglich."

Der Polizist winkt mir zu. „Würden Sie bitte mitkommen, Frau Sandvik, und uns sagen, ob Sie das Opfer kennen?"

Der Zweifel, den ich empfinde, hat keinen Bestand. Natürlich nicht. Warum sonst sollte Annikas Auto hier sein? Ich denke darüber nach, in Kreisen, in kreisrunden Bahnen, während ich mich langsam dem Wohnzimmer nähere. Sekunde um Sekunde, Meter für Meter. Dann verschwimmen die Sekunden, die Meter fransen aus, werden zu Zentimetern, Millimetern. Die Welt schrumpft. Dieses Gefühl von Erschöpfung ist anders als früher. Ich bin wie ein Ballon, bei dem die Luft entweicht.

Da sehe ich ein weißes Kleid und erinnere mich an ihre Worte: *„Ich habe ein schönes weißes Wollkleid in London gekauft. Das musst du sehen."*

Scheinwerfer leuchten das Wohnzimmer aus. Es ist hell im Haus. Die Konturen der Dinge sind scharfkantig und zum Greifen nah. Überall ist Blut.

An Annikas Arm ist eine Infusion angebracht. Neben ihr hockt ein Notarzt in einem roten Anzug, ein zweiter telefoniert. „Wir bringen sie ins Krankenhaus nach Drammen", sagt er zu seinem Kollegen.

„Nein, wir fliegen sie in das Ullevål-Universitätsklinikum nach Oslo. Sie hat ein schweres Schädel-Hirn-Trauma und muss sofort operiert werden. Ruf den Hubschrauber!", widerspricht der andere Notarzt.

Der Teppich ist rot getränkt. Rot wie der Wein, den ich gestern getrunken habe. Die Zeit hat sich aufgelöst. Ist verflossen, um nie wieder zurückzukehren. Für einen Moment stelle ich mir vor, einen Würfel Zeit in der Hand zu halten: genau den Würfel Zeit der letzten zwölf Stunden. Gleich werde ich sie neu auswürfeln ...

Wieder schaue ich Annika an, sehe das weiße Kleid, das blutüberströmte Gesicht und wende mich ab. Blicke durch das Fenster in die Winterlandschaft. Das Rot der Vergangenheit projiziert sich auf meine Iris. Ich kehre zurück.

Ein zweiter Polizist spricht mich an. Ich kenne ihn, erinnere mich daran, dass er vor einigen Wochen in Tores Haus mit einem Kollegen gesprochen hat.

„Hauptkommissar Lennart Haugen", sagt er und streckt die Hand aus. Sie liegt fest in meiner und entzieht sich ihr so behutsam, als wollte er sie in Wirklichkeit gar nicht loslassen. „Es tut mir leid, dass wir uns schon wieder unter solchen Umständen sehen, Frau Sandvik. Das ist Ihr Haus?"

Ich nicke.

„Kennen Sie diese Frau?"

„Es ist meine beste Freundin. Annika Bergström. Ich wähnte sie in Paris. Was ist passiert?"

„Sie wurde niedergeschlagen und befindet sich in einem sehr ernsten Zustand. Sie hat einen harten Schlag auf ihren Kopf bekommen." Er hält inne. „Wohnt Frau Bergström auch hier?", fragt Haugen nach einigen Sekunden des Schweigens.

„Nein."

„Hat sie einen Schlüssel zu Ihrem Haus?"

„Ja."

Wo waren Sie in der vergangenen Nacht? Haugen hat die unausgesprochene Frage auf seinen Lippen, die ich automatisch beantworte.

„Ich habe bei meiner Mutter übernachtet."

Haugen wendet sich an Bente. „Sind Sie ihre Mutter?"

„Nein. Ich bin Bente Kodrán, die Schwiegermutter." Sie drückt für einen Moment beruhigend meinen Unterarm.

113

„In Ordnung. Das wär's fürs Erste. Da kommt der Hubschrauber", sagt Haugen. „Hat Ihre Freundin Familie? Einen Mann? Eltern?"

„Einen Vater. Ihre Mutter ist tot. Er lebt in Drammen. Ich würde Annika gerne ins Krankenhaus begleiten?"

„Ich denke, es wäre das Beste, wenn Sie ihren Vater informieren und ihn bitten, sofort zum Ullevål-Universitätsklinikum zu fahren. Der Notarzt befürchtet, dass sie die Nacht nicht überleben wird."

Der Satz trifft mich wie ein Hammerschlag.

„Und sehen Sie sich bitte auch im Haus um, ob etwas gestohlen wurde."

Mein Blick verliert sich in dem Chaos, das ich erst jetzt wahrnehme. Er wird davon abgestoßen, weil er dieses Bild nicht mit meinem ursprünglichen Wohnzimmer in Einklang bringen kann. Ich suche Bentes Augen, sie nimmt mich sofort in den Arm. Einen Moment bleiben wir so stehen, dann löse ich mich von ihr, sehe weg und wieder hin, dorthin, wo Annika gelegen hat, die man jetzt mit dem Hubschrauber nach Oslo bringt und die in der Nacht vielleicht stirbt.

Der Fußboden ist mit dem Inhalt der Schubladen und den Büchern aus den Regalen übersät, die Kissen des Sofas sind im ganzen Raum verteilt. Ich hebe die Digitalkamera auf und spüre durch die rasche Bewegung sofort ein Stechen in meiner Brust.

Gelb, Rot, Blau, ein helles Grün: farbige Stifte, verteilt unter dem Zeichenbrett. Und dann sehe ich, was fehlt.

Der Laptop, auf dem ich meine ersten Entwürfe für das Klosterhotel gespeichert hatte, ist verschwunden.

KAPITEL 28

Der Krankenwagen fährt los. Bente hat Annikas Vater und Mom angerufen und sie informiert. Da es im Haus nur so wimmelt von Polizisten und Spurentechnikern, hat Malvi Oddbjørn uns zu einem Kaffee in ihr Haus eingeladen.

Mir ist kalt. Ich möchte mich unter meine Bettdecke kuscheln, einschlafen und beim Aufwachen feststellen, dass ich einen völlig absurden Albtraum hatte.

Ich will in mein imaginäres Flugzeug steigen und über den Wolken meine Runden drehen.

„Trink einen Schluck Kaffee, Jonte. Er ist stark und wird dir guttun."

Bente hat nicht übertrieben, mein Magen rebelliert nach dem ersten Schluck. Ich hoffe, dass Malvi auch einen Schnaps im Haus hat. Ich brauche dringend einen kräftigen Schluck, um mein Zittern zu bandigen. Ich sollte weniger trinken, aber das hat letzte Nacht auch nicht funktioniert.

Warum musste Annika nur bei mir vorbeikommen? Tauchte sie am Morgen auf, weil sie schon zurück war? Oder spätnachts, weil sie gar nicht erst geflogen ist? Aber wieso?

Weil sie sich Sorgen gemacht hat, antwortet mir Back-Vocal mit trauriger Stimme.

Aber sie hat mir doch selbst geraten, bei meiner Mutter zu übernachten, entgegne ich. Das macht alles keinen Sinn!

Ich wünsche mir nichts sehnlicher, als dass Annika diesen brutalen Übergriff überlebt. Das Bild des regungslosen Opfers auf meinem weinroten Teppich muss ich aus meinem Gedächtnis löschen. Ich möchte meine strahlende Freundin zurück, wieder ihr Lachen hören, mich über ihre Geschichten amüsieren, und ich werde nie wieder neidisch sein auf ihre zügellose Abenteuerlust.

Das blutbefleckte weiße Kleid huscht an meiner Iris vorbei, mir wird schwindelig, ich klammere mich an die Armlehnen meines Stuhls.

Bente berührt meinen Arm. „Deine Mutter ist da."

Sekunden später kommt Mom kreidebleich auf mich zu und nimmt mich in den Arm. „Du hättest dort liegen können", schluchzt sie.

Du hättest dort liegen MÜSSEN, stänkert Back-Vocal. *Das wäre fair gewesen. Aber du Feigling hast es mal wieder jemand anders ausbaden lassen.*

Ich stimme der Stimme hinter meiner Stirn zu. Aber ich frage mich noch immer, weshalb Annika gekommen ist. War sie um mich besorgt, weil sie dachte, ich sei ihrem Rat nicht gefolgt?

Natürlich, was sonst? Annika ist zu gut für diese Welt. Im Gegensatz zu dir!

Das weiße Kleid flattert wieder an mir vorbei. Meine Atmung stockt. Ich hätte auf dem weinroten Teppich liegen sollen. Dann wäre der Gerechtigkeit Genüge getan worden.

Die Spurensicherung hat ihre Arbeit beendet. Im Haus herrscht eine beklemmende Stille, das Chaos ist immer noch unübersehbar.

Meine Mutter hat mir ihre Hilfe beim Aufräumen angeboten, und Bente hat postwendend für den verschwundenen Laptop eine Lösung aus dem Hut gezaubert. „Malte, der älteste Sohn meines Mannes, hat vor ein paar Wochen einen neuen Laptop gekauft und mir gesagt, dass er mit dem alten vielleicht jemandem eine Freude bereiten könnte. Wenn ich zu Hause bin, werde ich ihn sofort fragen, ob du ihn haben kannst. Ist das in Ordnung?"

Bevor ich mich bedanken kann, will Mom wissen: „Was ist mit deinen Daten? Hast du sie denn auf einem USB-Stick gesichert?"

Ich nicke. Tatsächlich habe ich gestern aus einem unerklärlichen Gefühl heraus alle Pläne auf einen USB-Stick übertragen. Sollte ich Maltes alten Laptop bekommen, kann ich sofort an den Entwürfen für das Klosterhotel weiterarbeiten. Ich war noch nie ein Freund von Back-ups. Das hat Jonas immer auf die Palme gebracht. Er hat auf der Sicherung der Daten bestanden, und wir haben oft gestritten, weil ich es fast immer vergessen habe. Aber gestern drängte mich irgendetwas dazu.

Bente hat sich soeben von uns verabschiedet und fährt wieder nach Hause. Ich mag sie immer mehr und verstehe Jonas' abweisende Haltung nicht. Bente ist eine kluge, sympathische Frau, die ihren Sohn mit Sicherheit geliebt hat, ja vermutlich noch immer liebt.

Lennart Haugen sieht sich als Letzter noch ein wenig im Haus um. Er hat die Ermittlungen in diesem Fall recht eifrig aufgenommen, nennt den Übergriff auf Annika „versuchter Totschlag" – zwei Worte, die mich zusammenzucken lassen.

„Wieso versuchter Totschlag?", fragt Mom.

„Nun, wäre sie tot, wäre es Mord. Aber da Frau Bergström noch lebt, ist es versuchter Totschlag."

Ich stehe unter Schock. Der Sinn dieser Bezeichnung dringt zu mir durch, aber es fällt mir schwer zu begreifen, was heute passiert ist. Seit Monaten geschehen Dinge, die für mich keinen Sinn ergeben.

Und dann denke ich unvermittelt: Damals war das Kleid auch weiß. Es scheint plötzlich, als wäre keine Sekunde vergangen, obwohl so viele Jahre zwischen damals und heute liegen. Alles ist jetzt wieder da. Ich kann das Entsetzen und die Angst, die mich ruckartig überfallen, mit niemandem teilen, nicht mal ansatzweise, denn dann müsste ich etwas preisgeben, über das ich niemals sprechen darf.

„Der Schlag zielte eindeutig darauf hin, das Opfer zu töten, Frau Sandvik", erklärt Haugen.

Seine Worte erschüttern mich. Ein unfassbarer Gedanke drängt sich mir auf. Vielleicht galt der Übergriff auf Annika tatsächlich *mir*. Vielleicht wollte jemand in Wahrheit *diesen* Laptop. Vielleicht hatte jemand vor, mich zu töten – wie das Baby in meinem Bauch.

Ich hätte auf Jonas hören und den Laptop jeden Abend im Schrank einschließen sollen, anstatt ihn einladend vor dem Fenster auf den Tisch zu stellen, als wollte ich Einbrecher damit anlocken. Dann würde Annika jetzt nicht mit dem Tode ringen.

Es ist wie immer deine Schuld, dröhnt Back-Vocal hinter meiner Stirn.

Hauptkommissar Haugen hat das Haus für einen Moment verlassen, um sein Handy aus dem Fahrzeug zu holen.

Flammend rotes Abendlicht stochert mit neugierigen Fingern durch die halb geöffneten Lamellen der Jalousie ins Wohnzimmer und streicht sanft über Moms Gesicht. Sie lächelt, und ich glaube, den Grund dafür zu kennen.

„Ein sympathischer Mann, dieser Lennart Haugen", sagt sie.

Ich bin sofort auf der Hut. „Wie meinst du das?"

„Na wie ich es sage. Dass er ein sympathischer Mann ist. Er sieht deinem Vater ein bisschen ähnlich, findest du nicht auch?"

„Er gefällt dir?" Ich sehe sie argwöhnisch an.

Mom prustet vor Lachen. „Nun mach mal langsam, Jonte. Du glaubst doch nicht ernsthaft, dass ich mich blindlings auf jeden Mann stürze, der halbwegs aussieht wie dein Vater?" Sie schüttelt den Kopf. „Ich betrachte Männer nicht auf diese Weise, mein Kind", sagt sie ein wenig sanfter. „Schon lange nicht mehr. Aber ich mag es besonders, jemanden zu treffen, der mir zeigt, wie dein Vater jetzt wohl aussehen würde. Darüber hinaus möchte ich keinen Mann, ob mit dem Aussehen deines Vaters oder nicht."

„Du vermisst Papa immer noch?"

Sie nickt.

„Ich vermisse ihn auch, besonders wenn ich jemanden treffe, der ihm ähnlichsieht. Wie diesen Lennart Haugen. Das ist mir auch gleich aufgefallen, Mom. Zurzeit vermisse ich Papa ohnehin ganz schrecklich."

Wir sitzen eine Weile still da.

„Du hast alles richtig gemacht, Mom", breche ich das Schweigen. „Ich hatte so eine schöne Kindheit, und das habe ich größtenteils dir zu verdanken. Das wollte ich dir schon immer mal sagen."

Meine Mutter sieht mich überrascht an. „Danke, mein Schatz, wow, vielen Dank! Ich habe stets versucht, mein Bestes zu geben, dir Werte zu vermitteln und eine gute Ausbildung zu ermöglichen. Und jetzt sehe ich dich an und habe eine wunderbare Frau vor mir, du bist ein großzügiger und toleranter Mensch, Jonte. Liebevoll, fürsorglich. Manchmal zu fürsorglich für meinem Geschmack. Ich möchte, dass du dich ein bisschen mehr um dich selbst kümmerst, mein Kind. Dass du dein wahres *Ich* entdeckst. Ich habe schon so lange das Gefühl, dass du dich vollkommen ausblendest und immer nur für andere da bist."

„Du möchtest mir damit sagen, dass Jonas zu oft an erster Stelle kam?"

„Ehrlich gesagt, ja."

„Mach dir keine Sorgen, Mom. Das ist vorbei. Ab sofort soll endlich auch deine Jonte zu ihrem Recht kommen." Ich halte einen Moment inne und überlege, ob ich es meiner Mutter jetzt schon sagen soll. „Ich werde die Scheidung einreichen, Mom."

Sie lächelt selig. „Oh, das habe ich so gehofft, Jonte."

„Jonas möchte allerdings keine Scheidung. Noch nicht."

„Glaubst du, er ist sich seiner Gefühle gar nicht sicher, was seine neue Liebe betrifft?"

„Das nehme ich an."

„Kennst du sie denn?"

„Es ist ein *er*, Mom."

„Oh nein!" Sie starrt mich an, zuckt aber dann die Schulter. „Nun, um ehrlich zu sein, überrascht mich das nicht."

Wir sind wieder still. Warum über eine Affäre sprechen, über die ich nicht reden möchte? Die ich akzeptieren muss. Die mir längst egal ist.

Gegen meine sonstige Angewohnheit ziehe ich die Vorhänge zu. Niemand soll mich sehen. Das gibt mir das Gefühl von Sicherheit und Kontrolle.

Ich stelle überrascht fest, dass ich mich jeden Tag ein bisschen mehr zu einem seltsamen, fremden Wesen entwickle.

Hauptkommissar Haugen telefoniert in unserem Beisein mit der Universitätsklinik in Oslo. Er ist ein sympathischer Mann, er sieht meinem Vater wirklich sehr ähnlich. Das war mir bei unserem ersten Treffen gar nicht aufgefallen.

Ich schätze ihn auf etwa sechzig Jahre, so alt, wie mein Vater jetzt wäre, an den ich neuerdings häufiger denken muss. Ich kann mich nicht daran erinnern, dass ich mich jemals so sehr nach ihm gesehnt habe wie in den vergangenen Wochen.

Haugen beendet das Telefonat und sieht mich an. „Frau Bergström liegt auf der Intensivstation und wurde ins künstliche Koma versetzt. Ihr Zustand ist kritisch. Die Ärzte können nur noch abwarten. Wir haben zu ihrer Sicherheit einen Polizisten vor der Station postiert. Wenn sie aufwacht, kann sie den Täter vielleicht identifizieren."

„Darf man sie besuchen?"

„Die Ärzte sind der Meinung, dass das wohl erst in einer Woche möglich sein wird, Frau Sandvik."

Tief in meinem Herzen bin ich froh, dass ich noch nicht nach Oslo fahren muss. Ich möchte in meinem eigenen, vom Wald fast ganz umgebenen Haus bleiben und mich vom Treiben der Welt möglichst fernhalten.

Der Kommissar entschuldigt sich für die vielen Fragen, die er mir gestellt hat. „Tut mir leid, ich weiß, das war heute sehr schrecklich für Sie, aber alles kann wichtig sein", murmelt er. „Ist sonst noch etwas von ihren Sachen abhandengekommen, Frau Sandvik?"

„Meines Erachtens nur der Laptop. Ich habe überall nachgesehen, vermisse jedoch nichts weiter. Fernseher, DVD-Player, Stereoanlage, alles ist noch da. Selbst das Sparschwein mit meinen Kronen."

„Ich vermute, dass die Einbrecher durch Annika gestört wurden", wirft Mom ein. „Sie haben sie niedergeschlagen, damit Annika sie nicht identifizieren kann. Wir werden an der Küchentür eine Dreifachverglasung und neue Schlösser anbringen lassen."

„Sehr vernünftig", meint Haugen. „Haben Sie noch Fragen?"

„Können die Diebe mit meinem Laptop überhaupt etwas anfangen?"

„Den können sie im Handumdrehen verkaufen. Laptops sind sehr begehrt. Sollten sie aber feststellen, dass er gut gesichert ist, werden sie ihn einfach wegwerfen. Haben Sie ein Bios-Passwort verwendet?"

Ich hebe die Augenbrauen. „Was ist ein Bios-Passwort?"

Haugen lächelt nachsichtig. „Verlangt Ihr Laptop beim Start immer zuerst nach einem Passwort?"

„Ja, das hat mein Mann eingestellt."

„Dann hat der Laptop ein Bios-Passwort, und das bedeutet, dass der Laptop nicht einfach von jedem benutzt werden kann. Es ist schwierig, ein Bios-Passwort zu knacken. Denn das Passwort ist mit einem Bios-Chip verknüpft. Der muss geändert werden, die Programme können vorher nicht gestartet werden. Oder sie müssen eine neue Festplatte installieren. Für einen Hehler ist das recht aufwendig. Somit besteht die Möglichkeit, dass der Laptop direkt auf der Deponie landet. Oder irgendwo im Wald. Haben Sie Back-ups gemacht?"

„Ja. Auf meinem USB-Stick. Ich habe ihn immer in meiner Handtasche."

„Sehr klug von Ihnen. War das auch eine Idee Ihres Mannes? Oder wusste er gar nichts davon?"

Es vergehen Sekunden, bis ich den Argwohn hinter dieser Frage wahrnehme, und ich gerate kurz aus meinem seelischen Gleichgewicht, als ich begreife, dass er jemand konkret in Verdacht hat: Jonas.

Plötzlich mag ich Lennart Haugen nicht mehr.

Von den Rändern meines Bewusstseins her setzt sich ein Bild zusammen, um allmählich Form und Gestalt anzunehmen, so wie sich am Winterhimmel dunkle Wolkenberge sammeln: zwei Menschen, denen sich der Tod nähert. Mit voller Wucht dringt die Frage in mein Gedächtnis: Besteht ein Zusammenhang zwischen dem Tod meines Schwiegervaters und dem Übergriff auf Annika? Können zwei Einbrüche Zufall sein? Ich kann den Zusammenhang nicht mehr länger ignorieren. Dieser Gedanke hat sich in meinen Kopf eingenistet wie ein Übel, vor dem ich mich zutiefst gefürchtet habe. Eine grausige Vorstellung.

Die Ärzte haben bei Annika ein schweres Hirntrauma diagnostiziert. Sie liegt immer noch im Koma. Selbst wenn sie beatmet werden muss und völlig abhängig von Schläuchen und Geräten ist, so hat sie doch den Mordanschlag überlebt. Ich sage mir ständig, dass Annika wieder aufwachen wird, denn sie ist jung und stark und in einer guten körperlichen Verfassung. Sie war stets sportlich aktiv. Annika wird es schaffen. Sie kämpft, davon bin ich überzeugt.

Kommissar Haugen sucht uns häufiger auf. Sobald ich ihm die Haustür öffne, vermengt sich der Lärm der Straße mit der gedämpften Stille in meinem Haus, in das kurz darauf erneut seine seltsamen Fragen eindringen. Er bleibt stets einen Moment im Eingang stehen, als müsste er sich orientieren. Bei näherem Hinsehen halte ich ihn für einen eigenartigen Mann. Ich vermag jetzt auch keine Ähnlichkeit mehr mit meinem Vater zu sehen, dem mein Sinneswandel gewiss gefallen hätte, da er Haugen als einen unangenehmen Menschen empfinden würde.

Diesmal spricht der Kommissar plötzlich von Personen, die *mir* nicht wohlgesonnen sein könnten.

„Ich verstehe Sie und Ihre Fragen nicht, ich habe keine Feinde", entgegne ich entsetzt. „Jedenfalls nicht, dass ich wüsste. Ich komme mit meinen Kollegen gut aus, pflege einen guten Umgang mit meinen Nachbarn und habe ein freundschaftliches Verhältnis zu den Menschen, die ich kenne. Ich habe keine Feinde."

„Hm ... aber Sie lassen sich scheiden, Frau Sandvik. Könnte etwas aus dieser Richtung kommen?"

„Nein, auf keinen Fall! Jonas und ich sprechen noch in aller Freundschaft miteinander, sofern Sie das meinen."

„Sie sind sich demnach völlig einig über die Modalitäten der Ehescheidung?"

„Wir nehmen uns die Zeit, um diese Dinge vernünftig zu regeln."

Ich antworte gereizt, will, dass er aufhört, mir diese Art Fragen zu stellen. Dass er verschwindet und mich nicht mehr behelligt, und vor allem will ich, dass Annika aufwacht. Ich möchte das Bild des weißen Kleides für immer von meiner Netzhaut löschen. *Delete!* Weg damit!

Delete … Ich radiere später die Beichtstühle aus der Skizze der Klosterkirche, ersetze sie durch ein hypermodernes Kühlsystem aus Glas und Stahl für erlesene Weine und integriere das Regal in eine Bar. *Delete* – der Name der Bar. Perfekt und makaber.

Vielleicht hat Mom recht, und ich drehe allmählich wirklich durch. „Du ziehst dich zu sehr in dein Schneckenhaus zurück", wirft sie mir vor, „entziehst dich immer mehr der Realität und bist hinsichtlich Annikas Genesung viel zu optimistisch."

Oder meint sie vielleicht etwas ganz anderes? Ich will es gar nicht wissen und werde es gewiss nicht hinterfragen.

Ja, ich bin mir sicher, dass Annika wieder gesund wird. Es ist ein Gefühl, tief in meinem Bauch, eine Intuition, die ich nicht erklären kann. Und ich klammere mich fest daran.

Mom ist ständig um mich, dabei möchte ich lieber allein sein. Ihre Überfürsorglichkeit reizt mich immer mehr. Ich bin ruhelos, denn seit dem Einbruch samt Übergriff hat sie mich keine Minute mehr in Ruhe gelassen. Ich bin nie mehr allein gewesen. Das klingt undankbar, aber ich brauche Zeit für mich. Alle denken, dass ich mich nach diesem Vorfall vor dem Alleinsein fürchte. Natürlich habe ich Angst, aber ich sehne mich auch danach, nach der Arbeit wieder in ein leeres Haus zu kommen, in dem ich mich nicht verpflichtet fühle, mit jemandem ein Gespräch zu führen. Ich brauche Ruhe, um wieder klar denken zu können. Aber wie erkläre ich das einer Mutter, die es nur gut mit mir meint?

„Bente ist am Telefon", ruft Mom aus der Küche.

Ich zögere. *Nein!* Was soll ich denn jetzt auch noch mit Bente anfangen?

„Komm schon", drängt Mom, „rede einen Moment mit ihr. Sie macht sich große Sorgen."

Ich seufze und nehme das Gespräch an. Bente klingt in der Tat sehr besorgt. „Bekommt dir das denn, dass ständig jemand um dich ist?", will sie wissen.

Endlich spricht das mal jemand an!

„Eigentlich nicht", flüstere ich, weil ich vermeiden möchte, dass Mom mich in der Küche hört.

„Hör mal, Jonte. Wir haben hier in Hyggen auf unserem Landgut noch ein hübsches Gästehaus. Möchtest du nicht eine Woche dort verbringen?"

Endlich kommen die Tränen.

Zu meiner Überraschung stimmt meine Mutter Bentes Vorschlag sofort zu.

„Du musst mal raus, Jonte. Ich mache mir große Sorgen. Du entfliehst der Realität immer wieder. Das ist nicht gut. Für Annika kannst du nichts tun, indem du hier herumhängst. Wenn ich fort bin, wirst du bestimmt jeden Tag in die Klinik fahren und deiner Freundin etwas vorlesen. Wenn ich bei dir bleibe, wirst du die ganze Zeit mit mir über sie sprechen wollen. Annika wird dich dringend brauchen, sobald sie aus dem Koma erwacht. Also los, nutze die Zeit davor und erhole dich ein wenig. Nimm Bentes Angebot an!"

KAPITEL 30

Auf der Intensivstation 3 B herrscht eine beklemmende Stille. Nur das leise Piepsen der Monitore ist zu hören. Ich fühle mich benommen, als ich das Krankenzimmer betrete und Annikas reglose Gestalt sehe. Sie schläft nicht. Ihre Augen sind offen, doch sie bewegen sich nicht. Keine Reaktion auf das Geräusch meines Eintretens. Es schnürt mir die Kehle zu. Sie wirkt in dem großen Bett so zart und hilflos.

Ich bin erstaunt, wie sehr sie ihrem Vater ähnlichsieht. Warum ist mir das nicht schon früher aufgefallen? Das blonde Haar, die gleiche Stupsnase, die gleichen dunkelblauen Augen in dem schmalen Gesicht, das eine unnatürliche Blässe zeigt.

Ich ziehe leise einen Stuhl an ihr Bett, setze mich und streichle ihre Wangen. Annika, die Stille, die Seelenvolle, die Zerstreute. Aber auch die Lebenslustige und Wagemutige. Werde ich auch diese Annika eines Tages wiedersehen?

„Ach, Annika …"

Die Untersuchungen sind weitgehend abgeschlossen. Die Ärzte wissen nicht, ob Annika jemals aufwachen wird.

„Du kannst mich hören, hat mir die Ärztin versichert. Wache bald auf, Annika! Ich brauche dich so sehr."

Hinter der Glastür bewegt sich eine schemenhafte Gestalt. Eine Krankenschwester stürmt ins Zimmer und hängt eine neue Infusion an den Metallständer, an dem mehrere Tropfflaschen baumeln. „Bleiben Sie bitte nicht zu lange, Frau Sandvik", sagt sie. „Ruhe ist das Allerwichtigste für Annikas Genesung."

Ich nicke. Ein schwarzes Rechteck starrt mich aus dem Monitor an. Kein Lämpchen leuchtet in dem Kästchen auf, ein finsteres Loch, das Annikas Leben schlucken will.

Ich versuche, den Angstschauer in meinem Nacken zu ignorieren. Von draußen höre ich den Regen auf die Scheiben pladdern. Wie Finger, die nervös auf einer Tischplatte trommeln. Tausend Ängste um das Leben von Annika quälen mich. Der Regen wütet weiter, sein lautes Peitschen klingt, als käme es aus dem Zimmer selbst.

Ich beuge mich vor und streiche eine Haarsträhne aus Annikas Gesicht. Gleich darauf verlässt die Krankenschwester wieder das Zimmer und eilt den Gang hinunter.

Auch ich verabschiede mich nun und küsse Annika auf die Stirn. Plötzlich gehen die Impulse auf einem der Monitore in die Steilkurve. Annika blinzelt kurz. Ihre Augenlider zucken. Auf einem der Monitore über dem Bett spielt die EEG-Kurve verrückt. Dann ist alles wieder ruhig.

Ich küsse Annika noch einmal, aber sie zeigt keine Reaktion.

Ich bin aufgewühlt und setze mich einen kurzen Moment in den Aufenthaltsraum. Er wirkt gespenstisch. Die Stühle werfen lange Schatten. Kein Geräusch ist zu hören, lediglich das dunkle Summen des Kaffeeautomaten. Eine Lampe brennt auf einem Tisch in der Ecke. Das Mobiliar wirkt hastig montiert und lieblos hingestellt. Das Wartezimmer sieht hier genauso aus wie in der gynäkologischen Abteilung.

Ich bin allein mit meinen Gedanken, schließe die Augen, unterdrücke meine Tränen. Ich vermisse Annika so sehr und befürchte das Schlimmste. Ich rutsche auf dem Stuhl hin und her, blättere lustlos in einer Frauenzeitschrift und lege sie wieder weg.

Annika liegt nun schon seit einem Monat auf der Intensivstation und wacht einfach nicht wieder auf. Sie soll demnächst in ein Pflegeheim verlegt werden, das über eine Spezialabteilung für Komapatienten verfügt. Ich kann und will nicht glauben, dass es so weit kommen wird, und wünsche mir so sehr, dass meine Freundin bald die Augen öffnet. Annika will zurückkommen, davon bin ich felsenfest überzeugt. Wie ihr Vater spreche ich stets mit ihr, wenn ich neben ihrem Bett sitze, auch wenn ich anfangs eine gewisse Befangenheit überwinden musste.

Und jetzt dieses Lebenszeichen. Als wollte sie mir etwas mitteilen. Dass sie es schaffen wird.

Bentes Vorschlag hört sich verlockend an. Ich werde mir Urlaub nehmen. Mein Boss betont oft, wie sehr er es schätzt, dass ich so kurz nach der Fehlgeburt meine Arbeit wieder aufgenommen habe. Er weiß auch, was in meinem Haus geschehen ist und wird den Urlaub gewiss genehmigen. Ich habe natürlich mit keinem Wort erwähnt, dass meine Arbeit der einzige Weg ist, um nicht gänzlich durchzudrehen, und dass ich mich an einen strengen Zeitplan halte: im Kino arbeiten, Annika besuchen und jede Gelegenheit nutzen, die sich mir für das Klosterhotel bietet, obwohl das bedeutet, dass ich oft um sechs Uhr morgens vor dem Zeichenbrett stehen muss. Ich habe mir einen neuen Laptop gekauft, obwohl Bentes Stiefsohn mir seinen angeboten hat, und arbeite gerade an der Weinbar *Delete*.

Jonas hat sich noch nicht nach den Entwürfen erkundigt. Mein Noch-Ehemann stellt keine Fragen, ja er lässt überhaupt nichts von sich hören. Er ist wie vom Erdboden verschluckt.

Ich werde für eine Woche nach Hyggen fahren und meinen Laptop mitnehmen. Bentes feudales Landgut mit Gästehaus und einem atemberaubenden Blick auf den Drammensfjord – sie hat mir Fotos gemailt – ist jetzt genau das Richtige für mich. Am Telefon hat sie erwähnt, dass Malte mich gerne kennenlernen würde. Sie wird mich doch nicht bloß eingeladen haben, um mich mit ihrem Stiefsohn zu verkuppeln? Ich muss über meinen Argwohn lächeln.

Mein Leben wird bald wieder geordnet und normal verlaufen. Ich kann nur hoffen, dass Jonas nichts ausheckt. Unsere Scheidung soll schnell und sauber über die Bühne gehen. Aber meine Intuition sagt mir etwas anderes. Etwas Unangenehmes ist im Anmarsch. Verdammt!

Schon wieder etwas Unangenehmes?, knurrt Back-Vocal und gibt vor zu tänzeln. *Wo ist es, Jonte? Ich schlag es nieder!*

KAPITEL 31

Niemand ist auf der Straße unterwegs. Die meisten Häuser liegen im Dunkel. Nur bei Malvis brennt noch Licht. Ich sehe sie nicht, gehe aber jede Wette ein, dass sie jede meiner Aktionen genau beobachtet.

Ich parke mein Fahrzeug in der Parklücke vor meinem Haus. Wenn ich getrunken habe, fahre ich nie in die Garage. Aber ich musste mein Auto weiter weg abstellen, und als ich den Parkplatz vor dem Haus sah, bin ich hinausgehuscht, um das Auto umzuparken.

Es ist kalt draußen. Der Winter setzt sich in seiner gnadenlosen Heftigkeit immer mehr durch. Dicke Schneeflocken taumeln durch die Nacht. Meine Hände und Füße sind steif vor Kälte, und ich zittere.

Rein mit dir! Einmal überprüfen, ob die Tür richtig verriegelt ist und dann ab ins Bett! Back-Vocal macht heute auf Stimme der Vernunft.

Ich spüre, dass jemand in meiner Nähe ist und mich beobachtet. Ist es wirklich Malvi? Es passiert hin und wieder, dass sie urplötzlich hinter mir steht. Aber nicht heute. Meine Nachbarin löscht gerade das Licht und geht sicher ins Bett.

Wer beobachtet mich also?

Es ist wegen der Kälte, ich kann wegen dieser eisigen Kälte nicht mehr klar denken. Ich hätte einen Mantel anziehen oder überhaupt nicht nach draußen gehen sollen. Was spielt es denn für eine Rolle, wenn mein Auto nicht unmittelbar vor meinem Haus steht? Ich gehe schnell wieder hinein, schließe ab, überprüfe sämtliche Schlösser noch mal, ziehe die Vorhänge zu und sperre die Welt aus.

Das hast du dir wieder mal eingebildet in deinem Suff! Park dich in deinem Bett und schlaf deinen Rausch aus!

Ich kann nicht einschlafen. Mein Gehör bleibt fokussiert auf alle Geräusche in meiner Umgebung. Ich höre die Uhr im Wohnzimmer und die des Kirchturms weit draußen, die zu jeder halben und vollen Stunde schlägt. Ich höre Autos, die langsam vorbeifahren.

Bleiben sie vor deinem Haus stehen? Nein.

Vielleicht ist jemand im Garten hinter dem Haus?

Herrje! Der Mörder ist immer der Gärtner …

Ich denke an die riesige batteriebetriebene Taschenlampe, die ich heute im Baumarkt gekauft habe, nehme sie aus dem Küchenschrank, gehe ins Wohnzimmer, öffne die Terrassentür und leuchte den ganzen Garten aus.

Oh, wie clever! Du gehst raus, damit er dich besser anfallen kann! Legst du es darauf an? Willst du auch mal drankommen?

Es war niemand zu sehen. Ich schließe schnell wieder ab. Ich lege mich erneut ins Bett, aber ich kann nicht schlafen. Macht nichts. Ich ruhe mich auch aus, wenn ich nur daliege.

Draußen ist die Temperatur mit einem Mal angestiegen. Der Schnee ist in Regen übergegangen. Ich kann es tropfen hören. Ein Gewitter braut sich langsam zusammen. Der Wind rüttelt an den Bäumen, die sich von ihren letzten Blättern trennen. Die Natur ist bald nackt, alles ist kahl.

Nackte Bäume. In dem Roman auf meinem Nachttisch wird die Leiche im Wald erst entdeckt, als die Bäume keine Blätter mehr tragen.

Ich konzentriere mich auf die Geräusche der riesigen Standuhr aus Ebenholz. Ihr Pendel schwingt hin und her mit dumpfem, monotonem Klang; und wenn es Zeit wird, die Stunden zu schlagen, kommt aus den Messinglungen ein klarer, lauter, sonorer und harmonischer Schall, der sich aber doch so seltsam anhört, dass ich mich bei jedem Stundenschlag gezwungen fühle, den Atem anzuhalten, während ich dem Klang lausche.

Irgendwann befällt mich eine innere Unruhe, die Schläge der Uhr dröhnen nur noch lästig in meinen Ohren. Ich spüre, dass ich zittere. Sobald das letzte Echo verklungen ist, lache ich über meine Angst und meine Nervosität, und dann ängstigt mich auf einmal mein eigenes Lachen.

Selbst Back-Vocal scheint nun Muffe zu haben. Flüsternd versprechen wir einander, dass uns das nächste Schlagen nicht mehr verstören wird. Doch nach Ablauf einer Stunde, wenn die Uhr erneut schlägt, überkommt uns dieselbe Bestürzung und Angst wie zuvor.

Die Kirchenglocken haben gerade sechsmal geschlagen, ich sollte wohl besser aufstehen. Einen starken Kaffee trinken, etwas essen und dann wie abgesprochen nach Hyggen fahren.

Ich muss weg von hier, von all den Hirngespinsten, von den Stundenschlägen und der Leiche in meinem Buch.

Aber ich bleibe in meinem Bett liegen und reibe meine kalten Füße aneinander. Früher wachte ich stets von der Wärme auf und krabbelte bis an die Bettkante, um mich abzukühlen.

Bisweilen dachte ich dann über die Verhaltensweisen von Erwachsenen nach. Sie benehmen sich hin und wieder wie wilde Tiere im Schatten eines dunklen Waldes.

Manchmal merkte ich am Morgen, dass ich frierend in einer Art Fötusstellung lag und musste eine heiße Dusche nehmen, um mich wieder aufzuwärmen.

Mein Kopf klopft wie eine monströse Blase. Ich denke an all das, worüber ich niemals sprechen darf.

Plötzlich habe ich Heimweh nach der Vergangenheit.

KAPITEL 32

Bente wohnt am Blue Bay in Hyggen. Das Küstendorf an der Ostseite des Drammensfjord liegt nur vierzig Kilometer von Oslo entfernt, sodass ich ab und zu Annika besuchen könnte. Überall riecht es in der warmen Jahreszeit nach Früchten und Beeren, weshalb die Einwohner die Bucht am Jachthafen Blue Bay nennen.

Das Navi namens Balu wird mich zuverlässig zur Adresse führen. Bei seiner tiefen Stimme stelle ich mir eine Art Teddybär mit riesigem Bauch vor. Im Radio werden alte Hits gespielt. Ich drehe die Lautstärke ein wenig auf und singe mit. *Bridge over Troubled Water, Hey Jude, Danny Boy, Lady in Red, Sorry Seems to Be the Hardest Word.* Bei dem letzten Song haben Jonas und ich uns zum ersten Mal auf der Hochzeit meiner Nichte geküsst. Die Erinnerung daran – irgendwo in einem früheren Leben – ist mir nicht abhandengekommen.

Hyggen. Balu sagt mir, ich soll mich links halten.

Mit jedem Kilometer, den ich mich von meinem Zuhause entferne, werde ich fröhlicher. Eine Last fällt von meinen Schultern. Ich bin endlich frei, sieben Tage, eine ganze Woche lang. Ich weiß allerdings nicht, ob ich wirklich so lange in Bentes Nähe sein möchte, aber das werde ich dann ja sehen. Vielleicht fahre ich weiter in Richtung Süden und quartiere mich für ein paar Tage in einem Hotel in Hernestangen ein. Hauptsache erst mal weg von Drammen.

Vielleicht wäre es eine gute Idee, das Haus zu verkaufen. Dass mir das noch nie in den Sinn gekommen ist - ein neues Haus, ein Neuanfang.

Das wäre doch das Beste, um Jonas endgültig loszuwerden, deine Ehe und die ganze verdammte Vergangenheit hinter dir zu lassen ...

Ein neues Haus, in dem ich keine Schritte auf der Treppe höre, keine Hausschuhe verschwinden, keine Fenster offen stehen, die ich geschlossen habe? Ich grüble jetzt auch ständig darüber nach, was mit Annika passiert ist. Selbst in meinem imaginären Flugzeug hoch über den Wolken.

Dennoch ...

Ich will diesen Wechsel nicht.

Balu hat mich sicher nach Hyggen geleitet. Bevor Bente den Ort erwähnte, hatte ich noch nie von ihm gehört. Ich sehe überall schöne neue Häuser, umgeben von prächtigen Gärten. Balu erteilt mir klare Anweisungen: *Nehmen Sie im Kreisverkehr die dritte Ausfahrt.* Dann sehe ich das Schild *Blue Bay.* Ich habe mein Ziel erreicht.

Vor mir liegt das Anwesen *Kos* am Bakkekroken. Kos bedeutet so viel wie ein gemütliches Beisammensein und Dasein. Bente lebt wahrlich nicht schlecht. Das Anwesen ist so anders als mein Haus in Drammen. Aber …

Da ist etwas an diesem Gebäude, das mir nicht gefällt, obwohl es so idyllisch unter der Abendsonne liegt, von ihrem goldenen Licht umspielt. Vielleicht ist es die glänzende Blechgarage, die in keiner Weise zu dem klassisch-modernen Bauhausstil passt. Zwei Möwen trippeln auf dem Sims des großen Fensters herum, dann flattern sie davon. In der Ferne, ganz am Ende des weiten Gartens, liegt der Drammensfjord wie ein dunkelblauer Teppich, der gerade erst ausgebreitet worden ist, nur für mich und aus einem einzigen Grund. Damit ich ihn bemerke, den dunkelblauen Fjord. Den dunkelblauen Teppich, die Tiefe unter der glänzenden Oberfläche, die mich regelrecht anzieht.

In diesem Moment sehe ich Bente den Weg heruntergehen, sie kommt auf mich zu und schaut sehr glücklich aus. Hinter ihr steht ein Mann auf der Schwelle zur Eingangstür. Er winkt mir freundlich zu und lächelt.

Mein Herz setzt ein paar Schläge aus.

Bente öffnet die Fahrertür. „Wie schön, dass du da bist, Jonte", sagt sie herzlich. „Du kannst den Wagen vor der Garage parken."

Sie blickt mich schweigend an, abwartend. Auch ich sage kein Wort.

Dann strahlt Bente übers ganze Gesicht. „Der Kaffee wartet schon auf dich. Herzlich willkommen auf *Kos*, Jonte!"

KAPITEL 33

Es geschieht immer unerwartet, sodass ich mich nicht darauf vorbereiten kann. Plötzlich taucht jemand auf, der mich sehr stark an Aaron erinnert. Das letzte Mal passierte es, als ich einige Schlüssel für das neue Schloss meiner Haustür anfertigen ließ. Der Mann vom Schlüsseldienst hatte Aarons blonde Locken. Er stand da, wippte kaum merklich auf und ab mit seinen schlaksigen Beinen. Einen Augenblick sah er mich auf eine Weise an, als wollte er jetzt gleich den Knäuel meiner Gedanken entwirren – und zu einem glücklichen Ende führen.

Seit Jahren versuche ich, so wenig wie möglich an meinen verstorbenen Ex-Freund zu denken, und die meiste Zeit gelingt mir das auch. Es ist schon viel zu lange her, um mich ständig damit auseinanderzusetzen. Aaron ist an einem sicheren Ort abgespeichert, tief unter meinen anderen Erinnerungen, aber manchmal entkommt er dieser Zelle. Dann sucht die Vergangenheit mich so lange heim, bis ich ihr wieder entwischen und die Tür zuschlagen kann.

Der Mann, der hinter Bente in der Tür steht, erinnert mich an Aaron. In der kurzen Zeit, die ich brauche, um mein Auto vor die Garage abzustellen, rasen meine Gedanken durch den Kopf, meine Stimmung sinkt auf null. Ich sehe dieses Mal keinen lebenden Aaron. Ich spüre nicht die Liebe, die Leidenschaft, das atemberaubende Verlangen, das ständige Kribbeln in meinem Magen. Das könnte ich zumindest ein bisschen genießen, aber es bleibt alles weg. Nur das Verlustgefühl kehrt zurück, und ich sehe den Sarg, in dem er lag. Seine Hände mit den verschränkten Fingern, die mich so gestört haben. Ich empfand es als eine beleidigende Haltung. Ihm wurde Unrecht getan. Denn diese Hände erweckten den Eindruck, dass er betete, aber Aaron war ein überzeugter Atheist. Er ließ es sich nicht nehmen, dies bei jeder Gelegenheit kundzutun. Er würde sich für diese Hände schämen. Ich sah zu seiner Frau und durchbohrte sie mit meinem eisigen Blick. Es war ihre Schuld. Sie starrte mich ungerührt an.

Er trug einen dunkelblauen Anzug, ein schneeweißes Hemd und eine blau-weiß gestreifte Krawatte – seine Kleidung bei offiziellen Anlässen, aber eigentlich verabscheute er sie. Wie konnte sie ihn nur in einem Anzug in den Sarg legen? Er hätte seine Lieblingsjeans und den hellblauen Pullover tragen sollen. Er hätte dorthin als jener Mann gebettet werden sollen, der er war – ein Genießer, ein Draufgänger, ein charmanter Schurke, ein souveräner Lebenskünstler. Sie hätte ihn als den bösen Buben, den jeder kannte, ins Grab legen und ihn nicht wie ein elegantes Monster herausputzen sollen.

Ich hasste sie. *Liv*. Ich hasste ihren Status als Ehefrau, ihre zur Schau getragene Trauer und den überlegenen Ausdruck in ihren Augen. Ich wollte ihr zu verstehen geben, dass sie ihn monatelang mit mir hatte teilen müssen, dass seine Aufmerksamkeit im Grunde ganz auf mich gerichtet war, dass er sich zuletzt von ihr trennen wollte. Ich hätte ihr vorwerfen sollen, dass sie ihn vielleicht hätte halten können, wenn sie ihn mit meinen Augen gesehen und ihm gezeigt hätte, dass sie ihn liebte, statt diese Kälte an den Tag zu legen, die ihn in meine warmen Arme trieb ... Liv, die nur an der finanziellen Absicherung interessiert war, die er ihr bot. Sie hätte erfahren sollen, dass Aaron und ich geplant hatten, seine Arztpraxis gemeinsam weiterzuführen. Dass wir nicht mehr ohneeinander sein konnten ...

Aber kein Wort kam über meine Lippen. Ich konnte nur auf den Mann im Sarg schauen, den ich verloren hatte, auf diese traurige Persiflage meiner großen Liebe. Ich konnte nur auf die stille Brust starren, die sich nicht mehr hob und senkte und deren Anblick meinen Augen wehtat. Ich wollte meinen Kopf auf diese Brust betten, um wieder seine Atmung zu spüren. Ich wollte mich wieder durch die Wärme seines Körpers erwärmen.

Und dann sagte sie es.

Liv – ich nannte sie immer nur „die Schlange", wenn ich mit Annika über sie sprach. Meine Freundin hörte mir immer ruhig zu, versuchte aber meine Hasstiraden zu bremsen und legte mir beruhigend die Hand auf die Schulter, wenn ich Liv verfluchte.

Und jetzt kam die Schlange auf mich zu und zischte: „Du glaubst wohl, dass du etwas Besonderes mit ihm hattest. Das glaubten all seine Täubchen vor dir ebenfalls. Aber die Einzige, die ihm etwas bedeutet hat, war ich. Aaron war ein Fantast, ein leidenschaftlicher Liebhaber und ein unberechenbarer Polygamist, aber er liebte mich. Und ich liebte ihn. Das konnte niemand zerstören. Auch du nicht. Du am allerwenigsten."

Ich verspürte den Drang, sie zu schlagen.

Seit dem Moment, als ich erfahren hatte, dass Aaron an den Folgen eines Motorradunfalls noch an Ort und Stelle gestorben war, blockierte dieser Schock einen Großteil meines Körpers und meiner Seele. Alle Energie hatte mich verlassen. Ich bewegte mich träge, unsicher, zögernd. Ich konnte keinen klaren Gedanken mehr fassen. Bekam das Chaos in meinem Kopf nicht in den Griff. Meine Gedanken hatten weder Anfang noch Ende, drehten sich im Kreis, verblassten, nur schwer fassbar, und tauchten wieder auf. Ich verstand die Welt nicht mehr.

Bis zu dem Moment, als ich Aaron in diesem Sarg liegen sah. Da endete diese Lethargie abrupt, und mich ergriff die Wut über die betenden Hände und sein lächerliches Aussehen. Und als ich Livs eisige Worte vernahm, fletschte ich die Zähne.

„Du lügst, du falsche Schlange", schleuderte ich ihr entgegen. „Du hast ihm nichts mehr bedeutet. Er hat es ja nicht einmal mehr ertragen, dich zu berühren."

Sie lächelte. „Ach …?"

Ich stand aufrecht und fühlte mich ihr weit überlegen. „Er wollte mit mir leben, mit mir die Praxis weiterführen, mich heiraten." Die Worte sprudelten aus mir heraus, ich fühlte mich ja so stark.

Livs erwiderte kein Wort, sie streichelte nur ihren Bauch, und erst da nahm ich die leichte Rundung wahr. Sie lächelte giftig. „Und warum glaubst du, hat er mich dann geschwängert?"

Es standen peinlich berührte Leute um uns herum, die Liv ihr Beileid aussprechen wollten. Ich stolperte auf eine kleine Gruppe zu, die dies bereits getan hatte, weil ich dort eine junge Frau entdeckt hatte, die ein Tablett mit gefüllten Weingläsern trug, und kippte ein Glas Rotwein in mich hinein. Alkohol … Mein Realitätsverschöner. Mein Gruß an den Tod. Und an das Leben. Gleich darauf ein zweites Glas, während mich alle anstarrten. Fünf Minuten später noch eins, wo ich schon kaum einen mehr wahrnahm. So lange, bis ich nicht mehr in der Lage war, meinen Text klar und fehlerfrei aufzusagen. Immer denselben Text. „Hey! Noch ein Glas!" Schließlich torkelte ich in meinen Wagen und brauste davon. In meinem vernebelten Hirn war ich bereit zu sterben. So wie er. Dieser elende Verräter.

„Kommst du?" Bente holt mich in die Realität zurück. Ich schaue auf.

Sie sieht mich erstaunt an. „Da war aber jemand ganz weit weg. Jetzt steig schon aus, ich nehme dein Gepäck. Jonte, Mädchen, du bist auf einmal so verdammt blass."

Ich gehe auf das Haus zu, spüre ein Stechen im Magen. Der Kies knirscht unter meinen Schuhen. Ich werfe einen letzten Blick auf den tiefblauen Fjord. Meine Schritte werden schneller.

Renn zum Steg! Tauch ab in die Tiefe, dorthin, wo keine Gefahr lauert, wo sich alle Geheimnisse auflösen und sanfter Frieden herrscht.

Ich hätte damals schon sterben sollen.

KAPITEL 34

Der Mann steht allein in der Tür, er bewegt sich nicht. Ein Gedanke fängt mich allmählich wieder ein: *Es ist nicht Aaron.* Ich bin erleichtert über diese simple Wahrheit, aber auf eine Weise, die schmerzt. Spüre ein Brennen hinter den Augen, ein stummer Schrei vibriert auf meinen Lippen. Einige Sekunden lang, dann zieht er sich zurück, als die Erinnerung nachlässt.

„Ich bin Malte, Noahs ältester Sohn", sagt er. „Bente hat mich ziemlich neugierig auf ihre Schwiegertochter gemacht." Er küsst mich auf die Wangen.

Küsse - eine Berührung, die ich vor langer Zeit gespürt habe.

„Ex-Schwiegertochter." Ich frage mich, warum ich das richtigstelle.

Ex ist ein weites Feld. Die Liebe ist abhandengekommen. Niemand ist da, niemand, der tröstet, niemand, der zuhört. Niemand. Nichts bewegt sich, selbst die Psyche ist auf der Hut. Aber jetzt gleitet das Wort für getrennte Seelen zähflüssig durch meinen Kopf, teilt sich in *Ex* und *Schwiegertochter.* Ohne Bindestrich, ohne Bindung.

Ich folge ihm ins Innere des Hauses, in die Küche, wo Bente mir sofort eine Tasse Kaffee reicht. „Hier ... Der wird dir nach der Fahrt guttun." Sie hält einen Moment inne. „Ex? Sorry, ich habe das gerade mitbekommen. Du hast die Scheidung schon beantragt?"

„N ... Ja", antworte ich.

Mein Gehirn sendet mir unvollständige Sätze, wabernde Wortfetzen. Ich konzentriere mich, setze sie zusammen: ... eine schnelle Scheidung. Als wäre unsere Ehe in Windeseile durch einen Sommer gerast und am Herbstanfang zerbrochen. Jonas soll aus meinem Leben abhauen. *Delete.* Er soll es woanders mit seinem neuen Mann treiben, möglichst weit weg, am besten auf einem anderen Planeten. Ich hätte mich nie auf ihn einlassen, ihn nie heiraten dürfen, aber das ist eine müßige Erkenntnis. Weil es dafür zu spät ist. Ich habe nach seinem Outing den Herbst durchquert, aber meine Geschwindigkeit war zu gemächlich. Meine Gedanken kreisten, Stillstand und Tod kamen mir in den Sinn, während die Tage kürzer und die Nächte schwärzer wurden. Und Jonas ist immer noch da, irgendwo in meinem Leben.

Ich trinke den Kaffee und mustere Malte so beiläufig wie möglich. Ich suche nach der Ähnlichkeit mit *Aaron* – den Auslösern für diese Intensität des Wiedererkennens. Warum hat mich sein Anblick so sehr berührt?

Malte ist ein attraktiver Mann. Er hat fast den gleichen Körperbau, ist aber schlanker und größer als Aaron. Kurzes, weißblondes, stacheliges Haar. Keine Locken. Er blickt auf, schweigt. Auch wenn ich noch nicht alles verstehe, was um mich und mit mir geschieht – bei Weitem nicht alles

–, bildet sich ein zentraler Gedanke heraus: dass ich hier richtig bin. An einem Ort, an dem ich nie zuvor gewesen bin.

Er sieht mich an und lächelt. Ich stutze, sein Lächeln wärmt mich. Er *hat* Aarons Augen. Blaue, intensiv blickende Augen, die ein bisschen funkeln. Schelmische Augen. Kluge Augen.

Malte hält meinen Blick gefangen. „Schön, dich endlich kennenzulernen", sagt er. Es klingt aufrichtig und warm.

Und plötzlich gebe ich meine Reserviertheit auf und fühle mich wohl, geborgen, beschützt. Es fühlt sich gut an. Und richtig. Ich fliege der Sonne entgegen.

Bentes Stimme kommt wie aus der Ferne auf mich zu.

Ein wenig später führt sie mich durch das prachtvolle Haus. Malte begleitet uns.

Ich schließe kurz die Augen, um meinen Fokus neu einzustellen. Ein U-förmiges Wohnzimmer, der rechte Flügel ist in zwei Sitzbereiche unterteilt, von denen der letzte offenbar die Fernsehecke ist. Im linken Flügel liegt eine große Küche. Weiß lackierte hohe Schränke und eine Anrichte aus schwarzem Schiefer. Ich stoße einen tiefen Seufzer der Bewunderung aus.

Bente lächelt. Ungezwungen, ohne Vorbehalt. „Gefällt es dir?"

„Was heißt *gefallen*? Es ist ein fantastisches Haus."

Ich frage mich, warum ich vorhin beim Anblick der Garage diese seltsame Empfindung hatte. Dabei ist dieses Haus ein Wohlfühlort. Drammen ist weit weg, auf einem anderen Planeten.

Maltes Handy vibriert, er drückt die Hörertaste, lächelt. Ich will ihn nicht anstarren, aber ich kann nicht anders. Er ist so verdammt attraktiv, viel zu attraktiv.

„Möchtest du das Gästehaus sehen, Jonte?", fragt Bente.

Ich nicke.

„Dann komm, ich zeige es dir."

Ich folge ihr.

Das Gästehaus liegt unmittelbar hinter der merkwürdigen Garage. Es ist sehr geräumig: eine kleine Eingangshalle, ein helles, freundliches Wohnzimmer mit einer riesigen Fensterfront zur Seeseite. Ein Schlafzimmer, ein Badezimmer, eine in den Wohnraum integrierte Küche.

„Nun, was meinst du? Kann man es hier aushalten?", fragt Bente ironisch.

Ich umarme sie. „Es ist genau das Richtige für mich." Ich atme tief ein. „Du hast einen sehr sympathischen Stiefsohn. Wohnt er in der Nähe?"

„Ja, drei Straßen weiter."

Ich würde gern mehr über ihn erfahren, aber Bente zeigt mir den prall gefüllten Kühlschrank. Ich bin so gerührt und umarme sie ein zweites Mal. „Ich weiß gar nicht, was ich sagen soll. Du bist so großzügig. Danke!"

Sie lächelt und tätschelt meinen Arm. „Ach was. Ich habe deiner Mutter versprochen, dass ich mich ein wenig um dich kümmern werde."

Wir gehen ins Haus zurück. Malte bereitet Sandwiches in der Küche vor. „Ich habe einen Mordshunger", sagt er. „Und ich nehme an, du auch, Jonte." Er zwinkert Bente zu. „Danach mache ich mich an die Arbeit. Versprochen."

„Malte wird ein paar zusätzliche Steckdosen im Haus anbringen", erklärt Bente. „Wenigstens einer in der Familie, der einigermaßen technisch begabt ist. Das hat er gewiss nicht von seinem Vater."

Wir setzen uns an den großen Esstisch, und erst jetzt bemerke ich, wie hungrig ich bin. Zum ersten Mal seit Wochen verspüre ich Appetit.

„Schmeckt es?", fragt Malte.

Ich nicke mit vollem Mund.

„Du hast einiges durchgemacht, hat Bente mir erzählt. Ich weiß, wie es sich anfühlt, den Partner zu verlieren, auch wenn meine Situation anders war als deine. Vor ein paar Jahren habe ich meiner Frau erklärt, dass ich mich scheiden lassen will. Das war hart für sie, und kurz darauf war sie spurlos verschwunden. Ich hatte keine Ahnung, wo sie war oder ob sie noch lebte. Wir haben drei Kinder, die natürlich ganz besonders verstört waren."

Plötzlich ist mir kalt. Mit Mühe schlucke ich das Brot in meinem Mund hinunter. „Ist sie …?"

„Nein. Wir haben sie schließlich gefunden. Es ging ihr schlecht, Sie war krank – hatte einen Hirntumor."

Bente legt ihre Hand auf meinen Arm. „Er war gutartig, und sie konnten sie operieren. Aber sie ist schwer behindert."

„Geistig behindert?", erkundige ich mich.

Malte verzieht kurz das Gesicht. „Psychisch ist sie völlig gesund, haben die Ärzte erklärt. Aber sie ist querschnittsgelähmt, und die rechte Hand macht ihr auch noch Probleme. Isa wohnt jetzt in einem Pflegeheim in Kristiansund." Er bemerkt meinen überraschten Blick. „Ich weiß, das ist nun nicht gerade in der Nähe, aber dort leben viele behinderte Menschen, die noch nicht so alt sind, und werden bestens betreut. Isa wollte unbedingt dorthin, sie ist seit drei Jahren dort."

„Seid ihr geschieden?"

„Ja."

„Das ist wieder eine andere Geschichte", kommentiert Bente seine knappe Antwort. „Aber dafür ist jetzt nicht die Zeit."

Ich frage mich, warum er seine Frau verlassen hat, obwohl sie schwer behindert ist. Ich kann mir nicht vorstellen, dass er einen schäbigen Charakter hat. Er wirkt so sympathisch, zuverlässig und geradlinig, gar nicht schwammig. Sein Lächeln ist nicht gestellt wie das von Jonas, der es er immer nur für Fremde aufgesetzt hat. Mir traut allerdings auch keiner zu, dass ich mit einer Ladung Alkohol im Blut ins Auto steige. Ich bin mir sicher, dass Mom und meine Freundin ihre Hände für mich ins Feuer legen würden, um das zu bekräftigen.

Bente steht auf und räumt den Tisch ab. „Noah ist in unserem Gemüsegarten, er liegt paar Kilometer von hier entfernt, wir nutzen ihn gemeinsam mit Noahs Söhnen. Der Garten ist sein drittes Kind. Ich werde ihm ein paar Sandwiches bringen. Hast du Lust, mich zu begleiten? Noah würde dich gerne kennenlernen."

Bevor ich antworten kann, klingelt mein Handy. Ich hole es aus meiner Tasche, im Display steht *anonym*.

„Jonte Soren."

Stille.

„Hallo?"

„Jo…Jonas hier."

Ich höre ein leises Schluchzen. *Weint Jonas?*

„Ich muss mit dir reden, Jonte. So schnell wie möglich. Hier läuft einiges völlig aus dem Ruder. Ich brauche dich."

Jetzt höre ich es deutlich. Er weint wirklich.

Und wieder gerät ein Tag, der so schön begonnen hat, in Schieflage. Ich lasse die Jalousie in meinem Kopf herunterfallen. Schatten drängen sich aus allen Ecken. Ich verliere die Sonne aus dem Blick.

KAPITEL 35

Bente berührt meine Schulter. „Was ist los, Jonte? Du bist plötzlich so blass. Wer hat da angerufen? Geht es um Annika?"

Wer ist Annika?, will ich fragen. *Wer bist du? Wer bin ich? Lebe ich?* Ja, zu neunzig Prozent. Zehn Prozent zu wenig. Das macht mich unendlich traurig.

Ich versuche, etwas zu sagen, höre den Seufzer und das „Nein, nein", das meine Lippen verlässt.

Bente schaut auf mein Handy. „Soll ich lieber übernehmen?"

Ich schüttle den Kopf und zische: „Was ist los, Jonas?"

„Wo bist du?" Er hat seine Stimme wieder unter Kontrolle.

„Bei deiner Mutter", antworte ich barsch.

Dann ist da nur noch ein kurzes Klicken. Jonas hat aufgelegt.

„Das hättest du besser nicht erwähnen sollen", meint Bente. Ihre Worte hallen in meinem Kopf nach, während ich das Handy in meine Tasche schiebe.

Ich weiß immer noch nicht, wo Jonas wohnt. Wenn er sofort Hilfe braucht, dann kann ich nichts machen.

„Stimmt etwas nicht?" Das leichte Zögern in Bentes Stimme dringt zu mir durch. Ihr Blick ruht auf mir.

„Jonas hat geweint und gesagt, dass er dringend mit mir sprechen müsse. Ich sollte ihn wohl besser zurückrufen. Ich bin mir fast sicher, dass es etwas mit diesem Typen zu tun hat, mit dem er jetzt zusammenlebt. Vielleicht ist das ja doch nicht die große Liebe. Vielleicht ist er ja nicht mal ..."

„Zweifelst du an seiner Homosexualität?"

„Manchmal schon. Und dann auch wieder nicht", antworte ich und zucke die Schulter. „Hast du das denn geahnt? Du bist immerhin seine Mutter."

Meine Frage klingt verlogen, wie die Frage, die sich seit Tagen durch meine Hirnwindungen schlängelt und nicht an die Oberfläche kommen will.

Ich setze mich. Höre zu. Stelle keine Fragen, als Bente mir von Jonas erzählt und es klipp und klar ausspricht: „Jonas ist homosexuell. Schon lange"

Im Grunde weiß ich, dass es stimmt. *Er ist so was von schwul.* Bente hat es immer gewusst. Ich wollte es nie wahrhaben, habe die kleinen Anzeichen nicht miteinander verbunden wie sein Gekicher am Telefon, das Leuchten in seinen Augen, sobald ihn ein gut aussehender Mann anlächelte, sein Ekel vor meinem Körper.

„Jonas war seit frühester Kindheit stets von Jungen umgeben, und er hat sie angehimmelt. Ich habe das immer locker gesehen, aber als Jonas älter wurde, tobte er, sobald ich auch nur eine Andeutung darauf machte oder ihm ein paar Fragen stellte. Und Tore warf mir vor, ich sei gestört und habe eine schmutzige Fantasie. Er lehnte jede Diskussion darüber ab. Ich hätte keine Ahnung von Freundschaften unter Jungen, meinte er. Nicht nur Mädchen könnten sich nah sein. Mit Jonas würde alles stimmen! Er wurde geradezu rasend, denn Homosexualität war ihm zuwider."

Eine Erinnerung flackert in mir auf. Ein gemeinsamer Sommerspaziergang mit Jonas. Menschen schlenderten an der Uferpromenade entlang. Junge Männer, ältere Männer, gut aussehende, unattraktive und merkwürdige Männer. Und immer versuchte Jonas, ihre Blicke einzufangen, sie festzuhalten, sie loszulassen. Manche erwiderten sein Lächeln, die Mehrzahl verzog keine Miene.

Ich habe es gespürt und verdrängt, und das erklärt ein bisschen die undefinierbare Trauer, die mich seitdem tief in meinem Inneren erfasst und nie wieder losgelassen hat.

„Ich habe Tore davon zu überzeugen versucht, dass ein schwuler Sohn nichts Anstößiges ist, danach sprach er wochenlang nicht mit mir. Ihn widerte alles an, was mit diesem Thema zu tun hatte. Ich biss auf Granit. Auch Jonas lehnte jedes Gespräch ab. Er folgte seinem Vater treu in dessen Ideologie. Vielleicht hat er es damals sogar noch selbst geglaubt. Tore ignorierte mich, und Jonas schloss sich ihm freudig an. Er konnte ein verächtliches Schnauben nicht zurückhalten, wenn wir uns im Haus begegneten."

Bente schiebt nachdenklich ihr Glas Wasser auf der Tischplatte hin und her. „Er weigerte sich, den Tanzunterricht zu besuchen, und nahm niemals eine Einladung zu einer Party an, wenn sie von einem Mädchen ausgesprochen wurde. Von seinen Freundschaften erzählte er mir nichts mehr. Damals spielte Jonas oft mit Klassenkameraden Schach. Nur mit Jungen, nehme ich an."

Malte räuspert sich. Ich hatte seine Anwesenheit ganz vergessen. „Worüber machst du dir Sorgen, Jonte? Du bist doch nicht mehr für das Wohlergehen von Jonas verantwortlich."

„Ich frage mich, wovor ich sonst noch meine Augen verschlossen habe. Es ist mir einfach nicht in den Sinn gekommen. Wirklich nicht." Ich zucke mit den Schultern.

„Dann zieh einen Schlussstrich und hör auf, dich verantwortlich zu fühlen." Malte lehnt sich zurück. „Es hat nichts mit dir zu tun. Fällt es dir so schwer, zu akzeptieren, dass Jonas jetzt einen männlichen Partner hat?"

„Eigentlich nicht. Ich hatte nur Probleme damit, *wie* er es mir beigebracht hat. Er hat in all den Jahren nie ein Wort über seine Homosexualität verloren. Und jetzt, wo die Dinge zwischen den beiden aus dem Ruder zu laufen scheinen, braucht er mich plötzlich!"

„Bist du dir sicher, dass diese Beziehung die Ursache seiner Probleme ist?"

Ich verstehe nicht, was Malte damit andeuten will, und blicke zur Seite. Schatten spielen an den Wänden. Ein Spiel, das mir nicht gefällt. „Worum sollte es denn sonst gehen?"

Irgendwo ist ein Geräusch.

„Dein Handy, vermute ich", sagt Malte. „Wo hast du es hingelegt?"

Der dunkelblaue Fjord kommt mir in den Sinn und wie gern ich einfach darin abtauchen würde. Ich greife in meine Handtasche. Das Display kündigt einen anonymen Anrufer an.

„Das wird sicher wieder Jonas sein. Seid bitte einen Moment still." Ich hebe ab.

„Ich muss so schnell wie möglich mit dir reden. Bitte, es ist wichtig."

„In Ordnung." Eine klare Aussage. „Wo bist du?"

„Ich komme zu deinem Haus. Dort treffen wir uns." Dann legt er auf.

„Ich muss noch mal zurück, Bente", erkläre ich.

„Aber du kommst bitte so schnell wie möglich wieder her, denn ich denke, du hast wirklich eine Woche Ruhe nötig." Bente meint es aufrichtig, ich erkenne es auch daran, wie sie mich ansieht.

Malte hadert ein wenig mit meiner Entscheidung. „Ich denke nicht, dass es eine gute Idee ist, sofort zurückzufahren. Es ist schon dunkel. Soll ich dich nach Drammen fahren?"

„Nein danke. Aber das ist sehr lieb von dir."

Malte bringt noch immer Licht in mein Leben. Ich mag ihn, obwohl ich fast gar nichts über ihn weiß, außer dass er geschieden ist und eine querschnittsgelähmte Ex-Frau in einem Heim hat. *Hm* … Sofort kippt das sympathische Bild wieder aus der Verankerung. Vielleicht sollte ich mich erst mal zurückhalten und Malte nicht zu sehr anhimmeln. Immerhin habe ich mich schon viel zu oft in die falschen Männer verliebt.

KAPITEL 36

Jemand war in deinem Haus!

Der Gedanke trifft mich wie ein Knall. Ich steige aus dem Wagen. Es ist eine besonders dunkle Nacht. Winterliche Böen umfangen mich, die Kälte lässt mich schaudern. Die Vorstellung einer plötzlichen Gefahr verursacht mir eine Gänsehaut.

Ich weiß sofort, dass etwas nicht stimmt. Schattenhafte Bilder zucken auf, als ich mich dem Haus nähere und die Tür fokussiere. Sie ist angelehnt, dabei bin ich mir absolut sicher, sie abgeschlossen zu haben.

Erinnerungen flackern auf. Ferne Erinnerungen. Viele Jahre und Tausende Nächte weit entfernt, in einem anderen Monat, an einem anderen Ort. Ich weiß nur allzu gut: Erinnerungen sind wie Geschosse, manche zischen vorbei und erschrecken dich nur. Andere reißen dich in Stücke.

Ich halte diesen Erinnerungsfetzen in Händen, der auf der Schwelle zwischen Nacht und Morgen hängen geblieben ist. Die düster-traurige Geschichte eines Mädchens.

Langsam kehre ich aus meiner inneren Welt zurück, die mich immer wieder völlig vereinnahmt. Wühle mich nach oben aus dem Morast der Vergangenheit. Warum lässt mich die Erinnerung daran einfach nicht los?

Ich schließe eine Sekunde lang die Augen und versuche, die Bilder aus meinem Gedächtnis zu verdrängen. Verdrängen, fliehen, leugnen, darin bin ich wirklich Meister. Dennoch konnte das Mädchen Jonte den Bildern jenes Sommerabends noch immer nicht entkommen. Ich verirre mich lieber in meinem Gedankenlabyrinth, als mich der Wahrheit zu stellen.

Leise betrete ich mein Haus und schließe die Tür. Der Schirmständer neben der Garderobe wurde nach rechts verschoben. Auf der Treppe liegt eine Packung Papiertaschentücher. Vielleicht hat Mom im Haus nach dem Rechten gesehen? Das wäre eine mögliche Erklärung. Wenn ich sie jetzt anrufe, wird sie wissen wollen, weshalb ich nicht bei Bente bin. Ein Gedanke schält sich aus der Dunkelheit heraus: *Zuerst muss ich wissen, was Jonas mir zu sagen hat.* Ich halte kurz inne im Dunkel des Eingangs, dann schalte ich das Licht ein.

Im Haus hängt ein Duft, der mir vage bekannt vorkommt. Ich frage mich, woher ich ihn kenne. Mir ist kalt. Ich drehe die Heizung hoch. Draußen tobt jetzt der Wind ums Haus.

Ich möchte die Wintermonate am liebsten überspringen, insbesondere den Dezember, die Gedanken an wärmere Jahreszeiten kreisen wie Schneeflocken in meinem Kopf. Dabei wird auch noch etwas anderes aufgewirbelt, etwas Wichtiges von einem fernen Tag, das noch in meinem

Unterbewusstsein schlummert. Es muss mit dieser Garage zu tun haben, das ist die einzige Erklärung.

Draußen wird eine Autotür zugeknallt. Schritte kommen auf das Haus zu. Ich hole tief Luft und öffne die Haustür.

Jonas sieht mitgenommen aus und wirkt auf einmal alt. Viel älter, als ich ihn in Erinnerung habe. Er zieht mich an sich und küsst mich ein wenig zu heftig. Vorsichtig löse ich mich aus seiner Umarmung.

„Es läuft gar nicht gut, Jonte", sagt er traurig.

Ich lasse seine Stimme an mir vorbeigleiten, zusammen mit den Bildern einer gemeinsamen Vergangenheit samt all den hässlichen Szenen, die im Schatten spielten. Ich lenke ihn ins Wohnzimmer und warte, bis er sich gesetzt hat.

Er zittert am ganzen Körper. „Kannst du die Heizung nicht ein wenig aufdrehen?"

Noch höher? Seufzend gebe ich seinem Wunsch nach, obwohl es sich vermutlich einfach noch nicht richtig aufgewärmt hat.

„Es war jemand im Haus", sage ich und schaue ihm in die Augen. „Ich glaube, das ist schon einmal passiert, als ich nicht zu Hause war. Es passieren sehr seltsame Dinge, seit du nicht mehr hier wohnst."

„Glaubst du vielleicht, ich schleiche hier herum?" Er zittert nicht mehr. Ich höre die Verärgerung in seiner Stimme, und eine Frage liegt mir auf der Zunge.

„Hast du deine Schlüssel damals wirklich verloren?" Die Frage kommt mir heute zum ersten Mal in den Sinn.

„Was soll das? Ich habe doch extra ein neues Schloss anbringen lassen."

„Aber das beantwortet meine Frage nicht", beharre ich und fixiere ihn. „Hast du deine Schlüssel damals verloren oder nicht?"

Er sieht mich schuldbewusst an, und dann knickt er ein. „Nein, hab ich nicht", gibt er kleinlaut zu. „Sorry, ich habe mir die Ausrede ausgedacht, weil ich ..." Er schweigt.

Ich werde ungeduldig. „Weil du was? Sag es einfach!"

„Es ist nicht einfach, Jonte. Und es tut mir schrecklich leid. Das musst du mir glauben."

„Wovon redest du?"

„Ich war verwirrt und verliebt, blind vor Liebe. Hatte buchstäblich den Verstand verloren. Es war alles Haakons Idee." Er schluchzt auf. „Ich kann es dir nicht sagen."

„Verdammt, wovon redest du da, Jonas?"

„Der Schlüssel ist mir irgendwann abhandengekommen. Deshalb habe ich ja ein neues Schloss einbauen lassen. Punktum. Schluss. Lass mich in Ruhe!"

„Das neue Schloss hat aber nichts gebracht, Jonas." Er weicht mir aus. Ich frage mich, was er in Wahrheit vor mir verbirgt. Ein seltsamer Gedanke, der mich in diesem Moment durchfährt, hält mich davon ab, weiter nachzubohren.

„Wer könnte denn im Haus gewesen sein?" Jonas hat sich wieder unter Kontrolle.

„Nur meine Mutter, sie hat einen Schlüssel, aber sie war bestimmt nicht hier."

„Wieso bist du dir da so sicher?"

Ich lausche unwillkürlich dem Klang seiner Stimme. Etwas ist hier faul. Der Gedanke kreist noch in meinem Kopf, und dann verliere ich ihn. Denn etwas anderes zieht meine Aufmerksamkeit auf sich.

„Es ist der Geruch", antworte ich. „Ich habe ihn vorher schon einmal wahrgenommen. Ich werde weitere Schlösser im Haus anbringen lassen. Und dieses Mal kümmere ich mich selbst darum."

Jonas schweigt, sitzt da mit zusammengekniffenen Augen. Sein Blick streift die Wanduhr.

Meiner auch. *Zwanzig Minuten nach Mitternacht.*

„Du verrennst dich da in etwas …" Jonas hält inne, bewegt sich nicht. Ist auf der Hut.

„Du hast dich ja recht schnell von deiner bedrückten Stimmung erholt."

„Werden wir gegeneinander kämpfen, Jonte?"

Ich möchte etwas entgegnen, aber alles scheint verlangsamt, mein Herzschlag, seine Bewegungen, sein Lidschlag. Ich blicke einen Moment aus dem Fenster und sehe nur leere, ausgedörrte Weiten – ein Spiegelbild meiner inneren Leere.

Jonas beugt sich zu mir. „Jonte? Von welchem Geruch hast du gerade gesprochen?"

Ich stehe auf und blicke in das Gesicht meines Noch-Ehemanns, sehe darin eine beängstigende Flachheit. „Komm!", fordere ich ihn auf.

Jonas folgt mir in den Korridor, atmet tief durch die Nase. Hebt die Augenbrauen. Sieht mich überrascht an. Ich gehe die Treppe hinauf, und er folgt mir. Als wir auf dem Treppenabsatz stehen, atmet er wieder tief ein. Sein selbstbewusster Blick beginnt wieder zu kippen. Ich sehe leichte Panik in seinen Augen. Er geht weiter ins Badezimmer und dann zum Schlafzimmer. Der Duft ist überall. Nur ein Hauch, aber auf subtile Weise präsent. Als möchte mir jemand höhnisch sagen: Ich war hier.

„M…Meine Güte", stammelt Jonas. „Das darf doch nicht wahr sein. Das kann einfach nicht wahr sein."

Er ist kreidebleich, schüttelt den Kopf und muss sich an der Wand festhalten.

„Was willst du damit sagen, Jonas?"

Fast fluchtartig läuft er die Treppe hinunter und ruft zu mir zurück: „Lass gleich morgen früh ein weiteres Schloss anbringen, Jonte, und gib vorerst niemandem einen Ersatzschlüssel!"

Er ist schon an der Haustür, dreht sich noch mal um. „Ich muss jetzt gehen. Wir reden später. Ich muss zuerst etwas klären. Aber ich möchte dich noch um etwas bitten. Unser Bildband wird in zehn Tagen veröffentlicht. Ole Falk, unser Verleger, hat eine Präsentation im Verlag geplant und die Presse eingeladen. Die Vorbestellungen sind phänomenal, und es gibt bereits erste positive Kritiken von renommierten Architekturverbänden und Fachzeitschriften. Ich möchte dich bitten, auch dort zu erscheinen. Es ist wichtig, Jonte."

„*Unser* Bildband", sage ich verärgert. „Das sind alles meine Entwürfe. Es ist *mein* Bildband! Habe ich dir das nicht klargemacht?"

Im Bruchteil einer Sekunde ändert sich der Ausdruck in seinen Augen. Ich kenne diesen Blick. Er ist dunkel, unfreundlich, wütend. Er kommt immer dann, wenn Jonas sich in seinen Erwartungen getäuscht sieht.

„Ich weiß. Nach diesem Band brauche ich wahrscheinlich nur noch ein Projekt, Jonte. Nur noch ein einziges." Es hört sich fast flehend an. „Danach kannst du allein weitermachen."

„Wovon redest du, Jonas? Warum bist du in Wahrheit hier? Du weißt, zu wem dieser Geruch gehört, da bin ich mir ganz sicher! Los! Rede!"

Ich schreite wutentbrannt die Treppe runter. Er kommt plötzlich auf mich zugeschossen und packt mich so heftig an den Armen, dass es schmerzt. „Bitte, stell mir keine weiteren Fragen, Jonte. Es ist nur zu deinem Besten, glaub mir."

Seine Worte hallen nach. Er ist selbst überrascht von der Wucht, mit der er sie ausgesprochen hat. Er hat Angst, das kann ich sehen. Und das macht mir wiederum Angst. Ich bringe kein Wort heraus.

Der Gedanke, der mich vorhin gestreift, steht plötzlich wieder kristallklar in meinem Kopf: *An Jonas ist nichts, gar nichts mehr, woran ich mich klammern könnte. Dieser Mann ist nur noch ein gähnender Abgrund, und wenn ich mich nicht in Acht nehme, werde auch ich in ihn hineinstürzen!*

Jonas drückt schnell einen Kuss auf meine Stirn und rennt aus dem Haus. Eine Weile bleibe ich in der Tür stehen, schaue seinem Wagen hinterher und friere das Bild in meinem Kopf ein.

Ich würde jetzt gerne jemanden um Rat fragen, um mich beruhigen zu lassen. Ein Name kommt mir in den Sinn , aber ich verwerfe den Gedanken sofort. Ich muss mich endlich der Leere stellen, die diese Trennung hinterlassen hat. Ich bin diese ganzen Diskussionen leid, denn zwischen mir und Jonas gibt es nichts mehr zu sagen.

Ich gehe durch den fremden Duft und die Stille, die auf allem lastet, zu einem Glas Wein. Oder ein paar Gläsern mehr. Eine Wärmewelle brandet durch mich, die ich kaum beschreiben kann, brennend, versengend, schmerzlich und tröstlich zugleich. Ich habe diesen Moment schon oft durchlebt, der so einen wundervollen Namen trägt: Rausch. Ich mag diesen zärtlichen Freund, die mir sanft den Nacken streichelt, sich wohlig über meine Glieder ausbreitet und mein Gehirn süß betäubt.

Ich schlafe auf der Couch ein und schrecke in den frühen Morgenstunden aus einem Traum hoch. Ich saß am Ufer des Fjords und schaute auf das dunkle Wasser hinaus. Ein schlammverkrusteter Körper trieb auf der Oberfläche, ein zweiter schwamm auf das Ufer zu. Ich trat ein paar Schritte ins Wasser und starrte sie an. Da wurde auch ich in die Tiefe gezogen.

Ich stehe auf und gehe nach oben ins Bett. Ab morgen werde ich weniger trinken.

KAPITEL 37

Meine Urlaubswoche ist zu Ende. An meiner Haustür gibt es ein neues Dreipunktschloss, und bisher hat noch niemand einen Ersatzschlüssel von mir erhalten.

Zu Bente bin ich nicht mehr zurückgekehrt, aber ich saß drei Nachmittage mit meinem Laptop auf dem Schoß neben Annikas Bett, zeichnete weitere Pläne für das Klosterhotel und sprach dazwischen mit ihr. Annika wird in ein paar Tagen in ein Pflegeheim gebracht. Ihr Vater glaubt, dass sie nicht mehr aus dem Koma aufwachen wird. Das will ich wiederum nicht glauben. Ich bin mir absolut sicher, dass sie zurückkehrt. Es muss so sein. Ich will mir die dunklen Vorhersagen von Annikas Vater nicht länger anhören.

Anfangs trug Annika ein weißes Nachthemd. Ich habe es gegen ein farbentroheres ausgetauscht. Das weiße Nachthemd nahm ich mit nach Hause und legte drei neue in ihren Schrank. Ein sonnengelbes, ein blau getupftes, ein rosafarbenes.

Annika darf kein Weiß mehr tragen, nur dann wird es ihr besser gehen. In diesem Zimmer ist alles weiß, selbst das Badezimmer ist weiß gekachelt. Dagegen hat Annika eine Abneigung, das weiß ich. „Weiß ist steril und ohne jegliche Wärme. Es steht für hygienisch sauberen Sex, Jonte. Und das ist widerlich", hat sie einmal behauptet.

Dennoch hatte sie sich in London ein weißes Kleid gekauft und es an dem Abend des Übergriffs getragen. Auch ich verabscheue Weiß. Es ist die Farbe des Todes. Weiß bedeutet sterben.

Annika muss leben!

Ich habe meiner Mutter erzählt, dass der Verlag eine umfangreiche Buchpräsentation des neuen Architekturbandes geplant hat. Mom will sich das Spektakel nicht entgehen lassen und hat sofort einige Freundinnen eingeladen. Meine Mutter liebt es, eine ganze Schar um sich zu haben. Sie ist eine attraktive, fröhliche Frau und bei Events stets in Weiß oder Schwarz gekleidet, wobei Weiß bei ihr - anders als bei Annika – wie Sonnenlicht wirkt.

Mein Vorgesetzter stimmte nur mit Widerwillen einem weiteren Urlaubstag zu. Seinen Unmut zum Vorwand zu nehmen, um mich zu entschuldigen, kam aber nicht infrage. Jonas hatte dringend um mein Kommen gebeten.

Ich werde hingehen, um herauszufinden, was mit ihm los ist. Was ihn erschreckt hat. Und was es mit diesem kryptischen Satz auf sich hat. *Nach diesem Bildband brauche ich nur noch ein Projekt, Jonte.*

Nur noch *ein* Projekt? Und wofür *braucht* er es? Der Satz rollt immer wieder auf mich zu und schlägt krachend gegen meine Schädeldecke. Sobald ich die Augen schließe, sehe ich auch noch den Ausdruck auf Jonas' Gesicht. Es ist wie ein Rätsel, an dem ich mir die Zähne ausbeiße.

Ich überprüfe das Schloss meiner Haustür jetzt zweimal pro Nacht, aber alles ist ruhig, still. Ich nehme auch keinen seltsamen Geruch mehr wahr. Über alle anderen Vorkommnisse, die ich mir nicht erklären kann, denke ich nicht länger nach. Was das Leben zu kompliziert macht, verdränge ich. So bleibt alles übersichtlich. Und wenn es mir doch zu viel wird, kann ich immer noch vorübergehend in einen Alkoholrausch fliehen.

Das ist nicht gut, Jonte. Wie kommst du da nur wieder raus?, will meine innere Stimme wissen.

Ist es vielleicht notwendig, irgendwo wieder rauszukommen? Ich fühle mich doch eh jeden Tag beschissener. Meine Kollegen tuscheln bereits, ihnen fällt meine Blässe auf. Ob ich krank sei?, fragen sie immer öfter, und mein Boss hat mir nach meiner Rückkehr aus dem Kurzurlaub geraten, den Betriebsarzt aufzusuchen. Er deutete an, dass ich die Fehlgeburt mental wohl noch nicht verarbeitet hätte.

Ich kann ihm wohl kaum sagen, dass diese Fehlgeburt für mich nur ein übler Traum war, ein Trugbild. Ich habe widersprüchliche Gefühle in Bezug auf diese unerklärliche Schwangerschaft und den Abgang: Verleugnung und Angst. Es war alles nur eine Täuschung. Es *schien* nur so gewesen zu sein.

Ich war *nicht* schwanger.

Doch wenn ich an die Worte meiner Ärztin zurückdenke, an die zunehmende Wölbung meines Bauchs, an die leichte morgendliche Übelkeit, die höllischen Schmerzen vor der Fehlgeburt, an den kurzen Krankenhausaufenthalt, dann bekomme ich Panikattacken. Dann realisiere ich, dass etwas mit meinem Körper passiert ist, an das ich keine Erinnerung habe. Dass ich berührt, benutzt und geschändet wurde.

Sobald ich daran denke, bedeckt ein dünner Film aus Schweiß meine Haut. In meinem Kopf quietscht ein Bett, in einem Zimmer, in das ich nur mit Mühe hineinsehen kann. Da ist ein unterdrücktes Lachen, ein unterdrücktes Stöhnen. Jemand kommentiert die Vorgänge in einer monotonen, merkwürdig klaren Sprache. Ich möchte nach dieser Nacht greifen, sie wiederbeleben, um mich an alles zu erinnern. Immer wieder. Immer wieder dieselbe Nacht. Aber da ist nur ein schwarzes Loch, in das ich stürze.

Oder geschah es am helllichten Tag?

Seit Jonas den Versuch unternommen hat, mir etwas zu erzählen, das er bedauert, bin ich unruhig und angespannt und flüchte wieder zu oft in den Rausch. Der Teufelskreis ist nicht unterbrochen und wird es auch niemals sein. Noch halte ich alles in Schach, was sich bedrohlich anfühlt, und weiß, dass ich das nicht mehr lange durchhalten werde. Viele Jahre habe ich nicht zurückgeblickt. Zu lange habe ich alles verdrängt, aber seit der mysteriösen Schwangerschaft, dem Tod meines Babys, dem Suizid meines Schwiegervaters, Annikas Koma und den seltsamen Vorkommnissen in meinem Haus ist der Geist aus der Flasche entwichen. Alles, was ich hinter mir gelassen zu haben glaubte, kehrt zurück wie ein Bumerang. Es packt mich und droht mich zu zermalmen. Ich muss mit jemandem darüber reden, ich möchte ihm den Grund nennen, warum das alles passiert. Denn ich kenne den Grund.

Schuld ...

Als Jugendliche war ich unschuldig und schuldlos. Ein zwölfjähriges Mädchen mit einem Grübchen in einer Wange, ein Mädchen, das immer lächelte. Das gerne an den Fjord baden ging, im Sommer in einem luftigen Kleid, die dunkelblonden Haare zu einem dicken Zopf geflochten. Das Gesicht noch kindlich rund und doch bereits mit unverwechselbaren Zügen. Der Gedanke an das unbekümmert lächelnde Mädchen im Sommerwald, noch ahnungslos, welch bizarre Wende ihr Leben nehmen würde, stimmt mich traurig.

An einem sommerlichen Tag im Juni wurde ich zertrümmert. Auf dem Nachhauseweg vom Musikunterricht wurde ich von zwei Männern in einen Wagen gezerrt und im Sommerwald brutal vergewaltigt. Innerhalb weniger Minuten zerfiel mein bisheriges Leben zu Staub, verloren meine Bäume Blätter und Nadeln, welkten meine duftenden Sommerwiesen. Das, was ich gewesen war, gab es nicht mehr. Ich stürzte in ein Vakuum. Zuerst fiel mir während der Vergewaltigung das Atmen schwer, dann wollte ich es am liebsten ganz einstellen, während ich in die Welt blutete.

Ein Liebespärchen fand mich in jener Nacht in einer alten Garage am Fjord, mehr tot als lebendig. Zwei Ärzte haben mich anschließend zusammengeflickt, andere kümmerten sich um die seelischen Folgen. Körperlich bin ich zwar genesen, aber bis heute habe ich die tiefe seelische Demütigung nicht überwunden. Ich ging nicht mehr zum Musikunterricht und klemmte keine Geige mehr unter mein Kinn. Stattdessen wuchs in mir ein Tier heran: eine innere Stimme hinter meiner Stirn.

Jahre später habe ich mich selbst eines Vergehens schuldig gemacht. Ich wurde zur Mörderin. Bei dem Gedanken an all das spüre ich sofort Panik in mir aufsteigen. Ich kann weder meinen inneren Aufruhr noch meinen Atem beruhigen. Bilder überfallen mich, gegen die ich mich nicht wehren kann: eine Frau in meinem Alter, die allein im Dunkeln am Ufer entlangradelt. Kein Rücklicht an ihrem Fahrrad. Vielleicht wusste sie es, vielleicht auch nicht. Vielleicht glaubte sie, dass die Reflexion ihres weißen Kleides sie ausreichend schützen würde. In dieser Nacht war in mir alles dunkel, schwarz – die völlige Abwesenheit von Farbe und Gefühl. Diese Frau trug Weiß, die Summe aller Farben des Lichts, würde Mom sagen, und dennoch habe ich sie nicht gesehen.

Heute wabert ihr verletzter Körper, der auf dem Pflaster liegt, in meinem Kopf herum wie ein Nebel, ich sehe ihre Reglosigkeit und das viele Blut so deutlich, als würde ich neben ihr knien. Hätte ich sie rechtzeitig bemerkt, wenn ich nüchtern gewesen wäre?

Sobald die dunkle Flut dieser Erinnerungen wieder zur Oberfläche aufsteigt, ringe ich nach Luft, schließe ich die Augen. Dann gehe ich durch das Nichts, einen Schritt nach dem anderen, und fülle meine Lunge mit Waldluft. Ich versuche, mir gut zuzureden, meine Atmung zu verlangsamen und mir zu sagen: Das ist alles *nicht* passiert. Da war nichts, *keine* Frau in einem weißen Kleid, *kein* Blut. Kein Rot auf Weiß. *Keine* Vergewaltigung.

Da war nichts!

Seit ich weiß, wie instabil ich bin, begegne ich dem Leben sehr vorsichtig, bin eine wachsame Zuschauerin geworden, denn sonst droht bei jedem Schritt der Boden unter meinen Füßen nachzugeben. Ich weiß nicht, ob das normal ist. Aber normal ist auch gar keine passende Kategorie, wenn es um mich geht.

Seit Jahren überziehe ich das Leben um mich herum mit Dunkelheit und Lügen. Ich habe genug davon. Ich will endlich auch ans Licht.

KAPITEL 38

Geräuschlos tauchen die Schattenwesen der Erinnerung auf und beginnen ihr Spiel. Trugbilder und Wirklichkeit vermischen sich, Stimmen rufen mich, und die Vergangenheit kehrt zurück.

Fünf Tage bevor es passierte, rammte ich eine Straßenlaterne mit der vorderen Stoßstange. An jenem Tag erfuhr ich, was mit Aaron passiert war – dabei hatte der Tag so gut begonnen. Ich war früh ins Kino gefahren, die ersten Zuschauer warteten dort bereits um halb zwei an der Kasse auf mich.

Ich erinnere mich: Ich betrat das Kino, trällerte einen Song und sah mich mit einem triumphierenden Gefühl um, davon überzeugt, dass meine Beziehung mit Aaron bald kein Geheimnis mehr sein würde. Er kam immer häufiger spätnachts zu mir. Ich träumte von einem weißen Brautkleid und hatte bereits verschiedene Läden aufgesucht, um meinen Körper in weißem Tüll zu bewundern. Ich sprach mit meiner Mutter und Annika über meine Zukunft mit Aaron, aber sie verhielten sich zurückhaltend. Annika warnte mich mit sanfter Stimme: „Er ist noch nicht geschieden, Jonte. Pass bitte auf." Meine Mutter hingegen zeigte keine Spur von Diplomatie: „Ich hoffe, du bist nicht nur sein knackiger Snack in der Mittagspause, Jonte."

Ich reichte gerade einer jungen Frau zwei Kinokarten für *Der Honiggarten*. „Es ist ein Film, der zu keinem Zeitpunkt einen Zweifel daran lässt, wer die Guten und wer die Bösen sind. Das Böse verkörpert ein ehebrechender, zur Brutalität neigender Mann, der so abscheulich ist, dass man keine freie Minute mit ihm verbringen möchte. Wunderschöne Bilder, beschaulich, surreal", erklärte ich einer jungen Frau, als mein Handy vibrierte.

„Geh ruhig ran", sagte meine Kollegin.

Ich verließ den Kassenraum und drückte Sekunden später die grüne Hörertaste. „Jonte Sandvik."

„*Mein* Mann ist vor dreizehn Stunden mit dem Motorrad tödlich verunglückt!", herrschte mich Aarons Ehefrau Liv an und legte auf. Worte ohne Trost und Hoffnung auf Aarons Wiederkehr. Etwas Kaltes griff in meine Brust. Es drückte sich zwischen meinen Rippen hindurch und wühlte in mir herum.

Ich ging wieder in den Kassenraum. Eine leichte Taubheit breitete sich über meine rechte Wange bis zum Nasenflügel aus. Ich betastete mein Gesicht mit den Fingerspitzen und fühlte nichts und dachte: *Es gibt keine Stille, die dem Verlust eines Menschen gleichkommt.*

Meine Kollegin spürte, dass etwas nicht in Ordnung war. Sie stand auf, kam auf mich zu und lächelte mich an. Ihr Lächeln sollte mich aufbauen, aufmuntern, Zuversicht verbreiten. All das tun, wozu kein Anlass bestand. Danach weist die dunkle Flut der Erinnerung zahlreiche Lücken auf. Ich saß plötzlich in meinem Auto und fuhr durch die Gegend, wollte Mom sehen, aber sie unterrichtete zu dieser Stunde. Ich beschleunigte den Wagen und hörte Aaron in meinen Gedanken lachen. *„Wann lerne ich denn nun endlich meine zukünftige Schwiegermutter kennen?"*

Schwiegermutter, das klang damals hoffnungsvoll. Erinnerungen dröhnten durch meinen Kopf, leise gemachte Versprechungen, deren Auswirkungen Aaron und ich noch nicht kannten, still geschworene Treue.

Die Zeit musste zurückgestellt werden, damit all das wahr werden konnte.

„Aaron ist nicht tot. Er darf nicht tot sein." Ich hörte meine gedämpfte Stimme, mein Stöhnen, meine Schreie, aber nicht mein Weinen.

Ich empfand mich als Schatten in einem leeren Raum, den ich gefunden hatte, ohne danach zu suchen. Weiß war die gekachelte Wand, die mich umgab. Ein Tisch aus Stahl stand da. Medizinische Utensilien wie Skalpelle, Sägen. Auf dem Tisch lag Aaron unter einem weißen Laken. Tot! Kein Schlaf, kein Erwachen. Das Leben war aus seinen Händen, seinen Armen und Beinen, aus seinem Körper geflossen. Ich ging um den Tisch, während mein Schatten an den Wänden zusammenbrach …

Den ersten Aufprall habe ich kaum bemerkt, der zweite war ohrenbetäubend und brachte mich zur Besinnung. Ich hörte ein knisterndes Geräusch, ein Krachen, ein Schleifen.

Ich stieg aus. Ein Mann näherte sich meinem Wagen und sah mich grinsend an. „Ich hoffe, ihre Träume waren den Aufprall wert. Der Baum hat es heil überstanden." Er warf einen Blick auf die vordere Stoßstange. „Hm … Das wird ein teures Vergnügen!"

Ich hätte ihm gerne einen Tritt verpasst, seinen Kopf auf die Pflastersteine geschmettert. Ich wollte die ganze Welt vernichten.

Meine Mutter fuhr mich in die Werkstatt. Weder sie noch die Automechaniker ahnten, dass die Stoßstange bereits zweimal mit einem Hindernis in Berührung gekommen war. Als der Mechaniker die Stoßstange auswechselte, dachte ich an die brachiale Gewalt, die ich dem Autofahrer an der Unfallstelle zufügen wollte.

Alles Vertraute war aus mir gewichen, an seine Stelle war eine feindselige, vorwurfsvolle Stille getreten – und der Alkohol. Er verscheuchte das Unfassbare wie einen bösen Gedanken.

KAPITEL 39

In der dreistöckigen Kunstgalerie stolpere ich mehr oder weniger in jeder Ecke über einen Stapel unseres Architekturbandes *Grundriss*. Architekten, Presseleute, Kritiker und geladene Gäste halten ein Exemplar in den Händen und diskutieren über den Band.

Es ist warm, die Luft ist voller summender Stimmen. Leise Musik im Hintergrund. Der Geruch von Alkohol steigt mir in die Nase. Ich möchte mich umdrehen und gleich wieder verschwinden. Doch der Besitzer der Galerie kommt auf mich zu und begrüßt mich herzlich.

„Ich habe gehört, dass Sie nicht gerade nach dieser Art von Aufmerksamkeit suchen", schmunzelt er. „Umso mehr freue ich mich, dass Sie hier sind."

Er ist sympathisch, und ich spüre, dass er aufrichtig meint, was er sagt. Folglich werde ich mich heute *nicht* unnahbar geben, sondern mich ein wenig zugänglicher zeigen. Wenn ich später unter meinem eigenen Namen veröffentliche, muss ich mich ohnehin anders verhalten, aber noch ist es nicht so weit.

Ein paar Architekten zeigen auf mich. Ich möchte immer noch hier raus und meide den Blickkontakt mit den Gästen, die in *Grundriss* blättern. Vor einigen Tagen habe ich das Interview einer amerikanischen Fotografin gelesen, die gestand, dass sie es bei ihrem ersten Bildband kaum gewagt hatte, den Stapel in einer Buchhandlung anzusehen. Sie wollte davonlaufen, aber gleichzeitig wie eine Löwin um den Stapel herumschleichen. Ich empfinde ähnlich und möchte jeden Stapel *Grundriss* in der Galerie überwachen, ihn im Arm halten, jeden Band durchblättern und ihn vor der Außenwelt schützen. Ich möchte sämtliche Exemplare aus dieser Galerie mitnehmen. Das ist es, was ich jetzt *wirklich* tun möchte.

Neben mir schwatzt eine Frau in einem leuchtend gelben Hosenanzug. Das Bedürfnis, mich taub zu stellen, funktioniert nicht.

„Ich bin Haakons Schwester", schnattert sie mit schriller Stimme. „Ich war so stolz, als Haakon uns mit Jonas bekannt gemacht hat. Das war vielleicht eine Überraschung." Sie hört einfach nicht auf. „Ich glaube, es war im letzten Winter, Ende Februar, beim Schlittschuhlaufen."

Schlittschuhlaufen? Im letzten Winter? Ende Februar? Hatte Jonas nicht Mai erwähnt? Was schwätzt dieser nervige Kanarienvogel da nur?

Ein Mann, schmal und blass, starrt mich an. Über seine Lippen huscht ein unangenehmes Lächeln. Er geht auf Jonas zu und flüstert ihm etwas ins Ohr. Jonas schaut mich an, und ein breites Lächeln überzieht sein Gesicht, dann kommt er auf mich zu.

„Ah, da bist du ja, Jonte! Ich freu mich sehr, dass du gekommen bist", ruft er aus und flüstert mir dann ins Ohr: „Ole Falk hat vor einer Stunde verkündet, dass die erste Auflage des neuen Bildbandes bereits verkauft wurde. Die zweite Auflage ist schon in Vorbereitung."

Ich schaue an ihm vorbei zu dem seltsamen Mann, der uns anstarrt. „Wer ist das da, Jonas?"

„Das ist Haakon Jensen, mein Partner!", antwortet er mit einem Anflug von Stolz und winkt den Mann herbei.

Sein Anblick löst mehrere Reaktionen zugleich in mir aus, aber es passt alles nicht richtig zusammen. Müdigkeit, Nervosität, Panik, Angst, Schweißausbruch, Zittern. All das vermischt sich, während er auf uns zukommt. Seit der Trennung schlummert eine instinktive Abneigung gegen den bislang unbekannten Rivalen in meinem Körper, und in diesem Moment kommt all mein Abscheu hoch.

Ich versuche mich ihm zu entziehen, aber es gibt kein Entrinnen, ich muss Haakon die Hand geben. Sein Griff fühlt sich fest an, aber nicht unangenehm. Überraschend beugt er sich zu mir herunter, um meine Wange zu küssen. Ich will mich abwenden, erstarre aber gleich zu Beginn dieser Bewegung, als ich ihn rieche.

Dieser Geruch.

Es ist der Geruch auf der Treppe, der Geruch in meinem Haus. Der Geruch des Eindringlings. Der Geruch, der Jonas so erschreckt hat.

„Du warst in meinem Haus", zische ich.

Er hebt die Augenbrauen, und da erkenne ich ihn. Es verschlägt mir den Atem. Er ist schmaler, hat kürzeres Haar, aber ja, er ist es. „Du arbeitest in dem Schlüsseldienstladen", stoße ich heraus. „Ich habe neue Schlüssel bei dir machen lassen."

„Nicht mehr", antwortet Haakon lächelnd. „Habe dort aufgehört. Bin zu beschäftigt mit den Vorbereitungen für meine neue Firma. *Unsere* neue Firma." Er dreht sich um und flüstert Jonas etwas ins Ohr. „Wir werden einen Weinhandel eröffnen."

„Komm", sagt Jonas und nimmt meinen Arm. „Falco wartet. Es geht gleich los. Ich erkläre es dir später, Jonte."

Ich achte nicht weiter auf ihn, sondern frage mich, was Haakon Jonas zugeflüstert hat. Er hat große Macht über meinen Noch-Ehemann, das spüre ich. Oder ist es nur meine überbordende Fantasie? Werde ich gerade hysterisch? Gerate ich völlig außer Kontrolle?

Ich zwinge mich zu Gelassenheit. Über all das muss ich später in aller Ruhe nachdenken und in Betracht ziehen, dass ich vielleicht durchgedreht bin, weil ich hier unter Menschen sein musste.

Ich blicke mich um und entdecke Mom mit ihren Freundinnen, sie winken mir zu.

„Wie lange kennst du Haakon schon?" Meine Stimme zittert.

Jonas blinzelt. „Ich erkläre dir später alles. Aber nicht jetzt. Jetzt stellen wir unseren neuen Bildband vor, Jonte. Reiß dich zusammen!", zischt er.

Meine Mutter kommt auf mich zu und umarmt mich. „Schau dich nur an, Jonte. Du wirst noch eine weltberühmte Architektin. Wer ist dieser Junkie, der ständig Jonas hinterhertrottet?"

„Junkie? Wie kommst du den auf so was, Mom?"

„Da macht mir keiner was vor. Schau dir nur seine Augen an. Diese verengten Pupillen sind eindeutig. Und sieh doch mal, wie wacklig er auf den Beinen ist."

Ich taumle etwas, mir wird alles zu viel, ich fühle mich bei der bevorstehenden Präsentation überfordert. Mich widert diese ganze Öffentlichkeitsarbeit an.

Jonas fängt mich rechtzeitig auf. „Halte durch, Jonte. Heb dir die Panikattacke für später auf. So schlimm ist es doch gar nicht. Lächle!"

Er befürchtet, dass ich die Galerie fluchtartig verlassen könnte, ich kann es in seinen Augen lesen. Aber da ist noch etwas, das darüber hinausgeht: eine höllische Angst.

Wovor?

KAPITEL 40

Ole Falk macht den Anfang. Er lobt das Architektenduo *JO*, nennt uns den Traum eines jeden Bauherrn. Während seiner euphorischen Beschreibung unseres Werdegangs ist regelmäßig Applaus zu hören. Schließlich übergibt er Jonas das Wort, der eine beeindruckende Rede aus dem Ärmel schüttelt. Vielleicht hat er sie sich vorher zurechtgelegt, aber er hält sie so frei, dass er alle mitreißt. Ich kann es kaum fassen. Ist das derselbe Jonas, der schüchterne, unsichere Mann, mit dem ich verheiratet bin? Der zwar gut reden kann, aber nicht mit dieser rhetorischen Intensität. Seine Augen funkeln, seine Gestik unterstreicht die Worte, die nur so aus seinem Mund sprudeln. Er spricht von einem Kaminzimmer mit asiatischen Stilelementen, von einer Küche aus afrikanischen Holzarten, von einem Badezimmer aus italienischem Marmor und einer Bibliothek aus Muranoglas und Stahl, von Wasserelementen, die eine Ozeanwelle andeuten, von Purismus und Bauhausstil. Er zeigt ein Wissen und eine Wortgewalt, die ich ihm nie zugetraut hätte. Dieser Mann, der nur ein paar Schritte von mir entfernt steht, ist mir vollkommen fremd.

Er sieht Haakon häufig an, der ihm dann meist eine Kusshand zuwirft. Mir wird übel davon. Am liebsten würde ich zu meiner Mutter gehen und ihr leise alle meine Ängste gestehen: meine Selbstzweifel als Jugendliche, diese furchtbare Eröffnung der Gynäkologin über den Tod meines Babys und jene dunkle Macht um Haakon Jensen, die ich geradezu körperlich spüren kann, die mich zermalmen und zu Boden drücken will. Dabei sieht er mich nicht einmal an, sondern hängt mit den Augen an Jonas.

Ich möchte in die Arme meiner Mutter flüchten. Mich in den beruhigenden Duft ihres Parfüms schmiegen. Stattdessen starre ich auf Haakon Rückens, auf seine an den Körper gelegten Arme, den muskulösen Nacken, die raschen, knappen Bewegungen, wenn er sich zur nächsten Kusshand rüstet.

Mir ist nur zu sehr bewusst, dass ich mich jeden Tag ein wenig mehr einem gefährlichen Bereich nähere, aus dem es irgendwann kein Entkommen mehr geben wird.

Da höre ich wie durch Watte, wie jemand meinen Namen erwähnt. Jonas. Plötzlich bricht das Getuschel über mich herein. Das war nicht so abgemacht, Jonas. Du weißt doch, dass ich noch anonym bleiben möchte.

Im Raum wird gemunkelt, man dreht sich nach mir um. Ich fühle mich wie auf dem Präsentierteller. „*Sie* ist das?", flüstert jemand direkt hinter mir. „Nein, wirklich? Ich habe eine aufregendere Persönlichkeit erwartet."

Meine Mutter zwinkert mir zu und kommt näher. „Das ist nur der Neid", sagt sie leise. „Du bist hier der Star, mein Schatz."

154

Ich zucke mit den Schultern. „Wie kommen wir hier raus?", zische ich, aber sie legt mir beruhigend die Hand auf die Schulter.

Wenig später werden Sekt und Häppchen serviert, Jonas und ich signieren die Bildbände. Der Galerist strahlt, er ist am Umsatz beteiligt. „Ich hoffe, wir können das bald mal wiederholen."

Nach *Grundriss* wird das Architektenduo *JO* Geschichte sein, möchte ich ihm sagen. Es hat mich in meiner Entscheidung bestärkt, als ich Haakon offen mit Jonas flirten sah. Ich zwinge mich, nicht an diesen Mann zu denken. Heute ist Party-Time. Und ich bin eine Partylöwin.

Na dann lass mal sehen und blase hier nicht Trübsal. Das ist dein Auftritt, Jonte. Wenn du das Projekt in Zukunft allein durchziehen möchtest, kannst du nicht länger die graue Maus im Eck spielen. Showtime!, feuert mich meine innere Stimme an.

Back-Vocal hat recht! Ich werde nicht länger über Gerüche im Haus oder Schritte auf der Treppe nachgrübeln. Und es ist egal, ob dieser Dreckskerl einen Schlüssel zu meinem Haus hatte, denn ich habe nun ein neues Schloss.

Aber da ist noch etwas, das meine Feierlaune trübt. Etwas Hässliches. Etwas von Grund auf Böses, das mir keine Ruhe lässt.

Die Vergewaltigung.

Die zweite Vergewaltigung, um genau zu sein, denke ich bitter. *Ist sie der eigentliche Prolog dieser tragikomischen Farce?*

Aber ich will jetzt nicht daran denken. Nein! Jetzt ist nicht der richtige Moment, Jonte!

Stattdessen lächle ich all diese begeisterten Leute an, die mir sagen, dass sie unsere Projekte faszinierend finden und schon sehr neugierig auf unser nächstes Bauwerk sind. Ich geselle mich an Jonas' Seite. Meist überlasse ich ihm das Wort und staune, wie fachmännisch mein Noch-Partner über edle Baumaterialien aus der ganzen Welt spricht und über den Fortschritt in der modernen Architektur. Haakon, der uns nicht von der Seite weicht, kommentiert, dass es atemberaubende neue Pläne seien. Seine Stimme kommt mir vertraut vor, und zwar über die Erinnerung an den Handwerker hinaus. Wo habe ich sie schon mal gehört? Warum fällt mir nicht ein, wo das gewesen sein könnte?

Ich ignoriere mein zunehmendes Misstrauen. Blende auch das Bild der schwer verletzten Annika aus, das vor meinem inneren Auge immer wieder mal vorwurfsvoll aufflackert. Ich bin nervös, aufgewühlt und vollkommen irritiert. Das wird der Grund für die unbehaglichen Gedanken sein, die sich mir ständig aufdrängen. Aber ich lasse mir meine Unruhe nicht anmerken.

Meine Mutter drückt mir ein Glas Champagner in die Hand. „Stoß mit uns an, Kind. Oder hättest du lieber etwas Alkoholfreies?"

Ich nicke und bin erleichtert, als sie sich mit dem Champagner wieder zu ihren Freundinnen gesellt.

„Ich werde mich heute zur Feier des Tages betrinken", verkündet Jonas lauthals.

„Da bin ich dabei. Immerhin bringt Falk uns ja nach Hause", sagt Haakon und grinst.

Ich signiere ein weiteres Exemplar von Grundriss. „Wo ist Euer Zuhause?", frage ich beiläufig.

„Wir wohnen in Drammen", antwortet Jonas leise.

„In Drammen? Warum hast du mir das verschwiegen?"

„Aber, Jonte, ich habe nie ein Geheimnis daraus gemacht. Du hast mich einfach nicht danach gefragt." Sein Gesicht ist angespannt. Seine Augen blicken seltsam kalt. Aber das ist mir nicht neu.

Ich beuge mich tief vor, damit nur er mich hören kann. „Nach Grundriss war es das mit dem Architektenduo. JO ist finito! In Zukunft firmiere ich unter meinem eigenen Namen, denn ich werde diesen grotesken, beängstigenden Kerl, den du dir da geangelt hast, bestimmt nicht mitfinanzieren. Meine Mutter meint, dass er Drogen nimmt. Für den Dreck wirst du alleine aufkommen müssen. Ich werde gleich morgen einen Anwalt aufsuchen!"

„Wie du willst", flüstert er gepresst. „Aber die Konsequenzen wirst du selbst tragen müssen."

Mir läuft es eiskalt den Rücken runter, aber da drängen sich die Gäste plötzlich vor dem Signiertisch, und Haakon lacht laut auf. „Ruhe bewahren. Ihr kommt alle noch dran!", verspricht er.

An Jonas' Art ist wieder dieses Fiese, Hämische, dem ich mich instinktiv entziehen möchte. Als ich noch seine Ehefrau war, bin ich mit der Umgebung verschmolzen, wenn dieses grausame Funkeln in seinen Augen aufblitzte.

Mein Blick huscht über Haakon. Vielleicht bin ich in seinen Augen etwas Fremdes, Bedrohliches ... das er mit Jonas' Einverständnis beseitigen will.

„... war es das mit dem Architektenduo. "Haakon stand nahe genug, er muss es gehört haben. Und was schließt er daraus? Sein neues Zuhause, seine Zukunft – durch mich bedroht. Jonte die Zerstörerin. Die man aufhalten muss ...

Fick dich, Haakon Jensen!

Als ob er meine Gedanken hören könnte, bohren sich Haakons Augen in meine. Sein Blick ist eisig.

Ich glaube, er ist nur ein Maulheld, ein Jammerlappen, der Probleme mit Frauen hat und sich deshalb lieber homosexuell gibt. Ein Schmarotzer, der sich an Jonas' Erfolg dranhängen will.

Vielleicht unterschätze ich ihn aber auch gewaltig.

Ich habe das Licht eingeschaltet, bevor ich gegangen bin, denn ich möchte nicht, dass das Haus im Dunkel liegt, wenn ich zurückkomme.

Als ich mich meinem Heim nähere, spüre ich wieder das Stechen im Magen, doch meine Angst ist diesmal unbegründet. Das Haus begrüßt mich genauso, wie ich es verlassen habe.

Ich bin beschwipst, denn natürlich habe ich doch noch was getrunken. Berauscht, aber mehr von meinem Erfolg. Mein Atem bildet in der Kälte eine kleine Rauchwolke, und als ich die Haustür aufschließe, fühle ich mich längst ernüchtert.

Im Wohnzimmer genehmige ich mir ein letztes Glas Wein, während ich den atemberaubenden Blick auf den Drammensfjord genieße. Er schimmert schwarz in der mondklaren Nacht, der Wald wirkt wie ein Scherenschnitt. Sein Saum ist dunkelgrün, der Boden weiß, der Himmel funkelt nachtblau. Im Wald habe ich stets das Gefühl, allein auf der Welt zu sein. Die Augen der Nacht streifen mich nur. Gleiten ab. Niemand ist in Eile. Die Lebewesen beachten mich nicht. Sie laufen weiter und verschwinden, durch die Bäume dringt gedämpftes Quietschen, manchmal ein Stöhnen oder der Schrei einer Eule. In den Wäldern werde ich zu einem Schatten. Dort bin ich sicher.

Ich sollte die merkwürdigen Geschehnisse in meinem Leben aufschreiben. Um sie festzuhalten. Damit ich nichts davon vergesse. Das hätte ich schon viel früher tun sollen. Schon als Kind. Vielleicht hätte es mir viel mehr geholfen als die endlosen Gespräche mit der Psychologin, während meiner Jugend und auch später. Pflaster auf einer Wunde, die nur verdecken, aber nichts heilen.

Ich öffne die Terrassentür, der Winter fühlt sich plötzlich wie ein Sommer an, und für den Bruchteil einer Sekunde habe ich das Gefühl, dass die Zeit kein bisschen weitergegangen ist. Hier steht das zwölfjährige Mädchen, das vergewaltigt worden ist.

Ich gehe wieder hinein. Ich ertrage den Gedanken daran nicht und schenke mir ein weiteres Glas Wein ein, um die Zwölfjährige zu verscheuchen. Nur auf Alkohol ist Verlass.

KAPITEL 41

Ich habe noch immer keinen Anwalt konsultiert.

Seit ich Haakon Jensen getroffen, den kalten Ausdruck in seinen Augen gesehen, seinen Geruch wahrgenommen und die Bedrohung, die von ihm ausgeht, gespürt habe, fokussiere ich mich auf einen einzigen Gedanken: Ich möchte, dass Annika aufwacht, selbst wenn es weitere sechs Monate dauern wird. Sie muss aufwachen und sich wieder erholen. Vielleicht kann sie Haakon als Einbrecher und Angreifer identifizieren.

Ohne Annika stehe ich mit leeren Händen da. Dann muss ich diesen kriminellen Mistkerl in meiner Gegenwart erdulden und alle vor ihm beschützen, die mir am Herzen liegen. Ich muss äußerst vorsichtig sein, darf vor allem keine Fehler machen. Jede Entscheidung, die den Umgang mit diesem Bastard betrifft, muss wohlüberlegt sein. Wie gehe ich am besten mit ihm um?

Der Thriller auf meinem Nachttisch enthält ein interessantes Szenario, das ich auf ihn anwenden möchte: Jemand wird unter Drogen gesetzt, zu einem verlassenen Waldstück gebracht und unter einem Gestrüpp versteckt, unbekleidet, damit er abkühlt. Es ist eine saubere Art zu töten, sozusagen blutarm.

Willst dir wohl nicht die Hände schmutzig machen, stänkert Back-Vocal. *Aber dann vernichte lieber den Krimi, bevor ihn die Ermittler bei dir finden.*

Ich habe in diesen Tagen entsetzliche Gedanken. Und ich steigere mich in Dinge hinein. Aber egal was ich tue, es wird nie wieder so sein, wie es mal war. Ich denke immer noch an eine lebende Annika, obwohl ich es besser weiß, denn Annikas Vater hat mich angerufen.

Mit dieser Katastrophe habe ich nicht gerechnet, ich wollte nur nicht, dass Annika den Rest ihres Lebens als Gewächshauspflanze verbringen muss. Mom und Annikas Vater haben immer wieder versucht, mich davon zu überzeugen, dass sie wahrscheinlich nie wieder aufwachen wird, doch ich wies das jedes Mal empört von mir.

Nun ist Annika tot.

Diese Woche schleppte ich mich jeden Tag zur Arbeit. Dabei wollte ich nur neben Annikas Sarg sitzen, sie ansehen und mit ihr sprechen. Ihr Vater hat sie im Bestattungsunternehmen aufbahren lassen, damit ich nach Dienstschluss zu ihr gehen und bis spät in den Abend bleiben konnte.

Der Beerdigungsunternehmer brachte mir hin und wieder einen Kaffee und ein Sandwich. Ich habe ihm von Annika erzählt, und er hat mir zugehört.

Annika ist tot. Sie erlitt einen Herzstillstand. Ich frage mich, ob die Person, die sie getötet hat, jetzt wegen Mord angeklagt werden kann.

Haakon ist ihr Mörder, davon bin ich überzeugt.

Ich kann es immer noch nicht glauben. Obwohl ich gestern neben meiner Mutter und ihrem Vater in der ersten Reihe im Krematorium saß, will ich nicht an Annikas Tod denken. Ich möchte, dass sie heute Abend anruft und mir kichernd mitteilt, dass sie irgendwo in London oder in Paris wieder einen richtigen Mistkerl getroffen hat. Dass es verrückt war, was sie mit diesem Bastard erlebt hat. Dass das Wetter fantastisch war. Solche Dinge möchte ich hören.

Annika. Das blonde, schmale Smiley-Gesicht mit den funkelnden Pupillen. Nur wenn sie über ihre Mutter sprach, veränderte sich der Ausdruck in den fröhlichen Augen. Sie hatte ihre Mutter so sehr vermisst und musste mir das Gefühl nicht erklären. Ich weiß, wie sich das anfühlt. Nach dem Tod meines Vaters habe ich ebenso empfunden.

Unter Annikas fröhlicher Art verbarg sich ein nachdenklicher, sehr verletzlicher Mensch. „Ich bin außer Kontrolle geraten, Jonte", hat sie mir einmal gestanden. „Ich erkenne immer zu spät, was ich verloren habe." Annika wollte sich nicht binden. Sie hatte Angst. Angst davor, verlassen zu werden.

Als Mom mich nach der Einäscherung nach Hause brachte, lag ein riesiger Blumenstrauß mit einem Kondolenzgruß von Bente und Malte vor meiner Haustür.

„Wie nett von ihnen. Ich werde die Blumen in eine Vase stellen", sagte Mom.

Ich rief Bente an und erzählte ihr von der Beisetzung. Und während ich erwähnte, wie schön sie gewesen sei, fiel mir auf, dass ich unsinnige Dinge von mir gab. Eine schöne Beerdigung? Was soll denn daran schön sein? Es war schrecklich, widerlich, unfair. Jemand anders hätte in dem Sarg liegen sollen. Das schmale Gesicht mit den kalten Pupillen taucht vor meinem inneren Auge auf. Ich habe ständig seinen Geruch in der Nase. *Wer ist dieser Junkie?* Braucht Jonas Geld, um die Sucht seines neuen Partners zu finanzieren? Haakon hat in der Galerie sieben oder acht Gläser Champagner getrunken. Er hat demnach auch eine hohe Alkoholtoleranz. Wie ich auch.

Trotzdem konnte ich dieser Frau in ihrem weißen Kleid damals nicht mehr ausweichen. Auch sie ist tot.

Annika ist tot. Mein Schwiegervater ist tot.

Und ich habe es nicht verhindern können.

KAPITEL 42

Einmal eine Nacht durchschlafen …

Ich habe kaum ein Auge zugetan. Unentwegt glaubte ich, in der vergangenen Nacht Schritte im Haus zu hören. Ich saß auf der Bettkante, stampfte mit den Füßen auf den Boden und dachte: *Bitte lass mich schlafen*, dachte an mein wiederholtes Stoßgebet an alles Belebte außerhalb meiner vier Wände, an die Natur da draußen, die sich immer wieder bemerkbar machte.

Irgendwann ging ich in die Küche, nur um festzustellen, dass die Katze des Nachbarn sich wieder einmal auf meiner Terrasse mit einer Maus vergnügte. Später hörte ich ihr Kratzen an den Holzbohlen des Gartenhäuschens. Sie wetzte sich die Krallen, markierte ihr Revier – unermüdlich in der finsteren Nacht.

Das Kratzen und die eingebildeten Schritte verstummten irgendwann, und ich schlüpfte wieder unter die Bettdecke. Wenig später drang ein Flüstern in der Nacht zu mir durch: *Jonte …*

Ich zog die Bettdecke über meinen Kopf und vernahm von da an vertrautere Geräusche: das Knarzen des Lattenrostes, das laute, heisere Gekrächze der Nebelkrähen, den Wind, der heulend ums Haus fegte. Die Stille im Haus hingegen beunruhigte mich auch weiterhin. Ich weiß, dass das alles auf meinen labilen Zustand hindeutet, aber was nützt mir das, wenn ich einfach Angst habe.

Ich döste wieder ein. Zarte Farben raubten mir im Schlaf den Atem, bis ich Worte vernahm: hüpfende, knallende Ausrufe voller Staunen. Ein ersticktes, tiefes Stöhnen, als ränge irgendetwas mit dem Tod. Es ließ mich wieder hochschrecken und in der Küche nach dem Rechten sehen. Doch abermals war es nur die Nacht, die mir etwas vorgaukelte. Dafür brannten sich seltsame Worte wie Flammen in meinen Kopf. Meinen Mund verließen sie nicht, dem entwich nur wirres Zeug.

In der vergangenen Nacht überprüfte ich mindestens zehnmal den Riegel an der Haustür, leuchtete unzählige Male mit der Taschenlampe den Garten aus. *Dieses Haus beschützt mich nicht!* Selbst auf eine heiße Dusche habe ich verzichtet, denn dann hätte ich einen Eindringling auf der Treppe nicht mehr hören können.

Bente hat mich für den zweiten Weihnachtstag nach Hyggen eingeladen. Noahs Söhne werden auch mit ihren Familien kommen, und ich werde Malte wiedersehen. Er ist der wahre Grund, warum ich die Einladung angenommen habe. Ich muss zugeben, dass ich mich auf ihn freue. Ich mag ihn. Er schreibt mir E-Mails, in denen er mir von seinem Alltag berichtet.

Unsere zarte Freundschaft ergibt sich aus all den Kleinigkeiten, die uns beiden wichtig sind: gemeinsame Interessen, gegenseitige Sympathie, ein humorvoller Blick auf die Höhen und Tiefen des Lebens. Natürlich geht Letzteres nicht immer, aber für mich ist diese Fähigkeit eine Art Ideal, und ich glaube, für Malte auch.

Er besitzt ein kleines Hotel mit einem Fitnesscenter, das er um eine Sauna erweitern möchte, er hat mich als Architektin um Rat gebeten. Ich bin mir sicher, dass das nur ein Vorwand war, um mich nach Hyggen zu locken. Ich frage mich, woher er weiß, dass ich Architektur studiert habe. Ich kann mich nur daran erinnern, dass ich ihm von dem Job im Kino erzählt hatte.

Ich maile und chatte also mit einem Mann, den ich nur flüchtig kenne, der mich aber tief berührt. Es ist ein gutes Gefühl und gleichzeitig eine gefährliche Falle. Eine kreative Alkoholikerin und ein erfolgreicher Geschäftsmann: eine Pretty-Woman-Variante.

Meine Gedanken wandern oft zu diesem Mann, und ich weiß nicht, was ich davon halten soll. Mir gefallen seine E-Mails, die wie Sterne am nächtlichen Himmel meine innere Dunkelheit erhellen. Sobald ich meine Augen schließe, verlockt er mich mit der Verheißung von Aufregung und Abwechslung, verführt mich in Gedanken, indem er uns beiden ein Abenteuer in Aussicht stellt. Aber Malte ist mehr als nur ein Abenteuer, und mein Gefühl ist ganz anders als bei Aaron, der mit einem letzten Aufleuchten über den dunklen Himmel davongesaust ist, bevor er für immer aus meinem Leben verschwand. Malte soll nicht einfach so am Horizont verlöschen.

Ich würde gerne noch ein paar Stunden schlafen; in der verkrampften Position kippt mein Kopf zur Seite, dennoch fange ich ihn in Sekundenabständen immer wieder auf und begradige intuitiv meinen Körper.

Grübelnd sitze ich in der Stille, mit dem Kissen im Nacken, hoffe, auf die Fragen meines Lebens eine Antwort zu finden, während die Nacht sich unmerklich verabschiedet, auf einem schmalen Grat zwischen Schwarz, Rot und Blau, um mit dem Morgen zu verschmelzen. Wenn das Flammenmeer die Ränder der Nacht zu erhellen beginnt.

Worte sind unzuverlässig. Für mich gewinnen sie nur auf dem Papier an Bedeutung. Auch deshalb bin ich ein schweigsamer Mensch. Ich schweige über all das, was mir widerfahren ist und das mich zu dem Menschen gemacht hat, der ich jetzt bin – eine labile Kassiererin und hoffnungsvolle Architektin und heimliche Trinkerin. Niemand weiß davon. Der Alkohol wärmt und schützt mich vor der Welt und vor meiner Vergangenheit. Eines Tages wird er mich ganz aufsaugen, das weiß ich.

Wie viel Zeit bleibt mir noch?

Mein Kopf ist zu beschäftigt mit Verfolgungswahn und Mordkomplotten, und dabei bilden sich Fragen die überraschend in meinem Kopf auftauchen: Warum hat Jonas nicht auf einer genaueren Klärung der Todesursache seines Vaters bestanden? Trifft es zu, was Mom von Haakon Jensen behauptet hat? Ist er ein Junkie? Kann dieses Monster noch immer einen Schlüssel zu meinem Haus haben? Wann holt Jonas endlich seine persönlichen Sachen hier ab? Seine Zeugnisse, privaten Fotos, Bücher, Anzüge, alles ist noch da. Was soll ich damit?

Plötzlich erinnere ich mich an das, was ich mir vorgenommen hatte: Alles, was Jonas gehört … *Weg damit! Delete!* Ich möchte jede Spur von ihm aus diesem Haus entfernen, selbst die kleinste. Ab in den Müllsack, in den Kleidercontainer.

Spuren von Jonas entfernen … Der Gedanke fühlt sich gut an.

Die Standuhr im Korridor schlägt die zehnte Stunde. Ich sollte langsam aufstehen.

Ich warte lange, bevor ich näher an die Haustür trete. Setze meine Schritte behutsam. Ich habe den Schatten im Wagen beobachtet und, verborgen in einem Winkel am Fenster im ersten Stock meines Hauses, jede seiner Bewegungen studiert. Das Auto ist einige Male vorbeigefahren und hat dann vor dem Haus geparkt. Doch der Schatten blieb im Wagen, einige Minuten lang, erst dann stieg er aus und lief zum Haus, den Blick fokussiert auf …, ja worauf? Ich kann das Gesicht nicht genau erkennen. Es wird von den Bäumen überschattet. Aber alles ist eigenartig an der Gestalt. Vertraut und fremd zugleich.

Ich spüre einen Stich im Magen, ein Brennen hinter den Augen, als die Gestalt mit schnellen Schritten auf das Haus zukommt, und öffne ganz mechanisch die Haustür.

Ich schrecke zurück. *Haakon!*

„Du schmiedest die falschen Pläne, Schätzchen!", zischt er und drängt sich an mir vorbei.

Mir wird übel. „Habe ich dich gebeten, mein Haus zu betreten?"

Haakon ignoriert meine Worte und lässt sich im Wohnzimmer in den Sessel fallen. „Warum wolltest du wissen, wie lange Jonas und ich uns schon kennen?", fragt er und betrachtet das Picasso-Poster an der gegenüberliegenden Wand. „Ist das von Bedeutung?"

Ich atme tief ein. Ohne Jonas fühle ich mich freier, diesem Bastard zu sagen, was ich von ihm halte.

„Für mich schon."

„Und was dann? Willst du etwa die betrogene Ehefrau raushängen lassen? Werden Jonas und ich mit einer Portion Enttäuschung überschüttet, oder beabsichtigst du, vor aller Welt die beleidigte Unschuld zu spielen?

Ein Mann begibt sich nicht grundlos auf die Suche nach einem anderen Partner, Schätzchen. Und schon gar nicht nach einem *Mann*. Glaub mir, dann hat er zu Hause nicht viel geboten bekommen. *Du* hast nicht dein Bestes gegeben, um ihn zu halten."

Ich bin entsetzt und fühle mich völlig überrumpelt. Es gelingt mir nicht, ihm Worte an den Kopf zu werfen, die unter die Gürtellinie gehen. Ich möchte ihn zutiefst verletzen, verbal erwürgen, aber ich bin wie paralysiert.

"Wir kennen uns seit Dezember letzten Jahres. Hast du dich nie gefragt, wo Jonas übernachtet hat, wenn er nach einem Auswärtstermin nicht nach Hause kam? Oh, du dachtest bestimmt, in einem Hotel. Niemals hättest du es für möglich gehalten, dass es da noch etwas anderes geben könnte. Du dachtest bestimmt, du wärst alles für ihn."

"Das habe ich nie gedacht", sage ich leise.

"Frauen", schnaubt er verächtlich. "Es gibt keine dümmere Spezies." Er setzt sich aufrecht hin. "Es war mein Plan." Er klingt stolz.

"Wovon sprichst du?"

"Dir zu sagen, dass er mich erst im Mai getroffen hat, war mein Plan, Teil eines größeren Plans. Ich habe schon oft mit dieser Axt Holz gehackt, Schätzchen."

"Ich bin nicht dein Schätzchen!"

"Schätzchen ist meine Bezeichnung für Leute, die ich nicht ausstehen kann!"

Dieser Mann soll von hier verschwinden. Er soll gehen, ich will nicht hören, was er zu sagen hat. Wie bringe ich ihn nur dazu? Ich bin müde, möchte schlafen. Und vielleicht ein wenig von Malte träumen.

Dieser Mann ... Mir wird schwindlig, ich muss mich ebenfalls setzen und fixiere einen Punkt an der Wand. Etwas Eigenartiges passiert. Das Bild, das Haakon angestarrt hat, scheint aus der Verankerung zu kippen, als er zu sprechen beginnt. Picassos ineinander verschlungene blaue Gestalten drehen sich im Kreis. Ich kneife die Augen zusammen und verdränge die Halluzination.

"Deine Ausführungen interessieren mich nicht", zische ich.

"Aber *ich* möchte es dir gerne erklären; Jonte-*Schätzchen*. Und *ich* entscheide ... Ich entscheide immer, was passiert. Wenn die Leute das erst einmal begreifen und merken ..." Wieder hält er einen Moment inne. "... wer ich bin, widersprechen sie mir nicht mehr. Kapiert, Schätzchen!?"

Ich will ihm nicht zuhören und sollte auch besser still sein. Aber ich weiß auch, dass ich diesen Mann nicht gegen mich aufbringen darf. Er strahlt eine vernichtende Gewalt aus. Seine dämonischen Augen beobachten alles, was um ihn herum geschieht – er wittert sogar, was sich hinter ihm abspielt. Ich halte inne, bewege mich nicht. Bin auf der Hut vor ihm. Haakon schweigt, ist mit zusammengekniffenen Augen auf der Suche nach neuen Worten. „Jonas und ich trafen uns auf einer Baustelle", fährt er kalt fort. „Es hatte eine Besprechung mit einem Bauherrn, etwa eine Woche nach Erscheinen eines Artikels in der Zeitschrift *Berührungspunkte*. Es hat sofort zwischen uns gefunkt. Ich war gerade aus den USA zurückgekehrt, wo ich drei Jahre lang gelebt habe. Ich war bankrott, also kam mir eine Goldmine wie Jonas Soren wie gerufen."

Ich starre ihn an. „Wenn Jonas das erfährt …"

„Das weiß er längst, Schätzchen. Wir gehen offen miteinander um. Wenn man sich liebt, teilt man selbst seine Geheimnisse. Und wir lieben uns. Es ist pure männliche Liebe. Verstehst du?"

Ich finde keine Worte, weil ich mir beim besten Willen nicht vorstellen kann, dass jemand Lust auf diesen ekelhaften Mann verspüren könnte. Alles an ihm weckt Widerstand in mir. Mir wird übel, wenn ich daran denke, dass Jonas mit diesem Dämon im Bett liegt. Ihn berühren, sich von ihm … *Hör auf!* Vielleicht ist es genau das, was meinen Widerwillen erregt.

Ich schlucke ein paarmal und atme tief ein und aus.

„Jonas hat mir alles über deine Psychosen und Eskapaden erzählt", fährt Haakon fort. „Alles über deine Scheinheiligkeit, deine ständige Einmischung, die Art und Weise, wie du ihn mit deiner übertriebenen Fürsorge fast erstickt hast. Glaub mir, kein Mann, der solchem emotionalen Druck ausgesetzt ist, bringt im Bett noch was zustande. Dass du ihn mit deinen neidlos gesagt genialen Architekturentwürfen dafür entschädigt hast, ist deshalb mehr als gerecht, ebenso, dass Jonas und ich noch eine Weile hübsch davon profitieren werden."

Einmischung? Scheinheiligkeit, übertriebe Fürsorge? Psychosen? Und wovon will er profitieren? Worüber redet dieser Schlappschwanz eigentlich? Back-Vocal tost hinter meiner Stirn und peitscht mit Worten auf mich ein.

Ich finde meine Stimme wieder. „Vergiss es! Es spielt keine Rolle mehr, wie und wann ihr euch kennengelernt habt. Es war auch nie von Bedeutung!"

„Du irrst du dich, Schätzchen. Oh, wie falsch du da jetzt liegst."

Mir wird kalt. Da klingt etwas mit, das ich nicht hören und vor allem nicht wissen will. Ich stehe auf, mache einen Schritt nach vorne. „Verschwinde, Haakon, und lass dich hier nie wieder blicken! Du bist ein widerwärtiger Parasit, eine miese Krake, die sich nur allzu gern im Nacken anderer festbeißt, um sie auszusaugen. Ohne mich. Ich habe ein weiteres Schloss an der Tür anbringen lassen. Du kannst dich also nicht mehr in der Nacht an mich heranschleichen, du Arschloch. Und solltest du es dennoch wagen, werde ich die Polizei alarmieren." Ich erschrecke über meinen Mut.

„Das glaubst du wirklich?"

Der Raum beginnt sich zu drehen. Ich erinnere mich an die Schritte auf der Treppe, den Fernseher, die verschwundenen Hausschuhe, die ich später im Haus meines Schwiegervaters gefunden habe, die Streichholzschachtel, den Geruch in diesem Haus – den Geruch, den Haakon verströmt. All das überschwemmt mich, ich drohe daran zu ersticken. Dabei will ich nur Ordnung in meinem Kopf schaffen, keine Verwirrung und keine lächerlichen Schlussfolgerungen ziehen. Mit dem Restalkohol vom Vortag ist mir das aber kaum möglich. Der Mann vor mir hat etwas mit all den seltsamen Vorkommnissen der vergangenen Monate zu tun. Dessen bin ich mir sicher. Alles in meinem bisherigen Leben unterliegt einer Täuschung, nur darin täusche ich mich nicht.

Ich bin aufgebracht. Mein schnelles Atmen, das Versagen meiner Stimme, all das ist Ausdruck meiner Panik. Ich habe Angst. Und bin zugleich wütend.

In mir tost ein rasender Sturm.

Haakon grinst mich mit einem falschen Lächeln an.

„Ich soll gehen? Wie du willst, Schätzchen. Aber ich komme wieder. Sehr bald. Und ich bin sicher, dass du dann erneut die Tür öffnest, weil du ganz heiß darauf sein wirst, mit mir zu sprechen."

„Hör verdammt noch mal mit diesem *Schätzchen* auf!"

Er zuckt einen Moment zusammen. „Ich komme wieder", wiederholt er, und im nächsten Moment ist er verschwunden.

Heftig schluchzend torkle ich in die Küche, nehme eine Weinflasche aus dem Regal, entkorke sie. Meine Knie zittern, ich bebe am ganzen Körper und kann meine Tränen nicht länger zurückhalten. Wenn ich mich jetzt vom Alkohol betäuben lasse, wenn er sich den Weg durch meinen Körper bahnen darf, wird das Zittern aufhören.

Kein Traum, kein Monster heute Nacht, sondern etwas viel Schlimmeres. Ich fühle mich beklommen. Ein Satz hallt in meinem Kopf nach, den ich nicht recht zu fassen kriege. Es ist Haakons Stimme, die sich in meine Träume geschlichen hat.

Plötzlich begreife ich, weshalb sie mir von Anfang an so vertraut vorkam. Benommen schüttle ich den Kopf. Das kann nicht sein, das kann einfach nicht sein. Mein Herz zieht sich schmerzhaft zusammen. Mein Gehirn denkt: unmöglich. Aber meine Sinne wissen, dass es wahr ist.

Meine Welt erzittert. Die Gegenwart fällt wie ein Kartenhaus zusammen, ist Schutt und Asche. Was bleibt, ist die Vergangenheit.

Ich sitze aufrecht auf dem Küchenstuhl und fühle mich wie eine offene Wunde. Bin der Geruch von rohem Fleisch und klaffe weit auf. Ich greife mir ans Herz und will nur noch sterben.

Nach einigen Minuten explodiert etwas in meinem Hirn, eine Tür wird mit dem Fuß aufgestoßen, es entsteht ein mächtiger Luftzug, und jetzt habe ich ein loderndes Feuer vor Augen, dessen Flammen in die Höhe schießen und mich einzufangen drohen.

Mit einem Ellenbogen auf den Küchentisch und die rechte Hand am Weinglas, habe ich das Gefühl, alles sei aufgehoben worden, die Angst und die Erinnerungen. Die Raubvogelklauen, die meine Brust ständig zusammendrückten, haben sich endlich gelöst. Ich schließe die Augen, alles ist weggewaschen, ja, und alles kann beginnen.

Ich habe es verdrängt, geglaubt, ignoriert und wieder verdrängt. Doch die Tatsache, dass es wahr ist, hat mich seitdem nicht mehr losgelassen. Und dann ist sie plötzlich wieder da: die Angst. Mein Bauch verflüssigt sich fast vor Angst. Ich spüre das Böse. Es ist ganz nah und krallt sich wie einst die Dornen der verwilderten Rosen an der Garagenwand um meinen Körper.

Ich rufe verzweifelt nach Annika.

KAPITEL 43

Zu meiner Überraschung sprudeln die neuen Entwürfe für die Umgestaltung des Klosters zu einem Hotel trotz der bizarren Situation, in die ich geraten bin, weiterhin nur so aus mir heraus. Vielleicht treibt mich auch gerade diese aufdringliche Stimme in meinem Kopf an, die mir vorwirft, dass ich mich so verausgabe. Ich diskutiere mit ihr, verteidige mich, flüstere, dass ich Jonas bereits mitgeteilt habe, dass ich mich scheiden lassen und seine Anrufe zukünftig ignorieren werde. Und was ich hier tue, tue ich nur noch für mich.

Aber mein Aktionsdrang wird immer wieder ausgebremst, wenn ich Haakon vor Augen habe und die Bedrohung spüre, die von ihm ausgeht. Dann möchte ich am liebsten den Kopf in den Sand stecken.

Die Kirchenuhr schlägt achtmal. Es ist bereits stockfinster. Ich betrachte zufrieden meine Arbeit. Das Hotel atmet mit jedem Raum, jeder Nische, jedem Balken Leben. Die Querhäuser sind jetzt weniger filigran und großzügig.

Ich speichere die neuen Entwürfe auf dem USB-Stick und strecke mich. Jetzt habe ich das Bedürfnis nach einem Glas Rotwein. Heute Abend sind zwei Gläser Wein erlaubt für die brillante Architektin.

Zwei Gläser, Jonte, aber nicht mehr. Danach wandert die Flasche zurück in den Schrank, nörgelt meine innere Stimme vorwurfsvoll.

Ich liebe es, den Alkohol in meinem Körper zu spüren, und werde niemals den Moment vergessen, an dem alles begann. Mit einem Schluck Cognac zur Beruhigung, als ich ein Teenager war und glaubte, ich würde völlig untergehen. Das heimliche Trinken hielt mich nach der Vergewaltigung über Wasser. Ich rührte mich kaum. Nur so viel, wie zum Überleben nötig war.

Nach zwei Gläsern Wein vergewissere ich mich, dass alle Lampen ausgeschaltet und alle Türen verbarrikadiert sind. Dann gehe ich mit der Flasche in der Hand ins dunkle Wohnzimmer, setze mich und denke, dass ich meinem inneren Sterben einfach seinen Lauf lassen sollte. Niemand weiß von meiner Sucht, nicht einmal meine Mutter. Vielleicht ahnt sie, dass ich zu viel trinke. Den wahren Grund kennt sie nicht. Sie glaubt auch, dass ich die Vergewaltigung längst überwunden habe.

In der Nacht wache ich auf und folge dem Gedanken, der sich Stunden zuvor eingenistet hat. Es ist ganz selbstverständlich, dass ich die Treppe hinuntergehe, mit dem Gefühl, noch nie so zielstrebig in meinem Leben eine Flasche Wein angesteuert zu haben. Ich öffne den Kühlschrank und trinke innerhalb weniger Minuten drei Gläser, um meinen Schmerz zu betäuben.

Das Bild in meinem Kopf gewinnt an Schärfe, einzelne Elemente finden langsam zu einem Ganzen zusammen.

Ich flüstere seinen Namen. „Papa."

Papa ... Mein Vater schloss sich nach der Vergewaltigung tagsüber in seinem Zimmer ein und hörte Musik. Als ich aus dem Krankenhaus entlassen wurde, sah ich die Farbe seiner Haut und fragte mich, wie lange man ohne Tageslicht leben könne. Er wollte nicht mehr am Leben teilnehmen, weil er den Gedanken nicht ertrug, dass er mich nicht hatte beschützen können, und weil er als Einziger sah, wie sehr ich gebrochen worden war.

Drei Jahre nach meiner Rückkehr aus dem Krankenhaus nahm er sich an einem kalten Tag im Dezember das Leben. Ich konnte nicht weinen. Meine Augen blieben trocken, meine Lippen versiegelt. Aber ich nahm wahr, was um mich herum geschah, sah und hörte alles: die immense, nicht enden wollende Trauer meiner Mutter. Sie weinte sich viele Wintermonate in den Schlaf, sprach lange Zeit von meinem Vater in der Gegenwartsform.

Mit Papas und Aarons Tod habe ich gänzlich den Boden unter den Füßen verloren.

Der Tag liegt vor mir, eine weite freie Fläche. Im Zimmer ist es noch dunkel. Meine Augen sind verklebt, ich kann sie kaum öffnen und streichle mit den Fingerspitzen über die geschwollenen Lider. Noch schaffe ich es nicht, richtig wach zu werden, dabei will ich dem wirren, undeutlichen Befehl meiner inneren Stimme folgen, die mich über Nacht Hunderte Male gewarnt hat, bis ich das Weinglas gegen die Küchenwand geschmettert habe.

Ich springe auf, suche das Gleichgewicht und torkle ins Badezimmer. Nach einer kalten Dusche geht es mir besser. Ich zwinge mich, im Badezimmerspiegel mein vom Schlaf und Wein geschwollenes Gesicht zu betrachten. Tränen sammeln sich hinter den Augen.

Papa ... Ein Seufzen.

Der Tag endet wie viele andere: Ich lege den Zeichenstift beiseite und betrachte zufrieden meine Arbeit.

Gegen sieben Uhr schellt es. Ich öffne die Haustür, und Wärme und Geborgenheit betreten mein Haus, streicheln mein Gesicht. Meine Mutter nimmt mich in den Arm, und ihre Umarmung verspricht mir das Leben.

Während des Abendessens plappert Mom unentwegt über ihren Alltag mit ihren großen und kleinen Sorgen. Doch plötzlich hält sie inne. „Du bist so still. Stimmt etwas nicht, Jonte?"

„Nein, alles okay."

„Versuch's noch mal – und jetzt die Wahrheit, bitte."

„Ich bin nur müde, Mom, hab den ganzen Tag am Zeichenbrett verbracht."

Stille.

„Okay, ich arbeite an einem neuen Entwurf, den ich auch für den Architekturwettbewerb einreichen möchte", füge ich rasch hinzu. „Der Hauptpreis für zeitgenössische Architektur ist mit sechzigtausend Euro dotiert."

Dies ist ein Anfang. Ich kann einer begrenzten Anzahl von Leuten sagen, dass ich ein neues Projekt in Angriff genommen habe. Dann kommen gezielte Fragen. Und sobald es sich herumspricht, wird es schwieriger für Jonas, meinen Entwurf zu konfiszieren. Oder ich lasse Kollegen, denen ich vertraue, einen Blick auf die Skizzen werfen, ohne dass Jonas davon erfährt. Ich will stille Zeugen, die mitkriegen, dass ich unabhängig arbeite. So kann ich mich absichern. Dennoch frage ich mich, ob das klug ist.

Mom reagiert begeistert. „Großartig! Endlich! Es ist ja wirklich an der Zeit. Was ist es dieses Mal?"

„Ein Kloster aus dem 15. Jahrhundert mit einer monumentalen gotischen Kirche. Der Orden möchte, dass der Gebäudekomplex zu einem mit Fünf Sternen klassifizierten Designerhotel umgestaltet wird. Ich habe den Entwurf auch bei einem Wettbewerb eingereicht."

„Großartig. Welche Ideen hast du?"

„Es wird ein Zusammenspiel von Geschichte, Design und Kunst, und es soll am Ende den Eindruck von Gastfreundschaft, Kompetenz und Harmonie vermitteln. Es wird überwältigend."

„Wie wundervoll, Jonte. Du wirst ein wunderschönes Hotel gestalten. Ich werde der erste Gast auf dem Maibaumfest sein."

Ich lächle. „Mom! Ich weiß nicht, ob ich den Wettbewerb gewinnen werde, aber der Orden hat sich schon jetzt für meine Entwürfe entschieden."

„Du wirst ausgezeichnet werden. Da bin ich mir sicher. Welchen Beitrag leistet Jonas dazu?"

Plötzlich habe die Baustelle vor Augen und die Tafel mit den Bauherren und Architekten: Architekturbüro *JO*.

Ein anderer Name sollte dort glänzen: *Dr. Jonte Sandvik.*

„Bist du noch da?" Meine Mutter schnippt mit den Fingern vor meinem Gesicht. „Ich bin sehr neugierig auf den Entwurf. Wann wird er fertig sein?"

„Oh, das könnte noch ein paar Wochen dauern. Ich gehe nächste Woche wieder zur Arbeit."

„Es ist gut, dass du nicht in Trauer versinkst", sagt sie leise. „Es fällt auch mir schwer zu akzeptieren, dass Annika tot ist."

„Aber es ist doch erst passiert, Mom", widerspreche ich. „Wer kann von uns erwarten, dass wir es bereits akzeptiert haben?"

„Du hast natürlich recht. Hast du die Fehlgeburt einigermaßen verkraftet?"

Seltsam ... Sie hat nie gefragt, wie ich schwanger wurde.

„Ja, indem ich es als eine unabänderliche Tatsache akzeptiert habe", antworte ich und schenke mir ein fünftes Glas Wein ein. Das letzte, um mich zu entwöhnen.

Als Mom sich verabschiedet hat, entsorge ich die leere Weinflasche. Ich bekomme ein schlechtes Gewissen. Ich wiegle ab. *Nichts falsch gemacht.* Nur winzige Fehler und ein Gläschen über den Durst getrunken. Jeder Mensch macht manchmal einen Fehler.

Ich bin dabei, meine Alkoholsucht zu bändigen, ich behalte dieses Ziel im Auge, sage ich mir. Wenn ich jetzt ein weiteres Glas trinke, habe ich morgen einen Kater.

Das wird dich sicher nicht davon abhalten, nörgelt meine innere Stimme. *Du hast doch immer eine Ausrede parat.*

Morgen werde ich mich jedenfalls nicht über meinen Zustand beschweren. Ich bin eine erwachsene Frau, ich kann Verantwortung für meine Fehler übernehmen.

Ha! Kannst du das? Hicks!

Ich seufze. Wie kann ich mich nur von diesem nagenden Gefühl in der Brust befreien – und von meiner Angst?

Ich steige mit einer Flasche Wein in mein imaginäres Flugzeug und drehe meine Runden über den Wolken.

KAPITEL 44

Die Wettervorhersagen sagen für die kommende Woche nicht viel Gutes voraus. Ein kalter Ostwind. Ich mag keinen Ostwind. Er geht durch Mark und Bein, besonders hier am Drammensfjord.

Die Waage sagt mir, dass ich in vier Wochen sechs Kilo abgenommen habe. Das wird der Grund sein, warum mir immer kalt ist. Manchmal ziehe ich zwei Pullover übereinander an und trage eine dicke Strumpfhose unter meiner Jeans. Trotzdem zittere ich.

Sobald ich tagsüber über Annika grüble, wandern meine Gedanken blitzschnell in eine andere Richtung. Ich will es immer noch nicht wahrhaben. Noch lange nicht. Wenn Mom über sie sprechen möchte, blocke ich es ab. „Aber darüber sprechen hilft, Jonte. Nur so bekommt die Trauer einen Platz, und du kannst dein Leben weiterleben!", sagt sie dann.

Ich schweige, denn wie soll ich ihr erklären, dass ich bis ans Äußerste angespannt bin? Wie kann ich Mom wissen lassen, dass ich mich bedroht fühle? Wie mache ich das, ohne sie oder jemand anders zu gefährden?

Meine Entscheidung, Urlaub zu nehmen, fühlt sich mittlerweile auch nicht mehr so gut an wie in den ersten Tagen. Mein Haus ist kein sicherer Hafen mehr, seit Haakon Jensen hier eingedrungen ist. Ich habe an jenem Abend gespürt, dass ich nicht die Kraft habe, mich ihm entgegenzustellen.

Vielleicht sollte ich das Haus verkaufen. Und dann muss ich nur noch einen neuen Partner finden und mich vor allem von Freund Rotwein trennen.

Mein Stift flitzt wieder über das Zeichenbrett. Der architektonische Kontrast zwischen Vergangenheit und Gegenwart wird allmählich im gesamten Klosterhotel lebendig – vom Eingang aus Kupfer, dem Restaurant unter der Kirchenkuppel, der roten Weinbar *Delete* bis hin zu den luxuriösen Hotelzimmern, die einst Klosterzellen waren. Aber noch ist es nicht perfekt.

Ich bin eins mit meinem Entwurf, aber mir wird schwindlig vor Hunger. Ich sollte einen Happen essen und etwas trinken. Ich schätze meine Zeichenleidenschaft sehr, aber sobald der Magen knurrt, hasse ich sie zugleich. Dann kommt es mir vor, als konkurrierten zwei Persönlichkeiten um meine Gunst. Die Ideen sprudeln in einer Vielfalt, sodass ich jede Sekunde, Minute, Stunde und jeden Tag brauche, um sie zu Papier zu bringen. Aber der Hunger quält mich.

Mom beklagt sich telefonisch bei mir. „Ich sehe dich kaum noch. Du verkriechst dich in deinem Haus, wirst jeden Tag schmaler und schaust weg, wenn ich dich etwas frage. Und was ist mit deiner Scheidung? Warum tut sich da nichts? Was verschweigst du mir, was soll ich nicht wissen?

Warum diese Geheimniskrämerei? Verdammt, was ist denn nur los mit dir?"

Ich texte sie zu, sage, dass ich Zeit brauche, um alles zu verarbeiten, was in den vergangenen sechs Monaten passiert ist. Sage nicht, dass sie mich in einer kreativen Phase stört. Sage nicht, dass die Vergangenheit mich einzuholen droht. Sage nicht, dass ich mich verliere. Das würde sie nur verletzen.

„Hm ... Das mit der Zeit verstehe ich", sagt Mom, „aber deswegen musst du dich doch nicht verbarrikadieren? Ich mache mir Sorgen. Es würde mir gefallen, wenn du zumindest einmal pro Woche zu mir kämst und mit mir zu Abend isst. Du solltest mehr auf dich achten, Kind. Ich bin nicht die Einzige, die so empfindet."

„Ich weiß, Mom. Bente ruft auch oft an und schreibt mir regelmäßig eine E-Mail, um zu erfahren, wie es läuft. Ich glaube, sie hat mich auch aus lauter Sorge für den zweiten Weihnachtsfeiertag nach Hyggen eingeladen. Es ist ein gutes Gefühl, dass es Leute gibt, die sich für mich interessieren, aber ich kann das für eine Weile nicht ertragen. Verstehst du? Soziale Kontakte sind derzeit nicht bei mir vorgesehen."

Ich halte solche Gespräche nicht mehr aus. Sie bringen mich nur dazu, gleich danach zur Flasche zu greifen. Und das Schlimme ist, es hat keine Wirkung mehr. Wie oft habe ich mir schon gewünscht, ich hätte in einem entlegenen Winkel meines Hirns, zu dem ich jetzt die Tür ein wenig öffne, ein vages Trunkenheitsgefühl aufbewahrt. Ich suche in mir nach einer Spur von Betäubung, wünsche mir, ich könnte den Stempel des Alkohols noch in meinen Bewegungen spüren, eine Langsamkeit und Benommenheit, so winzig sie auch sein möge, aber es ist nichts mehr übrig. Er verleiht mir keinen Panzer mehr. Ich trinke nur noch, weil ich muss, aber der Schutz stellt sich nicht mehr ein. In der kalten Winterlandschaft meiner Seele habe ich alles verbrannt.

Ich bin wieder zu dem verängstigten Kind geworden, das mit einem Bauch voller Angst und dem Geigenkasten in der Hand von zwei Männern auf den schmutzigen Boden gedrückt wurde. Die Furcht steigt jeden Morgen aus dem betäubenden Schlaf auf, breitet sich in meinem ganzen Körper aus und legt sich lähmend auf mein Gehirn.

Zudem lässt der Gedanke an Haakons Rücksichtslosigkeit mein Herz rasen. Etwas Schreckliches wird geschehen.

KAPITEL 45

Kopfschmerzen zertrümmern mein Hirn. Ursprünglich wollte ich einige Stunden zeichnen, bevor ich heute Nachmittag zu Mom fahre, aber ich schaffe es nicht, aufzustehen. Ich habe gestern Abend wieder zu viel getrunken und habe furchtbare Schuldgefühle. Ich sollte einfach keinen Wein mehr kaufen, keine Vorräte mehr im Haus haben. Das wäre am vernünftigsten.

Im Regal stehen noch sechs Flaschen Weißwein. Ich könnte sie langsam leeren, Glas für Glas, tagein, tagaus. Oder den Inhalt aller Flaschen heute in die Spüle kippen.

Dass ich nicht lache! Das meinst du nicht ernst, oder? Bullshit, beinahe hätte ich es dir abgenommen!

Ich wanke ins Badezimmer und blicke in den Spiegel. Obwohl ich mich auf den Anblick vorbereitet habe, obwohl ich mich Dutzende Male vor Augen hatte, um mich daran zu gewöhnen und seit mehreren Monaten weiß, dass ich mich in diesem Zustand befinde, kann ich meinen Anblick nicht mehr ertragen. Ebenso wenig das nicht mehr kontrollierbare Zurückschrecken und dieses Gefühl von Ekel, das sich auf meinem Gesicht ausbreitet. Es wird jedes Mal schlimmer, ist immer schlimmer als in der Woche zuvor, offenbar ist es möglich, in der Selbstaufgabe tiefer und tiefer zu sinken. In einem Sekundenbruchteil registriere ich alles, das schmutzige T-Shirt, die Alkoholausdünstungen, die Pupillen, die sich weiten und verengen, die Grimasse, die der des Kummers ähnelt.

In Windeseile schlucke ich drei Kopfschmerztabletten, sie müssen jetzt ihre Arbeit erledigen. Danach lege ich mich wieder hin.

Nach vier Stunden Schlaf greife ich zum Telefon. Meine Mutter wird sich gewiss fragen, wo ich bleibe. Sie hebt sofort ab, nennt aber nicht ihren Namen.

„Bist du es, Mom?"

„Oh, Jonte! Es ist meine Tochter", höre ich sie sagen. „Katja ist fort", schluchzt sie. „Sie ist verschwunden."

„Katja? Wer ist Katja?"

„Das jüngste Enkelkind meiner Freundin Edith. Sie holt Katja manchmal vom Kindergarten ab und hat sich heute eine Weile mit ein paar Frauen unterhalten. Die Kinder spielten auf dem Spielplatz. Katja rannte einem anderen Mädchen hinterher. Einen Moment später war sie spurlos verschwunden. Die Polizei ist hier. Bitte, komm ganz schnell. Ich schicke dir Ediths Adresse per WhatsApp!"

In meinem Hirn ist die Wirkung von Alkohol noch immer spürbar.

Back-Vocals Schweigen ist irritierend.

Jetzt brauche ich einen klaren Kopf. Es wäre fatal, wenn ich auch noch die liebenswerte Edith oder ihre Enkelin in Gefahr bringen würde.

Ediths Haus ist voller Polizisten. Sympathische Männer und Frauen mit ernsten Mienen. Sie haben das Telefon im Visier.

Dann werde ich mit einer Flut an Informationen überschüttet. Ein Mann hätte sich in der Nähe des Kindergartens aufgehalten, aber niemand hat auf ihn geachtet. Niemand weiß, was für ein Auto er fuhr. Alle widersprechen sich in ihren Aussagen. *Der Mann ist schmal und hat kurzes blondes Haar*, behauptete eine Zeugin. *Der Mann ist fast kahlköpfig*, sagten zwei andere Mütter. *Es sind zwei Männer*, gaben wiederum andere zu Protokoll.

Edith hat auch nichts Auffälliges gesehen. Keinen Mann und kein Auto. Und keine Gefahr.

Wie perfide, am Nikolaustag ein Kind wegzulocken! Back-Vocal zeigt sich empört.

„Der Entführer könnte anrufen", behauptet eine Polizistin, die eine komplizierte Abhöreinrichtung installiert hat.

„Kidnapper?", frage ich ungläubig. „Kann das Mädchen sich nicht einfach verlaufen haben?"

Ich möchte, dass es sich verlaufen hat. Dass es in einer fremden Umgebung nach der Großmutter sucht. Ein kleines Mädchen, das orientierungslos alleine auf der Straße herumirrt, muss doch jemandem auffallen.

Mit *Alles in Ordnung* beschwichtige ich die Angst, die durch meinen Körper wütet. Katja wird in spätestens einer Stunde zurück sein. Und dann fragt sie ganz unschuldig, ob der Nikolaus ihr Geschenke bringt.

Edith zittert vor Aufregung. Katjas Vater ist mittlerweile auch eingetroffen und nimmt sie in den Arm, hält sie fest und versucht, sie zu beruhigen.

Ich sitze neben meiner Mutter, ich muss ihr nahe sein. Brauche ihren Schutz. Ich vermisse Annika. Sie sollte jetzt auch hier sein. Sie hätte in dieser Nacht nie zu mir nach Hause gehen sollen. Nein, ich hätte in dieser Nacht nicht so viel trinken und das Handy im Auge behalten sollen. Wenn ich umsichtiger gehandelt hätte, wäre Annika vielleicht nicht zu mir gefahren, und niemand hätte sie niedergeschlagen. Ihr Herz würde heute noch schlagen.

Es ist meine Schuld. Es ist alles meine Schuld.

Ich trinke zu viel, lasse mich bedrohen, achte nicht auf mich und spiele nicht mit offenen Karten. Ich glaube, dass ich so noch mehr Unheil und Unfälle verhindern kann, aber das Gegenteil ist der Fall.

Ediths Enkelin ist nicht einfach verschwunden. Welcher Irre hat es nur auf die Kleine abgesehen?

Die Zeugen sprachen über einen hageren Typ mit kurzen blonden Haaren. Ich kenne so einen Mann. Meine Magensäure sprudelt vor lauter Panik. Ich halte meine Hände vor den Mund, beuge mich nach vorn.

„Musst du dich übergeben?", fragt Mom besorgt. „Versuch es zu unterdrücken."

Ich schnaube resigniert, es ist zu spät.

KAPITEL 46

Eine junge, sympathische Polizistin bringt mich ins Badezimmer, hilft mir beim Ausziehen der Bluse, säubert sie unter der Dusche und holt mit Ediths Erlaubnis einen Pulli aus deren Kleiderschrank. Ich lasse alles mit mir geschehen. Meine Hose hat zum Glück nichts abbekommen. Der Pulli wärmt mich nicht, er kann meinen zitternden Körper nicht beruhigen.

Die Polizistin begleitet mich in Ediths Schlafzimmer und bietet mir eine weiße Strickjacke an.

Ich gerate in Panik. „Kein Weiß!"

Ich tauche in den Schrank und greife nach dem erstbesten Pullover, den ich sehe – blau. Blau ist in Ordnung. Nur kein Weiß

„Wie Sie wollen", sagt die Polizistin. Sie bleibt freundlich. Sie weiß, dass Menschen in einer Stresssituation seltsame oder widersprüchliche Entscheidungen treffen, denke ich.

„Geht es wieder? Ich lasse Sie jetzt einen Moment allein. Ruhen Sie sich noch ein bisschen aus." Sie mustert mich, nickt und verlässt das Schlafzimmer.

Ich setze mich auf die Bettkante nieder, meine Füße fest auf den Boden. Meine Knie flattern. Weiß …

Weiß, die Farbe jenes flirrenden Sommers. Die Wärme prallte an mir ab. Ich versuchte, sie aufzufangen, wie einen Ball, warf sie zurück an die Wände der Häuserfassaden. Mir war warm und kalt, kalt und warm. Flauschiger Stoff an meinen Oberkörper, ich betastete ihn mit den Fingerspitzen – mein weißer Sommerpulli. In der rechten Hand mein Geigenkasten. Auf dem Parkplatz vor der Musikschule herrschte Lärm, als ich das Haus verließ. Der weiße Pullover war mir ein bisschen zu groß und verhüllte die pubertären Veränderungen meines Körpers. Ich lief an den kreischenden Jugendlichen vorbei zu einem schmalen Waldstück.

Von allen Geräuschen, die das Grauen anzukündigen vermögen, vernahm ich das schlimmste: schnelle Schritte, die immer näher kamen.

Ich drehte mich um. Zwei Männer.

„Schöner weißer Pulli", sagte der Korpulente. „Ich liebe weiße Pullis. Darunter verbergen sich die unschuldigsten Knospen. Ausziehen!"

Ich fiel in Ohnmacht, während er mich vergewaltigte.

In einer Garage kam ich wieder zu mir. Die Stimme des anderen Mannes kam von unten. Strich an meinen Hüften entlang. Eine helle Stimme. Er betrachtete meine Nacktheit. „Ich möchte, dass du uns etwas auf deiner Geige vorspielst. Sofort!"

Ich gehorchte, kein harmonischer Ton verließ mein Instrument.

„Was ist das denn. Aufhören, das klingt ja furchtbar!" Er riss mir die Geige aus der Hand und warf sie auf den Boden. Dann schlug er mich, bis ich blutete. Er wurde immer wütender und schlug weiter auf mich ein, während der andere Mann ihn anfeuerte, in die Hände klatschte und schrie: „Und jetzt fick die kleine Fotze!"

Dieses Mal war die Vergewaltigung schlimm. Sehr schlimm. Ich starrte an die Decke. Er schrie mich an. „Wenn man ein Pferd nicht richtig zureitet, wird es nie gehorchen."

Meine Seele brach, zersplitterte in tausend Teile, als beide mich nahmen …

Ich unterdrücke meine Schreie in Ediths Schlafzimmer. Unzählige Male haben die Männer sich in den darauf folgenden Jahren in nächtlichen Träumen wieder erhoben, um mich in der Garage neben dem Erdbeerfeld zu missbrauchen. Ihre Gewalt hat meine Teenagerjahre vergiftet, mir meine Begeisterung für die Violine geraubt und mich Nacht für Nacht besudelt. Sie hat tiefe Wurzeln in meinem Herzen geschlagen.

Als ich meine Muskeln wieder unter Kontrolle habe, höre ich, wie unten im Haus die Haustür mit einem lauten Knall zugeschlagen wird. Kommt jemand herein, oder verlässt jemand das Haus? Überbringt jemand eine Hiobsbotschaft? Ich schaffe es nicht, aufzustehen.

Deine Schuld. Alles deine Schuld, hämmert es in meinen Kopf.

Ich hätte dem Verleger keine E-Mail über meinen Entschluss, alleine weiterzumachen, schicken dürfen. Katja ist der Preis, den ich für meine Rücksichtslosigkeit zahlen muss. Ein unschuldiges dreijähriges Mädchen ist verschwunden. Ich muss den Polizisten im Wohnzimmer erzählen, dass ich Haakon Jensen als Drahtzieher vermute. Nur er kommt für eine solche Tat infrage. Er ist überall. Er ist allmächtig. Er ist der Teufel.

Falls sich herausstellt, dass dieses Kind entführt und getötet wurde, um mich zu bestrafen, werde ich mir das Leben nehmen. Mit einer solch schweren Schuld kann selbst ich nicht mehr leben.

Ich beginne zu hyperventilieren.

„Du musst ruhiger und bewusster atmen, Jonte", höre ich meinen Vater sagen. Er steht neben mir und hält meine Hand. Nein, er ist nur ein Hirngespinst wie Back-Vocal. Mein Vater ist tot.

Mein Handy kündigt eine SMS an. Ich öffne die Nachricht.

Ich rate dir, deine E-Mail an Falk so schnell wie möglich zu widerrufen. Aber es ist natürlich deine Entscheidung …

Ich wähle Falks Rufnummer. Ein Knopfdruck, und ich habe ihn in der Leitung.

„Hey, hallo! Was für ein Zufall! Jonas kommt gerade ins Büro."

„Ich habe dir versehentlich eine E-Mail geschickt. Natürlich wird der nächste Band unter dem Namen des Architektenduo *JO* erscheinen. Mach dir keine Gedanken darüber."

„In Ordnung. Ich habe mich schon gefragt, was in dich gefahren ist. Wir haben jede Menge Interviewanfragen. Es ist wichtig, neue gemeinsame Projekte anzukündigen. Jonas hat mir bereits erzählt, dass ihr auf einem guten Weg seid und dass das Klosterhotel eine echte Sensation wird."

Ich schnappe nach Luft. Wie kann Jonas das wissen? Darüber möchte ich jetzt lieber noch nicht nachdenken. Mir geht es nur darum, dass Haakon schnell erfährt, dass ich meinen Entschluss rückgängig gemacht habe, damit er das Mädchen zurückbringt. Oder zurückbringen lässt, denn dieser Drecksack macht sich gewiss nicht selbst die Hände schmutzig. Er wird dem Mädchen doch nichts angetan haben? Schweiß bricht mir aus allen Poren.

Plötzlich sehe ich wieder meinen Vater neben mir stehen. Er sieht mich so traurig an. Aber er ist seit mehr als zwanzig Jahren tot! Ich kann unmöglich meinen Vater sehen. Und dennoch tue ich es. Er nimmt meine Hand.

Verliere ich allmählich den Verstand?

KAPITEL 47

„Man hat Katja in einem Einkaufszentrum aufgegriffen", sagt die Polizistin. „Sie hat sich wohl verlaufen." Ich will nicht weiter darüber nachdenken.

„Das muss erst noch bewiesen werden", sagt Mom knapp.

Ich beruhige mich wieder. Der Punkt ist, dass Haakon mir nur eine Lektion erteilen wollte. Er kann beruhigt sein. Das hier wird sich nicht wiederholen. Ab heute werde ich keinen Tropfen Alkohol mehr trinken.

„Woran denkst du?", will Mom wissen.

„Ich habe in letzter Zeit zu viel getrunken."

„Stimmt", sagt sie leise und mustert mich, ein schweigender Scanner, das Radar-Auge, sie kann wohl nicht anders. „Mir ist das auch aufgefallen, dass du noch nie so viel getrunken hast wie in den letzten sechs Monaten. Belastet dich die Trennung von Jonas so sehr?"

Ich würde ihr gerne ein Lächeln schenken, halte mich aber zurück. „Nachwehen, denke ich. Aber du hast recht, das Trinken bekommt mir nicht. Ich werde damit aufhören."

Ich wage es nicht, Mom meine Angst zu gestehen. Dass ich mich manchmal nur noch zurückziehen will, mich selbst ihrer Aufmerksamkeit entziehen möchte, um nur noch zu trinken, immer mehr, immer schneller zu trinken. Denn der Rausch bringt keine richtige Verdrängung mehr, der Schmerz wird nicht mehr betäubt, die Abstände von Glas zu Glas werden kürzer und kürzer.

„Vielleicht schmeckt dir das Essen dann besser", flüstert Mom. „Knochengerüste sind auch nicht gerade die Lieblinge der Männerwelt."

„Du findest mich zu dünn?"

„Vor allem wirst du immer dünner. Du hast doch keine Essstörung, oder?"

Ich kann nicht anders und muss grinsen. Sobald ich in eine bizarre Situation gerate wie in diesem Augenblick, lache ich in der Regel laut auf. Es ist unangebracht, aber Mom schenkt mir ein Lächeln.

„Nein, aber mach dir darüber keine Sorgen, Mom. Es sind nur meine Nerven."

Edith kommt auf uns zu, ihre Augen sind gerötet, die Lider leicht geschwollen. Die Anspannung der letzten Stunden ist von uns allen abgefallen.

„Wir fahren jetzt zur Polizeidienststelle. Katja ist unversehrt. Dieser Albtraum ist zu Ende."

Ich stehe auf und umarme sie. „Ich bin so froh, Edith. Das waren Horrorstunden."

Jetzt lächelt sie.

Plötzlich weiß ich, was zu tun ist. Ich muss mit Jonas über die Scheidung sprechen, mit dem Trinken aufhören, klar im Kopf werden, mir eine Strategie überlegen, ohne dass mein gesamtes soziales Umfeld in Gefahr gerät. Ich muss es ohne Hilfe schaffen. Weil etwas in mir nach Wiedergutmachung schreit. Und dieses *Etwas* heißt Ebba Hagebak.

Ebba Hagebak ... Ihre Asche wurde vor vierzehn Jahren im Drammensfjord verstreut. Sie starb an dem Abend, als ich erfuhr, dass meine Beziehung mit Aaron eine Lüge war, dass ich mich in eine Traumwelt hineinmanövriert hatte und dass mit seinem Tod gar nichts zu Ende ging, weil unsere Beziehung nie wirklich existiert hatte.

An jenem warmen Frühlingsabend fuhr ich wie von Sinnen vom Parkplatz des Bestattungsinstituts – und raste dabei in die falsche Richtung. Schatten. Alles war verschattet, die Straße, der Fjord, die Weite, verschattet, weil dunkelblau die Nacht anbrach. Ebba radelte die spärlich beleuchtete Uferstraße entlang, neben ihr schimmerte das Wasser bedrohlich schwarz.

Ebba trug ein weißes Kleid. Weiß ...

Meine Gedanken trieben mich zur Raserei, nur weg von der Beerdigung, mit hoher Geschwindigkeit und einem flüchtigen Blick zum Himmel, wo Aaron jetzt war – dann verlor ich plötzlich die Kontrolle über das Fahrzeug und raste in Ebba hinein, direkt in den weißen Fleck im Dunkel der Dämmerung.

Ich habe sie zu spät gesehen, im Grunde erst, als ihr Körper auf die Windschutzscheibe prallte und auf dem Pflaster aufschlug.

Ich bremste panisch, stieg aus, rannte zu ihr. Sie lag auf dem Rücken, Blut floss unter ihrem Kopf weg, Blut schuf ein Muster auf dem weißen Kleid. Rot auf Weiß.

Sie rührte sich nicht. Kein Atemzug, der den Brustkorb hob und senkte. Ich tastete nach ihrem Puls. Nichts.

Ich rannte durch die hereinbrechende Nacht zu meinem Wagen und sah mich immer wieder um. Keine Zeugen. Es gab keine Zeugen! Ich versuchte, nach dem erlösenden Gedanken zu greifen, so zynisch er auch war. Ich klammerte mich an die Vorstellung, dass ich normal weiterleben könnte, wenn niemand etwas erfuhr. Wie sehr ich mich doch irrte!

Ebba ...

Ich habe wochenlang nicht mehr an sie gedacht. Auch jetzt möchte ich mich nicht mit der quälenden Erinnerung auseinandersetzen. Ich versuche ein Lächeln. Versuche, es auf meine Lippen zu heben, aber ich habe keins mehr. Es ist mit Aaron mitgegangen. Mit Jonas verschwunden.

„Wer ist Ebba?", fragt Mom.

Ich erröte. „Wer?"

„Du hast gerade diesen Namen geflüstert."

„Ach, nur eine ehemalige Kollegin. Ich musste plötzlich an sie denken und hab das wohl laut ausgesprochen."

„Du siehst aus, als würdest du gleich umkippen. Komm, lass uns nach draußen gehen, du brauchst frische Luft."

KAPITEL 48

Ein neuer Tag. Ein neuer Morgen, der dem Mittag weicht. Ein neuer Mittag, der vergeht. Ich stehe am Fenster und starre auf das giftgrüne Wasser des Drammensfjord. Warte auf Haakon Jensen.

Wenn ich nicht aufpasse, wird auch dieser Nachmittag sich verabschieden, ohne dass die verdammte Sache mit dem Bastard erledigt ist. Kommt er, oder kommt er nicht? Soll ich ihn noch mal anrufen? Ich weiß es nicht. Meine Gedanken stehen still. Weil ich sie einfach nicht in Bewegung bekomme. Soll der verdammte Dreckskerl endlich untergehen. Aber nein, das wird er nicht. Nicht so bald.

Ich wende den Blick jetzt dem Schmutzfleck auf dem Fenster zu. Ein kleiner Kreis, der am Himmel zu kleben scheint und durch die Sonne verblasst. Ich stelle mir vor, es wäre Haakon und ich könnte ihn mit einem Lappen wegwischen wie den Fleck auf dem Fensterglas, und dann könnte ich den Lappen in die Tiefen des Drammensfjord werfen und den Bastard versenken. Auf Nimmerwiedersehen. Mitsamt den üblen Gedanken, und allem, was mich sonst noch so beschäftigt. Der Gedanke kommt und geht, verblasst, trübt sich ein, wie der Fleck auf der Fensterscheibe.

Ich höre seinen Wagen vorfahren, dann seine Schritte auf dem Kiesweg. Ich bin bereit für Verhandlungen und öffne die Haustür.

Haakon folgt mir schweigend, setzt sich und beginnt sofort das Gespräch. „Das war sehr knapp, Schätzchen. Du hättest Falk keine Sekunde später anrufen dürfen."

Bis zu diesem Moment war ich davon überzeugt, dass ich ruhig bleiben würde, aber ich habe mich getäuscht. Mir stockt der Atem. Ich schnaufe. „Du Bastard! Was hast du mit dem Mädchen gemacht?"

„Nichts. Ich mag keine kleinen Mädchen. Das weißt du doch."

Auch wenn ich noch nicht alles verstehe, bei Weitem nicht alles, hat sich ein zentraler Gedanke längst herausgebildet. Dass hier ein Monster zu mir spricht.

„Ich denke, niemand kann tiefer sinken als du. Ich verstehe beim besten Willen nicht, was Jonas in dir sieht."

„Ach Jonas, das ist eine Geschichte für sich." Haakon grinst. „Jonas kommt es nur darauf an, dass ich ihm seinen Stoff liefern kann."

Ich verstehe nicht, wovon er spricht, aber ich will es auch nicht wissen. Sein Mund ist eine Kloake.

Haakon lehnt sich lächelnd zurück, doch plötzlich beugt er sich tief vor. Seine Augen sind kalt, sein Blick überheblich. „Es ist für dich an der Zeit zu realisieren, dass du genau das zu machen hast, was ich dir sage", zischt er. „Du wirst weiter mit Jonas zusammenarbeiten und das Honorar mit uns teilen!"

„Das kannst du vergessen, du dreckiger Bastard! Du kannst mich nicht dazu zwingen. Ich habe keine Angst mehr vor dir. Ich werde dich anzeigen, du durchgeknallter Junkie! Du bekommst keinen Cent von mir, Haakon. Such dir ein anderes Opfer. Jonas wird schon wieder zur Besinnung kommen. Oder auch nicht. Jonas ist kein schlechter Mensch, und daran kannst du nichts ändern. Wenn er erfährt, was du getan hast …"

Stille. Todesstille. Haakon wirft mir wieder einen überheblichen Blick zu und trommelt mit den Fingern auf die Stuhllehne.

„Er weiß es. Und es hat ihn nicht gerade fröhlich gestimmt, wenn ich ehrlich bin. Aber er hat sich wieder beruhigt und wurde reichlich belohnt …"

„Was meinst du damit?"

„Er ist von uns beiden der wahre Junkie. Er wartet nur darauf, dass ich nach Hause komme, um ihn zu lieben. Er lechzt nach dem Sex mit mir, Schätzchen. So was kennst du von ihm gar nicht, oder?"

Ich habe das Gefühl, in einem Sumpf zu versinken.

„Jonas ist inzwischen in der Lage, Dinge zu tun, die du dir nicht im Entferntesten ausmalen kannst. Hast du mittlerweile herausgefunden, wie du schwanger werden konntest? Ich glaube nicht. Dann wird dir Onkel Haakon mal eine Gutenachtgeschichte erzählen."

Ich atme tief ein und aus, kneife die Augen zusammen, höre zu. Betrachte den Teppich, dann durch das Fenster den Fjord. Erinnerungen zucken auf, graue Bilder, Weiß auf Rot, Rot auf Weiß. Ich suche einen Ort, der nie existiert hat.

Worte bahnen sich einen Weg, klingen dumpf in mir nach. Worte, die Haakon mir an den Kopf wirft. Worte, die im Raum schweben, aber keinen Platz finden. Die Geschichte, die auf mich einstürzt, ist ein physischer Gewaltakt, der jede Sehne, jeden Muskel und jeden Nerv in meinem Körper in ein Bündel Schmerz verwandelt. Der jede einzelne Zelle in mir zerstört. Der meinen Körper zerstückelt und meine Seele in Stücke reißt.

Ich spüre nichts, frage mich nur, ob manches der Dunkelheit entspringt, unter einer finsteren Sonne heranwächst, gehegt und gepflegt von einem Gärtner mit einem Rechen aus Knochen.

Ich starre Haakon an. Will die Worte nicht aus diesem Mund hören. Doch blitzartig wird mir bewusst, dass er die Wahrheit sagt, und seine Worte durchbohren mein Herz wie Dolche. Ich zittere am ganzen Leib, das Pochen in meinem Körper will nicht aufhören. Meine Wangen stehen in Flammen.

Ich schüttle den Kopf. „Nein! Nein!"

Haakon steht auf. Er sieht widerlich aus, unappetitlich und schmutzig.

Ich brauche frische Luft und stehe ebenfalls auf. Laufe aus dem Haus in den Garten. Warte auf einen Lebensimpuls.

Doch da ist nichts.

Keine Sonne, keine Blume.

Ich bin tot.

KAPITEL 49

Ich sehe Jonas wieder vor mir, erinnere mich deutlich daran, dass er versucht hat, mir etwas zu sagen, dass er an dem Tag mitgenommen aussah und einen verzweifelten Eindruck machte.

Ich zwinge mein Gedächtnis in die Richtung seiner Worte. Einige Worte sind entschwunden, andere haben sich mir eingeprägt. „*Ich war verwirrt und verliebt. Habe den Verstand verloren. Es war Haakons Plan. Ich kann es dir nicht sagen. Aber zumindest habe ich ein neues Türschloss anbringen lassen.*" So ähnlich waren seine Worte.

Und das ist aus der Kloake rausgeflossen: „Kurz nachdem ich Jonas kennengelernt hatte, gestand er mir, dass du die Architekturentwürfe zeichnest und er das Architektenduo *JO* lediglich nach außen hin vertritt. Also brauchten wir eine Lösung für unsere Einkünfte nach der Scheidung. Jonas ahnte, dass du allein weitermachen und den Geldhahn zudrehen würdest. Schnell geriet er deshalb in Panik." Haakon seufzte. „Jonas hatte mir schon zu Beginn alles über deine Alkoholsucht erzählt. So kam ich auf die Idee, dich in eine kompromittierende Situation zu bringen und davon Fotos zu machen. Jonas meinte, dass du die Veröffentlichung solcher Fotos mit allen Mitteln verhindern würdest. Da er etwas weich veranlagt ist, protestierte er jedoch, er könne doch nicht seine eigene Frau vergewaltigen. Redete sich damit heraus, dass er ja gar keinen Sex mehr mit einer Frau wolle. Doch dann entdeckten wir dich an einem Samstagabend in einer Disco. Du warst sturzbetrunken. Wir sind dir auf dem Heimweg gefolgt, und Jonas hat dich ins Schlafzimmer gebracht. Er hatte ja noch immer einen Schlüssel."

Ich will das alles nicht hören. Es ist unmöglich, dass ich von meinem eigenen Ehemann ins Bett gebracht wurde, ohne mich daran erinnern zu können.

„Jonas bekam natürlich keine Erektion, aber für mich war es kein Problem, ihn zu erregen. Wir haben es neben dir miteinander getrieben, und du hast nichts davon mitbekommen. Dann drang er in dich ein, aber da er seine Erektion nicht aufrechterhalten konnte, musste ich ein bisschen Hand anlegen, damit er in dir kommen konnte. Es war schon eine verdammt geile Nummer!", schließt Haakon mit stählernem Gesicht. Er greift zufrieden in seine Jackentasche und wirft einige Fotos auf den Tisch.

Ich fürchte, mein Herz könnte jeden Moment versagen. Ich *will*, dass mein Herz jetzt sofort versagt! Ich möchte diese Worte und Sätze und Fotos nicht überleben, ich möchte keine Zukunft mehr, in der die Erinnerung an dieses Gespräch einen Platz hat.

Ich möchte auf der Stelle sterben, ich möchte zu meinem Vater. Warum sehe ich ihn jetzt nicht? Warum nimmt er mich nicht mit zu sich?

Haakon muss weg. Ausradiert werden. Ich muss als Erstes sicherstellen, dass er nie wieder dieses Haus betritt, aber er macht nicht mal Anstalten zu gehen. Sondern sieht mich mit finsteren Augen an.

„Irgendwas stimmt nicht mit dir, Jonte", sagt er. „Und niemand scheint genau zu wissen, was es ist. Nein, versuche nicht, zu protestieren. Ich habe Jonas gut zugehört. Du verbirgst etwas, und ich werde herausfinden, was das ist! Wenn du nicht spurst, zerstöre ich dich!"

Mein Herz setzt drei Schläge aus.

„Du bist schockiert, nicht wahr? Ich fange an, wirklich neugierig zu werden, was dein Geheimnis ist. Wir freuen uns schon auf den zweiten Entwurf des Klosterhotels. Der erste war ja sehr vielversprechend."

„*Wir*? Was verstehst du schon davon?"

„Du vergisst, dass ich auch vom Fach bin. Das alte Gemäuer könnte noch ein bisschen Pep vertragen, würde ich sagen. Lass dir was einfallen."

„Woher weißt du von dem Entwurf?"

Er lächelt, als wäre ich ein dummes Kind. „Du hast Jonas davon erzählt, Schätzchen."

„Nach der Scheidung werden sich unsere beruflichen Wege trennen."

„Sicher, Schätzchen. Aber erst dann, wenn *ich* davon überzeugt bin, dass die Zeit dafür reif ist. Das wird aber noch eine Weile dauern. Und so lange sind wir ein Team."

Ich schlucke ein paarmal und wechsle das Thema. „Ist Jonas auch süchtig?"

„Auch?"

„Ja, auch. Dir sieht man es an, aber ich kann mir beim besten Willen nicht vorstellen, dass Jonas drogenabhängig ist."

„Jonas war das einfachste Opfer, dem ich je begegnet bin", grunzt er und beugt sich dann drohend vor: „Du wirst das tun, was ich dir sage. Das nächste Mal gibt es keine Spielchen mehr. Oder willst du deine Mutter opfern, um deinen Kopf durchzusetzen? Ich würde mal *darüber* nachdenken!"

„Du hast dein Versagen und deine innere Wut an mir ausgelassen, du hast mich wie ein wehrloses Tier gequält, du hast meine Seele gefoltert. Du hast mir das Vertrauen in Jonas genommen, du hast alles zerstört, was Jonas und ich aufgebaut haben und was mir wichtig war. Und ich glaube, dass du auch Jonas' Vater in den Selbstmord getrieben und Annika ermordet hast. Du hast saubere Arbeit geleistet."

Ich schließe die Augen, damit ich sein Gesicht nicht mehr sehen muss. Die Wut übermannt mich, als ich mich erhebe und Haakon mit meiner letzten Kraft ins Gesicht schlage. „Verschwinde!", zische ich. „Verschwinde aus meinem Haus und aus meinem Leben!" Ich schleudere die Worte wie Geschosse aus meinem Mund.

Minuten später zittern die Wände immer noch von dem dumpfen Schlag, mit dem er die Haustür hinter sich zugeknallt hat. Ein Schlag, um mich einzuschüchtern.

Ich hasse ihn. Lange Zeit habe ich die beiden Männer gehasst, die mich vergewaltigt und meinen Vater in den Tod getrieben haben, aber ich wusste, dass dieses Gefühl mit der Zeit nachlassen würde.

Aber diesen Hass werde ich am Leben erhalten, dem möchte ich immer Nahrung geben, damit er meine Angst übertünchen kann.

Ich brauche frische Luft und verlasse fluchtartig mein Haus in Richtung Wald. Ich bin lange nicht an diesem Ort gewesen, dort, wo der Wald sich öffnet, als wollte er sich vom Dickicht befreien. Dort, wo der Wald einen freien Raum preisgibt, eine unerwartete Lichtung, einen hellen, lichten Moment, nur für mich. Hier habe ich mich nach der Vergewaltigung oft versteckt, wurde eins mit dem Wald am Drammensfjord. Hier habe ich als Jugendliche mit dem Trinken angefangen. Ein heimliches Spiel anfangs, nur für mich. Hier spürte ich, dass mit jedem Schluck der Schmerz nachließ. Als ich jedoch feststellen musste, dass meine seelischen Wunden am nächsten Tag nur noch heftiger bluteten, hörte ich mit dem Trinken auf. Damals besaß ich noch diese Kraft.

Doch jetzt spüre ich nur ein Kribbeln die Wirbelsäule hinunter, einen beschleunigten Herzschlag, einen Adrenalinstoß, der sich spürbar in meinem ganzen Körper ausbreitet.

Ich gehe wieder zurück zum Haus, im Kühlschrank erwartet mich der Rausch.

Dabei müsste ich einen klaren Kopf behalten.

KAPITEL 50

Im Fernsehen läuft eine Talkshow, an der drei Architekten teilnehmen, die für einen Architekturpreis nominiert worden sind. Ich liege mit einem Glas Wein auf der Couch und versuche, dem Gespräch zu folgen. Die Weinflasche ist fast leer. Ich sollte ins Bett gehen und den morgigen Tag mit Nicht-Trinken anfangen. Ab morgen wird alles besser.

Mir ist kalt, aber ich bin zu betrunken, um die Treppe hinaufzugehen und eine Strickjacke aus dem Schrank zu holen. Die Entfernung zum Thermostat der Wohnzimmerheizung erscheint mir auch unkalkulierbar.

Die Kälte in mir sagt mir mal wieder die alte Leier, dass ich auf dem Weg bin, meinen Körper zu zerstören. Wer wählt schon bewusst den Zerfall? Ich möchte über schöne Dinge nachdenken. Positive Dinge, die mir ein gutes Gefühl geben. Ich will doch leben. Jedenfalls meistens.

Aber meine Gedanken werden völlig von dem absorbiert, was Haakon mir erzählt hat. Das Bild drängt sich mir ständig auf: Ich, weggetreten im Bett liegend, Jonas, der sich auf mir abstrampelt, und ein nackter Haakon, der die Szene komplettiert und seinen Liebsten stimuliert. Ich könnte kotzen.

Warum bin ich nicht aufgewacht?

Das alles kann gar nicht passiert sein! Ich würde ja glauben, dass alles eine fiese Täuschung ist, wenn die Fotos es nicht aufs Widerlichste beweisen würden. Ich habe mich noch nie so elend, so gedemütigt, so missbraucht gefühlt.

Im Fernsehen reden und reden sie. „Es ist ein einsames Abenteuer", sagt eine Architektin, eine Frau mit spitzem Gesicht, unordentlichem Haar, offenen Augen. „Du zeichnest den Entwurf, landest in einer Welt, zu der noch niemand Zugang hatte. Das Schlimmste kommt erst, wenn du mit dem Entwurf fertig bist, wenn du auf die Erde zurückkehren musst. Dann fühlst du dich einsamer als je zuvor. Eine schreckliche Leere erwartet dich. Ich fülle diese Lücke, indem ich so schnell wie möglich mit dem nächsten Projekt beginne. Das Ausarbeiten einer ersten Idee – ob es nun nur eine Hütte oder ein ganzer Gebäudekomplex ist – reicht bereits aus, um mich erfüllt zu fühlen. Hauptsache etwas Neues entsteht."

Die anderen stimmen der Architektin zu.

„Demnach leidet der Architekt nicht, wenn er wie besessen zeichnet und sich kreativ völlig verausgabt?", fragt der Moderator.

Was für eine bescheuerte Frage!

„Nein!" Alle lachen laut auf. „*Leben zu schaffen* ist kein *leiden*. Architektur bedeutet, wertvollen toten Materialien wieder Leben einzuhauchen. Es ist ein extrem schöpferischer Prozess."

Leben zu schaffen vielleicht nicht, meint Back-Vocal nachdenklich, *aber Leben ist leiden, oder nicht, Jonte?*

Ich werfe die leere Weinflasche, die neben mir auf der Couch liegt, Richtung Bücherregal, wo sie zersplittert. Und jeder Splitter singt: Ja!

Aber muss das grundsätzlich so sein?, hakt er nach. *Könntest du das nicht ändern?*

Ich muss an Malte denken. Es passiert neuerdings oft, dass meine Gedanken in diese Richtung wandern. Er schickt mir weiterhin E-Mails, obwohl ich selten darauf antworte. Er erzählt mir alles über sein Leben, das Hotel, die Ausflüge mit den Kindern. Malte lebt, er leidet nicht. Er ist von Menschen umgeben, die ihm etwas bedeuten. Ich hingegen kam mir selbst während der gemeinsamen Urlaube mit Jonas unter all den Leuten stets verloren vor und dachte, es läge an mir. Heute weiß ich, dass das nicht stimmt. Ich war einsam mit Jonas. Ich litt. Und er auch.

Bei einem Architekturentwurf geht es um das Beleben, nicht um das Leben selbst. Ich aber will endlich leben. *Und* dabei schöne Häuser entwerfen. Genau in dieser Reihenfolge.

Morgen werde ich Malte ausführlich antworten. Morgen werde ich aufhören, Angst vor dem Gefühl zu haben, das aufkommt, wenn ich an ihn denke. Wir haben uns nur ein einziges Mal gesehen und uns nur kurz unterhalten. Aber etwas ist da zwischen uns passiert. Vielleicht das, was man das Sekundenglück nennt. Aber Maltes Versuch, mich zu kontaktieren, beweist, dass er es fortleben lassen will. Und meine Zurückhaltung letztendlich auch.

Ich habe keine Angst mehr vor meinen Gefühlen. Ich werde meine Chance ergreifen. Morgen werde ich zurückschreiben. Und definitiv mit dem Trinken aufhören! Und …

Ich nehme mein Smartphone und wähle Jonas' Rufnummer. Er nimmt sofort ab.

„Ich möchte mit dir reden. Morgen Abend. Und ohne Haakon!"

Er bittet mich um einen Kaffee und lässt sich in seinen alten Sessel fallen. Als er die Tasse nimmt, sehe ich, dass seine Hände zittern. „Brauchst du schon wieder einen Schuss?" Meine Stimme klingt hart.

Jonas senkt beschämt den Blick.

„Wie ist es nur möglich, dass du an diesen Dreck geraten konntest?" Diesmal ist der Klang meiner Stimme weicher.

Er zuckt die Achseln. „Ich habe es mal aus Spaß genommen, und es hat mir gefallen, weißt du."

„Nein, weiß ich nicht."

„Der eine nimmt Drogen, der andere trinkt."

„Mag sein. Aber lassen wir das. Wir reden jetzt über dich!"

„Über mich? Das brauche ich nun wirklich nicht. Lass es bitte endlich, mich beschützen zu wollen. Jeder von uns hat seinen Dämon, auch wenn der vielleicht manchmal jahrelang stillgehalten hat. Ich komme da schon allein wieder raus."

Ich sehe ihn an und frage mich, wie es möglich ist, dass ich diesen Mann heiraten konnte. An ihm ist nichts Anziehendes. Er ist von Kopf bis Fuß ein Versager.

Ich breche die Stille, die die Kluft zwischen uns verstärkt. „Ich kann nicht glauben, dass die Geschichte, die Haakon mir aufgetischt hat, wirklich wahr ist. Sag mir, dass es nicht stimmt, dass Haakon eine perverse Fantasie hat und ein niederträchtiges Bedürfnis, andere zu demütigen."

„Es ist alles wahr", sagt Jonas. „Und ich schäme mich wirklich dafür. Es hätte niemals passieren dürfen. Ich stand schwer unter Drogeneinfluss und wusste kaum, was ich tat. Wenn du das Kind bekommen hättest, hätte ich dir wirklich geholfen. Das habe ich dir damals gesagt, und das war die Wahrheit."

„Hättest du es mir irgendwann gestanden?"

„Niemals." Jetzt sieht er mich an. „Und ich nehme es Haakon verdammt übel, dass er es dir gesagt hat."

„Hast du eine Ahnung, wie ich mich jetzt fühle?"

„Jonte, ich kann nur immer wieder betonen, wie leid es mir tut, dass das passiert ist. Ich hoffe aufrichtig, dass es für dich wenigstens einen kleinen Unterschied macht, dass ich es war."

Jedes Gefühl in mir, das ich für diesen Dreckskerl einst empfunden habe, ist erloschen und einem Hass gewichen, der sich in der flachen Hand manifestiert, die ich ihm jetzt mit Wucht ins Gesicht schlage.

„Ihr habt mich vergewaltigt", zische ich. „Das ist eine Straftat. Ist dir das eigentlich klar? Was bist du doch für ein jämmerlicher Wicht!"

Wie ein Häufchen Elend kauert er im Sessel und meidet meinen Blick. Ich frage mich, wie er in diesem Zustand überhaupt noch arbeiten kann.

„Ich habe keinen Job mehr", flüstert er.

„Oh, hast du meine Gedanken erraten? Und wie kam es dazu? Hat man dich mit der Spritze auf dem Klo erwischt?"

Er zuckt die Achseln. „Umstrukturierung. Weniger Befugnisse. Ach was weiß ich. Ich hatte keinen Bock, mir da was vorschreiben zu lassen, also habe ich einer Kündigung zugestimmt und eine Abfindung kassiert. Das hat sowieso nichts gebracht. Und jetzt kann ich mich endlich ganz unseren Marketingplänen widmen."

„Aber das wird dauern, bis du da Geld siehst. Wie kommst du so lange klar?"

„Na ja, mein Geld ist bereits aufgebraucht. Wir leben über unsere Verhältnisse. Mit dem Arbeitslosengeld kommen wir kaum über die Runden."

„Was ist denn mit eurem Weinhandel?"

„Wir haben erst mal davon Abstand genommen. Mir blieb kein anderer Ausweg, als die Villa meines Vaters zum Verkauf anzubieten. Es gab fünf Besichtigungen und ein Gebot. Aber es ist nicht gerade berauschend. Ich bin mir sicher, dass ich für die Villa einen viel besseren Preis erzielen könnte. Aber wenn ich sie verkauft habe, kann ich eine Weile ruhiger schlafen. Und wenn du dich entscheiden könntest, auf einen Teil der Ansprüche zu verzichten, die dir nach der Scheidung zustehen, wäre das …"

„Darüber lasse ich durchaus mit mir reden, vorausgesetzt, du verzichtest auf die Hälfte unseres Hauses."

Jonas sieht betroffen aus. „Ähm, ich weiß nicht, ob Haakon damit einverstanden ist."

„Herrgott, Jonas, ich trenne mich nicht von Haakon, sondern von dir!"

„Haakon wird nicht lockerlassen."

„Er hat dich dazu animiert, mich zu vergewaltigen, Jonas. Er hat ein kleines Mädchen entführt, um Druck zu machen. Er hat angedeutet, dass er meiner Mutter etwas antun würde, wenn ich nicht kooperiere. Er hat mir mit jedem Wort gedroht, das er von sich gegeben hat. Dieser Mann ist ein eiskalter Psychopath."

Jonas lächelt – ein ekelhaft zärtliches Lächeln. „Du solltest nicht alles wörtlich nehmen, was er so von sich gibt. Du weißt doch: Hunde, die bellen, beißen nicht."

„Ich fürchte, da liegst du falsch, Jonas. Und ich rede nicht nur von der Vergewaltigung, die du vielleicht noch für einen seiner etwas geschmacklosen Scherze ansehen magst." Ich berichte ihm alles über den Morgen, an dem sein Vater starb. Die seltsamen Dinge, die mir aufgefallen sind, einschließlich der Hausschuhe auf der Treppe.

Jonas zuckt die Achseln. „Das ist in der Tat ziemlich seltsam. Aber was soll Haakon damit zu tun haben?"

Ich fasse es nicht. Mein Noch-Ehemann ist völlig verblendet. Hat der Stoff schon den letzten Rest seines Hirns vertilgt, oder ist die unterwürfige Liebe zu diesem Monstrum dafür verantwortlich?

Nach der zweiten Tasse Kaffee lässt sein Zittern ein wenig nach. Oder ich bemerke es nicht mehr, weil ich mich schon daran gewöhnt habe. Es ist auch egal.

Mir fällt auf, dass er immer wieder auf seine schwierige finanzielle Situation zu sprechen kommt. Er bemitleidet sich und versucht zugleich, mich zu manipulieren.

„Was ist denn mit den Ersparnissen deines Vaters?", werfe ich ein. „Habt ihr die auch aufgebraucht?"

„Ja, das ist schon weg. Es wäre sehr schön, wenn du vorübergehend auf deine Tantiemen bei dem Buch verzichten könntest. Denn davon kann ich gut leben, bis die Villa verkauft ist. Dann kriegst du es ja wieder."

„Wenn du so abgebrannt bist, frage ich mich, wie du deinen Drogenkonsum finanzierst? Was nimmst du eigentlich? Hängst du an der Nadel?"

Schweigen.

Ich kann Jonas nie wieder vertrauen. Ich habe ihn verloren. Definitiv.

Aber jetzt werde ich ihn überraschen: „In Ordnung. Ich verzichte auf die Tantiemen."

Er springt auf und will mich umarmen. Ich drücke ihn mit einer entschlossenen Geste von mir weg. „Danke, Jonte, danke, danke! Ich meine es ernst. Ich danke dir wirklich."

Ich fühle mich ausgelaugt. Als wäre ich einen Marathon gelaufen. Er muss hier raus, ich will ihn nie wiedersehen.

„Damit trennen sich aber unsere Wege endgültig. Es wird keine weiteren Geldspritzen geben. Dein Liebhaber kann sich einen Job suchen, und dir könnte eine Entziehungskur nicht schaden. Vielleicht wird aus dir dann wieder der Jonas, den ich kannte."

Er lächelt.

„Und sieh zu, dass Haakon nicht mehr in mein Leben eingreift. Er soll sich um seine eigenen Angelegenheiten kümmern."

Immer noch dieses verzückte Lächeln. „Das kann ich dir leider nicht versprechen, Jonte."

Siehst du es denn noch immer nicht? Fällst du jedes Mal wieder auf diese Hülle herein?, fragt mich Back-Vocal belustigt.

Jetzt erkenne ich es deutlich. Jonas existiert nicht mehr. Dort sitzt eine gut eingestellte Maschine, aus der nur Lügen quellen.

KAPITEL 52

Mir bleiben noch drei Tage, dann geht auch dieser Urlaub zu Ende. Bald muss ich wieder in der Lage sein, mich auf einen geregelten Tagesablauf zu konzentrieren. Die Kinowelt bringt mir aber auch die Ablenkung, die ich jetzt dringend brauche.

Annika wollte in diesen Tagen einen Kurztrip nach Oslo mit mir unternehmen, und sobald ich daran denke, füllt sich ein Tränenmeer hinter meinen Augen. Die Tränen kommen immer häufiger. Ich möchte jemandem davon erzählen, jemandem mein Herz ausschütten. Von dem Schmerz sprechen. Ihn teilen. Ich möchte, dass jemand erfährt, was mir angetan wurde. Dass ich als Zwölfjährige vergewaltigt wurde, dass mein Ehemann mich unter Anleitung seines Liebhabers im Schlaf missbraucht hat. Dass mir jemand Mifepriston-Tropfen verabreicht hat und ich deshalb mein Baby verloren habe. Mir fehlen aber die Worte für diese abscheulichen Taten. Vielleicht sollte ich weiterhin alles verdrängen, wie ich immer alles verdrängt habe, und nie wieder darüber nachdenken.

Ich frage mich, was passieren würde, wenn Haakon der Polizei in die Hände fallen würde und alles ausplaudert, was er über meine Vergangenheit herausgefunden hat. Oder wenn Mom es erfahren würde. Sie würde mich notfalls höchstpersönlich zur Polizei schleifen, wenn sie mich damit zu retten glaubte …

Die Nacht beginnt zu verblassen, der Morgen ist kühl, frisch und klar, ein Morgen, der wispernd vom beginnenden Tag erzählt. Ich habe den zweiten Entwurf für das Klosterhotel fast fertig und werde ihn bald einscannen. Als kurz darauf eine Mail vom Orden eintrudelt, in der er seine Begeisterung über die überarbeiteten ersten Entwürfe zum Ausdruck bringt, falle ich aus allen Wolken. Mein Magen zieht sich zusammen. Ich frage mich, wieso der Orden diese Entwürfe kennt, denn ich habe sie niemandem gezeigt und bislang auch keine E-Mails verschickt.

Die Schlussfolgerung erschüttert mich. Derjenige, der in meinem Haus war, ist im Besitz der Skizzen, die ich auf meinem gestohlenen Laptop gesichert hatte. Sofort projiziert sich Annika auf meine Iris, ich sehe die Blutlache, den leblosen Körper in einem weißen Kleid.

Meine Finger zittern. Zweimal versuche ich, Jonas Handynummer zu wählen. Erst beim dritten Mal gelingt es mir, die Mailbox meldet sich. Ich spreche wütend drauf.

„Hier ist Jonte. Der Orden hat meinen ersten Entwurf vorliegen, und er kann ihn nur von dir oder von deinem beschissenen Freund bekommen haben. Entweder du hast neulich, als du hier warst, meine Entwürfe kopiert, oder dein Haakon ist in Besitz meines Laptops. Und das würde bedeuten, dass er Annika auf dem Gewissen hat. Ich werde jetzt die Polizei anrufen."

Ich schnaufe. Das Atmen schmerzt. Ich muss mich beruhigen und einen klaren Kopf bekommen, um zu begreifen, dass ich nicht nur körperlich vergewaltigt, sondern auch geistig missbraucht worden bin. In der Küche trinke ich rasch ein Glas Wasser, Alkohol ist tabu.

Es ist ganz einfach. Man muss nur die Türen öffnen, die schon immer da gewesen sind, wenn auch manchmal verborgen. Aber dahinter verstecken sich die Geheimnisse.

Im Wohnzimmer klingelt mein Handy. Sekunden später drücke ich die grüne Hörertaste. Haakon meldet sich am anderen Ende der Leitung.

„Jonte, du gehst mir langsam auf den Sack! Dieser Anruf ist meine allerletzte Warnung. Stell dich mir nicht in den Weg, außer du möchtest gerne deine Mutter loswerden. Was passiert, wenn du nicht wieder Verstand annimmst, hast du dir selbst zuzuschreiben!"

Klick!

Unmittelbar danach klingelt mein Handy erneut.

„Ja? Was ist noch?", brülle ich in den Hörer.

„Oh!" Dann nach kurzer Pause: „Hallo, Jonte! Malte hier. Ich bin heute in Drammen. Wollen wir uns auf einen Kaffee treffen? Ich würde dich sehr gerne wiedersehen."

Ich stimme zu, sage ihm, wo ich wohne, und lege auf. Dann drücke ich sofort meinen Kopf zwischen die Knie. Ein Summen saust in meinen Ohren, die Welt dreht sich um mich herum. Ich schluchze und ertrinke fast in meiner Angst. Ich habe mich überschätzt, ich komme an Haakon nicht ran. Er sitzt am längeren Hebel. Ich habe das Bedürfnis, die Angst in Alkohol zu ertränken. Wieder mal.

Da wird mir plötzlich klar, dass nicht die verschlossenen Türen meiner Seele das Problem sind, nicht die Geheimnisse dahinter, die ich zu verbergen suche, sondern ich selbst. Und nun sehe ich auch endlich die Lösung. Die richtige Perspektive gewinnt an Kontur. Ich sehe die Angst, die eine Mauer um mich errichtet hat. Statt Löcher hineinzuschlagen, setze ich immer wieder einen neuen Stein drauf. Bis ich irgendwann darunter ersticke …

Sprenge die Mauer, und die Türen öffnen sich von selbst!, befiehlt mir die Stimme hinter meiner Stirn, und zum ersten Mal hört sie sich hoffnungsvoll an.

Ich nicke. Es flimmert vor meinen Augen. Ich brauche frische Luft. Ein Blick aus dem Fenster zeigt grauschwarze Wolken, die an der fahlen Wintersonne vorbeiziehen. Das Licht sickert durch die Äste der Bäume in meinem Garten und wirft Schatten.

Ich sehne mich nach einem Spaziergang durch den Wald. Er hat mir stets Trost gespendet. Tagsüber schlafen die Dämonen dort.

KAPITEL 53

„Hey!" Malte lächelt vorsichtig. Seine Augen suchen meine, sein Blick ist abwartend.

Ich seufze erleichtert. „Oh, Malte!"

Er streckt die Arme aus. „Darf man dich umarmen?"

Ich möchte in ihn hineinkriechen, tief in seine Wärme, unauffindbar für die ganze Welt. Obwohl ich ihn kaum kenne, habe ich ihn unglaublich vermisst.

Malte ist ein attraktiver Mann. Er hat dieses gewisse Etwas. Ich bin bestimmt nicht die einzige Frau, die das bemerkt hat.

Bilde dir also bloß nichts ein!

Aber da ist noch die behinderte Mutter seiner Kinder. Wurde sie einfach von ihm beiseitegeschoben? Ich mag dien Gedanken nicht, dass ein Jonas in ihm steckt.

Dennoch fühlt sich das, was zwischen uns aufkeimt, einfach gut an. In seiner Gegenwart spüre ich festen Boden unter meinen Füßen.

Malte bringt eine geballte Ladung Kälte ins Haus.

„Komm schnell herein, bevor wir hier draußen zu Eis erstarren", sage ich.

Er sitzt in meiner Küche, ich auf der einen, er auf der anderen Seite des Tisches, als ob er schon immer da gewesen wäre und hierhergehören würde. Ein Mann im Zentrum meiner Welt, der mir einen Kaffee einschenkt. Und eine zweite Tasse, eine dritte. Ich genieße seine Fürsorge.

„Ich soll dich ganz herzlich von meiner Familie grüßen, Jonte."

Sein Gesichtsausdruck bringt mich zum Lachen. „Aber sie kennen mich doch gar nicht."

„Na ja, ich hab viel von dir erzählt, und sie sind schon sehr neugierig auf dich."

„Wer sind *sie* überhaupt?"

Er schmunzelt. „Meine Kinder zum Beispiel. Ich erzählte ihnen, dass wir uns das erste Mal bei Bente getroffen haben und dass diese Begegnung etwas in mir ausgelöst hat. Sie wollen natürlich wissen, ob das auf Gegenseitigkeit beruht."

„Du hast aber neugierige Kinder." Leichtigkeit liegt in meiner Stimme.

„Das ist keine Antwort. Warum antwortest du nicht, Jonte?"

Ich spüre Unbehagen, gewinne den Eindruck, dass die großzügige Küche enger wird. Ich brauche ein weites, freies Feld. „Du kommst mir zu schnell sehr nah."

„Und ist das nicht erlaubt?"

„Ich kenne dich doch kaum."

„Was möchtest du denn wissen?"

Ich atme erleichtert auf, sehe ihn direkt an. „Hast du deine Frau verlassen, weil sie zur Invalidin wurde?", platzt es aus mir heraus.

Er verliert sein spitzbübisches Lächeln, aber er wirkt ehrlich auf mich, als er erwidert: „Ich habe einen Tisch in einem kleinen Restaurant reserviert. Lass uns dort zu Abend essen, dann werde ich dir alles erzählen."

Trotz meiner Zweifel werden meine Gefühle für Malte in diesem Moment noch stärker. Unsere E-Mails, unsere liebevollen Telefonate, all das zeigt mir, dass Malte für mich notwendig geworden ist, unverzichtbar.

Er ist bei mir. Und vielleicht brauche ich genau das: dass sich jemand ausschließlich für mich interessiert. Er besänftigt meine Angst, er lässt das wiederauferstehen, was ich unter ihr begraben zu haben glaubte: Zuversicht, Vertrauen, Liebe.

Als ich in Maltes Wagen einsteige, schiebt meine Nachbarin den Vorhang beiseite. Ich winke Malvi Oddbjørn lächelnd zu.

„Ist das der hiesige Straßenvoyeur?", fragt Malte amüsiert.

„Richtig, sie beobachtet jeden von sieben Uhr morgens bis elf Uhr abends. Aber sie ist völlig harmlos, nimmt Pakete vom Postboten entgegen und merkt sich, wer an der Tür war, wenn jemand mal nicht zu Hause ist. Sie ist ein guter Wachhund." Und ich füge im selben Small-Talk-Ton hinzu: „Neulich haben Kids aus der Nachbarschaft eine tote Katze in ihren Garten gelegt. Malvi hat panische Angst vor Katzen. Da hat sie mir wirklich leidgetan."

Malte ist entsetzt. Er sieht mich mit weit aufgerissenen Augen an. „Was? Wie grausam ist das denn?"

Das möchte ich auch können. Die Augen so unschuldig aufreißen, Worte aussprechen, die so schnell und laut nach draußen purzeln, weil man selbst mit dieser grausamen Parallelwelt in keiner Verbindung steht …

Plötzlich ist meine saloppe Stimmung dahin. Nun ist da wieder die Angst. Kälte umschließt meine Seele selbst an der Seite dieses Mannes. Hat vielleicht diese tote Katze etwas mit mir zu tun?, frage ich mich betroffen. Der Moment geht so schnell vorbei, wie er gekommen ist.

„Alles okay, Jonte?" Er klingt besorgt.

„Alles gut." Ich lehne mich entspannt zurück.

Von der Wärme seiner Stimme umfangen, möchte ich mit ihm nach Paris fahren, durch die Stadt der Liebe streifen, in einem Hotel mit ihm schlafen. Ich möchte … meine Gedanken bei mir behalten.

Das Erste, was ich beim Betreten des Restaurants wahrnehme, ist ein ausgestopfter Tiger über dem Kamin, die angenehme Wärme und der köstliche Duft der Speisen. Erst jetzt spüre ich, wie hungrig ich bin.

Der Kellner führt uns an einen Tisch am Fenster, mit Blick auf den Drammensfjord.

„Sie haben hier köstliche Krabben in Knoblauchsoße als Vorspeise", sagt Malte. „Sollen wir?"

Ich nicke. Mein Blick wandert zu den anderen Tischen, an denen fröhliche Menschen Wein zum Essen trinken. „Für mich bitte nur ein Wasser", sage ich der Kellnerin, als sie mir die Weinkarte reicht.

Während wir essen, erzählt Malte mir seine Geschichte. „Isa war meine große Liebe. Wir kannten uns seit der Schulzeit, besuchten gemeinsam die Universität in Oslo und machten beide den Master in Betriebswirtschaft. Es war von Anfang an klar, dass wir heiraten und drei Kinder haben würden. Und alles lief auch wie geplant. Ich habe damals oft gedacht, dass unser Leben zu perfekt war, um wahr zu sein. Isa wollte auch nie etwas von möglichen Rückschlägen hören. Sie glaubte an das Glück." Malte hält einen Moment inne.

Ich höre ihm zu, und die Zeit vergeht tröpfchenweise. Ich ersticke sie, halte sie an, und spüre, wie die Kraft in mich zurückkehrt. Wärme durchströmt mit ungeheurer Gewalt meinen Körper. Ich fühle mich lebendig.

„Wir wünschten uns ein Kind", fährt er fort, „und schon wurde Isa schwanger. Sie schien nie Schmerzen zu haben. Wenn ich mich jemals über etwas beklagte, lachte sie es hinweg. Dann hielt sie mich für zimperlich. Deshalb war es so schwer zu verstehen, als sie nach dem Hirntumor nur noch von körperlichen Beschwerden sprach. Selbst bei einem eingerissenen Nagel geriet sie auf einmal in Panik." Er schüttelt den Kopf. „Ihr Neurologe erklärte mir, dass es häufig vorkommt, dass sich jemand nach einem Hirnleiden verändert. Die Operation verlief erfolgreich. Der Tumor war gutartig und konnte vollständig entfernt werden. Aber Isa konnte plötzlich nicht mehr laufen und bekam Gewichtsprobleme. Doch der Arzt meinte, dass sie sich nach der Rehabilitation wieder erholen würde."

„War das eine Fehldiagnose?"

„Physisch geht es ihr viel besser. Aber sie kann nicht mehr ohne Hilfsmittel gehen und ist heute auf einen Rollstuhl angewiesen. Aber es ist unklar, ob der eigentliche Grund dafür psychischer Natur ist."

Ich werfe einen Blick auf den Tiger über dem Kamin. Er symbolisiert die Kluft zwischen Leichtigkeit und Bedrohung, im Leben eine gefährliche Bedrohung, aber hier nur noch ein schönes Schaustück von verführerischer Leichtigkeit. Ich lege mein Besteck beiseite.

Malte lächelt. „Die Portionen sind aber auch riesig."

Ich nippe an meinem Wasser.

„Isa hätte durchaus dauerhaft mit uns im Haus leben können. Ich schlug ihr sogar vor, alles behindertengerecht umzugestalten, aber sie lehnte das ab." Er hält einen Moment inne. „Sie ist nicht mehr die Isa von einst, und sie wird es nie wieder sein." Er muss mir angesehen haben, dass ich alles erfahren will.

Ich will wissen, worauf ich mich einlasse.

„Weißt du, Jonte, zuerst habe ich ja weiter mit ihr zusammengelebt. Ich habe mir gesagt, dass ich die Veränderungen akzeptieren muss, weil ich uns einst versprochen habe: in guten und in schlechten Zeiten. Aber die Isa, der ich das Versprechen gegeben habe, gibt es nicht mehr. Ich empfinde nicht mehr das, was ich einmal für sie empfunden habe. Irgendwann lebten wir beide zwar in unserem Haus, aber dennoch waren wir allein."

Ich spüre, dass er einen Moment abgleitet, in eine graue Welt. Und ich sehe das tote Lächeln des Tigers an der Wand und entdecke in Maltes vor Leben sprühenden Augen auch etwas Totes.

„Wie ist das passiert?", frage ich leise.

„Es ist nicht über Nacht passiert. Ich habe es erst im Nachhinein realisiert. Als sie nach der Operation nach Hause zurückkehrte, habe ich sie rund um die Uhr betreut. Ich habe sie gewaschen, sie angezogen, ihr auf die Toilette geholfen. Ich sagte mir immer wieder, das ist nicht Isa, es sind nur Körperteile, um die ich mich jetzt kümmern muss. Die wahre Isa kommt eines Tages zu mir zurück. So kapselte ich mich innerlich ab, das mag falsch gewesen sein, aber die ganze Situation war zu belastend."

Stille bricht ein. Ich warte.

Malte fährt sich durchs Haar. „Wir passten uns an, begnügten uns mit dem, was übrig blieb. Isa akzeptierte ihre Grenzen. Aber sie veränderte sich, geriet schnell in Panik, entwickelte eine grausame Angst, glaubte jede Minute sterben zu müssen. So ging sie auch mit den Kindern um, die sich irgendwann vor ihr fürchteten. Ich suchte eine Pflegerin für Isa und ging mit den Kids zum Psychologen. Das hat geholfen. Bente und mein Vater waren auch stets für uns da. Ohne sie wären wir verloren gewesen. Allmählich schienen wir uns stabilisiert zu haben."

„Und ab wann kamen die Probleme?"

Er seufzt tief. „Als Isa wieder mit mir schlafen wollte. Ich hatte monatelang davon geträumt und mich danach gesehnt. Aber sie schloss mich erst einmal aus, und ich überließ ihr die Entscheidung. Der Neurologe erklärte mir, dass der Sex anders sein könnte, dass sich Isa anders verhalten könnte. Aber er hat mir nie erklärt, dass sich meine Gefühle für Isa ebenfalls ändern könnten. Ich selbst habe auch nicht damit gerechnet und war schockiert, als ich feststellte, dass mein Verlangen nach ihr verschwunden war, dass ich gar nicht mehr wollte, dass Isa mich berührte."

Ich sehe, wie zerbrechlich Malte ist, als er versucht, das Erlebte in die richtigen Worte zu fassen.

„Du kannst alles sagen, Malte."

„Ich konnte die Erinnerungen an das Waschen, das Anziehen, den Gang zur Toilette nicht verdrängen", sagt er heiser. „Immer wieder sah ich es vor mir, sobald Lisa einen Annäherungsversuch startete. Ich dachte, es würde nachlassen, und bat sie um Zeit und Geduld. Isa hat es nicht verstanden. Sie sagte, sie sei immer noch dieselbe. Es dauerte Monate, bis ich ihr gestand, dass ich für sie nicht mehr dieselben Gefühle hegte wie früher, und danach war ich erleichtert. Aber Isa konnte es nicht akzeptieren. Sie verlangte, dass ich meine Gefühle wieder änderte, als ob das so einfach möglich wäre. Und damit hat sie mich letztendlich in die Scheidung getrieben. Schließlich wollte sie auch nicht mehr bei uns leben. Das ist die ganze Geschichte. Meine Ehe hat die Krankheit meiner Frau nicht überstanden. Die Leidenschaft ist erloschen. Ich möchte nicht in einer Beziehung alt werden, die der eines Geschwisterpaares ähnelt."

„Und eure Kinder?"

„Irgendwann stellte Isa Bedingungen. Sie wollte die Kinder nach der Trennung. Das wollte ich nicht. Isa war zu labil und die Kinder zu jung, um ihr ausgeliefert zu sein." Er sieht sich um. „Isa und ich haben hier ganz selten gegessen. Sie mochte das Lokal nicht. Nach der Trennung war ich oft mit den Kids hier. Für mich ist dieses Restaurant ein besonderer Ort, ich verbinde ihn mit einem Neuanfang."

Meine Augen suchen unwillkürlich den Tiger über dem Kamin. Suchen das Monster darin. Es hatte seine Klauen ausgestreckt, nach der Liebe zwischen Isa und Malte gegriffen.

Aber ich werde nicht zulassen, dass es mich mit seiner pelzigen Krallenhand packt.

Denn in Maltes Nähe komme ich endlich zur Ruhe.

KAPITEL 54

Wir verzichten auf ein Dessert, und ich schlage vor, zu Hause einen Kaffee zu trinken.

Ich bin froh, dass Malte das Gesprächsthema gewechselt hat und die Szenen der Vergangenheit hinter sich gelassen hat. Seine Offenheit hat mich beeindruckt und berührt.

Er hat mich berührt.

Ich einige mich mit der warnenden Stimme hinter meiner Stirn auf einen Moment der Stille. Wir gehen schweigend zum Auto zurück.

Im Wagen suchen meine Augen nicht die Dunkelheit hinter der Windschutzscheibe, sondern blicken immer wieder auf Malte. Eine Frage steht im Raum, er greift nach ihr.

„Was denkst du jetzt, Jonte?"

„Du hast vorhin erwähnt, dass dir jede Menge Unverständnis entgegengebracht wurde", erwidere ich.

„Das stimmt. Insbesondere von Isas Familie. Ihre Eltern wollen nichts mehr von mir wissen. Mein Vater hat sich auch mit meiner Entscheidung schwergetan, aber das legte sich später wieder. Nur Bente hat mich stets unterstützt. Sie weiß, was das Scheitern einer Liebe bedeutet und wie schwer es ist, jemanden zu verlassen." Malte schaut für einen Moment zur Seite. „War es okay, dass ich es dir erzählt habe?"

„Natürlich. Hast du noch immer Kontakt zu Isa?"

„Ja. Ich besuche sie ein paarmal im Jahr. Wir mailen manchmal. Wir sind einander noch immer freundschaftlich verbunden."

„Empfindet sie noch etwas für dich?"

„Ich weiß es nicht, ich frage nie danach."

Malte hält vor meinem Haus und stellt den Motor ab. „Ich habe in letzter Zeit viel an dich gedacht, Jonte. Ich würde dich gerne besser kennenlernen. Aber ich glaube, dass du zuerst ein paar Dinge abschließen musst. Ist das richtig?"

Ich nicke. Die Stimme hinter meiner Stirn ist still, sie hat sich in Maltes Nähe nach und nach verabschiedet. Meine Verunsicherung ist ebenfalls gewichen.

„Hast du schon die Scheidung eingereicht?"

Sofort ist die innere Stimme wieder da, die guten Gedanken werden wie von einer Schere abgeschnitten, weil ich seinen Blick aufgefangen und plötzlich wieder Angst habe. Mein altes Leben greift nach mir.

Er berührt sanft meinen Arm. „Komm, wir gehen erst mal ins Haus", sagt er sanft.

Die Frage nach der Scheidung hat mich erschüttert. Wie erkläre ich ihm das? Ich sitze am Küchentisch und beobachte ihn, wie er zwei Cappuccinos macht. Ein Außenstehender könnte annehmen, dass wir seit Jahren miteinander verheiratet sind. Die Anwesenheit dieses Mannes in meinem Haus hat etwas Selbstverständliches.

Ich will nicht, dass er geht.

Malte sitzt mir gegenüber, nimmt meine Hand. „Was ist los, Jonte?", fragt er.

„Viel. Zu viel."

„Möchtest du darüber reden?"

Die Worte umkreisen mich aus verschiedenen Perspektiven, die richtigen Worte sind nicht dabei. Aber das spielt jetzt keine Rolle. Malte ist dieser Jemand, dem ich endlich mein Herz ausschütten kann.

Deshalb erzähle ich Malte ohne Umschweife, warum ich schwanger geworden bin. Seine Hand bleibt still auf meiner, während die Worte aus mir herausprudeln. Ich muss alles loswerden. Möchte es teilen.

„Das ist ja schrecklich, Jonte. Das ist nicht nur ein widerlicher Betrug, das ist absolut abstoßend. Es ist ein Verbrechen. Und du solltest die beiden anzeigen. Sie haben das Schlimmste verdient."

„Aber ich kann nicht beweisen, dass es nicht einvernehmlich geschah", widerspreche ich. „Sie würden mich eine Lügnerin nennen."

„Aber es muss doch einen Weg geben." Malte ist so wütend, dass er nicht mehr ruhig sitzen kann. „Wem hast du sonst noch davon erzählt?"

„Niemandem. Es ist zu persönlich."

„Natürlich. Es ist entsetzlich, dass sie dir das angetan haben. Was sind das nur für Bastarde! Ich könnte beide mit bloßen Händen erwürgen. Aber das hilft dir nicht weiter. Du musst damit fertigwerden, um überleben zu können. Ich würde dir gerne dabei behilflich sein."

Ich schweige eine Weile, bin in meinem Trauma verloren. „Ich möchte es einfach vergessen."

„Verdränge es nicht, Jonte", warnt er mich. „Überlege lieber, wie du damit umgehen kannst. Ich meine es ernst. Verdrängen ist nie eine Lösung. Es wird dich irgendwann wieder einholen."

Er hat recht. Ich weiß nur allzu gut, wovon er spricht.

„Warum haben sie dir so etwas angetan, Jonte?"

Mit dieser Frage habe ich gerechnet. „Ich glaube, dass sie unter Einfluss von Drogen standen. Jonas muss vollkommen von Sinnen gewesen sein. Er hat mich kürzlich um Verzeihung gebeten."

Ich darf nicht weitergehen, sondern muss vorsichtig sein. Ich darf nicht zulassen, dass noch mehr Personen gefährdet werden.

„Nimmt Jonas noch immer Drogen?"

„Ich denke schon."

„Was für ein Chaos! Ich nehme an, du willst ihn so schnell wie möglich loswerden?"

„Stimmt. Aber ich befürchte, dass es eine Schlammschlacht wird, die Anwälte werden alles versuchen, es geht um Tantiemen, Bauobjekte, eben um viel Geld. Ich hasse diese Unruhe in meinem Leben. Ich werde gleich nach Silvester die Scheidung anstreben."

„Was macht dir Angst, Jonte? Ich spüre es doch."

Mit dieser Frage habe ich nicht gerechnet. Ich zögere die Antwort hinaus, und als der richtige Moment längst vergangen ist, breche ich in Tränen aus.

KAPITEL 55

Er hält mich, und ich möchte mich endlos an ihn schmiegen. Seine Arme beschützen mich nicht nur, sie trösten mich. Seine Wärme strömt in meinen Körper, selbst das Zittern lässt nach.

Ich spüre unser gemeinsam geschaffenes Territorium: das gegenseitige Erkennen und das schweigende Einverständnis. Dann ist da nur noch ein Gedanke, vielleicht von Anfang an, aber nie laut ausgesprochen. Stille ist um uns, als wir hinaufgehen. Oben auf der Treppe küsst er mich.

Ich lasse es geschehen, sehe Finger, die sich in meinen Händen verfangen und meinen Körper erforschen, Lippen, die mich bewundern, Augen, die mich beruhigen. Wir halten beide regelmäßig den Atem an, ich rieche das Verlangen und atme eine alles betäubende Leidenschaft ein. Ich fühle mich merkwürdig fokussiert. Konzentriert. Ich verspüre ein Lächeln, ein Bild stellt sich ein, ein Gedanke, der mich, auf dem Bett liegend, spiegelt. Ich sehe einen Wechsel der Farben, sich liebende Körper, süßes Gemurmel, das seine Lippen überschreitet. Ich denke einen Moment an Verhütung, aber Malte flüstert mir zu, dass er sterilisiert wurde. Und dann liebe ich ihn mit jeder Faser meines Körpers.

Und meiner Seele.

Malte liegt neben mir und schläft tief. Es ist zehn Minuten vor vier. Ich bin hellwach.

Das Bett ist angenehm warm. Eine sichere Wärme. Trotzdem halte ich es hier nicht aus, fliehe leise schleichend über die Treppe nach unten.

Das Licht ist noch an und heißt mich willkommen. Dies war einst das Zuhause von Jonas und mir, jetzt gehört es mir allein. Ich werde mich von einigen Dingen trennen. Die kleinen Bronzestatuen, die Jonas gesammelt hat, sein Sessel, die Fotos, auf denen wir beide zu sehen sind. Es ist alles noch da, doch plötzlich fühlen sich diese Dinge wie eine Verletzung meiner Privatsphäre an. Ich setze mich auf die Couch und schaue mich um.

Etwas hat sich geändert.

Ein anderer Mann hat mein Refugium betreten. Ich habe ihn nicht nur in mein Haus gelassen, sondern auch in mein Herz. Er ist Teil meiner Gefühle, meines Verlangens, meiner Verletzlichkeit. Dieser Mann ist kein Fremder mehr, er gehört jetzt zu mir.

Ich suche nicht mehr nach Worten, denn das Schweigen, das Ungesagte und selbst meine Scham ist ein Teil von uns. Ich sollte mich wohlfühlen. Seine Anwesenheit ist überall zu spüren, seine Atmung dringt durch das Bettlaken, alles an ihm wärmt mich.

Und doch glaube ich zu ersticken.

Angst! Sie ist langlebig, eine brennende, glühende Wunde an meiner Seele. Ich will ihr keine Macht mehr einräumen, aber sie lässt sich an meinem Gesicht ablesen, ist in meiner Stimme zu hören. Mit bloßem Auge sehe ich sie in meinen Adern pochen. Mein Blut fließt in einem geschlossenen Kreislauf der Angst. Schwärme düsterer Erinnerungen sind um mich herum, sie zwingen sich mir auf und können nicht vertrieben werden.

Mit jedem Gedanken entferne ich mich mehr von Aaron. Er ist tot, er war meiner Liebe nicht würdig. Er hat mich benutzt, getäuscht, betrogen. Wie Jonas. Ich möchte Aaron vergessen.

Dass ich dennoch immer wieder an ihn denken muss, liegt an der schmerzhaften Erinnerung, der ich mich trotz all meiner verzweifelten Versuche niemals entziehen konnte. Sie ist untrennbar mit Aaron verknüpft.

Das weiße Kleid in der Dunkelheit. Ein weißer Fleck im schwarzen Nichts, der Aufprall, die Gestalt auf dem Pflaster, die Blutlache um ihren Kopf. Rot auf Weiß. Die Totenstille, die seitdem in meinen Ohren kreischt …

Ich rannte zu ihr, nur um festzustellen, dass sie tot war. Meine Entscheidung, nach dem Unfall wieder in den Wagen zu steigen und wegzufahren, entbehrte jeder Logik. Ich geriet in Panik, konnte nicht klar denken. Ich floh und schaute nicht zurück – eine unbeschreiblich feige, kriminelle Tat.

Damals habe ich nicht zurückgeschaut, aber seitdem muss ich jeden Tag zurückblicken, sind meine Augen auf diesen Punkt in der Vergangenheit geheftet. Rot auf Weiß.

Aus der Zeitung erfuhr ich später, dass sie Ebba Hagebak hieß und vierundzwanzig Jahre alt war. So wie ich damals. Ein Leben voller Hoffnungen und Erwartungen. Wie meines. Beide auf einen Schlag für immer zerstört.

Eine zweite Anzeige hatte ein Ingmar Morano aufgegeben, der Mann, den Ebba zwei Wochen später hätte heiraten sollen. Die Polizei startete einen Aufruf, suchte nach möglichen Zeugen des Unfalls, aber niemand meldete sich. Mein rücksichtsloser Fahrstil, mein verantwortungsloses Trinken und mein blinder Zorn hatten ihr den Tod gebracht. Und mir die Schuld.

Dabei hatte die Uferstraße, die ihr zum Verhängnis wurde, nicht einmal auf meinem Weg gelegen. Ich fuhr Jahre später noch einmal dorthin, nur um festzustellen, dass ich mich in jener Nacht verfahren hatte.

Niemand kam je auf die Idee, dass ich diesen Unfall verursacht haben könnte.

Mittlerweile sind vierzehn Jahre vergangen. An manchen Tagen ist die Erinnerung so lebendig, als wäre es gestern passiert.

Mir ist kalt. Die Wärme liegt oben in meinem Schlafzimmer, aber ich kann nicht wieder zu Malte hinaufgehen. Sein Lächeln ist echt und unverfälscht, es leuchtet.

Ich fürchte mich davor, dass meine Erinnerungen in meinen Zügen sichtbar geworden sind.

Ich nehme die Wolldecke von der Couch und rolle mich darin ein. Vielleicht kann ich zumindest von Malte träumen.

KAPITEL 56

Jemand berührt mein Gesicht. Ich wache auf und seufze: „Malte."

„Du liegst auf der Couch. Habe ich zu sehr geschnarcht?"

Ich strecke mich. „Ja", lüge ich, „aber das hat mich gar nicht so sehr gestört. Ich musste darüber nachdenken, was mit uns gerade passiert. Und das kann ich am besten, wenn ich alleine bin."

Er küsst mich. „Grübel nicht zu viel, sondern genieße einfach unsere gemeinsam verbrachten Stunden. Ich tue es auch. Ich habe einen Kaffee für dich gemacht." Er küsst mich wieder. „Ich würde lieber den ganzen Tag bei dir bleiben, aber ich habe Termine und muss dich jetzt leider verlassen", flüstert er. „Aber ich melde mich, sobald ich kann. Okay?"

„Ja, das wäre schön."

Als Malte die Haustür hinter sich geschlossen hat, gehe ich zum Fenster und beobachte, wie er in sein Auto steigt und davonfährt, gleichzeitig kontrollieren meine Augen die gesamte Umgebung. Die Straße ist ruhig, weder hängt meine Nachbarin am Fenster, noch liegt Haakon auf der Lauer.

Meine Atmung stockt, und mein Puls schießt sofort in die Höhe, wenn ich an diesen Bastard denke. Haakon darf nichts über Malte und mich erfahren. Stundenlang gab es dieses Monster nicht mehr für mich, keine unangenehme Stimme, keine widerlichen Details, keine üblen Drohungen.

Es gab nur diesen wunderbaren Mann, der mich so intensiv berührt hat. Aber jetzt, wo er wieder fort ist, werde ich in die Realität zurückgeworfen.

Der gestohlene Laptop kommt mir wieder in den Sinn und der überarbeitete Entwurf, der dem Orden bereits vorliegt. Die Erinnerung lastet so schwer auf mir, dass ich zu ersticken glaube.

Hat Haakon ihn gestohlen, oder wäre auch Jonas zu diesem Einbruch in der Lage gewesen? Er hat sich verändert. Liegt es an seinem Drogenkonsum? Hätte Jonas Annika niederschlagen können? Die nächste Frage, die mir in den Sinn kommt, lähmt mich fast. Hat Jonas etwas mit dem Tod seines Vaters zu tun? Hat er mir bei seinem letzten Besuch die Mifepriston-Tropfen verabreicht? Er hatte den Tee in der Küche zubereitet.

Ich kann das nicht glauben. Wie enttäuscht er auch über die Ablehnung seines Vaters gewesen sein mag und wie sehr ihn womöglich der Gedanke an ein Produkt seiner Vergewaltigung belastet haben mag, solcher Taten hätte er sich nicht schuldig gemacht.

Ich werde unruhig und brauche einen Halt. Ich rufe Malte an. Er reagiert überrascht.

„Ich möchte nur wissen, ob es dir gut geht."

Er lacht. „Warum sollte es mir nicht gut gehen?"

„Auf der Autobahn", murmle ich, „passieren so oft Unfälle."

„Du bist süß", sagt er. „Mach dir keine Sorgen. Ich bin angeschnallt und übertrete nie die Höchstgeschwindigkeit. Was wirst du morgen machen?"

„Morgen ist mein letzter Urlaubstag. Ich habe mich mit meiner Mom zum Shoppen verabredet."

„Genieße es, Jonte. Und ruf mich bitte an, wenn du morgen nach Hause kommst. Egal, wie spät es ist. Ich möchte ab sofort jeden Tag deine Stimme hören."

„In Ordnung", verspreche ich.

Es ist riskant. Ich muss sicherstellen, dass Jonas nicht herausfindet, dass Malte und ich uns nähergekommen sind. Dieser Gedanke macht mir Angst. Drogen verändern Menschen, sie machen sie unberechenbar und aggressiv.

Plötzlich höre ich draußen Schritte und spähe hinaus in die Dunkelheit. Ich spüre ein Kribbeln auf der Haut.

Jetzt mach dich bloß nicht verrückt!

Die Schritte kommen auf mein Haus zu. Wie paralysiert stehe ich Sekunden später vor meiner Wohnungstür. Jemand befindet sich auf der anderen Seite der Tür. Als die Klingel schrillt, löst sich der Bann.

Eine Klingel ist Normalität.

Psychopathen und Einbrecher klingeln nicht.

Dennoch spähe ich diesmal durch den Türspion, um nicht wieder Haakon reinzulassen. Ich kann aber nichts sehen.

Ich zögere, dann öffne ich.

Doch da ist wirklich nichts.

Nur Dunkelheit.

Ich versuche ein Lächeln, versuche es auf meine Lippen zu heben, aber es missglückt.

Ich gehe ins Schlafzimmer und lasse die Jalousien herunter. In meinem Bett kann mich niemand beobachten, wenn ich an die Stunden mit Malte zurückdenke. Diese Erinnerungen gehören nun auch zu mir.

Ich nehme die Gedanken an sein Lächeln und seine Liebkosungen mit in den Schlaf.

KAPITEL 57

Früh am Morgen brechen Mom und ich zum Shoppingcenter auf. Meine Mutter fährt, und die Welt gleitet an mir vorbei. Der Tag ist so blau, und blau ist auch der Drammensfjord, auf dem eine kleine Fähre von Ufer zu Ufer eine Trennlinie auf die Wasserfläche zeichnet. Blau und Blau, zwei Farben. Die Stadt breitet ein malerisches Winterbild vor mir aus, fast als wollte sie mich veranlassen, etwas dazu zu sagen. Ich denke an Malte und spüre ein Lächeln auf meinem Gesicht.

Nach der Einkaufsorgie meiner Mutter essen wir am Hafen zu Mittag.

„Ich habe seit Ewigkeiten nicht mehr so gelacht, Mom", sage ich und lege das Besteck beiseite.

„Und ich habe dich schon lange nicht mehr so fröhlich gesehen wie heute, Jonte. Ich bin froh, dass du das Problem Jonas angehst", fügt Mom leise hinzu und umarmt mich. „Und wenn du im neuen Jahr keinen netten Kerl suchst, mache ich das für dich."

„Du drohst mir doch nicht etwa, Mom?" Meine Wangen glühen plötzlich.

„Warum errötest du, Jonte?", fragt sie und sieht mich aufmerksam an. „Du willst mir doch nicht sagen …"

„Es gibt nichts zu sagen, Mama."

Sie lächelt. „Darf ich dir eine Frage stellen?"

„Natürlich", sage ich beiläufig.

„Wie ist sein Name?"

Ich zucke sofort zusammen, blicke sie misstrauisch an. „Was meinst du?"

Sie beugt sich zu mir rüber. „Kind, jedes Mal, wenn du dich unbeobachtet glaubst, hast du einen gewissen Ausdruck in deinen Augen, du bist dann ganz woanders. Du errötest ständig, möchtest hübsche Kleider kaufen, du strahlst richtig. Also: Wie ist sein Name?"

„Es darf nicht sein", sage ich leise.

„Warum nicht? Ist er verheiratet?"

„Nein, geschieden."

„Schwul?"

Ich denke an den Sex mit Malte. *Schwul?* Ich muss kichern.

„Nicht schwul. Sehr gut. Und anscheinend hattest du mit ihm bereits guten Sex. Kenne ich ihn?"

„Es ist einfach unmöglich. Gib endlich Ruhe, Mom!"

„Ich komme darauf zurück", droht sie. „Du wirst keinem Kerl die Tür zeigen, der dich zu schätzen weiß. Ich werde mich darum kümmern." Sie umarmt mich. „Ich wünsche es dir so sehr, Jonte."

Als ich nach Hause komme, erwartet mich eine ausführliche Mail von Malte. *Sie fragen mich, was mit mir los ist. Ich wäre jetzt gerne bei dir, aber ich möchte auch nichts überstürzen. Wir sehen uns Weihnachten. Allerdings stimmt es mich traurig, dass du im Gästehaus meines Vaters schlafen wirst und nicht bei mir. Ich umarme und küsse dich. Malte.*

Plötzlich kommen mir die Worte meiner Mutter in den Sinn: *Du strahlst richtig …*

Obwohl ich Malte versprochen habe, ihn heute Abend anzurufen, habe ich plötzlich Zweifel, ob ich mir dieses Glücksgefühl gönnen soll. Wenn Mom es mir ansieht, sieht Haakon es auch. Er wird es gegen mich einsetzen. Oder gegen Malte. Oder gegen dessen Kinder. Ich muss sie alle schützen.

Du grübelst schon wieder!

Ja! Ich gehe ins Badezimmer, putze mir die Zähne. Das Wasser läuft gurgelnd in den Abfluss. Aber das ist nicht das einzige Geräusch. Ein penetrantes Knistern und Rascheln dringt an mein Ohr. Sehr nah. Beharrlich. Von überall. Die Kälte ist auch wieder da.

Ich verlasse das Bad. Ich lausche. Das Knistern und Rascheln scheint näher zu kommen. Vorsichtig spähe ich ins Schlafzimmer. Nichts zu sehen. Alles steht an seinem Platz, und doch stimmt etwas nicht. Ich setze mich aufs Bett. Mein erschöpftes Gehirn braucht eine Weile, um in Gang zu kommen, schließlich nimmt es Fahrt auf. Ich sehe mich um.

Plötzlich sind die Ereignisse des heutigen Tages verblasst, die Panik hat sie weggefegt. Vielleicht habe ich zu sehr versucht, Haakon zu vergessen. Fast höre ich ihn flüstern: „*Hast du gedacht, du könntest einfach das Haus verlassen und mit deiner Mutter herumbummeln, ohne dass ich davon Wind kriege. So läuft das nicht, Jonte. Hast du noch immer nichts dazugelernt? Ich weiß alles, was du tust. Vergiss das nie!*"

Mein Blick schweift zum Computer, der leise vor sich hin summt. Mich fröstelt. Denn ich weiß, dass ich ihn ausgeschaltet habe. Mich beschleicht eine schlimme Ahnung. Haakon muss schon wieder im Haus gewesen sein, er muss noch immer einen passenden Schlüssel haben.

Meine Nerven liegen blank. Ich schüttle das Frösteln ab, treffe eine Entscheidung. Es wird mir guttun, ein wenig frische Waldluft zu schnuppern.

Ich stelle den Wagen auf dem Parkplatz am Waldrand ab und steige aus. Ein starker Wind kommt auf, und der Mond unternimmt mal wieder einen vergeblichen Versuch, die Wolken zu durchbrechen. Ich ziehe mir die Kapuze meiner Windjacke über den Kopf und mache mich auf den Weg. Der Duft des Waldes tut mir gut. Ich laufe den Pfad entlang in Richtung Drammensfjord. Alles ist dunkel. Undurchdringlich schwarz. Laut lärmt die

Stille. Die geübte Wanderin in mir übernimmt die Führung und ignoriert die Schmerzen in meinem Schädel.

Der Wald verschlingt mich. Je tiefer ich in ihn eintauche, umso lauter wird er. Jetzt ist er nicht mehr leise. Tiere rascheln im Gebüsch, eine Eule ruft, Vögel kreischen durch die Nacht. Ich laufe und verliere jegliches Zeitgefühl. An einer Lichtung bleibe ich stehen und halte den Atem an. Eine Sekunde lang halluziniere ich und glaube, dort einen Schatten zu sehen.

Irgendwann wollen meine Beine nicht mehr weiter, ich setze mich auf eine windgeschützte Bank am Ufer des Drammensfjord. Denke sofort wieder an Malte.

Wir haben uns leidenschaftlich geliebt. Es waren ehrliche Gefühle, und sie beruhten auf Gegenseitigkeit. Ich sehne mich nach ihm, aber ist mein Verlangen nicht zu gefährlich?

Ich muss es beenden, es darf nicht sein, obwohl allein der Gedanke an den Verlust schon schmerzt. Ich werde ihn heute nicht anrufen. Er darf nicht mit hineingezogen werden. Es ist eine Entscheidung aus Liebe. Wenn ich nach Hyggen fahre, werde ich ihm klarmachen, dass es zwischen uns keine Beziehung geben kann. Ich muss stark sein.

Müdigkeit, Nervosität, Trauer, Hoffnung. Angst. Kein Lachen mehr, nur Weinen. All das begleitet mich, als ich eine Stunde später über den schmalen Pfad nach Hause laufe, mit einem Brennen hinter den Augen.

KAPITEL 58

Das XD Cinema Norge ist heute ein Irrenhaus. Die Kinobesucher stehen Schlange, um sich die Premiere von *Motherless Brooklyn* anzusehen, eine Romanverfilmung von und mit Edward Norton, der einen Privatdetektiv mit Tourette-Syndrom spielt und unablässig dem Mord an seinem Mentor nachgeht. Ich bin verrückt nach den Filmen mit Edward Norton, seit ich den amerikanischen Schauspieler in *Die üblichen Verdächtigen* zum ersten Mal gesehen habe. Endlich mal wieder eine US-Produktion mit Sinn, Handlung und Spannung, ohne Raserei auf einem Highway, ohne Explosionen, ohne Menschen, die aussehen, als hätte man sie durch den Fleischwolf gedreht. Keine abgedrehte, zusammengeklaute Superhelden- oder Märchen-Magie-Geschichte. Der Film spielt im New York der Fünfzigerjahre mit seinen Jazzclubs und Cadillacs. Die Zuschauer werden ihn mögen, da bin ich mir sicher. Ich liebe ihn.

Ich helfe meinen Kollegen an der Kinotheke und merke, wie gut es mir tut, dabei körperlich zu ermüden. Eine Stunde lang verteile ich hektisch Cola, Popcorn, Limonade, Wasser, Wein und Sekt. Verzweiflung und Angst rücken dabei unmerklich in den Hintergrund.

Ich höre, wie zwei Frauen, die eine Cola bei mir ordern, über die Zusammensetzung des Weihnachtsmenüs diskutieren. Sie machen es zu einem Megaproblem. Ich muss mir dieses Jahr keine Gedanken mehr machen, was Weihnachten auf den Tisch kommt. Jonas war an den Feiertagen immer wortkarg, schlecht gelaunt und trübsinnig. Seine Kindheit lag ihm auf dem Magen und die angespannte Atmosphäre in seinem Elternhaus, als würden diese früheren Weihnachten alle zukünftigen überlagern. Da war kein Platz für eine fette Weihnachtsgans. Es gelang mir nie, Jonas an solchen Tagen aufzumuntern.

Das vergangene Jahr hat unser Leben verändert. Wir haben uns mit den Architekturbänden, den Bauhaus-Projekten und den dafür erhaltenen Auszeichnungen einen Namen als Architektenduo gemacht. Wir gehören jetzt zur Spitzengruppe. Ich werde das Klosterhotel nicht nur mit einem atemberaubenden Design ausstatten, sondern ihm am Ende auch noch einen Hauch von Hoffnung verleihen, als wäre das Hotel ein Aufenthaltsort zwischen Himmel und Erde.

Ich freue mich schon jetzt darauf, heute Abend an meinem Zeichenbrett zu stehen, das Telefon abgeschaltet, die Vorhänge geschlossen und für niemanden erreichbar. Ich werde die Außenwelt ausschließen und selbst das verzehrende Verlangen nach Malte verdrängen. Und ich werde nur Wasser oder Fruchtsäfte trinken. Der Kühlschrank quillt schon über davon.

Ich weiß, dass meine zitternden Hände, meine angespannten Nerven, meine Schweißausbrüche und meine Schlafstörungen Entzugserscheinungen sind. Der Alkohol wird mich trotzdem nicht mehr betäuben, er wird aus meinem Körper verbannt. Ich bin Stammkunde im Internet, wenn es um Suchtinformationen geht. Ich werde keinen Schluck mehr trinken. Ich möchte heute Abend mit klarem Kopf an dem Hotelprojekt arbeiten und dabei ein bisschen an Malte denken. Ein Lächeln huscht über meine Lippen.

Plötzlich weht mir *sein* aufdringliches Aftershave entgegen, ich blicke hoch. An der Kasse kauft Haakon zwei Kinokarten und unterhält sich mit einem Mann. Ich erkenne den Fremden nicht, er steht mit dem Rücken zu mir, aber Jonas ist es ganz sicher nicht.

Ich gerate in Panik. Meine Hände sind feucht vor Schweiß. Im nächsten Moment fällt mir eine Flasche Cola aus den Händen und zerbricht mit einem ohrenbetäubenden Knall auf dem Boden. Die braune Flüssigkeit spritzt auf meine Beine, der Colageruch dringt in meine Nase.

Haakon wird durch den Lärm auf mich aufmerksam und kommt schwungvoll und zielstrebig auf mich zu.

„Was machst du denn da, Jonte? Hast wohl deinen Rausch nicht ausgeschlafen?" Er grinst. „Wie schön, dass wir uns hier treffen. Mein Halbbruder und ich werden uns *Motherless Brooklyn* ansehen. Vielleicht kann man aus dem Streifen etwas für das wahre Leben mitnehmen. Was meinst du?"

Als ich hochblicke, überlappen sich die Zeiten. Mein Blick stellt sich scharf. Ich zucke zusammen, blinzle. Begreife es nicht. Benommen schüttle ich den Kopf. Das kann nicht sein, das kann einfach nicht sein. Ich traue meinen Augen nicht, blinzle erneut, hektisch, als könnte das Haakon und seinen Halbbruder vertreiben.

Mein Herz bricht auseinander, und flimmernde Bilder fügen sich wie Puzzleteile zusammen: eine schmale graue Straße, Abendrot, ein Schatten, zwei Schatten. Ein verängstigtes Mädchen mit einer Geige.

„Darf ich dich mit meinem Halbbruder Björn bekannt machen?"

Für den Bruchteil einer Sekunde streift mein Blick ein dunkles Augenpaar. Es ist ein Blick in den Abgrund der Hölle.

Diese Augen, dieses Gesicht, ich ertrage es nicht. Ich will den Blick abwenden, aber es ist unmöglich, ich bin wie versteinert. Die Welt um mich herum wird zu Eis, in meinem Inneren tobt ein rasender Sturm. Mein Herz pocht mit ungeheurer Wucht. Meine Welt erbebt, die Wände der Wirklichkeit geraten ins Wanken, brechen am Ende in sich zusammen. Getränke fallen aus den Regalen, Popcorn explodiert, Glas splittert, an der Decke bilden sich fingerdicke Risse. Alles stürzt ein, der Lärm ist unbeschreiblich, und dennoch ist es plötzlich still, ganz still.

Ich bin wieder das zwölfjährige Mädchen, das in einer dreckigen Garage vergewaltigt wird, ein nacktes kleines Mädchen, das Geige spielt. Ein weißer Sommerpulli liegt im Staub. Ein Messer. Schläge. Blut. Rot auf Weiß.

Ein paar Augenblicke verharre ich, die Augen geschlossen, die Finger krampfhaft umeinander geklammert, das Gefühl für Raum und Zeit habe ich verloren. Eine ferne Stimme ruft etwas, erst leise, dann immer lauter und fordernder, allmählich dringen die Worte mit solcher Wucht in mein Bewusstsein, dass es schmerzt.

Back-Vocal ist außer sich vor Wut.

Die Worte beginnen in mir zu kreisen, laut und deutlich, während ich schweige.

Seine Stimme ist jetzt ganz nah. „Hallo! Ich bin Björn Jensen, Haakons Halbbruder. Freut mich, Sie kennenzulernen, Frau Sandvik."

Was labert er da? Er kennt dich doch bereits.

Es ist die Stimme aus der Garage. Mir stockt der Atem wie damals, als meine Unschuld gemordet wurde.

Haakon mustert mich. Er spürt, dass meine Reaktion anders ausfällt als meine übliche Feindseligkeit. Diese Begegnung trifft mich wie ein Kinnhaken. Wie tausend Ohrfeigen.

Und Haakon fragt sich, warum.

Ich drehe mich abrupt weg und verlasse das Kino, fliehe hinaus in die eisige Kälte. Wo ist mein imaginäres Flugzeug?

KAPITEL 59

Eine üble Wetterfront kündigt der Wetterfrosch im Radio an. Winterstürme und Eisregen, kein Wetter, das zum Weihnachtsfest passt.

Mit Mühe gelingt es mir, auf dem Heimweg den Überblick über mein inneres Chaos zu behalten. Ich rase nicht über die Straßen, bleibe vor jeder roten Ampel brav stehen und halte mich an die örtliche Geschwindigkeitsbeschränkung. Fünfzig Stundenkilometer.

Ich fluche innerlich. Die Welt ist von Gedankenlosigkeit umgeben. Die Leute, die aus den Geschäften kommen, laufen, ohne sich umzusehen, so sorglos über die Straße, als wäre es Sache der Autofahrer, ihnen auszuweichen. Das macht mich rasend.

In meinem Viertel ist dreißig erlaubt, aber ich schleiche mit zehn dahin und finde Björn Jensen in jedem Gesicht, an jeder Straßenecke, an Ampeln stehend, Straßen überquerend, ich sehe ihn überall: Björn Jensen, der mich als Zwölfjährige mit seinem Kumpel überfallen und stundenlang in der Garage missbraucht hat. Nur ein Augenblick hat gereicht, um sicher zu sein. Ich kenne mich mit dem Bösen aus. Das Ungeheuer in der Garage hat mich damals genauso angesehen wie vorhin an der Kinotheke – bevor es mich vergewaltigt und halb tot geschlagen hat.

Ich fahre in die Garage, lasse den Motor laufen. Die Scheibenwischer kratzen und schaben.

Ich bin eine offene Wunde. Ich bin der Geruch von rohem Fleisch, klaffe weit auf. Es blitzt in meinem Kopf, schmerzhaft und gleißend hell. Mein Gesichtsfeld färbt sich rot, ich habe eine Panikattacke, Schweißausbrüche, gleich werde ich ohnmächtig, hoffentlich werde ich ohnmächtig.

Endlich erlöst mich ein Weinkrampf.

Ich muss wohl für einen kurzen Moment vor Erschöpfung eingenickt sein. Ich friere, schalte den Motor ab und steige aus.

Grauschwarze Wolken ziehen am fahlen Mond vorbei. Sein Licht sickert durch die Äste der alten Bäume, die gespenstische Schatten auf den Vorgarten werfen. Diese Nacht ist noch viel schwärzer als alle anderen. Überall lauern feindliche Augen. Mein Gehör spielt mir einen Streich, ich höre Schritte näher kommen, sehe Schatten, wo keine sind.

Nur noch zehn Meter bis zu deiner Haustür.

Ein Dilemma, sage ich mir. Genau das ist Björn Jensen, ein Dilemma – wie Haakon. In den verschwendeten Tagen, in den verzweifelten Nächten hatte ich mich einigermaßen gefangen.

Dachtest du zumindest!

Als ich die Haustür öffne, habe ich urplötzlich das Gefühl, dass sich unsichtbare Hände um meinen Hals legen. In mir tost die Angst eines zwölfjährigen Mädchens. Hyperventilierend verbarrikadiere ich die Tür.

Klick, klick, klick, klick!

Endlich in Sicherheit. Mein Herz pocht wie nach einem Marathonlauf. Ich blicke aus dem Fenster. Mir fällt ein Schatten auf, der die Straße überquert und geradewegs auf mein Haus zukommt, dann aber in der Dunkelheit verschwindet.

Ich entscheide mich, bis spätestens elf Uhr an den Plänen zu arbeiten und dann ins Bett gehen. Spätestens Anfang Januar werde ich das Hotel digital präsentieren und dem Orden eine Miniausführung des Klosterhotels zeigen. Ich setze mich an meine Plantafel, beginne zu zeichnen und blende die Realität aus.

Das Klingeln an der Haustür reißt mich aus meiner Klosterwelt. Mir ist kalt. Ich hole tief Luft, lege den Bleistift zur Seite. Meine Armbanduhr zeigt zehn Uhr. Davon überzeugt, dass Haakon oder Jonas vor der Haustür stehen, entscheide ich mich, sie nicht zu öffnen. Aber als ich doch durch den Türspion spähe, schlägt mein Herz schneller. Es ist Malte.

Wir tauschen einen Blick. Ich spüre die Röte in meinem Gesicht aufsteigen. Vor knapp sechsunddreißig Stunden habe ich in seinen Armen gelegen, seinen Körper an meinem gespürt.

„Ich musste einfach vorbeikommen", sagt er. In seiner Stimme liegt Sehnsucht.

Ich schmunzle. „Das höre ich gern."

Seine Umarmung ist innig, die schönste Liebkosung, und sie hält eine gefühlte Ewigkeit an. Dann führt er mich ins Schlafzimmer. Heiß und leidenschaftlich pressen sich seine Lippen auf meinen Mund. Seine Küsse sind voller Verlangen, seine Hände überall. Wellen der Lust durchzucken mich. Als er sich neben mich legt, strafft sich jeder Muskel meines Körpers. Er schlingt seine Arme um mich und zieht mich fest an sich.

Ich öffne meine Lippen, möchte etwas sagen, aber sie werden sogleich von seinem Mund versiegelt. Ich genieße einen Liebesakt, in dem der Geschmack, der Duft und die Farben der Liebe lebendig werden. Spüre seine Erregung, sein Drängen, seine Lust.

Ich verjage das Übel aus meinem Gedächtnis, schiebe den Tag und die Angst beiseite und ergebe mich ihm.

Ich weiß nur allzu gut, dass Liebe hungrig macht, und bereite uns ein herzhaftes Omelett zu.

„Ich kann dir leider nur ein Wasser oder eine Cola anbieten. Ich habe keine alkoholischen Getränke im Haus", entschuldige ich mich. „Ich will keinen Alkohol mehr trinken."

„Ist es zum Problem geworden?", fragt er vorsichtig.

„Ja, seit geraumer Zeit. Ich habe versucht, die Gläser Wein zu reduzieren, aber es hat einfach nicht funktioniert. Deshalb habe ich ganz damit aufgehört."

„Eine gute Entscheidung. Ich bin kein Alkoholiker. Im Sommer, wenn es heiß ist, trinke ich gern ein Bier oder ein Glas Wein auf der Terrasse. Aber ich kann es auch sein lassen."

Ich zögere. „Für mich … Für mich musst du das nicht tun."

„Doch. Denn es ist sehr wichtig in der ersten Periode des Entzugs. Das ist ein Versprechen, Jonte."

Plötzlich kommen mir Haakons Worte wieder in den Sinn. Sofort schnürt mir meine Angst vor den möglichen Folgen dieser Beziehung die Kehle zu.

Du möchtest also nicht auf diesen Mann verzichten?, fragt Back-Vocal.

Nein!

Malte streichelt mein Gesicht. „Lass mich dich lieben, Jonte", sagt er zärtlich.

Ich beruhige mich wieder. Sein Auto steht ein paar Häuser entfernt. Niemand kann sehen, dass er bei mir ist. Meine Vorbehalte verflüchtigten sich, und ich vergesse die Welt um mich, es gibt nur noch uns.

Nachdem er neben mir eingeschlafen ist, bleibe ich bei ihm. Ich beobachte sein ruhiges Atmen, küsse sanft seine Fingerspitzen und lausche gleichzeitig, ob ich merkwürdige Geräusche höre, doch da ist nichts.

Ich horche in die Nacht, bis der Schlaf auch über meine Augen seine dunkle Decke legt. Im Traum starre ich das Monster aus meiner Kindheit an, während ich wieder unter ihm liege. Mir ist klar, dass ich träume, und deshalb versuche ich, aufzuwachen und zu sterben.

KAPITEL 60

Bente ist nervös. Ich sehe es sofort, als sie auf mich zukommt. Sie umarmt mich herzlich, aber ich spüre ihr Zittern. „Herzlich willkommen auf Gut Kos! Schön, dass du da bist." Sie mustert mich. „Wir werden dich in den nächsten Tagen mästen. Noah und Malte kochen wunderbare, kalorienreiche Gerichte. Ein paar zusätzliche Pfunde auf den Rippen werden dir nicht schaden. Du bist so schmal geworden. Alles gut? Wie war der Verkehr? War es voll auf den Straßen?"

Wir gehen ins Haus. Auch in der Küche redet Bente ununterbrochen. Und dennoch ist da etwas an ihrer Art, sich leicht gebückt zu halten, sich dem Blick zu entziehen, das kenne ich. Das kenne ich nur zu gut, diese Art, mit der Umgebung zu verschmelzen, transparent zu werden. Aber bei ihr funktioniert das so wenig wie bei mir. Sie kann mir nichts vormachen. Da ist diese Unsicherheit, die all ihren Bewegungen anhaftet, man muss sie nur sehen, wie sie erstaunt die Augen aufreißt oder mir mit zitternden Händen eine Tasse Kaffee reicht, die ihr prompt aus den Händen fällt.

Ich legte eine Hand auf ihren Arm. „Was ist los, Bente? Ist etwas passiert?"

Sie setzt sich mir gegenüber. „Nein. Diese Tage machen mich immer ein bisschen nervös."

„Quälen dich Erinnerungen?"

Sie schluckt. „Ich will nicht darüber nachdenken, und ich denke trotzdem an nichts anderes. Seit Tore tot ist, sucht die Vergangenheit mich zu oft heim. Noah sagt, dass es besser ist, keinen Widerstand dagegen zu leisten, sondern sich damit auseinanderzusetzen. Er ist davon überzeugt, dass jeder für seine Geister selbst verantwortlich ist."

„Wie praktisch", erwidere ich. „Noah hat gut reden."

„Noah hat sein Kind nicht im Stich gelassen", sinniert Bente und sieht mich an. „Ich denke zu viel an das Kind, das Jonas einmal war, besonders an diesen Tagen." Sie rührt wütend mit dem Löffel ihren Kaffee um. „Als er klein war, war er ein liebevolles, anhängliches Kind. Wenn Tore nicht da war, kam er immer wieder zum Knuddeln zu mir. Manchmal habe ich den Duft des Jungen noch in der Nase, diesen herrlichen Duft seines Kindershampoos."

„Sind das die Geister, die dich quälen?"

Sie hört auf, den Kaffee umzurühren, und lässt den Blick auf mir ruhen. „Es ist hauptsächlich meine sentimentale Natur." Sie springt plötzlich auf. „Da ist ja Noah. Jetzt lernt ihr euch endlich mal persönlich kennen." Sie wirkt erleichtert, das Thema ruhen lassen zu können.

Maltes Vater ist eine ältere Version seines Sohnes, und ich mag ihn auf Anhieb, vielleicht weil er mich auch ein wenig an meinen Vater erinnert. Er ist herzlich, fröhlich und sprüht vor Energie. Ich muss Noah immer wieder ansehen, und er spürt es.

„Habe ich mein Hemd falsch zugeknöpft, Jonte?" Er grinst.

Ich fühle mich ertappt. „Entschuldigung, aber du bist meinem Vater sehr ähnlich."

Er überprüft den Braten im Ofen. „Lebt er noch?", fragt er.

„Nein, er ist seit über zwanzig Jahren tot."

„Hm … Der Braten braucht noch fünf Minuten. Dann können wir essen. Inwiefern ähnle ich ihm?"

„Es ist nicht dein Aussehen." Ich seufze. „Wie soll ich es sagen? Es ist deine Art, ich fühle mich wohl in deiner Nähe."

Er sieht mich ernst an. „So geht es mir auch mit dir, Jonte."

Bente ist ruhiger geworden. Sie hat im Wohnzimmer den Esstisch festlich gedeckt. Überall brennen Kerzen, das einzige elektrische Licht spendet die Weihnachtsbaumbeleuchtung. Es ist angenehm warm im Haus. Ich möchte ihr helfen, aber sie lehnt das Angebot entschieden ab.

„Unsere Gäste werden von uns verwöhnt. Das ist eine Tradition in diesem Haus", sagt sie leise. „Und Traditionen soll man niemals brechen. Das bringt Unheil."

Das Essen war köstlich, aber jetzt rumort mein Magen. Ich bekomme keinen Bissen mehr runter und möchte an die frische Luft, aber ich befürchte, dass jemand dort draußen mich warten könnte. Ich hatte schon auf der Hinfahrt das Gefühl, dass mir ein Wagen gefolgt war. Ich kann das Gefühl nicht abschütteln, ständig beobachtet zu werden.

Ich hätte nicht hierherkommen sollen, denn ich gefährde die Menschen um mich herum. Haakon ist unberechenbar. Ob er weiß, dass ich in Blue Bay bin? Ob er ahnt, was sein Halbbruder für ein Mensch ist? Ich bin zu sorglos, gehe zu viele Risiken ein, treffe die falschen Entscheidungen, drehe mich ständig im Kreis und lenke mein Leben nie in die richtigen Bahnen. Haakon schmiedet indessen fatale Pläne, um Jonas weiterhin zu manipulieren und mich um mein Geld zu bringen.

Ich werde morgen wieder abreisen und muss mir rasch einen vernünftigen Grund einfallen lassen, denn ich möchte weder Noah noch Bente vor den Kopf stoßen, auch Malte soll sich nicht zurückgewiesen fühlen. Sie alle geben ihr Bestes, um mich glücklich zu machen. Ich fühle mich hier zu Hause, bin hier willkommen. Ich würde so gerne bleiben, aber ich muss gehen, bevor etwas Schlimmes passiert.

Gegen ein Uhr nachts leert sich das Haus endlich. Malte hat es mit den Kindern bereits verlassen. Sie haben mich sofort akzeptiert, und wir haben viel miteinander gelacht. Bente und Noah räumen den Tisch ab. Ich biete ihnen meine Hilfe an, aber davon will Bente nichts wissen.

Sie streichelt meine Wange. „Sag mal, Jonte, du bist mit deinen Gedanken manchmal so weit weg. Worüber grübelst du denn?"

„Jonas hätte euch beide als Eltern haben sollen", antworte ich spontan. Bente zuckt zusammen und wirft mir einen seltsamen Blick zu. „Danke", sagt sie leise. „Soll ich dich zum Gästehaus begleiten?"

Ich lehne ihr Angebot ab, ich kenne ja den Weg. Und ich möchte jetzt allein sein.

Die Nacht ist still, nirgendwo ist ein Geräusch zu hören. Die Luft ist kalt und trocken, der Himmel bedeckt. Kein einziger Stern ist weit und breit zu sehen. Nach und nach werden auch die Lichter im Gutshaus gelöscht.

Erst als ich den Schlüssel ins Schloss meiner Haustür stecken will, fällt mir auf, dass sie nur angelehnt ist. Erinnerungen stürzen auf mich ein: die offene Haustür in dem großen, finsteren Haus in Lierstranda, Jonas' Vater, der in einem Blechsarg hinausgetragen wird; die offene Tür meines eigenen Hauses, Annika, die dort mit dem Tod rang. Nein! Ich will nicht wieder ein Déjà-vu-Gefühl. *Ich will das nicht!*

Ich lausche und versuche, Geräusche auszumachen, die aus dem Gästehaus kommen.

Totenstille.

Ich drücke die Tür ein bisschen weiter auf, schiebe die Hand hindurch und betätige den Lichtschalter. Warmes Licht durchflutet den Raum.

Meine Wochenendtasche steht neben der Couch, dort, wo ich sie hingestellt habe. Ich atme erleichtert auf und schließe die Haustür. Dann gehe ich sicherheitshalber ins Badezimmer. Öffne die Tür. Niemand zu sehen.

Vergiss nicht das Schlafzimmer, knurrt Back-Vocal missmutig.

Ich gehe hinein, sehe mich um. Nichts.

Ich bin allein. Vermutlich habe ich die Tür einfach nicht richtig zugezogen. Bente hatte mich gewarnt, dass sie schon mal aufspringt, wenn man sie nicht richtig hinter sich zuzieht. Also alles in Ordnung.

Sicher?

Blue Bay ist ein friedliches Küstendorf. Hier kann man die Tür eines Gästehauses stundenlang offen stehen lassen, ohne dass jemand auf die Idee kommt, einen Blick ins Haus zu werfen.

Oder einzubrechen?

Plötzlich halte ich inne. Im Schlafzimmer war irgendetwas seltsam. Ich sehe noch einmal nach. Erst jetzt fällt mir auf, dass die Tür des Kleiderschranks einen Spaltbreit aufsteht.

Ich hatte mit Mom drei schöne Kleider für diese Urlaubstage gekauft und sie im Kleiderschrank ordentlich auf einen Bügel gehängt. Doch der Schrank ist leer.

Als ich mich umdrehe, liegen die Kleider sorgfältig nebeneinander auf dem Bett. Erst bei genauerem Hinsehen erkenne ich die feinen Linien, dort, wo eine Schere sie in Länge und Breite durchtrennt hat. Sie liegen da wie bizarre Puzzles, scheinbar intakt und doch völlig zerfetzt. Auf dem schwarzen Kleid liegt ein Blatt Papier. Meine Hände zittern, als ich die Zeilen lese:

Das kann auch mit jedem passieren, den du liebst! Schnipp-schnapp!

Ich schließe die Augen, sehe die Verletzungen meiner Seele, so deutlich, als würde sie wie meine Kleidung zerrissen vor mir liegen. Ich ringe nach Luft und höre das Stöhnen, das meine Lippen verlässt, wie einen fremdartigen Ton. Der Schmerz hinter meiner Stirn lässt nicht nach. Back-Vocal tobt, als stünde er im Fegefeuer.

Ich setze mich aufs Bett, versuche klar zu denken. Es gelingt mir nicht. Ich wollte für Malte schön und attraktiv sein, wollte all das, was mich belastet, loslassen und die Zeit mit Malte und seiner Familie in einem wunderschönen schwarzen Kleid genießen.

Aber das Kleid wurde so zerfetzt wie meine Seele. Ich werde heimfahren und Haakons Spiel spielen. Weinen bringt mich nicht weiter.

Ich packe sofort meine Sachen zusammen und lasse nur eine Notiz zurück.

Liebe Bente, ein Familienfest ist momentan zu viel für mich. Ich bin dafür noch nicht bereit. Der Schmerz und die Gefühle um meine bevorstehende Scheidung sind noch zu frisch. Können wir es um ein Jahr verschieben? Es hat nichts mit dir zu tun. Ihr seid die wunderbarsten Menschen der Welt. Es liegt nur an mir. Entschuldigung! Ich kann einfach nicht anders. Jonte.

Draußen kann ich wieder frei atmen. Der Regen prasselt auf den Asphalt, und ich trete beim Verlassen des Hauses mitten in eine riesige Wasserpfütze. Auf dem Weg zu meinem Auto blicke ich dreimal zurück. Es würde mich nicht überraschen, wenn Haakon irgendwo in der Nähe ist, um mir zu folgen. Oder Jonas.

Rasch lade ich meinen Koffer ein. Die Welt schläft, und es ist fast unangemessen, die Stille der Nacht mit dem Starten des Autos zu durchbrechen. Auf der Landstraße schalte ich das Radio ein und gerate mitten in eine Talkshow. „Du wirst dieses Gefühl niemals verlieren", höre ich eine Frau sagen. „Du arbeitest ständig daran, aber es gelingt dir nicht. Denn irgendwo da draußen läuft der Mörder meines Kindes ungestraft herum. Vielleicht hat er seine Tat schon längst vergessen und genießt sein Leben. Aber als Mutter habe ich eine lebenslange Haftstrafe bekommen."

Ich schalte das Radio wieder aus. Hinter mir hupt jemand ungeduldig. Sekunden später rase ich durch die Nacht.

KAPITEL 61

Es ist halb fünf Uhr morgens, als ich in meine Garage fahre. In einigen Häusern brennen noch die Weihnachtsdekorationen im Garten. Was für eine Energieverschwendung!

Auf der Straße bewegt sich etwas. Es ist eine Katze, die unter einem Busch davonschießt. Sonst regt sich nichts. Um diese Zeit lauert selbst Malvi Oddbjørn nicht mehr hinter ihren Gardinen.

Im Haus ist es kühl. Ich drehe sofort die Heizung auf. Bin ich allein? Die Frage drängt sich mir automatisch auf. Es bringt nichts, meine Angst abzustreiten. Ich durchsuche das Haus, beginne auf dem Dachboden und überprüfe systematisch jeden Raum, aber weit und breit ist kein Feind zu sehen, alles ist so, wie ich es hinterlassen habe. Im Schlafzimmer liegen auch keine zerschnittenen Kleidungsstücke auf dem Bett.

Die Standuhr schlägt fünfmal. Mir ist kalt, und ich möchte mich hinlegen und einschlafen. Eine heiße Dusche wird mich entspannen und meinen Körper wärmen. Ich fühle mich entsetzlich einsam.

Die Stimme hinter meiner Stirn wird plötzlich laut. Sie spricht Warnungen aus, so schnell, dass ich ihnen kaum folgen kann. *Hörst du denn nichts? Ich fordere dich auf, etwas dagegen zu unternehmen. Wir sind hier nicht sicher! Du denkst immer nur an Haakon, aber hast du schon mal an Björn Jensen gedacht?!*

Meine Ohren dröhnen. Meine Augen brennen. Ohne mich auszuziehen, krieche ich ins Bett. In der Ferne schlägt eine Kirchenuhr. Dann wird es still in meinem Kopf.

Irgendwo vibriert ein Geräusch. Ich krieche tiefer unter die Bettdecke, um ihm zu entkommen. Aber auch da muss ich horchen. Es ist mein Handy.

Ich zögere. Vielleicht ist es Malte, der versucht, mich zu erreichen. Nach einer Minute höre ich das Signal, dass auf der Mailbox eine Nachricht hinterlassen wurde.

Die Nachricht ist von Jonas. „Jonte, würdest du mich bitte so schnell wie möglich zurückrufen? Oder direkt zum Haus meines Vaters kommen? Ich muss mit dir reden, es ist dringend." Ich höre die Panik in seiner Stimme. Wieder mal. „Es ist in deinem eigenen Interesse", schiebt er noch nach einer Atempause hinterher.

Was kümmert mich eine Panikattacke meines Ex-Mannes machen. Im Gegenteil: Ich gönne ihm diese Angst, soll er doch daran ersticken. Außerdem könnte es eine Falle sein.

Nach der heißen Dusche und einer Tasse starken Kaffees entscheide ich mich, Jonas zumindest anzurufen.

„Danke, dass du zurückrufst."

Sein unterwürfiger Ton macht mich sofort hellhörig. „Was ist los?"

„Bitte komm zu mir, Jonte. Ich bin im Haus meines Vaters und kann hier nicht den ganzen Tag bleiben. Ich habe Haakon eine Notiz hinterlassen, dass ich dort einige persönliche Gegenstände abholen möchte. Wenn ich zu lange wegbleibe, wird er misstrauisch."

„In Ordnung, ich fahre sofort los."

Als ich das Haus verlasse, sehe ich mich um. Alles ist normal, selbst Malvi Oddbjørns Spitzenvorhang bewegt sich.

Ich winke ihr zu.

Es ist ruhig am Vitbankveien 22. Das Verkaufsschild steht einsam mitten im Garten.

Jonas muss mich gesehen haben, denn bevor ich auf die Glocke drücken kann, öffnet er schon die Haustür.

Ich zeige auf das Schild. „Hast du es bloß vergessen, oder ist der Verkauf gescheitert?"

„Das Haus wurde unter Vorbehalt verkauft, die Finanzierung muss noch geklärt werden." Er drückt hinter mir die Tür zu.

Ich gehe schnell ins Wohnzimmer. Die Vorhänge sind geöffnet. Jonas läuft zum Fenster und schließt sie.

„Wer darf uns hier nicht zusammen sehen, Jonas?"

Er macht eine abwehrende Geste, als wäre das ja wohl klar. „Möchtest du einen Kaffee?"

„Nein. Ich möchte gleich zur Sache kommen. Warum wolltest du mich so dringend sprechen?"

„Setz dich bitte." Er zeigt auf die Stühle am Esstisch und nimmt Platz. Seine Finger spielen mit der Tischdecke. „Du hattest recht", beginnt er.

Ich warte, ich werde es ihm nicht leicht machen.

„Ich spreche von deinem Verdacht, dass Haakon dich stalkt. Er hat tatsächlich einen Schlüssel für dein Haus. Ich weiß nicht, woher, vermutlich durch seine Kontakte zum Schlüsseldienst."

Meine Wut kommt wieder hoch.

„Er ist in der Nacht, als mein Vater Selbstmord beging, bei ihm gewesen. Sie gerieten in Streit, und mein Vater warf ihn aus dem Haus. Später kehrte Haakon noch einmal zurück, und da stand die Haustür offen. Er hat ihn tot aufgefunden. Er rief mich sofort an. Ich riet ihm, er solle sich von dem Haus fernhalten, weil der Verdacht auf ihn fallen könnte. Er versprach, sofort zurückzukommen, aber es dauerte ein paar Stunden, bis er heimkehrte. Ich habe ihm geglaubt, als er sagte, er hätte sich zuerst von dem Schock erholen müssen."

Ich sehe den Mann an, mit dem ich noch verheiratet bin, und suche den freundlichen Blick in seinen Augen, die unbeholfene Art, sich zu bewegen, den Jungen, der einst seine Mutter brauchte. Ich finde nur ein beängstigendes, unheimliches Gesicht, seine Haltung strotzt nur so vor Gleichgültigkeit, er hat die Sensibilität einer Wanze. Dieser Mann gleicht in keiner Weise dem Jonas, den ich kannte. Oder sehe ich jetzt sein wahres Gesicht?

„Woran denkst du, Jonte?"

„Wer zum Teufel bist du?"

„Ich verstehe deine Frage nicht. Du kennst mich, sei nicht so theatralisch. Haakon war verwirrt, er hatte sich nicht mehr unter Kontrolle. Da macht er manchmal komische Sachen."

„Zum Beispiel?"

„Sich auszudenken, wie er dir Angst einjagen könnte, in dein Haus zu schleichen, deine Hausschuhe zu stehlen und sie neben der Treppe im Haus meines Vaters abzustellen."

„Deine ganze Geschichte ist Bullshit. Glaubst du wirklich, dass Haakon mitten in der Nacht auf die Idee kommt, zu mir zu fahren, um aus Jux meine Hausschuhe zu stehlen und dann zu deinem Vater zu fahren, wo passenderweise die Tür offen ist, und sie dort reinzustellen? Oh nein, er hat deinen Vater nicht tot aufgefunden, Jonas, er hat ihn getötet! Dein Vater hatte vor, dich zu enterben? Und ich vermute langsam, er hatte dafür triftige Gründe. Das war Haakon natürlich bekannt. Also hat er Tore aufgesucht, um ihn umzubringen, und er wusste ganz genau, wie er mich in diese Sache verwickeln könnte. Er hat nur nicht damit gerechnet, dass ich mit deinem Vater verabredet war und die Hausschuhe vor Eintreffen der Polizei finden würde."

Jonas schüttelt den Kopf. „Nein, nein, Haakon hat nichts mit dem Tod meines Vaters zu tun."

Ich sehe für eine Sekunde seine Panik, aber meine erste Reaktion, ihn zu beruhigen, wird von der Schlussfolgerung abgewürgt, dass er bereits gewusst haben muss, dass sein Vater tot war, als er von der Polizei angerufen wurde.

„Du hast mich zum Narren gehalten und versuchst es immer wieder. Warum bin ich hier, Jonas? Warum bist du hier? Was fällt dir ein, dich so aufzuführen? Stehst du unter Drogen? Was nimmst du eigentlich? Koks, Ecstasy?"

„Heroin. Aber ich habe es unter Kontrolle."

Seine Worte erschüttern mich. „Was willst du von mir? Warum musste ich hierherkommen?"

„Ich war in Panik. Haakon hat gestern gesagt, dass er deine Vergangenheit durchleuchten will. Er hat sogar schon Kontakt mit der Frau deines verstorbenen Liebhabers aufgenommen."

„Wie kann Haakon etwas über meine Vergangenheit wissen?"

„Ich habe es ihm erzählt. Tut mir leid, aber wir sind ein Paar. Wir haben keine Geheimnisse."

Ich kann ein höhnisches Lächeln nicht unterdrücken. „Dein Urteilsvermögen war schon mal besser, Jonas. Aber das muss wohl an dem Dreck liegen, den du einnimmst. Klar, du erzählst Haakon alles, auch wenn es ihn gar nichts angeht. Was fällt dir ein, ihm solche Intimitäten anzuvertrauen, und warum will er dem nachgehen? Was ist das für ein schmutziges Spiel? Glaubst du, dass sich dadurch etwas ändern wird? Dass ich mit dir verheiratet bleibe und dir weiterhin ein gutes Einkommen verschaffe, um Sex und Drogen zu finanzieren?" Ich atme tief ein. „Zum letzten Mal: Das Spiel ist vorbei, Jonas. Haakon kann meinetwegen mit jedem reden, der je etwas mit mir zu tun hatte. Soll er doch. Das wird meine Entscheidung nicht ändern. Ich werde einen Anwalt aufsuchen, und ich sorge dafür, dass du keinen Cent mehr von mir bekommst. Du kannst ja auf den Strich gehen, um deinen Heroinkonsum zu finanzieren. Schieß dir doch den gesamten Erlös dieses Hauses in die Venen, aber behellige mich nicht mehr damit. Ich verbiete mir weitere weinerliche Anrufen. Setz dir das nächste Mal einen Schuss, wenn du eine Panikattacke hast, aber lass mich zufrieden!"

Ich sehe, wie sehr ihn der letzte Satz trifft. Das ist gut, denn ich möchte ihn verletzen. Er widert mich an.

„Du darfst Haakon nicht wütend machen." Jonas winselt geradezu. „Benutze deinen Verstand und gib ihm, was er verlangt."

„Ach ja? Ich nehme an, du sprichst aus Erfahrung. Wie ist es möglich, dass du dich diesem Mann vollständig auslieferst, der dir nichts als Elend gebracht hat und bringen wird?"

„Er hat meinen Vater nicht getötet!", schreit er mich plötzlich an. „Er hat ein loses Mundwerk, aber er ist kein Mörder."

„Die Untersuchung ist eh abgeschlossen, oder? Bis eine Neuentwicklung eintritt."

„Wovon redest du?" Er beugt sich zu mir rüber. „Weißt du etwas? Hast du etwas zurückgehalten? Mir etwas verschwiegen?"

„Ich weiß nichts, und ich will auch nichts wissen. Aber ich bin überzeugt, dass du mit einem abartigen Menschen zusammenlebst. Und dass du ziemlich tief in der Scheiße steckst." Die letzten Worte speie ich ihm entgegen.

„Du verstehst nichts von Haakon und mir. Du bist zu stumpfsinnig, um auch nur irgendetwas von wahrer Liebe zu begreifen. Ich wollte dich warnen und nicht gegen dich arbeiten, Jonte. Aber weißt du was, ich brauche dich nicht. Ich unterschreibe die Scheidungsurkunde gern. Aber zu unseren Bedingungen!"

Ich stehe auf und gehe zur Tür. Er kommt hinter mir her. „Wenn du es wagen solltest, Haakon öffentlich zu beschuldigen, dann mache ich dich fertig!"

Ich zucke mit den Schultern und schließe die Haustür hinter mir.

KAPITEL 62

Ich könnte nach Portugal fliegen und mich einfach Mom und ihrer Freundin anschließen. Sie werden mich in Ediths Ferienhaus mit offenen Armen empfangen, und sie werden respektieren, dass ich nichts erklären will. Das bedeutet aber auch, dass von mir erwartet wird, dass ich mich in angenehmer Atmosphäre an ihren Gesprächen beteilige. Bei dem Gedanken bricht mir der Schweiß aus. Da ist mir eine Tiefkühlpizza und aufgetautes Baguette lieber. Ich bin nicht in Weihnachtsstimmung. Was bleibt, ist das Gefühl, dass mir mein Leben entgleitet und dass ich in jede Falle tappe, die man vor mich hinstellt.

Mein Schwiegervater hat mich bis zu dieser bewussten Nacht nie angerufen. Er wollte mir etwas sagen, und es muss etwas sehr Wichtiges gewesen sein, sonst hätte er nicht zum Hörer gegriffen. Wurde er von Haakon bedroht? Oder von Jonas? Hat er Hilfe gesucht und sie ausgerechnet von mir erwartet?

Jonas ist der festen Überzeugung, dass Haakon seinen Vater tot aufgefunden hat. Ich erinnere mich vage, dass Lennart Haugen sagte, dass Tore wahrscheinlich geschlafen hat, als in das Haus eingebrochen wurde. Die Haustür stand offen. Hatten die Einbrecher sie offen stehen lassen? Konnte Haakon deshalb problemlos eintreten? Ich sollte Hauptkommissar Haugen meine Bedenken mitteilen, aber noch wage ich es nicht. Das Risiko von Vergeltungsmaßnahmen ist zu groß. Wenn ich jetzt ein paar Gläser Wein getrunken hätte, wäre ich gewiss mutiger und weniger unsicher.

Eine Erinnerung macht mir bis heute zu schaffen. Auch sie hält mich davon ab, Kommissar Haugen aufzusuchen. Eine männliche Stimme hinter mir – an einem Abend vor vierzehn Jahren – will nicht schweigen. Eine wütende, empörte Stimme.

Sie wollen doch wohl nicht mit einem solch hohen Alkoholpegel ins Auto steigen?

Ich kannte den Mann nicht, ignorierte ihn und stieg erst dann ein, als er aus meinem Blickfeld verschwunden war.

Komisch, ich habe lange nicht mehr an diese Szene gedacht. Warum kommt sie mir jetzt zu Bewusstsein? Hätte ich auf diesen Mann gehört, wäre sie noch am Leben.

Ebba Hagebak, die Frau im weißen Kleid, die genauso alt war wie ich damals. Sie wäre jetzt ebenfalls fünfunddreißig, könnte Kinder haben, vielleicht besaß sie auch besondere Talente, die sie hätte weiterentwickeln können. Ich weiß es nicht und werde es nie erfahren.

Dennoch frage ich mich, ob Schuldgefühle wirklich niemals nachlassen? Oder ob sie nur irgendwann die scharfen Kanten verlieren und im Hintergrund verharren? Bestimmen sie, ohne dass es dir bewusst ist, in deinem Leben deine Reaktionen, Gefühle, Ängste?

Ich kann sie nicht abschütteln, obwohl ich das möchte, weil ich nach vorne blicken will. Ich möchte die Chance haben, zu beweisen, dass es nie wieder passieren wird. Dass ich etwas daraus gelernt habe.

Aber wer vergibt mir meine Schuld?

Würde ich denn einem Täter jemals vergeben?

Das Gespräch mit Jonas ist in den Hintergrund gerückt. Ich frage mich immer noch, warum er mich angerufen hat und was er im Schilde führt. Ich komme nicht dahinter, und irgendwann möchte ich mich auch gar nicht mehr damit auseinandersetzen. Ich habe gesagt, was es zu sagen gibt, und werde jetzt meinen Plan in die Tat umsetzen. Ich will die Scheidung, ich will weg von dem durchgeknallten Junkie, zu dem mein rechtmäßig angetrauter Ehemann wurde. Meine Liebe ist erloschen. Oder das, was ich für Liebe gehalten habe. Ich möchte diese Episode abschließen.

Es gibt da einen Mann, nach dem ich mich sehne, aber für den momentan in meinem Leben kein Platz ist. Ich werde ihm eine E-Mail schreiben und ihm sagen, dass ich eine Auszeit brauche, um einige persönliche Dinge zu erledigen. Ich werde ihn bitten, mich in Ruhe zu lassen, aber auf mich zu warten. Es muss gelassen klingen, unaufgeregt. Ich will nicht, dass er misstrauisch wird und die Angst bemerkt, die mich beherrscht, sobald ich darüber nachdenke, was Haakon anrichten könnte. Deshalb darf Malte nicht in meiner Nähe sein. Er darf nicht zur Zielscheibe werden. Dasselbe gilt für meine Mutter, aber für sie kommt eine Mail nicht infrage. Ich muss ihr persönlich erklären, was vor sich geht, sie muss gewarnt werden. Zum Glück ist sie gerade in Portugal.

Vielleicht sollte ich mit Kommissar Haugen Kontakt aufnehmen, der den Angriff auf Annika untersucht hat. Ich bin überrascht, dass ich mich noch an seinen Namen erinnere. Ich könnte ihn anrufen und ihm sagen, dass Haakon Jensen mich bedroht und dass ich ihn anzeigen möchte. Aber vielleicht sollte ich lieber noch einmal eine Nacht darüber schlafen.

Ein stummer Schluchzer zerreißt meine Brust, als ich an Malte denke.

KAPITEL 63

Bislang gab es noch keine Reaktion aus Hyggen. Vielleicht sind sie wütend, aber es ist auch möglich, dass sie Verständnis aufbringen und mich nur in Ruhe lassen wollen. Ich überprüfe alle fünfzehn Minuten meine E-Mails, lese aber immer wieder: *Keine neuen Nachrichten*.

Zuerst werde ich eine E-Mail an Malte senden, aber wie mache ich ihm plausibel, dass ich jetzt keinen Kontakt will, dass das aber nichts mit meinen Gefühlen für ihn zu tun hat? Wie kann ich verhindern, dass er mich wieder unverhofft besucht?

Während ich eine Nachricht schreibe, kommt mir plötzlich ein Gedanke, der mich zutiefst beunruhigt. Haakon hatte mich im Kino gewarnt. Hat Jonas auf dem Treffen bestanden, weil er wissen wollte, wo ich Weihnachten verbringe?

Ich überprüfe mein Postfach noch einmal. Jonas hat mir soeben eine seltsame E-Mail geschrieben.

Jonte, dein Widerstand ist zwecklos. Es wird sowieso passieren. Haakon ist stärker, als du glaubst. Er hat merkwürdige Gedanken. Unheil braut sich über deinem Kopf zusammen. Ich warne dich: keine Scheidung. Zuerst machen wir einen neuen Bildband und dann noch ein weiteres Projekt. Besser sogar zwei weitere, vielleicht drei! Jonas
PS: Wann bekomme ich die Pläne?

„Niemals!" Ich brülle den Bildschirm an wie eine Furie, die Wörter kommen wie schneidender Hagel aus meinem Mund. „NIE WIEDER!!!"

Später erinnere ich mich nicht daran, was ich alles gebrüllt habe, aber es klingt mir noch in den Ohren. Das Toben war wohltuend, meine Wut fällt von mir ab.

Ich lege mich auf die Couch und schlinge ein Stück Pizza hinunter. Der Fernseher läuft, ich bringe den Ton zum Schweigen und schaue mir nur die bewegten Bilder an. Es ist ein Film über ein Kind, das versucht, seine Eltern zusammenzuhalten, weil Weihnachten ist. Ich zappe weiter. Ein Konzert. Ein Ballett. Ein Theaterstück. Ich drehe die Lautstärke auf. Eine Schauspielerin spricht. „Wenn sie es herausfindet, wird sich alles zwischen uns für immer ändern."

Der Satz ist wie ein Schlag ins Gesicht.

Nach Mitternacht liege ich immer noch auf der Couch, mit einem Glas Fruchtsaft in Reichweite. Ich sehne mich nach Alkohol, ich kann mich nicht erwärmen. Auf meiner Haut glänzen Schweißperlen, auf meinem Hals und meiner Stirn sind kleine rote Flecken, meine Lippen zittern leicht. Nie zuvor in meinem Leben habe ich mich so allein, so von allen verlassen und so verletzlich gefühlt. Selbst der schrille Ton hinter meiner

Stirn beginnt sich zu entfernen. Back-Vocal befolgt neuerdings andere Spielregeln. Er übt sich in Schweigen.

Eine sanfte Welle überläuft mein Rückgrat, während meine Gliedmaßen, von einer Art leichter, weicher Watte erhoben oder getragen, an Festigkeit verlieren. Nein, so ist es nicht. So ist es nur, wenn ich trinke. Ich spüre, dass in meinem Inneren die Welle dabei ist zu schwinden. Doch sobald ich meine Augen schließe, sind da die Einsamkeit und das weiße Kleid, das mahnend im Wind flattert.

Wenn sie es herausfindet, wird sich alles zwischen uns für immer ändern.

Wenn Mom herausfindet, was ich vor vierzehn Jahren getan habe, wird sie mich mit Sicherheit nicht im Stich lassen. Sie ist meine Mom, sie ist loyal. Aber sie wird mich nie wieder mit dem gleichen Ausdruck in den Augen ansehen, da bin ich mir sicher. Ich fürchte mich nicht vor Abneigung in ihren Augen, sondern vor Enttäuschung. Ich weiß nicht, was schlimmer ist.

Wenn sie es herausfindet, wird sich alles zwischen uns für immer ändern.

Die Worte kreisen in meinem Kopf, als ich schließlich doch anfange, nach Alkohol zu suchen. Ich tauche in alle Schränke ein, überprüfe jedes Versteck, an dem ich noch etwas finden könnte, schaue sogar in den Mülleimer. Aber alles ist weg, ich habe gründlich aufgeräumt.

Plötzlich wird mir bewusst, dass ich ein viel größeres Problem habe, als ich dachte.

Ich habe zehn Tage lang keinen Tropfen Alkohol getrunken, habe mich tapfer den Entzugserscheinungen gestellt. Sie sind noch nicht vollständig verschwunden, aber sie hielten sich bislang in Grenzen. Ich darf nicht mehr den Fehler begehen, zu glauben, dass der vorübergehende Verzicht auf Alkohol den Weg zu einem normalen Trinkverhalten ebnen könnte. Ein Glas zum Abendessen oder zu einem guten Gespräch. Dosiert und mit Verstand. Ich dachte, ich könnte diesen Zustand erreichen. Womit ich nicht gerechnet habe, ist die Tatsache, dass beim Gedanken an Wein der Schweiß auf meinem Körper perlt, dass meine Hände zittern, weil sie ein volles Glas halten wollen, und dass mich ein fast unaufhaltsames Bedürfnis nach Alkohol quält.

Ich habe ein Alkoholproblem und löse es sicher nicht mit meiner Absicht, mäßiger zu trinken.

Ich darf keinen Schluck mehr trinken, sonst geht alles wieder von vorne los!

Bist du sicher, dass du das ohne professionelle Hilfe hinkriegst? Back-Vocal ist zurück und gibt sich besorgt.

Ich gehe nach oben und betrachte mich im Badezimmerspiegel. Meine Augen sind glanzlos, meine Haare stumpf, die Fältchen um meine Augen tiefer. Ich nehme eine heiße Dusche, wasche mein Haar, creme mein Gesicht ein, und treffe eine Entscheidung.

Ich werde mir keine professionelle Hilfe holen, ich helfe mir selbst und präge mir als Ansporn einen Namen ein: Ebba Hagebak. Sie ist mein Geheimnis und gleichzeitig mein geheimes Maskottchen. Ich schulde ihr, dass mir so etwas nie wieder passieren darf. Denn indem ich ihr Leben genommen habe, bin ich verpflichtet, aus meinem etwas zu machen. Das schulde ich ihr. Sie ist meine Energiequelle, brennend und wärmend, versengend und beschützend, schmerzend und heilend.

Ich muss aufhören, gegen die Erinnerung anzukämpfen, sondern werde sie zukünftig zulassen. Ich benutze sie als Waffe gegen meinen Alkoholismus. Es ist der einzige Weg, mein Leben wieder in Ordnung zu bringen.

Mom werde ich nichts davon erzählen. Es würde nichts lösen, sondern alles nur zerstören. Mom ist nicht die richtige Person, um meine Schuld zu kommunizieren. Ich werde ihr nur sagen, dass Haakon mich bedroht und dass ich ihn anzeigen werde.

Ich spüre, wie sich meine Muskeln langsam lösen, Beine, Arme, Füße, Finger, selbst mein Herz schlägt langsamer. Meine Hände und Füße sind noch kalt, aber auch das wird sich irgendwann geben.

Ich rolle mich zusammen, ziehe die Bettdecke fest um mich und lausche der Stille der Nacht.

Obwohl ich allein bin, fühle ich mich geborgen.

Ich bin schwerelos, umgeben von Nebel, der in der Weite der Dunkelheit brodelt. Die Erde bebt leicht. Noch sind die Umrisse des Mannes undeutlich und fern, aber ich weiß, dass ich bald in der Lage sein werde, ihn zwischen dem Nebel, den Bäumen und der Finsternis zu unterscheiden. Bald wird er vor mir stehen.

Der Wald wirkt düster und entrückt. Das fahle Licht des Mondes, die Nebelschwaden und die Schatten spielen miteinander: Sie wechseln sich ab, werfen das Licht wie einen Ball hin und her. Der Mond badet die Nacht und verleiht ihr einen irrealen Glanz.

Ich lausche und erwarte meinen Peiniger, warte auf das Flüstern seiner heiseren Stimme. Noch ist kein Laut zu hören. Später, denke ich, später werde ich es hören.

Und dann, als wäre er ein formloser Nebelstreif, entdecke ich ihn zwischen den Tannen. Ich höre sein Schnauben und mache mich bereit. Entferne mich von der Lichtung, gehe tiefer in den Wald. Betrachte ihn von Weitem.

Ich habe Angst, obwohl ich in mir eine ungeheuerliche Kraft spüre. Aber Angst zu haben, ist normal, das weiß ich nun.

Jahrelang habe ich von diesem Moment geträumt, dies hier ist die Wirklichkeit, kein Traum. Er und der Wald sind die reale Welt. Mondlicht schlängelt sich durch die Bäume, als er auf mich zukommt. Die unzähligen Geräusche der Dunkelheit dringen an mein Ohr, das kristalline Wispern der Wintertannen, der Ruf eines Uhus, das Knacken der Zweige unter meinen Füßen. Ich zittere und bereite mich vor, schmiege mich eng an diesen Augenblick.

Plötzlich steht er vor mir, dieser Mann, den ich vor seiner Gräueltat nicht gekannt habe, höchstens flüchtig, vielleicht ein im Gedränge der Straße wahrgenommenes Gesicht.

Finster ragt er vor mir hoch, die Stimme dunkel und drohend. „Was willst du von mir, Jonte?"

„Für dich war ich nur das Mädchen in der Garage, ein bedeutungsloses Kind, das du quälen und in dem du explodieren konntest, ein lebendiges Sexspielzeug, an das du später keinen weiteren Gedanken verschwendet hast."

Der Mann erinnert sich nicht an mich, ich kann es sehen. Er ist jedoch hoch konzentriert, denn wie ein Tier wittert er die Gefahr, die von mir ausgeht. Ich schleudere ihm wütend Worte in sein überraschtes Gesicht, das sich jetzt zu einer Grimasse des Unmuts zusammenballt. Die schmalen Lippen zucken feucht, und eine gereizte Röte färbt die ungesund teigigen

Wangen. Stumpfsinnig starrt er mich an. Dann dreht er sich um, will gehen. Vielleicht, weil er sich vor der Auseinandersetzung drücken will. Vielleicht, weil ich ihm als Erwachsene zuwider bin. Er mag Kinder.

Ich betrachte dieses Monster, das sich von mir entfernen will, und ziehe das Messer. Noch während er sich wegdreht, steche ich zu. Er will fliehen, will trotz der Wunde fort von hier, doch er kann sich nicht rühren, ich habe ihn jeder Fähigkeit zur Bewegung beraubt. Er steht wie versteinert da, sodass ich mit dem Messer nach Belieben wüten kann: in Bauch und Brust, die mich als Kind erdrückt haben, in das Gesicht, das mir den Atem geraubt hat, in die Arme, die mich gefangen hielten, die Hände, die mich blutig geschlagen haben, und am Ende in den Penis, der mich immer wieder durchstochen hat.

Erst als sich die Welt in einem Meer aus Blut verdunkelt, dringen seine Schreie zu mir durch. Dann folgt ein allerletzter Schrei – animalisch, wild und gierig –, der das Dunkel wie einen Vorhang hinweghebt. Er ist meinen eigenen Lippen entwichen. Es war ein Befreiungsschrei.

Nun gehe ich ruhig davon – und Nebel begleitet mich in den Schutz des Waldes.

Ich wache schweißgebadet auf, blicke mich entsetzt um, schockiert über meinen grauenvollen Traum, und schreie mir den Hass aus der Seele, bis ich nur noch krächze.

Mir ist schwindlig, als ich aufstehe. Die Welt dreht sich. Ich lege mich wieder hin, bis meine Atmung sich beruhigt hat. Als sie wieder ruhig dahinfließt, ist es halb neun Uhr morgens.

Ich rufe Mom an, die sich mit einer schläfrigen Stimme meldet. „Mädchen, so früh? Ist etwas passiert?"

Es gelingt mir nicht, mit fester Stimme zu antworten.

„Was ist passiert, Jonte? Wo bist du?"

„Zu Hause, Mom."

„Zu Hause? Du wolltest doch die Feiertage bei Bente verbringen."

„Ich war auch dort." Meine Gedanken sind im Moment nur schwer fassbar. Ich möchte Mom nicht beunruhigen und bereue es bereits, sie angerufen zu haben.

„Bitte, Jonte, sag mir, was los ist."

„Ich habe geträumt, dass ich meinen Vergewaltiger massakriert habe."

„Oh, Jonte … So schlecht geht es dir?"

Die Stimme meiner Mutter zu hören, tut mir gut. Ich werde ruhiger.

„Wann bist du übermorgen zu Hause. Ich möchte dich sehen, Mom."

„So gegen drei Uhr am Nachmittag. Ich könnte sofort zu dir kommen."

„Nein. Ruf mich an, wenn du zu Hause bist. Ich komme lieber zu dir. Keine Sorge, ich habe mich schon wieder beruhigt und die Situation voll im Griff."

„Welche Situation?"

„Das sagt man halt so. Ich hatte einen schrecklichen Traum und bin noch etwas verwirrt."

„Hast du schon wegen der Scheidung einen Anwalt aufgesucht?"

„Ja, habe ich."

„Und denkst du noch genauso über diese Entscheidung?"

„Ja, natürlich, es ist absolut notwendig. Ich … ich werde Haakon Jensen anzeigen, Mom. Er stalkt mich." Diese entschlossene Antwort überrascht mich. Aber es ist wahr, die Scheidung berührt mich nicht, und die Anzeige verschafft mir ein befreiendes Gefühl.

Stille.

„Ich wusste, dass da etwas gewaltig schiefläuft. Warte, bis ich wieder da bin, Jonte. Dann kannst du mir alles in Ruhe erzählen. Ich werde dich auch zur Polizei begleiten."

„Danke, Mom! Du bist super. Ich liebe dich", antworte ich und lege auf.

Wenig später sitze ich in der Küche mit einer dampfenden Tasse Kaffee vor meinem Laptop. Noch immer keine Nachricht von Malte. Ich versuche, erleichtert zu sein, weil ich mir keine Gedanken mehr machen muss.

Aber ich bin überhaupt nicht erleichtert, sondern enttäuscht und wütend. War es nur ein Flirt für ihn? Nein, diese Schlussfolgerung will ich nicht zulassen.

Der Schock nach dem Erwachen steckt mir noch immer in den Knochen. Björn Jensen ist wieder in meiner Nähe aufgetaucht, steht zwischen mir und der Dunkelheit, und der Hass auf dieses gefühllose Tier kommt wieder hoch. Im Traum hatte ich Macht und Kontrolle. Ich besaß Fertigkeiten, die im Wachzustand undenkbar sind, denn ich könnte niemals einen Menschen töten. Mir bleibt nichts anderes übrig, als den Traum beiseitezulegen.

Der Albtraum treibt mich wieder an mein Zeichenbrett. Vor ein paar Tagen zweifelte ich daran, ob ich dem Orden die Pläne präsentieren könnte. Ich war mir nicht sicher, was die Ausstattung des Klosterinnenhofs betraf. Diese Ungewissheit liegt hinter mir. Die Lösung sprüht förmlich aus mir heraus. Ich nehme den Zeichenstift und vergesse die Welt um mich herum.

Als ich den Stift beiseitelege, ist es bereits halb fünf. Draußen wird es dunkel. Ich schließe die Vorhänge, schalte die Stehlampen an, dimme ihr Licht und zeichne fieberhaft weiter.

KAPITEL 65

Meine Angst verblasst am Morgen zu einer fernen Erinnerung. Meine innere Stimme lacht lauthals über diese Angst, die jetzt nur noch ein harmloser Gedanke ist. Back-Vocal lacht meine Angst aus.

Gut.

Nach zwei Tassen Kaffee spüre ich eine Kraft, die mich überrascht. Eine unbändige Energie. Ich steige in meinen Wagen und breche zu meiner Mutter auf, um die finalen Pläne für das Klosterhotel, den Laptop und den USB-Stick mit den Back-ups in Moms Safe zu deponieren. Sie sind dort besser aufgehoben als bei mir. Selbst über das Licht der Sonne, das mich während der Autofahrt blendet, lacht Back-Vocal. Er meint, die Sonne sei schlimmer als die Nacht, weil sie alle Widerwärtigkeiten auskoste.

Ich werde Anzeige gegen Haakon Jensen wegen seiner Drohungen erstatten, die Vergewaltigung werde ich aber nicht erwähnen. Mom wird mich zu Hauptkommissar Haugen begleiten. Ich habe schon zu lange gewartet. Manchmal frage ich mich, wie lange ein Mensch braucht, um Böses zu tun. Björn Jensen benötigte nur eine Minute, um das Mädchen Jonte zu überrumpeln und in eine Garage neben dem Erdbeerfeld zu zerren. Und später? Wie viele Sekunden teuflischer Freude hat er bei der mehrfachen Vergewaltigung gehabt?

Ob Haakon und sein Bruder schon immer böse Menschen waren? Die Frage hallt nach, ich habe keine Antwort darauf.

Lennart Haugen hat sich meine Probleme mit Haakon zwar angehört, aber gleich angedeutet, dass er nur etwas unternehmen könne, wenn Haakon seine Drohungen nachweislich in die Tat umsetzen würde.

„In den meisten Fällen bleibt es bei der Drohung, Frau Sandvik", versucht er mich zu beruhigen. „Ich werde aber die Streife bitten, hin und wieder bei Ihnen vorbeizuschauen. Kann ich sonst noch etwas für Sie tun?"

Mom rutscht auf dem Besucherstuhl hin und her. „Wir sind auch in einer anderen Sache hier, Herr Haugen", sagt sie leise.

Ich trete ihr sofort gegen das Schienbein, sie sieht mich verständnislos an. Björn Jensen läuft mir nicht davon. Um dieses Monster werde ich mich später selbst kümmern. Eins nach dem anderen.

„Ich habe meinen Laptop und Pläne bei meiner Mutter im Safe deponiert", falle ich ihr ins Wort. „Meine Mutter will wissen, ob Sie das auch für eine gute Idee halten?"

Lennart Haugen hebt irritiert die Augenbrauchen und sieht meine Mutter an. „*Das* wollten Sie mich fragen, Frau Sandvik?"

Mom errötet. „Ja, natürlich", antwortet sie.

„Sicher, das ist eine gute Idee. Würden Sie mich jetzt bitte entschuldigen. Meiner Abteilung wurde kurz vor Ihrem Eintreffen ein Mord gemeldet." Er sucht meinen Blick. „Sollte Ihnen etwas verdächtig vorkommen, Frau Sandvik, dann rufen Sie bitte an. Aber wie gesagt, es kommt sehr selten vor, dass jemand seine Drohungen wahr macht. Vielleicht beruhigt Sie das ein wenig."

Selten ist kein beruhigendes Wort, stänkert Back-Vocal.

Wir verabschieden uns von Lennart Haugen. An seiner Bürotür drehe ich mich noch einmal um. „Wer wurde denn ermordet?"

„Ein Kinderschänder, den wir seit Jahren auf der Fahndungsliste hatten."

„Um den tut es mir nicht leid. Auf Wiedersehen, Herr Haugen!"

Draußen hole ich tief Luft. Über meine Haut kriecht eine Gänsehaut.

Meine Mutter möchte, dass ich vorerst bei ihr einziehe, aber das kommt nicht infrage. Haakon weiß, wo sie wohnt. Ich darf gar nicht daran denken, dass er auch sie belästigen könnte. Mom soll nicht noch mehr in diese Geschichte hineingezogen werden.

Ich bin davon überzeugt, dass Haakon in Kürze wieder bei mir auftauchen wird, denn ich habe das Geschäftskonto *JO*, das ohnehin nur auf meinen Namen läuft, aufgelöst. Ich werde Jonas' Anteil mit einem Scheck ausgleichen. Doch er nimmt meine Anrufe nicht entgegen, und ich weiß auch nicht, wo er sich im Moment aufhält. Mein Anwalt hat ihm offenbar eine Nachricht über die Auflösung des Kontos zukommen lassen und ihn darüber informiert, dass infolge der bevorstehenden Scheidung die Basis für gemeinschaftliche Projekte nicht mehr gegeben ist. Haakon wird ausrasten, wenn er das hört, aber das spielt keine Rolle. Es ist mir egal. Nun agiere ich und werde nie wieder nur reagieren. Mein imaginäres Flugzeug habe ich ins Meer stürzen lassen, denn ich will nie wieder die Flucht vor dem Leben ergreifen. Nie wieder. Selbst wenn ich tatsächlich zum Messer greifen muss, um mich zu verteidigen.

Meine Rachegefühle gegenüber Haakon und Björn Jensen nehmen eine konkrete Gestalt an. Ich beginne meine Fantasien über die Zerstörung der beiden, zu genießen. Um nicht selbst unterzugehen, müssen die beiden untergehen. Mein Hass auf die Brüder ist eine Waffe, wie meine Schuld wegen Ebba. Wenn ich an sie denke, verspüre ich keine Panik mehr, sondern Entschlossenheit. Ebba ist da. Sie wird immer da sein. Wenn ich mit ihr leben will, muss ich sie als Freundin betrachten, die mich durch mein

Leben geleitet. Aber notfalls muss ich auch mit ihr sterben, denn angesichts ihres Opfers steht es mir nicht zu, mich feige davor zu drücken.

Es ist gut, dass niemand ahnt, wie es in dir drinnen aussieht. Back-Vocal läuft in meinem Kopf zur Höchstform auf. *Ich weiß wirklich nicht, ob du jetzt endgültig verrückt geworden bist oder geistig stabiler als je zuvor.*

Such dir Hilfe, Jonte!, würde Mom sagen und versuchen, mich davon zu überzeugen, dass ich aufgrund einer depressiven Verstimmung eine Therapie brauche. Aber sie weiß ja nichts von Ebba.

Ich schließe mit meiner Vergangenheit ab und akzeptiere Ebbas Tod als ein erschreckendes Beispiel dafür, was passieren kann, wenn man sich volltrunken ans Steuer setzt.

Und Björn Jensen? Werde ich eines Tages eine Schlinge aus meiner Handtasche nehmen, um sie ihm um den Hals zu legen und einfach zuzuziehen? Werde ich ihn und Haakon töten, damit die Geister nicht länger über mein Leben bestimmen?

Sie werden mich nie wieder erpressen, nie wieder meinen Schlaf stören, nie wieder meine Angst oder Panik schüren. Das habe ich beschlossen.

Ich werde auch ALLEIN wachsen, und Jonas kann dabei zusehen.

Wir werden gemeinsam berühmt, hat er gesagt.

Vergiss es!

Nur noch zwei, drei gemeinsame Projekte.

VERGISS ES!

KAPITEL 66

Als ich am nächsten Abend vom XD Cinema Norge nach Hause zurückkehre, fahre ich nicht in die Garage, sondern parke den Wagen vor meinem Haus. Der Schnee und das Eis sind geschmolzen, stattdessen nimmt ein böiger Wind zu, Büsche und Bäume rauschen in der düsteren Stimmung, die Wolken plustern sich auf, als würden sie gegen irgendetwas oder irgendjemanden einen mächtigen Groll hegen. Die Temperaturen liegen fünf Grad Celsius über dem Gefrierpunkt.

Ich bleibe für eine Weile still im Wagen sitzen und suche hinter der Frontscheibe in der Dunkelheit nach Anzeichen seiner Anwesenheit. Vielleicht versteckt er sich hinter einer der Hecken.

Im Haus brennt Licht. Ich habe begonnen, morgens, wenn ich gehe, das Licht einzuschalten. Ich mag keine Häuser, die im Dunkeln liegen. Haakon ist weit und breit nicht zu sehen. Ich steige aus, nehme die Post und die Zeitung aus dem Briefkasten und gehe ins Haus.

Noch einmal lese ich den Artikel in der NEWSTRAL-Zeitung Drammen.

Am Abend des 30. Dezembers 2019 wurde im Haus der Familie N. der fünfzigjährige Björn J. schwer verletzt und nicht mehr ansprechbar aufgefunden.

„Björn J. ist der Kriminalpolizei Drammen bekannt. Dem Mann werden mehrere Straftaten vorgeworfen, insbesondere wurde er wegen Kindesmissbrauchs in zehn Fällen per Haftbefehl gesucht", so Hauptkommissar Haugen. „Mutmaßlich war die dreizehnjährige Stina N. ein neues Opfer für den Triebtäter."

Die Mutter des Kindes berichtete unserem Reporter vor Ort, dass Stina allein zu Hause gewesen sei. „Das Mädchen hat ferngesehen und gehört, wie die Tür aufgebrochen wurde. Daraufhin hat sie sich in die Küche geschlichen und ein Messer aus der Schublade genommen. Als der Mann plötzlich hinter ihr stand und sich an ihr vergreifen wollte, hat sie ihm das Messer in die Brust gestoßen", so die Mutter des Mädchens.

Der Täter ist noch im Rettungswagen seiner schweren Verletzung erlegen.

Ich lege den Artikel zur Seite. Stina N. hat das getan, was ich hätte tun sollten, als ich an der Kinotheke auf dieses Monster traf.

„Stina ist ein mutiges Mädchen."

Der Bastard hat seine Strafe bekommen, knurrt Back-Vocal. *Das Mädchen hat dir die Arbeit abgenommen.*

„Ich hoffe, sie verkraftet es gut. Aber ich muss zugeben, es ist ein beruhigendes Gefühl, dass ich nicht zum Messer greifen musste. Mom hätte vermutlich einen Herzinfarkt bekommen."

Und ich hätte mit dir viele Jahre in einer Gefängniszelle verbringen müssen. Obwohl es hinter deiner Stirn ja fast wie im Knast ist …

Ich muss schmunzeln. „Du bist ja richtig witzig heute. Aber mach dir mal keine Sorgen. Jetzt, wo ich die Entscheidungen selbst treffe ...“

... scheint es dir endlich besser zu gehen.

Ich führe jetzt Selbstgespräche mit Back-Vocal, um mich zu beruhigen, zu trösten und mir Mut zu machen. Für Mom wäre das wohl ein besorgniserregendes Zeichen. Doch Back-Vocal wendet sich neuerdings zuversichtlich und besänftigend an mich. Meine innere Stimme kennt eben auch meine guten Seiten. Ich mag sie, obwohl sie meistens das letzte Wort behalten will. Back-Vocal neigt auch nicht zur Panik. Das ist gut. Wenn ich abends zu Bett gehe, wünscht er mir nun eine gute Nacht. Wir sind wie gute Freunde, die sich genau kennen.

Es ist ruhig im Haus. Nur draußen tost der böige Wind. Ich schalte den Fernseher ein und verzichte auf den Ton. Die Tür zum Korridor ist nur angelehnt, damit ich es höre, falls jemand näher kommt. Die Fenster sind geschlossen, die Vorhänge zugezogen. Das Telefon ist in Reichweite.

Ich frage mich, warum ich Jonas nicht erreichen kann. Vielleicht ist er verreist, oder die beiden hecken gerade einen Plan aus, wie sie mich zur Zusammenarbeit zwingen können. Ich spüre am ganzen Körper eine undefinierbare Unruhe, die ich auf die Entzugserscheinungen zurückführe. Das ist nicht gut, aber ich habe es im Griff. Im Internet sind genug grausame Beispiele aufgeführt, wie gefährlich eine Sucht ist, um mich bei der Stange zu halten.

Malte und Bente haben mir noch immer nicht gemailt. Sie sind vermutlich enttäuscht wegen meiner hastigen Abreise, vielleicht sind sie beleidigt, weil ich ihre Gastfreundschaft abgelehnt habe. Aber so muss ich mir wenigstens keine Gedanken um ihre Sicherheit machen, falls Haakon Rachepläne schmieden sollte. Ob der Tod seines Halbbruders ihn getroffen hat? Im Cinema Drammen machten sie einen vertrauten und verbundenen Eindruck. Vielleicht ist er ja erschüttert.

Als es an der Haustür schellt, denke ich spontan, dass sich nun ein unveränderliches Schicksal erfüllt. Ich habe niemanden kommen hören, weil der Wind an den Fenstern gerüttelt und alles andere übertönt hat. Meine Knie zittern, als ich aufstehe.

Ich wage mich nicht an den Spion – das ist mir zu nah –, sondern laufe die Treppe hinauf und öffne das Fenster im Badezimmer. Der Wind stürmt herein, zerzaust mein Haar, peitscht es mir wild um den Kopf. Die frische, stechend scharfe Nachtluft reinigt sofort meine Lunge. Mit halb geöffneten Augen schaue ich nach unten. An der Haustür steht Malte.

„Bin ich willkommen?“, ruft er herauf.

Einen Moment lang staune ich über mich selbst, dann sind alle Absichten, ihn von mir fernzuhalten, ihn nicht einmal hereinzulassen, von einer Böe in die Ferne getragen worden. Ich renne runter, öffne die Haustür und verspüre sofort den Impuls, ihn zu umarmen und fest an mich zu drücken, bis uns beiden die Luft wegbleibt.

Als er mich küsst und ich den Geschmack von Schokolade in seinem Mund schmecke, legt sich ein sanfter Schleier um mein Herz.

„Du hast genascht", keuche ich zwischen zwei Küssen.

„Ich habe eine Tüte Schokonüsse im Handschuhfach gefunden", lächelt er.

Wir gehen nach oben. Ich lasse das Licht im Wohnzimmer an, obwohl ich jetzt in Sicherheit bin.

Ich gebe mich Malte völlig hin, bin unersättlich. Noch nie habe ich so empfunden, seine Worte sind sanft, liebevoll, nie zuvor war der Sex so innig, so nah und intim, so selbstverständlich, so vorbehaltlos. Als wir erschöpft nebeneinanderliegen, kullern mir die Tränen über die Wangen.

Malte küsst sie fort. „Nicht weinen, Liebling", flüstert er. „Es sei denn, es ist vor Glück."

Ich möchte sagen, dass es so ist, aber ich kann diese Lüge nicht aussprechen. Ich weiß nicht genau, welche Art von Tränen gerade fließen, aber für Glück ist es noch zu früh. Es gibt zu viele andere Gründe, warum ich weine, meine Emotionen sind aufgewühlt, Angst und Freude wechseln sich ständig ab.

Malte zieht mich an sich und streichelt meinen Rücken. Ich werde ruhiger.

„Ich habe dich völlig überrumpelt", sagt er zärtlich. „Aber ich konnte nicht anders. Ich hatte Angst, dich zu verlieren, falls ich zu lange warte. Und ich muss wissen, ob in deinem Leben ein Platz für mich ist. Es spielt für mich keine Rolle, ob du viel Zeit dazu brauchst. Ich kann warten, wenn ich nur weiß, dass es einen Platz für mich gibt."

„Er gibt ihn", sage ich leise.

„Das ist wunderbar." Er küsst mich sanft. „Aber leider habe ich noch eine weniger gute Nachricht."

Ich erstarre.

„Ich kann nicht bleiben. Ich muss meine Tochter morgen früh zum Flughafen nach Oslo bringen. Sie geht für ein Jahr nach Amerika. Ich muss leider noch heute Nacht zurück nach Hyggen."

„Aber das ist doch selbstverständlich", murmle ich erleichtert, dass es nichts anderes ist, und spüre, dass der Schlaf mich fast übermannt.

Malte küsst meine Augenlider. „Ruh dich aus", flüstert er. „Ich werde morgen auf deinen Anruf warten. Das kann auch mitten in der Nacht sein. Du darfst nur nicht wieder kneifen."

Ich schließe die Augen, als könnte ich so die Erinnerung an seine Berührungen länger festhalten, und spüre, dass er das Bett verlässt. Irgendwo ist ein Rascheln zu hören. Malte zieht sich an. Dann sind da wieder seine

Lippen auf meinem Mund, meiner Nase, meinen Wangen. Und noch mal auf meinem Mund. „Bis bald, mein Liebling!"

Ich lausche den Schritten, die die Treppe hinuntergehen. Ich höre, wie er die Haustür öffnet, aber nicht, wie die Tür wieder ins Schloss fällt.

Stille. Auf der Schwelle zwischen Nacht und Morgen.

Ich warte. Suche in der Stille das Klicken des Schlosses. Die Müdigkeit nähert sich. Sie ist so schwer, so bleiern.

Schritte auf der Treppe. Ich lächle. Sie sind eine Melodie in meinem Ohr.

Er kommt zurück.

KAPITEL 67

Meine Augenlider sind schwer, aber ich bin wach. Ich höre die Schritte näher kommen und warte, dass Malte mich wieder in die Arme nimmt, mich küsst und mir sagt, dass er noch ein paar Stunden neben mir liegen möchte.

Doch dann spüre ich die Spitze einer Nadel auf meiner Haut, spüre, wie sie meine Armvene durchbohrt. Es kommt völlig unerwartet, der Schock lässt mich zusammenzucken. Gleichzeitig nehme ich einen vertrauten Geruch wahr. Ich brauche einige Sekunden, um mich zu orientieren. Um zu begreifen, dass es nicht Malte ist. Ein zweiter Geruch dringt in meine Nase, den ich aber nicht einordnen kann.

„Nun öffne schon deine Augen, *Schätzchen*", haucht eine Stimme in mein Ohr. Hass und Gewalt in einem Atemzug.

Ein Schauder setzt in meinen Zehen ein und breitet sich in meinem Körper aus. Meine Beine sind wie gelähmt, ich versuche sie zu bewegen, aber Haakon liegt auf mir. Ich bin keines Gefühls oder Gedankens mehr fähig. Will nur mein imaginäres Flugzeug aus dem Meer ziehen. Ich brauche es wieder.

Nein, Jonte!, ruft Back-Vocal. *Tu es nicht! Du hast es uns beiden versprochen!*

Ich bin in einem Albtraum gefangen. Das ist alles nicht real. Ich muss aufwachen. Aufwachen!

Aber ich wache nicht auf.

Bitte, lass das hier nur einen Albtraum sein ..., flehe ich.

„Öffne deine Augen, Schlampe!" Der Hass in seiner Stimme trifft mich wie ein Peitschenschlag. Mein Mund ist trocken.

„Du weigerst dich? Oder fällt es dir so schwer? Würde mich nicht wundern! Denn ich habe deinem Körper gerade eine gewaltige Dosis Valium verpasst. Du wirst gleich einschlafen und zuckersüß träumen."

Valium?

Ich höre ein Rascheln. Im nächsten Moment legt er mir Fesseln um die Handgelenke und befestigt sie an beiden Seiten des Kopfteils, sodass ich mit ausgebreiteten Armen vor ihm liege. Ich zwinge mich, meine Lider zu öffnen, und lese Hass in seinen Augen, sehe seine ungezügelte Freude, mich zu quälen.

Er geht zum Fußteil, umfasst meine Beine, zieht sie weit nach unten, fesselt die Fußknöchel und verknotet die Seile an den Bettpfosten. Ich atme tief durch, winde mich unter den Fesseln, drehe meinen Körper, versuche mich zu befreien, mich loszureißen.

Die Nacht ragt durch das Fenster ins Zimmer herein, wie in einer schiefen Ebene. Nichts stimmt. Alles kippt. Ich bebe vor seelischer Qual.

Tränen schießen mir aus den Augen. Mein Körper windet sich in dem Bedürfnis zu entkommen. Es ist sinnlos. Die Fesseln sind so unnachgiebig wie Haakon selbst. Ich liege nackt vor ihm, möchte schreien. In meinem Kopf wirbelt das Geräusch einer Brandung, in meine Nase dringt ein penetranter Geruch. Ich versuche, ihn zu bestimmen. Es gelingt mir nicht.

Plötzlich ist Haakons Gesicht direkt über mir. Ich muss den Drang hinunterschlucken, ihm ins Gesicht zu spucken, ihn anzuschreien und die Stille nach der demütigenden Fesselung mit Worten zu füllen. Ich presse die Lippen fest zusammen.

Er will dich gefügig machen, dich brechen, flüstert Back-Vocal. *Aber du bist stärker, Jonte! Denk an Ebba! Du bist es ihr schuldig, dich jetzt nicht unterkriegen zu lassen!*

Niemals wird er mich brechen. Niemals. Niemals. Niemals. Niemals …

„Dein Freund hat mir netterweise die Tür geöffnet. Ich habe den perfekten Moment gewählt. Er hat nun wahrlich nicht mit einem Schlag auf den Kopf gerechnet, der ihn zu Fall bringen würde, der Ärmste. Ich habe ihn ordentlich zusammengeschnürt und wie ein Postpaket in den Flur gelegt, Schätzchen. So könnt ihr Turteltauben zumindest gemeinsam im Feuer brennen. Ich bin einfach zu sentimental."

Benzin!

Es ist Benzingeruch, den ich wahrnehme.

Ich hebe den Blick, suche seine Augen, in denen ein Höllenfeuer brennt; halte stand, bis er sich abwendet. „Ich habe den Flur und die gesamte Treppe bis zu deinem Bett mit Benzin gesprenkelt. Wenn ich das Haus verlasse, werfe ich ein brennendes Streichholz hinein, und du und dein Ficker werdet eine heiße Nacht zusammen haben, Schätzchen. *DU* wirst mich nie wieder provozieren! Denn *DU* bekommst keinen Cent von Jonas' Vermächtnis, und *DU* wirst zukünftig auch keine satten Architektenhonorare mehr kassieren. Du elende Hexe landest auf dem Scheiterhaufen, wo du hingehörst!" Haakon starrt mich mit hassverzerrtem Gesicht an. „Ich habe dich gewarnt, mich nicht in Rage zu versetzen, aber du wolltest einfach nicht hören. Du wirst bald einschlafen und kannst mir dankbar sein, dass ich dich nicht bei lebendigem Leib schmoren lasse. Du wirst nichts spüren, wenn das Feuer dich liebkost. Und deine Mutter …" Er sieht mich kalt an. „… kann sich auch noch deine Einäscherung ersparen." Er lacht.

Das Valium entfaltet bereits seine lähmende Wirkung. Meine Augen schließen sich. Ich spüre meine Arme und Beine nicht mehr, mein Oberkörper wird leicht, ich schwebe.

Er steht auf und schaut auf mich herab. „Was bist du nur für ein hässliches Knochengerüst. Keine weichen Kurven. Es war eine kluge Entscheidung von Jonas, dir die Mifepriston-Tropfen in den Tee zu kippen. Mit der Dosis hat er es zwar ein wenig übertrieben, aber kann man es ihm verdenken, dass er seinem Balg in deinem Bauch einen Abgang bescheren wollte?"

Ich öffne mit letzter Kraft meine Augen und gewähre ihm einen Blick in meine Seele, in der Dämonen in Hohngelächter ausbrechen.

„Vorsicht!", mahnt er mich. „Hör endlich damit auf, mich zu provozieren, du dumme Schlampe!" Wut flammt in seinen Augen auf. Dann schlägt er zu. Mitten in mein Gesicht. Meine Haut brennt. Mein Mund öffnet sich. Ich schmecke Blut. Back-Vocal flucht hinter meiner Stirn. Meine Lippen bewegen sich nicht. Meine Zunge liegt taub auf dem Boden meines Mundes.

Er lacht laut auf. „Grüße Jonas von mir, Schätzchen!"

Ich gleite in eine unergründliche Tiefe ab, habe keine Kontrolle über meinen Körper. Dann ist alles anders. Vor meinen geschlossenen Augen nimmt das Bild von Haakon Gestalt an, der mich in die Garage verschleppt, dann ist da Björn, der mich anzündet. Dann steht alles still. Ich bin die Einzige, die das sieht. Haakon hat das Bild nicht verändert. Natürlich nicht. *Er* ist ein Nichts. *Er* ist ein Niemand. *Ich* kenne die Geschichte, weiß, wie sie ausgeht.

In der Ferne sind plötzlich Stimmen, ich kann ihre Worte nicht verstehen. Ich drehe den Kopf zur Seite, blinzle und versuche, mit letzter Kraft an dem Licht vorbeizusehen, das mich plötzlich blendet. Dann stürze ich in einen dunklen Abgrund, in dem ein weißes Kleid meinen Aufprall auffängt. Ebba ist da!

„Sie kommt zu sich", sagt jemand.

Ich halte meine Augen geschlossen und überlege, wo ich bin. In meiner Nase ist noch immer Benzingeruch. Dann erinnere ich mich an das Monster, das auf mir lag, und versuche, dieses Bild zu verdrängen.

„Ich glaube, ich habe mich geirrt", sagt die Stimme, ihr Klang verflüchtigt sich im Raum.

Ich werde berührt, jemand streicht sanft über meine Stirn. Das ist schön, ich fühle mich sicher. Ich bin in einer Nahtodphase, das grelle Licht gewährt mir einen Blick ins Jenseits.

Die Benzinluft drängt sich mir auf, umarmt mich, dann strömt ein Meer brennbarer Flüssigkeit heran, und ich schwimme mittendrin. Ich höre das Geräusch eines zündenden Streichholzes. Das schrecklichste Geräusch der Welt.

„Bist du wach, Jonte?" Die Stimme ist nah und lädt mich ein, meine Augen zu öffnen. „Oh, mein Mädchen, mein Mädchen."

Es ist Mom, sie weint. Ich sehe Tränen über ihr Gesicht rinnen. Fassungslosigkeit ist in ihren Augen. Was sieht sie? Bin ich verbrannt und entstellt? Warum fühle ich dann keinen Schmerz?

Ich blicke vorsichtig auf meine Hände. Sie sind unversehrt. Ich kann meine Beine wieder bewegen. Und meine Arme. Ziehe meine Bauchmuskeln an. Ich bin weder verletzt noch nackt.

„Warum weinst du, Mom?"

Sie lächelt mich unter Tränen an, schluchzt erneut.

Ich versuche, einen klaren Kopf zu bekommen, blicke aus dem Fenster. Die Wintersonne brennt auf das Glas, sie prangt schillernd am Himmel wie ein besonders heller Mond. Der Benzingestank hängt vor meinem Gedächtnis, wie eine Sperre, die ich durchbrechen muss.

„Malte liegt auch hier in der Klinik", sagt meine Mutter.

Eine Schockwelle überwältigt mich. Ich schlage um mich, schreie, als die Erinnerungen mit einem Paukenschlag aufflammen.

„Beruhige dich, Jonte", ruft meine Mutter. „Bitte, beruhige dich, ich rufe eine Krankenschwester."

Back-Vocal tobt vor Angst, er vermisst mich. Wieder stürze ich ins Dunkel. Schreie in ein Vakuum hinein, in dem Haakon und Björn sitzen, Seite an Seite. Grinsend.

Ein Mann hockt neben meinem Bett. „Aha, ich freue mich, Sie wieder bei uns zu haben. Das wurde aber auch Zeit. Ich bin Erik Lansson, ihr behandelnder Neurologe."

Ich versuche, den Arzt an meinem Bett klar zu erkennen, doch mein Kopf rebelliert.

Lansson nickt mir freundlich zu, dann blättert er in einer Krankenakte. „Sie haben einige Tage verschlafen, aber das ist in Ordnung und völlig normal nach einem so traumatischen Erlebnis. Sie haben etwas Schreckliches hinter sich."

Er beugt sich zu mir. „Soll ich Sie ein bisschen aufrichten? Die Infusion können wir entfernen, jetzt, wo Sie wach sind." Lansson lächelt, es ist ein sympathisches, warmes Lächeln.

„Wie lange bin ich schon hier, Dr. Lansson?"

„Zwei Tage. Sie sind ein paarmal aufgewacht, aber immer gleich wieder in die tiefen Abgründe des Bewusstseins abgetaucht. Aber keine Sorge, es war kein Koma. Nennen wir es einfach ein Schlafdefizit. Das passiert häufiger nach einem Schock."

„Meine Mutter war hier?"

„Sie ist immer noch hier und isst gerade mit einer Freundin im Klinikrestaurant zu Mittag. Soll eine Schwester sie holen?"

„Bitte."

Dr. Lansson misst meinen Blutdruck und fühlt meinen Puls. „Alles perfekt. Wach bleiben und so weitermachen, dann können Sie bald nach Hause. Ich sehe heute Abend noch einmal nach Ihnen. Okay?"

Er lächelt und verlässt das Zimmer.

Nach Hause? Ich betrachte das Nachthemd, das ich trage, es gehört mir. Meine Nachthemden liegen in meiner Schlafzimmerkommode. Hat das Monster mein Haus doch nicht niedergebrannt?

Pflegerinnen gehen in meinem Zimmer ein und aus. Sie sind freundlich, beruhigen mich und sagen, dass ich Glück gehabt hätte mit einer so aufmerksamen Nachbarin. Sie scheinen ganz in Ordnung zu sein, doch ich traue ihnen nicht. Es ist nichts Persönliches – ich traue niemandem mehr, nicht einmal mir selbst.

Dann wird die Tür mit einem Schwung geöffnet, Mom und Edith stürmen auf mich zu und erdrücken mich fast. Mom weint wieder. „Mein Mädchen, oh, mein Kleines, endlich bist du wieder bei uns."

„Erzählst du mir bitte, was passiert ist, Mom?"

Edith reicht meiner Mutter ein Taschentuch und sieht mich an.

„Du verdankst es deiner Nachbarin, dass du …", erklärt Mom.

„Malvi Oddbjørn?"

„Ja, sie hat diesen Haakon Jensen mitten in der Nacht vor deinem Haus gesehen und beobachtet, wie er – als deine Haustür geöffnet wurde – den Mann, der herauskam, niederschlug. Sie hat keine Sekunde gezögert und sofort den Notruf gewählt. Zum Glück fuhren in der Gegend zwei Polizeifahrzeuge Streife, die sofort zur Stelle waren. Die Beamten verschafften sich Zugang zum Haus und überwältigten Haakon, bevor er dein Haus in Brand setzen konnte."

Ich will nach Malte fragen, aber meine Stimme versagt.

„Malte hat eine Gehirnerschütterung und wurde gestern in sein Haus nach Hyggen gebracht. Er hat dich hier kurz besucht, aber du hast geschlafen. Du bist einfach nicht aufgewacht. Tagelang. Ich habe zweimal mit ihm telefoniert. Er ist sehr besorgt um dich. Ruf ihn bitte an, sobald es dir besser geht, Jonte. Er ist so ein sympathischer Mann. Genau der Richtige für dich, wenn du mich fragst."

Ich höre Mom zu und schweige. Die Worte, die in mein Ohr dringen, beruhigen und erschöpfen mich zu gleichen Teilen. Ich verspüre den Drang, wieder in einen tiefen Schlaf abzutauchen. Ich will Ruhe, Stille, Abgeschiedenheit.

Und ich will hier raus.

„Wie lange muss ich noch hierbleiben?", frage ich Dr. Lansson bei seiner abendlichen Visite.

„Sie können nach Hause gehen, soweit es mich betrifft. Ich rate Ihnen jedoch dringend, sich professionelle Hilfe zu suchen, um sich mit diesem Trauma auseinanderzusetzen. Ich werde Ihrer Hausärztin den Befund mailen. Sie kann Sie dann an einen Psychologen überweisen."

Meint er etwa diese Ärztin hinter ihrem rosa lackierten Schreibtisch, die dich bei deinem letzten Besuch angesehen hat, als hätte sie einen Volltrottel vor sich?

„Vielen Dank! Ich werde das selbst entscheiden."

„Sie brauchen wirklich Hilfe", betont Dr. Lansson.

„Ich werde darüber nachdenken."

Heute habe ich unverwandt in den Badezimmerspiegel geschaut und sah nichts anderes als meine Augen, die mir fragend entgegenstarrten und selbst meine Erinnerungen an die Ereignisse anzweifelten. Ich erinnere mich an den Benzingestank. Und an *seinen* Geruch. Wie das eine zum anderen geführt hat. Zumindest glaube ich, mich daran zu erinnern. Mein Gedächtnis war schon immer unzuverlässig, und angesichts des Grauens hinter diesen Bildern frage ich mich, ob das alles wirklich so passiert ist oder ob es einfach nur das ist, was mein Verstand im Augenblick bewältigen kann. Vielleicht werden die Lücken in meinem Gedächtnis sich später schließen, wenn ich besser mit anderen Wahrheiten umgehen kann.

Hoffentlich nicht. Wir haben hier in deinem Kopf schon genug Baustellen, Jonte …

Wie komme ich hier schnellstens raus? Es stürzen zu viele Wörter auf mich ein. Befürchten alle, dass ich wieder einschlafen könnte, wenn sie einen Moment schweigen?

„Die Polizei möchte dich sehen", sagt Mom, die nicht von meiner Seite weicht. Ich winke ab, aber der Mann steht bereits hinter ihr. Ich kenne ihn.

Er streckt die Hand aus. „Es tut mir leid, dass wir uns unter diesen Umständen wiedersehen, Frau Sandvik."

„Hallo, Herr Haugen", sage ich leise.

Mom seufzt selig. „Ihr Gedächtnis funktioniert anscheinend immer noch einwandfrei."

„Ich freue mich, dass es Ihnen wieder besser geht", sagt er. „Sie müssen keine Angst mehr haben. Sie sind hier sicher."

Ist das nicht der Typ, der gesagt hat, dass Drohungen selten in die Tat umgesetzt werden?, stänkert Back-Vocal.

Ich kann mich kaum auf seine Fragen konzentrieren. Es gelingt mir schlicht und einfach nicht, mit Haakon Jensen abzuschließen. Ich spüre wieder, wie er auf mir liegt, bin wieder der Überwältigung, dem Schrecken und der Hilflosigkeit ausgesetzt.

Adam Haugen stellt eine Frage, aber ich höre sie nicht. Denn Haakons Stimme erfüllt mich. Er hat mir etwas gesagt, an das ich mich zu erinnern versuche, aber die Worte sind schwer fassbar. Aber ich muss sie fassen. Es ist sehr wichtig. Ich muss.

„Was ist los, Jonte?" Mom berührt meinen Arm. Dann wirft sie Kommissar Haugen einen hilflosen Blick zu und umschließt meine Hand noch fester. „Das läuft überhaupt nicht gut."

Es war der Klang in seiner Stimme, Jonte, meldet sich Back-Vocal. *Es war etwas mit einem Gruß. Ich komm selbst nicht drauf.*

Mein Schweigen ist durchdrungen von einem einzigen Gedanken. Ich erinnere mich jetzt und schnappe nach Luft. „Jonas ist tot!"

Meine Mutter zuckt zusammen, wird kreidebleich. „Aber … aber Jonte."

Haugen zieht einen Stuhl ans Bett und setzt sich zu mir. „Versuchen Sie mir bitte alles zu erzählen, woran Sie sich erinnern." Er sieht mich aufmerksam an, wie es mein Vater oft getan hat.

„Malte war bei mir, aber er musste wieder nach Hyggen", beginne ich.

KAPITEL 69

Ich habe das Angebot meiner Mutter, eine Weile bei ihr zu bleiben, dankbar angenommen. Sie hat eine Firma für Tatortreinigung beauftragt, die Kommissar Haugen uns empfohlen hat, mein Haus zu säubern und den Teppichboden auf der Treppe und im Schlafzimmer zu entsorgen. Selbst die Bettwäsche wurde entfernt. Ich will nichts davon jemals wiedersehen. Tief in meinem Herzen bin ich mir sicher, dass ich nicht mehr in dem Haus leben möchte, spreche aber den Gedanken noch nicht aus. Ich ertrage keine Diskussion, bin immer noch schnell erschöpft, schlafe viel.

Mom kümmert sich rührend um mich. „Wenn die Rettungskräfte nicht im Nu vor Ort gewesen wären, würdest du jetzt auf dem Friedhof liegen. Ich *will* mich jetzt um meine Tochter kümmern!", begründet sie ihre Fürsorge.

Das ganze Haus ist ein einziges Blumenmeer. Selbst der Orden hat einen riesigen Blumenstrauß geschickt und mir den Auftrag für das Klosterhotel *Zwischen Himmel und Erde* erteilt. Mein Boss ruft mich regelmäßig an, und jeden Tag treffen Genesungswünsche von den Cinema-Kollegen ein.

Bisher hat Haakon im Verhör stets behauptet, dass Jonas eine Urlaubsreise machen würde. Allerdings ist sein Name zum Zeitpunkt seines angeblichen Abflugs nach Spanien in keiner Passagierliste einer Flugzeuggesellschaft aufgeführt. Lennart Haugen hat mich mehrmals gefragt, ob ich mir sicher bin, dass Haakon die Worte gesagt hat: *Grüße Jonas von mir.*

Ich weiß es genau. Er hat es gesagt, als er dabei war, mich ins Jenseits zu befördern. Jonas muss also tot sein. Andernfalls ergäben seine Worte keinen Sinn. *Grüße Jonas von mir … im Jenseits.*

Ich habe Haugen alles erzählt, was in den vergangenen Monaten passiert ist, bis auf die Vergewaltigung. Sie ist zu peinlich, zu ekelhaft und zu intim. Der Vorfall, mit den Mifepriston-Tropfen kam ebenfalls zur Sprache, aber diese Tat war bereits aktenkundig, da meine Gynäkologin in der vergangenen Woche Anzeige gegen unbekannt erstattet hatte.

Vielleicht wird Haakon die Vergewaltigung im Verhör selbst erwähnen und daraus eine schmutzige Geschichte machen. Ich traue es ihm zu. Dessen ungeachtet wird er in Untersuchungshaft bleiben, bis das Gerichtsverfahren eröffnet wird. Die Staatsanwaltschaft hat ihn des versuchten Mordes angeklagt. Vielleicht kommt ja noch eine richtige Mordanklage dazu. Ich bin davon überzeugt, dass er Jonas umgebracht hat und dass die Behörden dessen Leiche bald finden werden.

Mom möchte wissen, was dieser Gedanke in mir auslöst. Mir fällt keine vernünftige und für sie akzeptable Antwort ein. Ich lasse diese Bilder an mir vorbeifliegen. Ohne einzugreifen, ohne eines anzuhalten und näher hinzusehen.

Ich will keine Gedanken an Jonas verschwenden, und mir wird bewusst, dass das schon lange so ist. Jonas existiert nicht mehr in meiner Wirklichkeit, sondern in einem bösen Traum. Seit dem Tag, an dem er mir die Tropfen gegeben hat. Einfach so.

Das Gefühl der inneren Leere ist zurück. Ich fürchte, wahnsinnig zu werden. Wie sonst lässt sich erklären, dass ich in der vergangenen Nacht das Flüstern meiner beiden brüderlichen Schänder gehört habe? Haakon und Björn Jensen sind präsent wie eh und je. Meine Stimme klingt flach, wenn ich über beängstigende Dinge spreche, und der Angstschweiß perlt auch nicht auf meiner Stirn. Mein Herz schlägt normal, ich stehe emotionslos und fest auf meinen Beinen.

Ich bin nicht hier.

Ich bin irgendwo abgetaucht und für niemanden erreichbar.

Nur im Schlaf kommen die Ereignisse zurück. Ich wache jede Nacht aus meinen Albträumen auf: Träume, in denen Haakon mich stalkt und lodernde Flammen meine Haut versengen. Manchmal bin ich im Albtraum das zwölfjährige Mädchen, das in der Garage neben dem Erdbeerfeld nach der Vergewaltigung auf seiner Geige spielt.

Von alldem erzähle ich Mom nichts. Ich erzähle ihr auch nicht, wie ich die Zeit manchmal verliere. Ganze Sekunden, Minuten – und manchmal kommt mir sogar eine Stunde abhanden – verschwinden spurlos in meinem Kopf. Und wenn die Realität mich wieder einholt, hat sich nichts verändert, außer dem Zeigerstand auf der Uhr. Es ist besser, dass das ungesagt bleibt. Ich fühle nichts und hänge zwischen Licht und Dunkelheit in der Schwebe.

Mom arbeitet tagsüber am Computer. Ich liege auf der Couch. Dabei würde ich mich gern im Haus nützlich machen, um mich ein bisschen abzulenken. Aber ich bin und bleibe erstarrt, habe keinen Funken Energie in mir. Selbst die allabendlichen Telefonate mit Malte erschöpfen mich.

Ich habe ein paar Tage meines Lebens verloren, die mir dieses Monster geraubt hat. Wo sind sie? Ich möchte nicht auf die Vergangenheit zurückblicken, aber der Umgang mit der Gegenwart fällt mir gleichermaßen schwer. Ganz zu schweigen von der Zukunft.

Mom kommt auf mich zu und wedelt mit einem Blatt Papier vor mir. „Ich muss dir etwas zeigen. Die Online-Seite der NEWSTRAL-Zeitung hat einen Artikel veröffentlicht. Sie schreibt, dass heute Morgen ein Toter in einem Waldstück am Drammensfjord gefunden wurde. Eine Joggerin hat die Leiche zufällig entdeckt, weil sie von ihrer normalen Route abgewichen ist."

„Weiß man Näheres über den Toten?"

Jeden Moment sagt sie es, Jonte. Hab ein bisschen Geduld!

„Nein, da steht nur, dass die Leiche in die Rechtsmedizin gebracht wurde." Mom zögert. „Könnte es vielleicht …?"

Der Gedanke erregt meinen Widerwillen. Vielleicht will ich, dass er im Dunkel bleibt. Dessen ungeachtet antworte ich mit „Ja, Mom".

Ich weiß nicht genau, warum ich davon überzeugt bin, dass meine Antwort der Wahrheit entspricht. Ich besitze keine hellseherischen Fähigkeiten, ich weiß nichts über den Mann im Wald. Gleichwohl bin ich mir sicher, dass es Jonas ist.

KAPITEL 70

Jonas lebt nicht mehr. Hauptkommissar Haugen hat uns mitgeteilt, dass er nicht ermordet wurde. Er starb an einer Überdosis Heroin. „Das passiert häufig bei Drogenmissbrauch. Abhängige können nicht mehr beurteilen, was ihr Körper verkraftet. Die Obduktion hat unsere Annahme bestätigt."

Ein DNA-Abgleich hat seine Identität erwiesen. Sein Tod berührt mich nicht, ich habe keine Tränen. Er hat mich vor Monaten verlassen und mich vergewaltigt. Er hat den Tod unseres Babys zu verantworten und mit meinem Leben gespielt. Und obwohl er unter dem Einfluss von Drogen stand, obwohl er mich um Vergebung gebeten und mich vor seinem Freund gewarnt hat, habe ich keine Emotion für ihn übrig. Er ist es nicht wert. Ich möchte nichts spüren, was Jonas betrifft. Auch dann nicht, wenn meine Mutter mich beschwört, mir die guten Zeiten meiner Ehe in Erinnerung zu rufen.

„Es war Jonas' Entscheidung, sein Leben mit Heroin zu zerstören, Jonte. Dich trifft daran keine Schuld. Aber du musst trotzdem den Schmerz zulassen, sonst gehst auch du zugrunde."

Ich habe mich entschlossen, die Beerdigung für Jonas zu organisieren. Es gibt niemanden, der das sonst tun könnte. Immerhin war er offiziell noch mein Ehemann. Sein Tod macht mich zu seiner Witwe. Ich werde ihn einäschern und seine Asche im Drammensfjord verstreuen lassen. Das hätte ihm gefallen.

Haakon wurde noch nicht angeklagt. Er leugnet vehement seine Taten. Seit er in meinem Leben aufgetaucht ist, musste ich mich von drei Menschen verabschieden: Annika, Jonas' Vater und nun auch noch Jonas. Ich verspüre das Bedürfnis nach Rache. Ich möchte Blut sehen.

Lennart Haugen erklärte mir, dass er und sein Kollege Logulf den Tod von Jonas' Vater und auch Jonas' Tod mit größter Sorgfalt untersuchen werden. Haakon wird immer wieder verhört, und Kommissar Haugen ist sich sicher, dass er bald ein Geständnis ablegen wird. Die Beweise sind erdrückend. Haakon ist ein narzisstischer Psychopath. Kompromisslos, skrupellos und nur an seinem eigenen Vorteil interessiert. Ein Monster, das nur schwer zu fassen ist. Pech für ihn, dass er auf frischer Tat ertappt wurde, als er mich töten wollte. Damit kommt er auf keinen Fall durch.

Meine Mutter hat Bente angerufen. Sie wollte wissen, was ich plane. „Jonas' Leiche wird eingeäschert", hat Mom geantwortet. Das ist Jonas jetzt für mich, ein Körper. Nicht mehr. Ich sage seinem Körper Adieu, nicht ihm.

In den vergangenen Tagen habe ich gar nicht an Bente gedacht. Dabei ist sie seine Mutter, wie konnte ich das nur vergessen. Sie wird zur Beerdigung kommen, Malte habe ich hingegen gebeten, ihr fernzubleiben. Er arbeitet noch nicht, weil er an den Folgen der Gehirnerschütterung leidet und ihm immer noch schwindlig und übel ist. Seine Tochter hat ihre Abreise nach Amerika verschoben und kümmert sich um ihn und um das Hotel.

Malte ruft mich jede Nacht an. Dann lege ich mich ins Bett und erzähle ihm jedes Mal von Jonas, von dem Mann, der er einmal war, als ich ihn kennenlernte. Und während ich das alles erzähle, zeigt sich die alte Jonte, die ich in meiner Ehe war: flach, dozierend, langweilig. Ich frage mich, ob Malte es auch bemerkt hat.

Jonas hat kein Testament hinterlassen. Das macht mich zur einzigen Person, die befugt ist, seine Angelegenheiten zu regeln. *Das nenne ich Gerechtigkeit*, war der Kommentar meiner Mutter. Im Moment fühlt es sich nicht nach Gerechtigkeit an, sondern wie ein weiterer Ballast, den ich abwerfen will. Nach der Einäscherung werde ich mein Haus verkaufen. Ich möchte es nie wieder betreten.

In den späten Abendstunden stehe ich in meinem Zimmer oft nur da, grüble über Jonas, straffe mich, atme durch. Gehe hinunter in die Küche und öffne die Hintertür. Die Kälte der anbrechenden Nacht umfängt mich, hüllt mich ein. Dann fliegen die Gedanken, kreisen nicht mehr. Ich stoße einen Schrei aus, der vielleicht meine Mutter aufwecken könnte, aber es ist mir egal.

Ich schließe das Kapitel Jonas ab.

Ich fange wieder von vorn an.

Aber wohin mit dem weißen Kleid? Wohin mit Ebba Hagebak?

In der Trauerhalle haben ein paar Männer Platz genommen. Sie sind mir fremd und gehören vermutlich zu Jonas' neuem Leben, einem Leben, das ihm zum Verhängnis wurde.

Ich sitze zwischen meiner Mutter und Annikas Vater. Im Hintergrund läuft Jonas' Lieblingssinfonie: Dvořáks Neunte Sinfonie aus der Neuen Welt. Ich höre sie, und doch dringen die Klänge nicht wirklich zu mir durch. Ich betrachte den Sarg mit dem bescheidenen Blumenarrangement und den Blumensträußen, die auf dem Boden liegen – weiße Blumen. Die Farbe der Reinheit, obwohl ein schmutziger Dunst über dieser Bestattung liegt.

In mir toben destruktive Gefühle: die Abneigung gegen diesen Mann im Sarg, die Wut über seine Täuschung, über seine Drogensucht und was sie aus ihm gemacht hat. Selbst der Mordgedanke wäre mir nicht fremd, würde Jonas noch leben. Es fällt mir schwer, meine Gedanken in eine andere Richtung zu lenken. Sie kreisen grau hinter meiner Stirn.

Bente und Noah sitzen hinter uns. Als sie vorhin für einen Moment mit meiner Mutter sprach, flüsterte Noah mir zu, dass Jonas' Tod sie schwer getroffen habe und sie es immer noch nicht fassen könne. Ich werde Bente später alles erzählen, was ich erfahren habe. Insofern es ein *Später* gibt.

Als der Trauerredner seine Ansprache hält, driften meine Gedanken immer wieder weg. Ich drehe mich kurz zur Seite und sehe, dass Jonas' Freunde ein paar Tränen wegblinzeln. Ich sehne mich nach Malte, bin beinahe blind vor Sehnsucht nach ihm und fiebere nach seiner Wärme, seiner Berührung, nach seinem Körper. Trotzdem ist es gut, dass er nicht hier ist. Bei dem Gedanken spüre ich sofort wieder eine innere Unruhe. Mich beschleicht immer noch dieser Zweifel und eine Traurigkeit lähmt mich, weil ich einen endgültigen Abschied vor mir sehe.

Warum grübelst du auf solche Weise über die Zukunft?, fragt die Stimme hinter meiner Stirn . *Warum probierst du es nicht einfach aus?*

Vielleicht sollte ich nach dieser Chance auf Glück greifen. Vielleicht …

Ich spüre Mom neben mir und fasse nach ihrer Hand. Oder sie nach meiner. „Versuche mal, ruhiger zu atmen", sagt sie leise „Es läuft doch gut. Nimm ein wenig Abstand. Lass Jonas gehen." Dann richtet sie den Blick wieder nach vorn.

Jonas ist die letzte Person, um die ich mir im Moment Gedanken mache.

Dann ist es vorbei. Niemand hat ein Wort gesprochen. Ich hielt eine Rede für eine heuchlerische Idee. Es gibt nichts zu sagen, schon lange nicht mehr.

Der Bestattungsunternehmer gibt uns ein Zeichen, wir erheben uns. Ich werfe einen letzten Blick auf den Sarg, dann sinkt er in die Tiefe. Der Boden schließt sich über den weißen Blumen.

Unverhofft spüre ich die Tränen auf meinen Wangen.

Meine Mutter drückt meinen Arm. Natürlich glaubt sie, Jonas sei der Grund meiner Tränen. Vielleicht sind auch ein paar Tränen für ihn bestimmt. Tränen für eine gemeinsame Vergangenheit, in der Jonas liebevoll war, mich umsorgte und mir seine Verwundbarkeit zeigte. Tränen für einen Jonas, den ich in mein Leben gelassen habe, weil er Aaron nicht ähnlichsah.

Du weinst nicht um Jonas. Back-Vocal wünscht einen inneren Dialog, aber mir ist nicht danach.

Nun gut.

Ich treibe meine Gedanken voran, fange sie wieder ein. So geht es die ganze Zeit, während ich aus dem schummrig-schattigen Eingangsbereich ins Freie trete, in die enervierend helle Wintersonne, so hell, als wollte sie alles enthüllen und meine Gedanken entblößen. Als ich über den Kies zu meinem Wagen gehe, werfe ich einen letzten Blick auf das Krematorium.

Ich weine nicht *um* Jonas oder *um* irgendetwas, sondern *wegen* eines Gefühls, das mir in diesem Moment schmerzlich bewusst wird: aus Verzweiflung.

Sie beherrscht mich, hält mich unter Kontrolle.

Back-Vocal feiert ein kleines Fest hinter meiner Stirn. *Die Wahrheit ist ein mieser Verräter.*

KAPITEL 72

Mom hat mir angeboten, bei ihr zu bleiben, bis ich eine passende Unterkunft gefunden habe, aber ich denke, es ist Zeit zu gehen.

Ich habe einen Immobilienmakler beauftragt, mein Haus zu verkaufen. Ich habe mir eine wunderschöne Dachterrassenwohnung am Drammensfjord gekauft, da der Makler bereits einen Käufer für mein Haus gefunden hat. Die Wohnung hat einen Ausblick auf den Drammensfjord. So kann ich zumindest, wenn mir danach ist, die Welt von oben betrachten und muss dazu nicht mehr in mein imaginäres Flugzeug steigen. Es wird endgültig verschrottet.

Ich muss oft an Malte denken, besonders nach seinem letzten Anruf. Er hat mich nach Jonas' Einäscherung sofort angerufen und sich nach Bentes Verhalten erkundigt. Eine seltsame Frage, zumal sich eine Mutter ja von ihrem Sohn verabschieden muss. Als ich Malte um eine Erklärung gebeten hatte, wechselte er das Thema und schlug vor, ein gemeinsames Wochenende in Oslo zu verbringen.

Mir wird übel von dem permanenten Dualismus, der mich beherrscht, wenn ich an uns denke, als wären wir beide Elemente, die stets in einem Spannungsverhältnis zueinanderstehen. Ich möchte den Rest meines Lebens mit diesem Mann verbringen und gleichzeitig verspüre ich den Drang, die Geschichte mit ihm sofort zu beenden. Ich verstehe meine Zweifel und meine Gedankenwelt nicht mehr. Es verunsichert mich, es ist irritierend, es lähmt mich und macht mich traurig. Wie ist es nur möglich, dass ich nach Jonas' Tod geglaubt habe, unter das Ganze einen fetten Schlussstrich ziehen zu können? Dass die Entscheidung, nicht mehr zu trinken, die Erinnerung an einen Rausch auslöschen würde? Dass die Sucht keineswegs besiegt ist, wenn ich den Alkohol aus dem Haus entferne.

Seit ich mich vom Alkohol fernhalte, sind unzählige Gespenster der Vergangenheit entsprungen. Das Bild von Aaron, der lächerlich gekleidet im Sarg liegt, taucht zu oft in mir auf, zu oft hallt die Stimme eines anderen Mannes in mir nach.

Sie wollen doch wohl nicht mit einem solch hohen Alkoholpegel ins Auto steigen?

„Wo bist du mit deinen Gedanken, Jonte?" Meine Mutter schnippt mit den Fingern vor meinen Augen. „Du bist ja völlig weggetreten."

„Ich habe den Auftrag für den Umbau des Klosterhotels erhalten, und es ist ein großartiges Projekt. Im Moment bin ich auch noch nicht auf das Honorar angewiesen, das ja erst später ausgezahlt wird. Ich werde im Cinema Drammen kündigen, Mom. Ich riskiere es."

Meine Mutter ist restlos überrascht. „Meine Güte, Jonte. Das ist großartig." Ihre Stimme überschlägt sich. „Ja, ja, ich meine es ernst."

„Drehst du jetzt durch, Mom? Das ist mein Part." Ich strecke meine Arme aus und umarme sie. „Wie ist das nur möglich, dass es so gut läuft?"

Sie umarmt mich und küsst meine Wangen. „Das liegt daran, dass ich endlich die Tochter zurückbekommen habe, die du einmal warst. Die Tochter, die Entscheidungen trifft."

Ich hebe den Blick.

Mom weint, und dieses Mal tröste ich sie.

Ole Falk sitzt mir gegenüber und zeigt mir den Coverentwurf für den neuen Architekturband *Zwischen Himmel und Erde*. Er sprüht vor Begeisterung, ist überwältigt von dem Klosterhotel.

„Deine Pläne kommen in dem Band wundervoll zur Geltung und zeigen Architekturkunst vom Feinsten", schwärmt er. „Das alte Kloster werden wir in seinem jetzigen Zustand mit Hochglanzfotos einfangen und das neue Klosterhotel digital visualisieren. Das ist unglaublich, Jonte, was du aus dem alten Kasten gemacht hast. Mich würde es nicht wundern, wenn dein Projekt mit Preisen überschüttet wird."

Falk erinnert mich in seiner Begeisterung an die Zeichentrickfigur Dagobert Duck, der mit leuchtenden Augen in einem Haufen Taler badet. Falk hat den gleichen Ausdruck in den Augen. Er wittert hohe Auflagen.

Soll er doch das Einrichtungsbuch für Ikea machen, dann könnte er es gleich eine Million Mal drucken lassen. Back-Vocal ist wieder der Alte – in Stänkerlaune.

„Wir werden den Bildband im Oktober veröffentlichen, die Genehmigung des Ordens habe ich bereits eingeholt. Der Oktobertermin wird mit einer durchdachten Marketingoffensive möglich sein." Er räuspert sich. „Wir sollten diesen Band unter *JO* auf den Markt bringen. In memoriam an Jonas Soren. Was meinst du?"

„D...das wäre ein scheußliches Lügengespinst", stammle ich. „Jonas ist tot, und ich werde in der Öffentlichkeit kein negatives Wort über ihn verlieren. Aber das *JO* war eine einzige Lüge. Ich bin die Architektin und der kreative Kopf. Das Klosterhotel ist ganz und gar *mein* Projekt. Nein! Du gehst zu weit!"

Das alles fühlt sich nicht richtig an. In Bezug auf *Bauhaus* habe ich dem Kasperltheater zugestimmt, aber jetzt bin ich nicht mehr dazu bereit. Ich bin die Architektin des Klosterhotels und werde es auch bleiben. Ich werde auch nie wieder den Namen eines Mannes annehmen.

Falk verabschiedet sich und bittet mich, mir die Sache noch einmal zu überlegen. „*JO* ist eine Marke, Jonte Sandvik kennt niemand!"

Dann sieh doch zu, dass Jonte Sandvik eine Marke wird, du Trottel!, ruft Back-Vocal ihm nach.

„Du grübelst wieder", kommentiert Mom nach Falks Abgang. „Du hast vollkommen recht. Nimm deine Chance wahr. Auf der Tafel vor der Baustelle soll nur Dr. Jonte Sandvik stehen, und da gehört er auch hin. Und wenn Falk nicht mitzieht, suchst du dir einen anderen Verleger für deine Architekturbände. Und jetzt geh ich zum Bäcker und hole uns Apfeltorte mit Sahne. Und was machst du?"

Ich setze mich an den Computer und starte das Animationsprogramm für Gebäudeplanung. „Ich werde dem Restaurant in der Kirchenkuppel ein Tüpfelchen auf das i geben", antworte ich lächelnd. „Und ich genieße die Stille, wenn du eine Stunde fort bist."

„Du wirst mich vermissen", grinst Mom und umarmt mich. „Alles wird gut, Jonte. Ich bin mir sicher. Es ist dein eigener Zug, auf den du da aufspringst."

Ich möchte, dass Mom endlich geht. Und dass sie vor allem nicht solche Dinge sagt. Ich bleibe sitzen, eine Minute, zwei Minuten lang. Es ist ein Gebot der Stunde, das zu tun. Ich betrachte den leeren Raum und nehme nur entfernt wahr, dass Mom mal wieder irgendetwas sucht. Dann stehe ich auf. Spüre unmittelbar die Energie und setze mich in der Küche an den Laptop – mit dem Gefühl, allein auf der Welt zu sein.

Als Mom die Haustür öffnet, höre ich Stimmen.

„Jonte ist in der Küche und arbeitet an einem neuen Projekt. Ich gehe schnell zum Bäcker, und danach machen wir es uns bei Kaffee und Kuchen gemütlich. Komm schon mal rein. Ich werde höchstens eine halbe Stunde fort sein."

Ich möchte zur Tür gehen, um den Besucher zu begrüßen, aber ich kann mich nicht bewegen und verstehe nicht, was in diesem Moment mit mir passiert. Mein Körper wird mit einem Mal schwer. Ich lehne mich zurück. Bleibe so. Dann versuche ich aufzustehen, aber meine Beine verweigern den Dienst, meine Finger klammern sich an die Rückenlehne. Ich kann mir meine Starre nicht erklären, ebenso wenig die Angst, die mich mit einem Mal überwältigt. Es ist eine Angst, die mich hyperventilieren lässt.

Ich starre den Türknauf an und warte.

Ich habe mit Bentes Kommen gerechnet. Diese Erkenntnis überrascht mich. Ich erinnere mich wieder an den Vorfall in der Trauerhalle, als Jonas' Vater eingeäschert wurde. Als ich nach meiner Trauerrede zu meinem Platz zurückging und Bente neben der Eingangstür erblickte. Ihr Anblick war für mich ein Schock. Mom zog damals an meinem Arm und sagte, ich solle mich setzen. Jetzt erst begreife ich, dass ich in diesem Moment bereits wusste, wer sie war. Ich erkannte sie, obwohl ich sie noch nie gesehen hatte.

Es waren ihre Augen. Augen, die Jonas unzählige Male beschrieben hatte. Dunkle, wütende, finster aufflackernde Augen, die ein ungutes Gefühl vermittelten. Augen, die sie nie in Gegenwart einer dritten Person zeigte. Ihr bedrohlicher Blick traf mich mit Wucht, er machte mir Angst und schürte meine Abneigung. Trotzdem habe ich alles infrage gestellt, was ich gesehen habe, als ich später mit ihr sprach und erneut in diese Augen blickte. Bente war freundlich, einladend und beruhigend. Sie machte einen positiven Eindruck, ich fand dieses bedrohliche Aufflackern in ihren Augen später nicht wieder und glaubte, es mir nur eingebildet zu haben.

Bis zu dieser Sekunde.

Zuerst bleibt Bente still. Ihr Gesicht ist regungslos, ihre Körperhaltung starr vor Anspannung. Sie steht in der Tür und sieht mich an. In ihren dunklen Augen lodert vernichtender Hass, der mich lähmt und mich festhält. Sie kommt näher. Erst da sehe ich es. Verstehe mit einem Mal, wovor Jonas mich stets gewarnt hat. In ihren dunklen Augen ist kein Flackern mehr, keine Drohung, keine Wut, ja kein Funken menschlicher Regung, nur Finsternis und eisige Kälte, die in meine Knochen dringt und meinen Körper erzittern lässt.

Dann entweicht ihrer Kehle der Ausdruck einer mörderischen Wut, ein Schrei löst sich, dem Worte folgen, die wie Pistolenkugeln durch die Luft davongetragen werden. „Es ist deine Schuld", zischt sie mit einer mir fremden Stimme. „Es ist deine Schuld, dass Jonas tot ist."

Ich sehe eine Wut, die stärker ist als alles, was ich zuvor bei einem Menschen erlebt habe, und erschaudere. Ich würde ihr gerne den Rücken zukehren, um nicht in diese Augen sehen zu müssen, aber ihr Blick hält meinen gefangen. Ich versuche, langsamer zu atmen, und denke fieberhaft darüber nach, wie ich ihr entkommen kann. Die einzige Fluchtmöglichkeit bietet die Küchentür, aber ich könnte sie nur erreichen, indem ich an ihr vorbeiliefe.

Sie kommt näher. „Es ist deine Schuld, dass Jonas tot ist", wiederholt sie krächzend.

Ich schüttle wütend den Kopf. „Du irrst dich, Bente. Damit habe ich nichts zu tun. Jonas ist selbst dafür verantwortlich. Oder Haakon. Haakon Jensen, dieser Bastard, der deinen Sohn drogenabhängig gemacht hat."

„Haakon ist völlig in Ordnung."

Hast du das gehört? Hat sie dieses Monster wirklich gerade verteidigt?

„Du kennst Haakon nicht, sonst würdest du anders über ihn sprechen."

„Ich kenne Haakon sehr wohl, und *ihn* mag ich sehr. Er wollte mir helfen, den Kontakt zu Jonas wiederherzustellen. Aber *du* warst ja dagegen. *Du* hast es mir nicht gegönnt, *du* hast dich auch Haakon gegenüber in ähnlicher Weise geäußert. Du warst eifersüchtig!" Ihre Wut zersetzt die Luft in der Küche.

Mir bricht der Schweiß aus allen Poren, ich drücke meinen Rücken gegen die Stuhllehne. „Ich habe nie mit Haakon über dich gesprochen", erwidere ich wütend. „Wenn er das behauptet, lügt er. Dieses Monster hat mich bedroht und Jonas für seine Zwecke missbraucht. Als Jonas' Vater starb, erschien dein Sohn mit einem blauen Auge auf der Bildfläche und erzählte mir, dass es zwischen ihm und Haakon gerade gar nicht gut lief."

„Lüg mich nicht an!" Ihre Stimme ist ein messerscharfer Angriff, ihre Gesichtszüge sind verzerrt. „Wenn du Jonas erlaubt hättest, nebenher mit einem Mann zu schlafen, anstatt ihn aus dem Haus zu werfen, hätte Tore seine Vorliebe für Männer nie bemerkt. Er hätte unserem Jungen nicht gedroht, ihn zu enterben, und Jonas wäre auch nicht in Panik geraten. Dann hätten Haakon und ich auch nicht eingreifen müssen."

Was redet sie da? Meine innere Stimme ist in Aufruhr.

Nein, ich habe mich bestimmt verhört, ich muss mich irren. Das ergibt doch keinen Sinn.

„Ich glaube, dass Haakon Jonas' Vater getötet hat", sage ich leise. Diese Wahrheit ist für mich so unverrückbar wie ein Fels in der Brandung. Indem ich sie ausspreche, mache ich sie real.

„Haakon hat nur alles im Auge behalten", erwidert Bente. Aus ihrer Stimme ist jetzt weder Zorn noch Kapitulation, sondern kalte Gleichgültigkeit herauszuhören. „*Ich* habe das Haus betreten. Haakon hat draußen aufgepasst. Später habe ich dort auf Haakon gewartet."

„Haakon ist an dem Abend in mein Haus eingedrungen, hat meine Hausschuhe gestohlen, um sie in Tores Haus neben die Treppe zu stellen. Ich sollte für etwas verdächtigt werden, das Haakon getan hat."

Sie lächelt. Ich traue meinen Augen nicht. Wieso lächelt sie jetzt?

„Haakon hatte viele solcher nützlichen Einfälle. Es war auch seine Idee, dass ich mich mit dir anfreunde."

„Hast du etwa deinen Ex-Mann getötet? Hast du mit Haakon gemeinsame Sache gemacht? Wie ist das nur möglich, Bente? Warum? Und zu welchem Zweck?" Ich höre die Verzweiflung in meiner Stimme, die Tränen, das Entsetzen.

„Ich hätte alles getan, um meinen Jungen zurückzubekommen", antwortet sie. Der Schall ihrer Stimme dringt aus der Ferne auf mich zu. Ihre Worte treffen mich wie Schläge. Panik keimt in mir auf, nein, es ist Angst. Ich blicke zur Küchentür.

„Vergiss es!", brüllt sie.

Ich kneife die Augen zusammen und stelle meinen Fokus neu ein. Der blaue Himmel könnte sich herabsenken, die grelle Wintersonne ihre Arme ausstrecken und Bente zermalmen. So sollte es sein, aber das Bild hängt schief in meinem Hirn, unvollendet. Naturkatastrophen kommen unverhofft, nicht nach Bedarf oder Aufforderung. Ich frage mich, woher diese Bilder kommen. Bin ich hysterisch? Nein! Außer Kontrolle? Nein!

Es ist ganz einfach. Ich muss ihr nur entkommen.

KAPITEL 74

Ihr massiger Körper überragt mich. Sie blickt auf mich herab wie eine Drohung. Ihr sprudelnder Wortschwall prallt auf mein Hirn. Ich höre eine Vielfalt an Emotionen in ihrer Stimme, die eine Geschichte preisgibt, die nicht von der Bente handelt, die ich kenne, die aber ihre schwarze Seele entblößt. Ich versuche, ihre Worte zu fassen. Sie atmet und spricht und ist zugleich beängstigend weit weg, irgendwo in einem Abgrund, abgestützt in ein tiefes, finsteres Loch.

Es ist die Geschichte einer Mutter, die ihr Kind verloren hat. Sie verflucht Jonas' Vater, den sie dafür verantwortlich macht, der die alleinige Liebe des Kindes für sich beanspruchte und es in Besitz nahm. Der ihre Gefühle ignorierte und torpedierte, der sie demütigte und verletzte. Der sie zwang zu gehen, weil er sie als eine Gefahr für sein Kind ansah.

Ihr Klagelied nimmt mich gefangen, ich kann dem nicht entkommen, bin wie betäubt von ihrer Ohnmacht, dem Zorn, der Trauer, dem Bedauern. Ich erfahre, dass es viel mehr ist als eine Schilderung dessen, was geschah. Es ist viel mehr. Es ist ein Schuldbekenntnis.

Sie scheint in Trance zu sein, und ihre Flut an Worten ist nicht aufzuhalten. „Es war wegen dieser drei verdammten Tage, die mich jeden Monat überwältigten und mich niederschmetterten. Es passierte mir immer wieder, und ich habe es nie kommen sehen. Aber Tore hat das nicht verstanden, niemand konnte es mir erklären. Ich wurde unruhig, alles fiel mir aus den Händen: Ich fühlte mich minderwertig, von allen missachtet, und tobte vor Wut, wann immer mein Kind sich mir widersetzte. Ich habe ihn geschlagen und war jedes Mal schockiert über meine Reaktion. Und seine Angst. Ich sehe immer noch die Angst in seinen Kinderaugen, erinnere mich an sein Zurückschrecken, seine Versuche, meinen Händen zu entkommen. Das war grauenvoll."

„Ich verstehe", versuche ich sie zu besänftigen.

Das Aufflackern in ihren Augen lässt mich sofort schweigen.

Bente holt tief Luft. „Du verstehst gar nichts. Du hast keine Kinder. Du weißt nicht, was es bedeutet, ein Kind zu verlieren, ständig das Gefühl zu haben, dass du versagst, deinen guten Absichten hinterherzulaufen und immer wieder von deiner Ohnmacht, deiner Angst und dem Wissen eingeholt zu werden, dass du sowieso fällst und versagst. Du hast noch nie deinen Kopf gegen eine Tür geschlagen, weil du nicht wusstest, wo du nach Reue und Scham Ausschau halten solltest, nachdem du dein Kind wieder einmal verprügelt hattest. Mein eigenes Kind, meinen kleinen lieben Jungen." Sie schluchzt. „Mein Arzt diagnostizierte eine besonders schwere Form einer prämenstruellen dysphorischen Störung. Davon hatte ich noch nie gehört. PMS-Syndrom, eine Form von Wahn, der bei Frauen während des Eisprungs auftreten kann. Er sagte mir, dass die Lösung bei mir selbst läge, dass ich mein Bewusstsein schärfen müsse, um rechtzeitig Maßnahmen zu ergreifen. Er hat mir empfohlen, mich in diesen Tagen von meiner Familie zu isolieren. Ein typisch männlicher Rat. Ich habe abgelehnt. Er verschrieb Ovulationshemmer, Aspirin, Antidepressiva. Aber nichts hat wirklich geholfen. Dann verabreichte er mir Prolaktin. Ich wurde unfruchtbar. Die Anfälle traten in immer kürzeren Abständen auf und wurden immer heftiger."

Bentes immense Wut und ihr Wahn machen mir Angst. Sie tobt, lacht zu laut, zu leise. Schreit. Für sie gibt es keine beruhigenden Worte, ihre Wut ist zu groß für einen Besänftigungsversuch. Ich fange ihren Schrei ein, dämpfe ihn ab, lasse ihn in meinem Hirn verweilen, nur wir beide, der Schrei und ich.

„Therapien ...." Wieder lacht sie hysterisch. „Ach, als wenn alles so simpel wäre. Dann könnte ich alles in eine kleine Schachtel packen." Sie wirft hektische Blicke durch den Raum, lächelt. Nicht freundlich, sondern freudlos und kalt. „Aber du, du wirst es niemals verstehen!", faucht sie mich an.

Ich versuche, ihren Wortfluss in eine andere Richtung zu lenken. „Du hast meiner Mutter und mir eine völlig andere Geschichte erzählt."

Sie lacht beschämend. „Natürlich habe ich dir eine andere Geschichte erzählt. Glaubst du, ich bin stolz auf die wahre Version?"

Ich muss erreichen, dass sie weiterspricht, bis Mom zurückkommt. Hoffentlich trifft sie niemanden beim Bäcker. Ich kann kaum noch atmen, mein Herz stolpert unregelmäßig in meiner Brust. Wieder spähe ich zur Küchentür.

Bente drückt fest gegen meine Schulter. „Hey! Vorsicht, heute keine Mätzchen! Kapiert?! Benimm dich und hör auf mit dem Theater! Du hast uns allen lange genug etwas vorgemacht."

Wovon redet diese Furie?

Ihr Gesicht ist wieder ganz nah an meinem. „Ich habe mich in all den Jahren nach meinem Sohn gesehnt, hörst du? Ich hoffte immer, dass Jonas eine Frau finden würde, die ihn dazu bringt, seine Mutter wieder zu besuchen. Frauen können solche Barrieren überwinden, Frauen sind Brückenbauerinnen. Das ist aber nicht passiert. Kein Jonas, keine Frau."

Ich fühle, wie Wut und Trauer in mir überschwappen. Ich rühre mich nicht, starre sie nur an. Wir sind allein, und ich weiß: Ich bin ihr körperlich nicht gewachsen.

„Manchmal erstickte ich fast vor Reue", fährt sie fort, „ich bekam Magenbeschwerden wegen dieser verdammten unverdaulichen Schuld, die mir auferlegt wurde und die ich schlucken musste. Und dann las ich von dir und Jonas in der Zeitung, erfuhr von den Auszeichnungen, die *JO* erhalten hatte, und stellte fest, dass *JO* das Pseudonym von Jonas und Jonte Soren war. Ich konnte ab da an nichts anderes mehr denken als an mein Kind, und an meinen Wunsch und eine Gelegenheit, Jonas wiederzusehen. Ich kaufte den ersten Architekturband und rief im Verlag an."

Bente verstärkt den Druck gegen meine Schulter. Ich empfinde ihre Worte als das unwillkommene Eintreten in den Raum qualvoller Erinnerungen. Als Kind hatte ich auch den Druck von Händen gespürt, die mich auf den Boden drückten. Sekunden, Minuten, Stunden. Und Jahre danach in meinen Träumen.

„Ich kontaktierte Falk und erfuhr, dass er keine persönlichen Informationen über seine Klienten zur Verfügung stellen könne", fahrt Bente fort. „Aber er rief Haakon an, und der versprach, Jonas von meinem Anruf und meiner Bitte um ein Treffen zu erzählen, aber dann hat sich Haakon anders entschieden. Er rief mich an. Jonas habe eine schwere Zeit, weil sein Vater drohte, ihn zu enterben. Jonas war schockiert, fühlte sich zurückgewiesen. Er könne nicht mit seiner Frau darüber reden, weil sie nichts mehr von ihm wissen wolle. Er habe nie vorgehabt, sie zu verlassen, aber sie habe ihn rausgeworfen, als er ihr gestand, dass er auch auf Männer stand. *Du* hast ihn in die Arme seines Liebhabers getrieben. Du hast triumphiert, weil dir klar war, dass Tore dem Ganzen auf den Grund gehen würde. Du wolltest Jonas' Erbschaft für dich allein und hattest dein Ziel erreicht, weil du wusstest, dass Tore die Homosexualität seines Sohnes niemals akzeptieren würde. Du hast den Bruch zwischen Jonas und seinem Vater verursacht!"

Diese Geschichte ist Haakons krankem Hirn entsprungen. Ich möchte protestieren, aber die Worte bleiben irgendwo in meiner Kehle stecken. Ich bin zu fassungslos, zu verärgert, zu schockiert. Ich schaue auf Bente und sehe, dass sich kein Verteidigungsversuch durchsetzen wird. Was hat sie vor? Warum ist sie in Wahrheit hier? Um mir ihre Geschichte zu erzählen und mich zu beschuldigen? Um mir zu sagen, dass sie mich nie wiedersehen will, und mir auch den Umgang mit Malte zu untersagen? Weiß Malte etwas darüber? Und was ist mit Noah, hat Bente ihm von diesem Besuch erzählt?

Bente war im Haus meines Schwiegervaters und hat ihren Ex-Mann getötet. Vielleicht will sie mich auch töten. Ich nehme ihr Gemurmel wahr, ohne die Worte zu verstehen. Sie hat etwas vor. Ich muss aufstehen, muss fliehen. Als ich mich aufrichten will, verspüre ich einen starken Druck gegen meine Schultern. Bente streckt die rechte Hand aus, ohne mich aus den Augen zu lassen, und legt sie mir auf den Kehlkopf.

Ein Schauder durchläuft meinen Körper. „Bleib sitzen. Ich rede noch. Und wenn ich fertig bin, werde ich mit dir abrechnen."

Ich sehe abermals das Flackern in ihren Augen. Sie greift nach meinen Armen, hält sie fest. Ich versuche sie abzuschütteln, aber Bente lässt nicht locker, bis ich verstumme und meine Gegenwehr nachlässt.

Mein Gehirn arbeitet verbissen. So ist es immer gewesen. Aber es fällt mir zunehmend schwer in Gegenwart ihrer Kälte.

Wenn, dann richtig, flüstert Back-Vocal hinter meiner Stirn. *Ganz oder gar nicht.*

Ich muss etwas sagen. Bente ablenken, die abwechselnd stöhnt und schreit. Die Geschichte, dass sie in Tores Haus war, während Haakon auf der Lauer lag, kann nicht stimmen.

Stell ihr Fragen. Hol sie in die Realität zurück. Sag etwas!

„Überlege doch mal, Bente. Du lebst in Hyggen und kannst wohl kaum mitten in der Nacht unbemerkt das Haus verlassen. Das wäre Noah aufgefallen."

„Bist du so blöd, oder tust du nur so. Ich habe dir doch erzählt, dass ich regelmäßig meine Schwägerin im Pflegeheim in Drammen besuche. Manchmal nehme ich mir ein Hotelzimmer und bleibe über Nacht. Ich bin die Einzige, die sich um die Ärmste kümmert. Weil *ich* auch am besten weiß, wie es ist, von allen im Stich gelassen zu werden."

Ich schlucke, atme tief ein. „Ich glaube nicht, dass du eine Mörderin bist, Bente. Du steckst nicht den Lauf einer Waffe in den Mund eines alten Mannes. Das kannst du mir nicht weismachen."

„Ach nein?" Sie beugt sich tiefer, unsere Nasenspitzen berühren sich fast. Der Wahn lodert in ihren Augen. „Ich habe es genossen! Eine wahre Genugtuung. Tore wollte mein Kind enterben. Auch wenn es ihm nur teilweise gelungen wäre, so war es dennoch eine Ablehnung. Mein Junge hat das nicht verkraftet, er hat schon zu oft Ablehnung erfahren müssen: erst von mir, dann von dir. Tore sollte diese Möglichkeit nicht mehr bekommen. Darum habe ich mich gekümmert. Ich habe diesen Scheißkerl getötet, hörst du? ERMORDET! Und jetzt bist du dran. Jonas hat das Geld für seine Drogen gebraucht. Haakon wollte ihn davon abbringen, aber er hat meinen Sohn nicht mehr erreichen können. *Du* hättest mit ihm sprechen und ihn zu einem Entzug überreden müssen. *Du* hättest ihm helfen sollen, du warst seine Frau. Du hast ein Ehegelübde abgegeben: *in guten und in schlechten Zeiten.* Und hast es gebrochen. Du wolltest das Geld, das ihr verdient habt, nicht mit ihm teilen. Du hast es genossen, ihn zu quälen und ihn wegen Geld unter Druck zu setzen. Hast dich auch noch mit Jonas' Erbe auseinandergesetzt, auf das du überhaupt keinen moralischen Anspruch hast. Du hast nur Geld und Machtmissbrauch im Kopf. Fickst sogar meinen Stiefsohn, du widerliches Stück Scheiße."

Ich zucke zusammen. Malte hat wohl nicht nur seinem Vater von uns erzählt. Es ist vorbei, ich sitze in der Falle. Wenn Mom nicht bald zurückkommt, wird Bente mich töten. Worte sind jetzt haltlos. Ich stehe auf der Schwelle zwischen Tag und Nacht, kann es nicht mit der massigen Gestalt aufnehmen, die vor mir steht. Ich spüre meine Beine kaum und bin nicht mehr in der Lage, langsam ein- und auszuatmen.

Bente fährt fort, und leise bohren sich ihre Worte in mein Hirn. „Ich habe Haakon versprochen, ein wachsames Auge auf dich zu haben. Als du zu Weihnachten nach Hyggen kamst, wollte er, dass ich dir absage. Er hätte dich lieber in seiner Nähe gehabt, weil er dir nicht traute, besonders als du anfingst, Malte anzumachen. Gemeinsam haben wir einen Weg gefunden, dich zu erschrecken. Zuerst hat Haakon dafür gesorgt, dass du bemerkt hast, dass dich jemand in der Kirche beobachtet, und dann haben wir deine Kleider zerfetzt. Ich wusste, dass du davonlaufen und zumindest an den Feiertagen nicht in der Nähe von Malte sein würdest. Ihr habt wirklich geglaubt, dass Noah der Einzige war, der etwas über euer Verhältnis wusste. Noah hat es mir natürlich gesagt, er kann kein Geheimnis für sich behalten. Ich habe deine Panik gesehen, als du den Wagen gestartet hast, und ich habe zugesehen, wie du davongerast bist. Es war eine wundervolle Weihnachtsfeier - ohne dich in der Nähe."

Sie ist verrückt. Sie ist völlig durchgeknallt. Sie ist genauso, wie Jonas sie beschrieben hat: ein Dämon, eine tickende Zeitbombe.

Sie ist eine Mörderin.

„Haakon und ich waren wütend, als du die Scheidung beantragen und Jonas finanziell in der Kälte zurücklassen wolltest. Er wollte sich sogar um dich kümmern, weil er wusste, was du für ein Häufchen Elend bist, längst bereit zum Abtransport ins Jenseits. Es war Haakons Idee, dir eine Überdosis Mifepriston zu verpassen, dazu ein blutverdünnendes Mittel. Perfekt. Es sollte dein Todestag werden. Jonas hat versagt und dir leider zu wenig verabreicht."

Ich stehe am Abgrund, blicke in die Tiefe einer schwarzen Seele, in der mich aufgewühlte Wellen stürmisch umbrausen. Suche krampfhaft nach einem Ausweg. „Haakon ist im Gefängnis und wird dort auch eine ganze Weile ausharren müssen. Glaubst du, dass er darüber schweigen wird, was ihr beide ausgeheckt habt? Dass er dich deckt? Es gibt gewiss Beweise für seine Anwesenheit in Tores Haus. Er wird keine Verantwortung für einen Mord übernehmen, den er nicht begangen hat. Haakon ist ein krimineller Psychopath. Er wird dich nicht schützen, er wird dich reinlegen. *Du* steckst fest, Bente. Vermutlich wird er dich auch noch für den Übergriff auf Annika verantwortlich machen. Und da sie an den Folgen dieses Übergriffs starb, ist es kein Mordversuch mehr, sondern ein Mord."

Sie schnaubt verächtlich. „Annika, na ja ... Sie hätte ihre Nase besser nicht in die Angelegenheiten anderer Leute stecken sollen."

Worte wie ein Hammerschlag, so hart, unerbittlich, gewaltig. Dann eisige Stille, die in mir mit jeder Zelle meines Körpers die Gier nach einer verstörenden Lust weckt. Der Lust zu töten. Ich friere. „Was meinst du damit?"

„Haakon wollte nur deinen Laptop, um zu überprüfen, ob du an einem neuen Projekt arbeiten würdest. Als du bei deiner Mutter warst, habe ich ihm eine SMS geschickt, damit er ungestört den Laptop checken konnte. Annika war ein unvorhersehbares Hindernis. Sie war zur falschen Zeit am falschen Ort."

Ich will ihre letzten Worte verdrängen, aber ich schaffe es nicht. Tränen schießen mir in die Augen. „Was bringt es dir, mich zu töten? Davon wird Jonas auch nicht wieder lebendig." Meine Stimme zittert.

„Es wird mir helfen. Es ist mir egal, ob ich den Rest meines Lebens hinter Gitter verbringen muss. Du hast mein Kind im Stich gelassen, und es zur Verzweiflung getrieben. Jetzt habe ich Jonas endgültig verloren. Nichts ist mehr wichtig."

„Aber was ist mit Noah? Und seinen Kindern und Enkelkindern? Sie mögen dich."

„Ach, Noah, das ist nicht genug", flüstert sie resigniert. „Und es ändert nichts an der Tatsache, dass ich Jonas' Leiche gefunden habe."

„*Du?* Du hast Jonas gefunden? In der Zeitung stand, dass es eine Joggerin war."

Eigenartig. Alles ist eigenartig. Alles. Selbst die Geschichte, die sie mir erzählt hat. Selbst dass ich ihre letzten Worte mit einem Mal glaube: *Ich habe Jonas' Leiche gefunden.*

„Dieses Bild hat sich für immer in mein Gedächtnis gefräst", fährt Bente fort. „Ich werde es immer vor Augen haben. Jonas war so einsam in diesem Wald. Vielleicht hat er mich ja dort gesucht. Er wusste, dass ich da oft jogge."

Ich sehe sie an. Die Kälte, die von ihr ausgeht, ist kaum zu ertragen. Ihr Gesicht ist vom Wahn verzerrt.

Jetzt!

Ich muss handeln und springe auf. Strecke die Hände aus, um sie wegzustoßen. Ihre Fingernägel krallen sich in meine Haut. Für einen Moment starren wir einander in die Augen. Ich bemerke die Spucke, die ihr übers Kinn rinnt. Ihre Mundwinkel sind nach unten gezogen. Sie sieht fast ein wenig gekränkt aus. Ich schreie vor Schmerz. Falle in meinen Stuhl zurück.

„Du würdest mich gerne brennen sehen? Hm? Dann könntest du endlich in dein kleines, beschissenes Leben zurückkehren!", schreit sie. Ihr Gesicht ist wutverzerrt. „Und dich auf die Brust schlagen wie ein Affe." Sie lachte laut auf. „Du amüsierst mich."

Mit einer Hand hält Bente mich fest, mit der anderen greift sie nach dem schweren Kerzenleuchter auf dem Tisch und zielt damit auf meine Nase. Ich kann nicht ausweichen. „Ich hätte dir schon längst den Schädel zertrümmern und dich im Drammensfjord versenken sollen", zischt sie. „Auf diese Weise macht die Vergänglichkeit aus allem, was uns widerfährt, Geister und Schatten. Deine Tage sind unwiederbringlich gezählt!" Der zweite Schlag trifft meine Stirn, der dritte meinen Hinterkopf.

Ich spüre nichts, tauche ein in eine dunkle schwarze Welt, in der nur entfernt Bentes Keuchen zu hören ist. Ich sehe Annika lächeln, und Ebba streckt in ihrem weißen Kleid die Arme nach mir aus. Dann sind auch sie nicht mehr da.

KAPITEL 76

Ich schlendere durch eine mit Blumen und Wassertropfen gesprenkelte Wiese. Es ist hell, zu hell. Die Nacht hat hier keinen Zugang. Ich suche die Sonne, finde sie nicht. Woher kommt das helle Licht?

Ich betrachte mich, sehe an meinem Körper herunter, der Teil des Ganzen ist, spüre ihn aber nicht, obwohl ich mich bewege. Ich weiß nicht, wo ich bin. Ich blicke in die Ferne, streichle im Gehen mit den Händen das hohe Gras und die Blumen. Mein Blick streift einen Wald, dann einen smaragdgrünen Fjord.

Im Gras schimmert etwas gespenstisch weiß. Sofort dringt der Gedanke an Ebba in mein Bewusstsein, im nächsten Moment gehe ich Hand in Hand mit ihr über die Wiese. Sie lächelt mich an und streicht mir zärtlich übers Haar, doch ich empfinde bei ihrem Anblick Panik und Angst. Sie verschwindet wieder im Wald. Will sie mich in den Wahnsinn treiben? Ich bezweifle es. Aber ich bin erleichtert, ihr erst mal entkommen zu sein.

Der Nebel lichtet sich. Alles ist wieder hell und schön, friedlich und vollkommen. Hier ist alles, was Menschen brauchen, um sich glücklich zu fühlen.

Der weiße Fleck bewegt sich, er zieht mich magisch an. Ich gebe diesem Bedürfnis nach.

Ebba liegt auf dem Rücken, ihre Hände hat sie hinter den Kopf gelegt. Ich umkreise sie. Ihr Blick folgt mir, ernst, aber auch neugierig. Um ihren Mund ist ein vages Lächeln.

Ich knie neben ihr nieder, sehe sie an, wie sie totenstill daliegt, das weiße Kleid wellenförmig um den Körper. Meine Augen erfassen die Stelle an ihrem Kopf. Kein Rot ist zu sehen, nicht einmal ein Blutspritzer auf dem weißen Kleid. Doch sie ist es, ich bin mir ganz sicher. Ich hocke neben Ebba Hagebak und spüre, dass hier etwas nicht stimmt. Ich habe schon einmal neben ihr gekniet, nahm ihr Handgelenk und fühlte ihren Puls. Nichts. Kein Puls. Sie lag auf dem Bauch und ihr blondes Haar war zu einem Pferdeschwanz zusammengebunden. Diese Ebba ist zwar blond, aber das Haar umspielt sanft ihr Gesicht. Hier ist auch keine Spur von Blut zu sehen.

Es ist ein seltsames Gefühl, in einer mir unbekannten Umgebung Ebba berühren zu können. Vor vierzehn Jahren geriet ich in Panik, als ich nur noch ihren Tod feststellen konnte, und wusste sofort, dass sie mich vor Gericht stellen und verurteilen würden, dass mein Leben für immer ruiniert war. Ein Unfall mit Todesfolge infolge von Trunkenheit am Steuer.

Mir ist nie zuvor klar gewesen, dass ich *nicht* gedankenlos weggefahren bin. All die Jahre habe ich geglaubt, dass es eine unüberlegte Handlung, eine Panikreaktion, ein unbesonnener Affekt gewesen sei. Eine Entscheidung, die sich wegen meiner Trunkenheit der Kontrolle entzog. In diesem Moment, inmitten einer imaginären Blumenwiese, inmitten dieser Unendlichkeit, wird mir bewusst, dass es anders war.

Ich traf eine vorsätzliche Entscheidung und schätzte die Folgen vollkommen falsch ein. Ich dachte, ich könnte mich mit Fahrerflucht den Folgen meiner Tat entziehen, und nahm ein mögliches Schuldgefühl als selbstverständlich hin.

Ich habe die Wucht der Schuldgefühle unterschätzt. Ich habe nicht damit gerechnet, dass ich Ebbas Tod für den Rest meines Lebens mit mir tragen muss, dass ich nie in der Lage sein werde, meine Schuld zu begleichen, dass ich durch mein Abtauchen vor einer Verurteilung über mich ein eigenes Urteil verhängt habe. Hier, an diesem vollkommenen Ort, in dieser friedlichen Zwischenwelt, erkenne und verstehe ich, dass ich auch hierbleiben kann. Ja, ich möchte an diesem Ort bleiben.

Ebba sieht mich immer noch an, dennoch spüre ich die Gegenwart einer zweiten Person im Gras. Es ist Annika, sie trägt ebenfalls ein weißes Kleid. Ihre Gesichtszüge sind vollkommen entspannt. Sie schläft.

Ich möchte, dass sie aufwacht. „Annika?" Ein Flüstern.

Irgendjemand zieht mich hoch. Ich will das nicht. Ich werde Annikas Schlaf nicht stören, aber ich muss zu Ebba, ihren Kopf sanft berühren. Meine Finger streicheln ihre Wangen, ihre Nase, ihr Kinn. *Verzeih mir.* Die Worte meiner inneren Stimme sind wie eine Kapitulation.

„Komm zurück, Jonte!", flüstert eine Stimme.

Papa? Er ist hier, ich kann ihn spüren, aber ich sehe ihn nicht.

Das unentwegt von den Blättern tropfende Regenwasser klingt wie Musik, und die Heftigkeit der Worte hallen in der Luft nach. Plötzlich verschleiert sich mein Blick. Nebel steigt aus dem Wald auf. Er verwandelt die blühenden Wiesen in geisterhafte Weiden, kriecht über den Boden: rauchige Finger, die sich um die Bäume ringeln und sie in geheimnisvolle Schemen verwandeln. Dann umhüllt der Nebel meinen Körper. Der helle Himmel ist jetzt grau.

Ich schlendere in die Unendlichkeit und suche nach einem Weg. Es gibt keinen Weg, dem ich folgen kann, nirgendwo ist ein Hinweis. Ich irre über Wiesen, laufe wahllos durch den Wald, und blicke nicht zurück.

Wie aus dem Nichts verliere ich die Kontrolle, taumle und spüre meine Beine nicht mehr. Sie sind wie totes Treibholz. In einem dunklen Raum sinke ich zu Boden, den Blick auf die gegenüberliegende Wand gerichtet.

KAPITEL 77

Der Schrei explodiert in meinem Kopf. Ich kämpfe gegen die Versuchung an, wieder in der Bewusstlosigkeit zu versinken, und hebe die Lider. Keine Dunkelheit, nur verwischte Farben und Licht. Allmählich schälen sich Gesichter heraus. Fremde Menschen in Blau, die auf mich herabblicken. Ich blinzle, spüre, dass mir jemand eine Hand auf die Stirn legt, und schrecke hoch. Mir wird schwindlig.

„Ruhig, ganz ruhig, Frau Sandvik. Diazepam, fünf Milligramm, Schwester." Eine warme männliche Stimme.

Jetzt berührt jemand meinen Arm.

„Nein! Nur fünf Milligramm", wiederholt die warme Stimme.

Still! Bitte nicht sprechen.

Das Geräusch verursacht mir höllische Schmerzen. Zögerlich öffne ich die Augen. Keine unendliche Weite, keine saftige, blumengesprenkelte Wiese. Keine Annika, keine Ebba, keine strahlend weißen Kleider.

Die Wände in diesem Zimmer sind nicht unendlich, sondern sehr nah und in einem satten Cremeton gehalten, die Beleuchtung ist indirekt. An der gegenüberliegenden Wand hängt ein zartes Landschaftsaquarell.

„Ganz ruhig, Frau Sandvik, ganz ruhig."

Verwirrt blicke ich um mich.

Ein Mann in einem weißen Kittel leuchtet mit einer kleinen Lampe in meine Augen. „Sie hatten einen Albtraum. Lassen Sie los. Ganz gleich, was es war, lassen Sie los", sagt er leise.

Ich schaue verwirrt auf die Schläuche, die an meinen Armen befestigt und mit diversen Infusionsflaschen an einem Ständer verbunden sind. „Wo bin ich?"

„Sie sind im Krankenhaus Drammen. Mein Name ist Erik Lansson. Wir kennen uns bereits."

Ich versuche, den Arzt an meinem Bett klar zu erkennen, doch mein Kopf rebelliert.

„Sie wurden vor fünf Tagen hier eingeliefert. Das ist jetzt das zweite Mal innerhalb kurzer Zeit." Er blättert in einer Krankenakte. „Da hat es schon wieder jemand nicht besonders gut mit Ihnen gemeint. Erinnern Sie sich an das Geschehen?"

Ich sehe ihn unsicher an.

„Ist schon in Ordnung", beruhigt mich der Arzt. „Das ist völlig normal nach einem schweren Schädel-Hirn-Trauma."

„Was ist passiert?" Ein Flüstern.

„Ihre Mutter hat sie rechtzeitig gefunden. Sie haben eine sehr schwere Kopfverletzung, hatten einen Herzstillstand ..."

Ich sehe ihn entsetzt an.

„Nein, nein! Alles ist gut. Wir haben sie rechtzeitig zurückgeholt. Meine Kollegen sind Meister ihres Fachs. Sie sind so gut wie neu, Frau Sandvik. Na ja, fast. Sie liegen auf meiner Station, weil wir sie für fünf Tage in ein künstliches Koma versetzen mussten. Um den Druck vom Gehirn zu nehmen." Lansson holt sich einen Stuhl und setzt sich an mein Bett. „Und jetzt ruhen Sie sich bitte aus. Meine Fragen können warten." Er wirft einen Blick auf den Monitor und nickt der Krankenschwester zu; dann erhebt er sich und verlässt leise das Zimmer.

Plötzlich verschwindet der Raum vor meinen Augen. Ich will nur noch schlafen.

Das Pflegepersonal flüstert. Laute Geräusche ertrage ich auch nicht. Sie waschen mich, messen meine Temperatur, legen Infusionen an, und streichen mir über den Arm. Ich sage mir, dass eine andere Person hier liegt. Das bin nicht ich.

Ich nehme Abstand.

„Du bist so weit weg", seufzt meine Mutter. Ihre Lippen berühren sanft meine rechte Hand. „Komm zurück, meine Kleine. Ich vermisse dich so sehr."

Ich will wieder über die Wiese laufen, das Gras berühren, die Blumen pflücken und mich neben Annika und Ebba legen. Sobald sie mich in diesem Zimmer in Ruhe lassen, suche ich mit geschlossenen Augen nach den beiden – und nach meinem Vater. Er war auch dort, ich konnte ihn spüren. Ich versuche einzuschlafen, hoffe, dass ich dort ankommen werde. Es gelingt mir nicht.

Ich frage Dr. Lansson, warum das so ist, aber er hat keine Antworten. Er schweigt, lächelt. Er besitzt andere Fähigkeiten, und das ist auch gut so. Er war nicht auf der Wiese, niemand aus meiner unmittelbaren Umgebung war dort. Sie können mir keine Antworten geben, ich werde es selbst herausfinden müssen.

Mom sagt, dass mein Zustand sehr kritisch war, dass ich fast gestorben sei. Keine Ahnung. Meine Erinnerungen an das Geschehen spielen mir einen Streich. Ich erinnere mich nur daran, dass Bente in die Küche kam, aber nicht mehr an ihre Worte. Ich würde gerne darüber sprechen und auch über die beklemmende Leere, wenn es mir helfen würde. Aber wie soll ich über das Gesprochene reden, wenn ich mich überhaupt nicht daran erinnere. Ich saß vor dem Laptop, und dann waren da plötzlich diese dunklen, beängstigenden Augen. Mehr ist da nicht.

Dr. Lansson hat mir erklärt, dass dies ein normales Phänomen bei einem Schädel-Hirn-Trauma sei und dass ich damit rechnen müsse, dass dieser Teil meiner Erinnerung für immer verloren sei.

Malte hatte nur eine leichte Gehirnerschütterung. Er litt dennoch partiell unter Gedächtnisverlust.

„Malte wird dich besuchen, sobald es die Situation mit seinem Vater zulässt."

„Was ist denn mit Noah, Mom?"

„Du wurdest von Bente übel zugerichtet, Jonte. Sie hätte dich getötet, wenn ich nicht zurückgekommen wäre." Mom kann ihre Tränen nicht mehr aufhalten. „Ich hatte mein Portemonnaie vergessen und kehrte deshalb um. Als Bente mich sah, floh sie durch die Hintertür. Ich habe den Notruf gewählt und danach Kommissar Haugen angerufen. Bente wurde kurz darauf verhaftet und hat zwei Morde gestanden."

Ich verspüre plötzlich einen ungeheuren Drang, die Augen zu schließen. Ihre Stimme ist nicht mehr ganz nah. Ich schirme mich ab, bin von einer Kapsel umgeben, als Mom fortfährt.

„Bente ist völlig verwirrt. Es war ein bizarrer Zufall, dass sie an dem Tag in dem Wald joggte, in dem Jonas' Leiche lag. Noah hielt es immer für eine unsinnige Laune, dass sie eine Dreiviertelstunde mit dem Auto fuhr, nur um in diesem Waldstück am Drammensfjord zu joggen. Aber sie ging immer wieder hin. Noah hat mir auch von Bentes beängstigenden Wutausbrüchen erzählt."

Moms Worte dringen einen Moment zu mir durch, dann fliegen sie wieder davon. Ich verliere das Interesse an den Dingen, die um mich sind. Es interessiert mich auch nicht, dass das CT keine Einblutungen im Gehirn gezeigt hat, dass ich vermutlich eine Zeit lang Aufmerksamkeitsdefizite haben werde. Dass ich neue Eindrücke und Informationen nicht schnell verarbeiten kann. Ich darf vorerst nicht lesen, am Laptop arbeiten oder Sport treiben. All das erklärt mir Dr. Lansson immer wieder.

„Es wird ihnen auch schwerfallen, Lösungen für komplexe Zusammenhänge und verwirrende Situationen zu finden. Es gibt nur eine einzige Therapie, und die heißt Ruhe, Ruhe und nochmals Ruhe. Nur so werden Sie sich erholen", sagt es bei jeder Visite.

Mom möchte mich wieder bei sich aufnehmen und eine Pflegerin einstellen. Ich will nicht von Fremden abhängig sein, aber ich möchte auch nicht länger als notwendig im Krankenhaus bleiben.

„Was möchtest du denn, Jonte?", fragt meine Mom.

Ich lächle in mich hinein. Ich möchte im hellen Licht über die Blumenwiese gehen. Ich möchte die friedliche Unendlichkeit bestaunen, meine Augen über den Himmel schweifen lassen und den Duft der Blumen einatmen. Ich möchte, dass mir der Himmel auf den Kopf fällt und Gott gleich mit. Doch vor allem möchte mich auf der Wiese ausruhen – neben Annika und Ebba.

KAPITEL 78

Das Haus ist verkauft, und ich bin die stolze Besitzerin einer großen Dachterrassenwohnung an der Strandveien in Drammen. Es ist ein dreistöckiges, gepflegtes Haus mit sechs Wohneinheiten, einer Ligusterhecke und einer adretten Reihe von Briefkästen. In dieses Viertel ziehen die Leute mit mittleren Einkommen. Jede Menge Sicherheit und Fahrthindernisse auf der Straße, sodass man auch nicht über dreißig Stundenkilometer fahren darf. Das Fenster im Wohnzimmer hat einen phänomenalen Blick auf den Drammensfjord und vom Schlafzimmer aus sieht man eine Weide, auf der Kühe grasen. Wenn ich meine Augen schließe, erblicke ich meine eigene Wiese, sie ist unerreichbar geworden, aber in Gedanken verweile ich manchmal dort. Das fühlt sich gut an.

Meine Mutter hat den Umzug organisiert und meinte, ich solle erst in meine neue Wohnung gehen, wenn ich mich vollständig erholt habe, aber niemand kann mir sagen, wann das sein wird. Ich kann zwar ohne Hilfe wieder duschen und mich anziehen, und ich schlafe auch nicht mehr nach der kleinsten Anstrengung sofort ein, aber dennoch habe ich das Bedürfnis nach Stille und Abgeschiedenheit. Meine Merkfähigkeit ist durch das Schädel-Hirn-Trauma immer noch eingeschränkt, ich ertrage keine Menschen um mich herum; selbst eine Diskussion im Radio stört mich. Ich schaue höchstens mal fern, obwohl ich mich nicht länger als fünf Minuten auf den Bildschirm konzentrieren kann. Mein Laptop ist immer noch verbotenes Terrain, aber hin und wieder google ich ein wenig. Und ich war noch nie so glücklich darüber, dass ich blindlings die Tastatur bedienen kann. So bin ich in der Lage, morgens eine Viertelstunde und eine Viertelstunde am Abend an einem neuen Projekt digital zu arbeiten. Ich möchte die aktive Zeit langsam verlängern. Sehr langsam, denn sonst würde ich den Anschluss an meine Arbeit verlieren. Ein Kollege beaufsichtigt in meinem Auftrag die Baustelle des Klosterhotels, das gut voranschreitet und im kommenden Winter eröffnet werden soll.

Malte hat mich dreimal bei meiner Mutter besucht. Als er mich das erste Mal sah, war er zutiefst erschüttert, streichelte mich immer wieder und weinte stille Tränen. Ich muss wohl ziemlich übel ausgesehen haben. Das zweite Mal erzählte er mir, wie bestürzt sein Vater gewesen war. Noah war nie aufgefallen, was wirklich in Bente vorging, niemand ahnte, dass es viel mehr war als eine hormonelle Stimmungsschwankung, nämlich eine schwere psychische Störung. Es war ein tragischer Zufall, dass Bente bei ihren Joggingrunden im Wald die Leiche ihres Sohnes entdecken musste. Vermutlich hätte sie sonst nicht die Kontrolle über sich verloren. Dr. Lansson hat mir erklärt, dass Frauen mit einem schweren prämenstruellen, dysphorischen Syndrom, sich wie Psychopathinnen aufführen können. „Die meisten von Frauen begangenen Morde werden in den PMDS-Phasen verübt."

Bentes Taten wiegen schwer, meine hingegen liegt noch außerhalb meines Erfassungsvermögens. Ich weiß jetzt, dass ich mich vorsätzlich vom Unfallort entfernt habe, nicht aus Panik. Dessen ungeachtet habe ich dabei keinerlei Empfindungen. Es scheint mir um eine andere Person zu gehen, es berührt mich kaum.

Mom behauptet, dass der Gedächtnisverlust einerseits von Vorteil sei, andererseits aber auch ein Hindernis darstellt. Durch den Gedächtnisverlust kann ich nicht damit abschließen. Ich stimme ihr nicht zu. Da ist nämlich nicht nur dieser Gedächtnisverlust, da ist auch noch eine andere Erinnerung, die ich bewahren möchte und an die ich mit einem guten Gefühl zurückdenke, eine Erinnerung, nach der ich mich immer noch sehne. Mein imaginärer Aufenthalt auf der schönen Wiese und die Begegnung mit Annika und Ebba haben mein Leben bereichert. Auf die Erinnerung an Bentes Übergriff kann ich gerne verzichten. Was mich betrifft, so kann dieser Teil meines Gedächtnisses für immer im Dunkeln bleiben. Ich muss nichts beenden, was ich nicht verursacht habe.

Malte schickt mir wunderschöne Ansichtskarten und liebevolle Briefe aus Hydden. Er berichtet von seinem Vater und den Kindern. Sie sind manchmal wütend, oft traurig, aber sie lachen auch wieder. Wenn Noah darüber schreibt, habe ich das Gefühl, mitten unter ihnen zu sein.

Bente wurde kurz nach ihrer Verhaftung in eine forensische Klinik gebracht, wo sie auf ihre Unzurechnungsfähigkeit untersucht wird. Sie hat Noah um die Scheidung gebeten. Malte hat seinem Vater geraten, ihr zuzustimmen. Er ist überzeugt, dass Bente nie wieder gesund wird, und hofft, dass Noah irgendwann eine neue Liebe findet.

Ich kann auch seine Wut zwischen den Zeilen herauslesen, Vorwürfe in Richtung seiner Stiefmutter. Als ich das letzte Mal mit ihm telefoniert habe, bestätigte er meinen Eindruck. „Durch sie hätte ich dich fast verloren", sagte er. „Ich mache mir Vorwürfe und bin wütend, weil ich Bentes negative Stimmungen immer wieder heruntergespielt habe, wie es auch mein Vater getan hat. Wir wollten ihre dunkle Seite ignorieren. Ihre Tobsuchtsanfälle uferten immer wieder aus, aber kurz darauf war sie so sanft wie eh und je. Wir hätten mehr auf sie eingehen müssen, statt ihre Niedergeschlagenheit durch Ignoranz zu nähren. Wir waren blind, naiv, bequem und schwach."

Ich stimme dem nicht zu. Ich habe Jonas unzählige Male über seine Stiefmutter sprechen hören, und jedes Mal spürte ich seine Ohnmacht über das Unfassbare. Ich glaube auch, dass Bente und Noah nicht füreinander bestimmt waren und dass Malte die beiden einfach zu selten gesehen hat, um das Ganze wirklich beurteilen zu können.

Malte hat mich bei unserem letzten Telefonat gefragt, wann ich ihm meine neue Wohnung zeigen werde. Ich spüre, dass er bei mir sein möchte, aber ich schiebe die Entscheidung vor mir her, und es fällt ihm auf.

„Was steht da zwischen uns, Jonte?", wollte er wissen. „Hat es etwas mit Bente zu tun?"

Nein, ganz sicher nicht, habe ich ihm versichert. Bente bleibt vorerst in der forensischen Strafanstalt, ich denke kaum noch an sie. Die Menschen um mich herum sind aber immer noch mit ihr beschäftigt, insbesondere meine Mutter. Sie hat Bente immerhin davon abgehalten, mich zu töten. Das muss sehr schockierend für Mom gewesen sein.

Mein Gesicht sieht jetzt wieder normal aus. Meine gebrochene Nase ist wieder gerade, die Prellungen und Hämatome sind verschwunden. Ich habe zwei Monate lang nicht in den Spiegel geschaut, deshalb habe ich keine Erinnerungen an dieses beschädigte Gesicht. Und die Geschichten, die über Bentes Taten und Motive im Umlauf sind, dringen nicht bis zu mir durch. Ich erlaube es nicht. Ich gebe dem keinen Raum. Die Toten dürfen auf die Lebenden keine Schatten werfen.

Ich blicke auf den Fjord und sein stilles Wasser und denke an Malte. Habe ihn vor meinem inneren Auge.

Ich gehe Malte aus dem Weg.

Haben sich deine Gefühle für ihn verflüchtigt?

Nein, ganz im Gegenteil.

Bedauerst du eure letzte Begegnung?

Überhaupt nicht.

Möchtest du die Beziehung mit ihm beenden?

Ich darf nicht einmal an so etwas denken.

Und dennoch gehst du ihm aus dem Weg.

Ich führe es auf meine Unsicherheit und meine Angst zurück. Nicht auf die Angst vor der Vergangenheit.

Ich bin jetzt gefangen in einer allgegenwärtigen Angst vor der Zukunft.

Der Frühling geht zu Ende. Ist irgendwann einfach fort. In diesem Jahr habe ich meine Lieblingsjahreszeit verpasst.

„Du verschanzt dich in deinem hohen Turm. Wenn du so weitermachst, verpasst du auch noch den Sommer", grummelt Mom. Sie glaubt, dass ich nicht allzu oft an die frische Luft gehe und mich zu sehr isoliere. „Ist dir bewusst, dass ich dich überall hinfahren würde, Jonte?"

Natürlich weiß sie das. Wie sollte sie das auch nicht mitkriegen, wo du ständig davon anfängst. Sie fühlt sich sogar schuldig, weil sie dein Angebot fortlaufend ablehnt.

„Ich bin noch nicht bereit, Mom", protestiere ich. „Für mich ist die Welt da draußen immer noch zu unruhig, ich bin noch nicht in der Lage, ein Gespräch mit mehreren Leuten gleichzeitig zu führen. Aber ich stehe mit allen in Kontakt. Mit dem Orden, mit meinen Kollegen, mit Falk."

Und ich reagiere auf die Posts im Gästebuch der Architektenwebsite SANDVIK & PARTNER. Mir ist allerdings nicht ganz wohl dabei, denn es erzeugt in mir zweierlei Empfindungen: Angst und die Neigung zur Panik. Auf der Website ist ein aktuelles Foto von mir, ich habe meine Identität preisgegeben, bin nicht mehr anonym.

Was würde passieren, wenn dieser Mann, der in jener Nacht hinter mir herlief, mich erkennt?

Auf dem Foto sehe ich wesentlich älter aus, aber dessen ungeachtet bin ich leicht zu identifizieren. Vielleicht weiß dieser Mann nichts von dem Drama, das sich später abgespielt hat. Vielleicht weiß er es doch, sieht aber keinen Zusammenhang. Was wäre, wenn wir uns zufällig auf der Straße begegnen würden? Ob er dann in sich geht, um Schlussfolgerungen zu ziehen? Um Unruhe zu stiften? Um sicherzustellen, dass ich unter Verdacht gerate?

Ich versuche, all diese Gedanken von mir fernzuhalten. Es hat keinen Sinn, gespenstische Szenarien zu kreieren. Wenn es dazu kommt, kann ich immer noch reagieren. Ich will meine Medienangst überwinden.

Jeden Tag werden im Gästebuch neue Kommentare veröffentlicht, und fast alle beziehen sich auf das neue Klosterhotel. Auch der dritte Band *Architektur zwischen Himmel und Erde*, eine Bilddokumentation über das ursprüngliche Kloster und das jetzige Klosterhotel, wird gut angenommen. Ich kann mich als Architektin vor Aufträgen kaum noch retten, bin aber nicht in der Lage, sie zu bewältigen. Ich habe einen jungen Architekten eingestellt, er macht seine Sache im Home-Office gut. Ich arbeite jetzt zweimal täglich eineinhalb Stunden an der Zeichentafel, mehr geht nicht. Noch nicht. Es erfordert viel Kraft.

Falk möchte auch meine nächsten Projekte veröffentlichen, vielleicht Ende nächsten Jahres, sofern mich keine neuen Probleme aus der Bahn werfen. Es muss funktionieren. Den Namen *JO* habe ich für immer zu den Akten gelegt. Auf der Tafel vor der Baustelle des Klosterhotels steht mein Name: *Dr. Jonte Sandvik.* Und das erfüllt mich mit Stolz.

Der Nachmittag schleicht sich an. Mom bereitet in der Küche einen Kaffee vor. Ich bin im Schlafzimmer und sehe den Kühen beim Grasen zu. Schließe irgendwann die Augen. Dichter Wald hinter der Wiese. Plötzlich ziehen sich die Bäume zurück, wie auf ein stilles Kommando. Eine Lichtung tut sich auf. Nichts steht meinem Blick mehr im Weg. Zwei winzige Gestalten tauchen am Horizont auf, werden nach und nach größer, bis ich Annika und Ebba erkenne. Sie werden mir zuwinken, mir vielleicht sogar zurufen. Weiter gedeiht meine Fantasie nicht. Das lasse ich nicht zu. Die Farben werden schwächer, verschieben sich wie ein Filter vor meinem Sichtfeld. Ich öffne die Augen und lasse mich von Zeit und Landschaft umfangen. Obwohl mir Tränen übers Gesicht laufen, schluchze ich nicht und verliere auch nicht die Beherrschung.

„Jonte! Der Kaffee ist fertig", ruft Mom.

Rasch gehe ich ins Bad und mache mich frisch. Alles gut.

„War Malte schon mal hier?"

Ich glaube, die Frage soll beiläufig klingen, ich kichere. „Du bist so durchsichtig wie eine Glasscheibe, Mom. Bist wohl ziemlich begierig darauf, etwas zu erfahren."

„Ich mag Malte und sehe, wie verrückt er nach dir ist." Sie hält einen Moment inne. „Und mir ist auch aufgefallen, was mit dir geschieht, wenn du ihn ansiehst. Es ist wie …"

„… Aaron?", ergänze ich. „Das wolltest du doch sagen. Eine Liebe, wie ich sie für ihn empfunden habe? Du irrst dich, Mom. Es ist sehr viel mehr, es ist tiefer, es fühlt sich so viel besser an."

„Weshalb zweifelst du dann noch?"

Ich zucke mit den Schultern.

„Versuch nicht, mich glauben zu lassen, dass *du* das nicht weißt." Meine Mutter steht auf und greift nach ihrer Handtasche. „Ich habe heute Nachmittag einen Termin. Soll ich vorher noch ein paar Einkäufe für dich erledigen, mein Schatz?"

Ich stehe ebenfalls auf, umarme sie still.

„Ich möchte nur, dass mein Kind wieder glücklich ist", sagt sie zärtlich. „Brauchst du noch Kosmetika, um dich aufzuhübschen, falls er kommt?"

Ihre praktische Frage lässt mich laut auflachen. „Oh, Mom, mein Badezimmerschrank quillt über von den vielen Pröbchen, die du mir immer wieder mitbringst."

Sie küsst mich fest. „Weißt du, ich bin stolz auf dich. Ich betone es zu selten, aber ich meine es ernst und bin nicht nur stolz auf deine Entscheidung, dich von JO zu trennen. Ich finde es auch großartig, dass du keinen Alkohol mehr trinkst."

„Ich muss nur durchhalten, Mom", murmle ich.

Sie lässt mich los und schaut mich an. „Das wirst du auch, mein Kind. Du bist eine starke Frau. Und darüber hinaus solltest du jetzt auch weniger Angst vor der Liebe haben."

Als sie die Haustür hinter sich geschlossen hat, überfällt mich eine innere Unruhe. Ich streife durch die Wohnung, bewege Dinge, bleibe am Schlafzimmerfenster stehen. Unten auf der gegenüberliegenden Weide grasen noch immer Kühe. Ich schaue mir ihre eckigen Hintern an. Kühe achten auf nichts, drücken ihre Nasenspitzen ins Gras, zupfen und kauen. Sie heben ihre Schwänze an, um sich zu entleeren. Die Weide ist ihre Welt. Ein schönes Leben. Ich wäre gerne eine Kuh.

Es reicht, Jonte!, ermahnt mich Back-Vocal. *Du willst doch nicht wirklich als Rindvieh enden …*

Der Klang der Türklingel reißt mich vom Fenster weg. Mom hat vermutlich mal wieder etwas vergessen. Ihren entschuldigenden Blick habe ich bereits vor Augen, als ich lächelnd die Tür öffne.

„Die Geschichte wiederholt sich", sagt Malte. „Wenn der Prophet nicht zum Berg kommt, muss der Berg eben zum Propheten … Bin ich willkommen?"

Ich stürze mich in seine Arme.

Meine spontane Reaktion bereue ich fast sofort und entziehe mich seinem leidenschaftlichen Kuss wieder. Ich löse mich aus seiner Umarmung und gehe ins Wohnzimmer. Malte schließt die Tür und folgt mir schweigend.

Die Verzweiflung ist wieder da, obwohl die Worte meiner Mutter in meinem Kopf nachhallen: *Du solltest jetzt auch weniger Angst vor der Liebe haben.* Aber ich habe keine Angst vor der Liebe, ich habe Verlustängste. Das muss ich Malte erklären und vieles mehr. Aber wie? Wo fange ich nur an?

Malte setzt sich auf die Couch und zieht mich neben sich. „Ich werde mich auf dich stürzen", beginnt er. „Entschuldige, aber ich denke, es war an der Zeit, sich zu sehen und zu sagen, was gesagt werden muss."

Was weiß er? Er darf nichts wissen. Niemand darf etwas wissen, und das ist mein Problem. Ich will da raus, alles hinter mir lassen und an einen Ort fliehen, an dem mich niemand finden kann. Dieser Gedanke hat sich so massiv festgesetzt in meinem Hirn, dass alles andere verblasst. Wie Treibgut, das diesen einen, alles beherrschenden Gedanken umspielt.

Treibgut, das belanglos herumplätschert? Sag etwas!

„Schau mich an, Jonte. Bitte bleib bei mir. Ich liebe dich."

Ich liebe dich.

Drei Worte, die alles verändern. Der Abend wird taghell in meinem Kopf, die Nacht gleicht einer Morgendämmerung. Der Mond wird, sobald er aufgegangen ist, der Sonne zum Verwechseln ähnlichsehen. So wird es sein.

Malte sitzt schweigend neben mir. Er wartet, er wird immer warten und mich nicht unter Druck setzen. Er ist ein großartiger Mann, mit einer eigenen Vergangenheit, und der Mann, den ich liebe und der meine Liebe erwidert. Ich hatte stets Angst davor, mich wieder in jemanden zu verlieben, und habe jede Chance auf eine neue Liebe gemieden, die Aaron auch nur im Entferntesten ähnlich war. Jetzt ist Malte da, und er ist nicht wie Aaron, denn alles, was ich für ihn empfinde, ist stärker, besser, ausgeglichener und sicherer als die Gefühle, die ich für einen Mann empfunden habe, an den ich geglaubt und den ich verloren habe. Einen Mann, der im Nachhinein meiner nicht würdig war. Die Erinnerung an Aaron wird immer mit der Erinnerung an Ebba verbunden sein. Bis zu dem Moment, als sie wie ein Blitzschlag in meinem Leben einschlug, um nie wieder daraus zu verschwinden.

Ich atme tief durch. Und noch einmal.

Ebba ist da, damit du nicht mehr davonläufst. Siehst du denn nicht, dass du es ihr schuldig bist, dein Leben zu leben?

Das Unbehagen, das in mir gegärt hat, legt sich allmählich. Je weiter ich mich von der Angst entferne, die mich zu Treibholz auf dem Meer des Lebens gemacht hat, desto leichter fühle ich mich. „Ich muss dir etwas sagen", fange ich an. „Es ist eine Geschichte, die ich lieber aus meinem Leben verbannen würde, weil ich mich dafür schäme. Seit Jahren versuche ich, die Erinnerung daran aus meinem Gedächtnis zu löschen, aber sie kommt immer wieder zu mir zurück. Und bisher hat das nur Unheil verursacht." Ich stocke.

Malte schweigt. Wartet.

„Wenn du erfährst, was damals geschah und welche Verantwortung ich daran trage, kannst du dich von mir abwenden, wenn du das möchtest. Die Geschichte ist traurig, abscheulich und unumkehrbar. Sie lässt mich in keinem guten Licht dastehen und wird mich nie wieder loslassen, aber auch du könntest in ihren Sog geraten."

„Erzähl mir einfach davon", sagt Malte leise. „Ich liebe dich."

Ich liebe dich ... Drei Worte, die das Dunkel durchdringen, alles mit sich reißen, die Schreie zum Schweigen bringen und die Stille zum Schreien.

Drei Worte, die mir ein Leben an Maltes Seite versprechen.

ÜBER DIE AUTORIN

Das Spezialgebiet der Bestseller-Autorin sind Suspense-Thriller, Psychothriller und Romane. Bei ihrer akribischen Recherche lässt sie sich von Forensikern, Psychologen, Gentechnologen, Pathologen und Medizinern beraten. Ihre Thriller erreichten alle die Top-Ten-Bestsellerlisten vieler E-book-Plattformen. Die Autorin ist Mitglied im Schriftstellerverband Syndikat, im BvjA und den Mörderischen Schwestern.

Auszeichnungen und Nominierung:

2016: Stefko, From Sarah with love: Halbfinale der Int. Writemovies Contest, Los Angeles.

2015: Sibirien – Die aus dem Eis erwachen: Finale der Int. Writemovies Contest, Los Angeles.

2019: Seelen unter dem Eis – Finale der Int. Writemovies Contest, Los Angeles und einem honorable mention

Weitere Romane der Autorin:

Thriller / Psychothriller: Eiskalte Umarmung, Eiskalter Schlaf (Print: Jasper, das Böse in Dir), Tödliche Perfektion (Print: Die Sekte), Wintermorde, Die Behandlung des Bösen, Am Ende das Böse, Wo ist Jay?, Lilith-Eiskalter Engel, Gleis der Vergeltung, Puppenmutter, Seelen unter dem Eis. Weitere Romane folgen.

Roman: Café de Flore und die Sehnsucht. Trilogie: Perlen der Winde.

Anthologie: Winterküsse, Nix zu verlieren, Summer in my Pocket

Kurzgeschichte: Sibirien – Die aus dem Eis erwachen

Mehr über Astrid Korten:

Website: www.astrid-korten.com

Facebook: www.facebook.com/Astrid Korten